THE EYE

OF THE

BEHOLDER

a suspense novel

By
Richard Taylor Boswell

PublishAmerica
Baltimore

© 2005 by Richard Taylor Boswell.
All rights reserved. No part of this book may be reproduced, stored in a retrieval system or transmitted in any form or by any means without the prior written permission of the publishers, except by a reviewer who may quote brief passages in a review to be printed in a newspaper, magazine or journal.

First printing

This book is a work of fiction. Names, characters, and incidents are the product of the author's imagination or are used fictitiously. Any resemblance to actual events, locales, or persons living or dead is coincidental.

ISBN: 1-4137-8159-4
PUBLISHED BY PUBLISHAMERICA, LLLP
www.publishamerica.com
Baltimore

Printed in the United States of America

The Eye of the Beholder

To Richard & Vivian

1-7-07

I hope you both like this novel. Perhaps life experiences will mirror some of the characters herein.

May the Lord bless you.

Anthony Dunphe Burrell

I

"Not only are the many accusations against my client unfounded, but, as has been pointed out several times, both by the court and by us, they have no value in this hearing. They don't address the issue here being considered. This is a custody hearing, and while the plaintiff would have you believe that all those allegations go to his character and ability to raise the child, the fact is, there has been no substantive evidence presented to show that Mr. Coleman has been or will be a bad parent. We have clearly shown that he is both the biological father and has raised and nurtured this child since birth. He has done an excellent job. Provided the child with a good home, food, and clothing."

Robert sat quietly thinking that the attorney didn't seem to have a clue. He obviously didn't answer Robert's testimony that Mr. Coleman had participated in an armed robbery, or that he had filmed Coleman selling coke to a girl at a high school. The judge can't be stupid enough to believe that those elements have nothing to do with raising Jackson. The attorney's conclusions seemed to be argument for argument's sake. It was probably because he had no real rebuttal against the allegations.

Hansen, the defense attorney, went on and on and on talking about how the father had provided for both Jason and Jackson and how he had a good job and was giving the children a great childhood. It was hot outside and the courtroom was not well air-conditioned. Robert figured the judge must be hot too; he seemed a little out of patience with the defense attorney. Especially his lengthy conclusions, which did not address any of the contentions made by the plaintiff.

Robert looked over at the grandparents. Jason appeared really nervous and Marge's face got red every once in a while, especially when the defense would assert that Mr. Coleman was the better of the two parents. They occasionally would shake their heads and then whisper something into the ear of the other. They didn't understand the legal process at all and seemed extremely anxious. Robert mused, *I remember the first time I suffered in court like them. Now it seems so many years ago. Like the years that have passed in the Bradleys' life. I wonder what brought Golden to California. It seems strange to me.*

Robert's mind drifted back to Golden's childhood. She came from a good couple. Farmers in Minnesota, good stock, good working people. Why had she come to California? Perhaps the excitement or the adventurous spirit of Wendy, her new girlfriend. Perhaps just a chance to get away from the farm and see the world.

Even after she married and settled, Goldie had said she really loved her parents and sometimes she'd asked her husband to take her back home for a vacation.

II

BEGINNINGS

It was late in the summer and Jason hadn't made the last hay cut. On a good year he could get four cuts. It looked like an Indian summer this year, so with a little luck the alfalfa would get up to 12 or 14 inches before the cut. Jason decided to give it another week.

"Hope it don't rain the day after you cut it. You know how unpredictable the weather is this time of year," Margie said as she took another bite of the hot homemade apple pie.

Marge and Jason went to the dinner every Friday night at 6:30 p.m. They had been doing it for three years, regular as clockwork. But this night was different. Jason had plans.

"Marge, you know I love you. We've been going together for more than three years."

He shifted in his seat and took a drink of water.

"I don't have much, a little house and only 130 acres. Ya can't do much on a hundred and thirty 'cept Herefords. I've got a good production count and good cream percentages. We got a contract with Meadow Cream Milk, so we'll be all right. Most farms nowadays have thousands of acres and machinery and help. But it's hard to get help up here and the growing season's short. Just the same, I got a little in the bank and don't owe nobody. So I was thinking, life'd be better if ya married me. Ya don't have to answer right now, but I think you love me and we ain't gettin' any younger."

He reached into his coveralls and pulled out a ring box. It wasn't wrapped but when he opened it, Marge was surprised at the size.

"I don't have to think about it, Jay. I've been hoping for this moment for a long time. O'course I'll marry you. Ya obviously need to get some fat on ya, so let me get some good food in the house and I'll cook ya up some real tasty meals." She leaned over the table and whispered, "I promise they'll be better than this one."

Leaning back she reached over and took the ring out of the box. "When?" she asked.

"I figure we don't need a big party or anything. How about inviting your mom and my mom, a couple of friends, and having the ceremony at my place two weeks from today?"

"Sounds great. I'll see if Mom and me can make a dress that fast. I'll talk with her and if it's okay, I'll get out some invitations tomorrow."

You might think she was too dependent on her mother, but the truth was her mother was old and really needed to be taken care of. Marge asked her for help because it kept her alive and working.

Jason knew when she said "a couple of friends" that it meant more than a couple of friends. Marge would send out invitations by the dozens. *Oh well*, he thought, *I'll go with whatever she needs to make her happy.*

"My mom'll have to stay with us, I got no place to send her, and I wouldn't even if I could, so we'll be upstairs and she'll keep the bedroom downstairs. I hope that's okay with you, sweetheart." Jason knew it was okay; it just needed to be said. He shifted again and looked into Marge's eyes. She didn't flinch.

"You know I love Lil. She and I have spent many a day talking, mostly about you." She smiled and winked. "It's no problem."

"Guess you'll want that Lutheran minister to do it?" Jason asked. He had been raised a Baptist, but really didn't care.

"If that's okay with you," Marge responded. She loved this kind of conversation; she could make any arrangements she wanted and knew Jason would go along. It was great and it was about time.

"'Course, and ya know, I think I'll start going with you on Sundays."

"Oh, honey, thanks, I know you'll enjoy it, an' I'll be so proud to have you there with me."

Jason had gone twice in the past year with Marge to church. He said he didn't get it, if God loved us all, what difference did it make if you went to church? But he knew how much it meant to Marge. It was his way of saying how much he loved her. He picked up the bill and left a bigger tip than usual. Not that the country-fried steak was any better than it always was, Jason was just thinking about Marge cookin' for him. She was a great cook. Usually nothing fancy, but really good down-to-earth food. They had done lots of barbeques at his place. He usually cooked the steaks and she made a great potato salad. She always brought chips and drinks and rolls and, of course, really great dessert.

It will be nice to have Marge home with me, Jason thought again as he looked at her shining face in the dim light of the car. *I love her and it's time to get going with my life.* The car approached Marge's house. Jason pulled up the dirt driveway and swung around the circular patch of dirt that had been worn out of the grass by cars turning around in the front yard. It was now a driveway, albeit dirt. Jason turned off the car and leaned over and pulled Marge close to him.

"I love you, Marge. Good night." He kissed her. It wasn't the passionate kiss of a teenager; it was a kiss of love. A kiss of promise.

She got out of the car and walked up the front steps of her mom's place. The porch light was still on and Mom was sitting in the living room reading a romance novel. It didn't matter her daughter's age,

Mom waited up for her faithfully as she had when Marge dated in high school.

"Jason proposed to me tonight, Mom," she said with a smile broader than a rainbow.

"It's about time," Mom said dryly and then smiled and took Marge's hand. "I think it's wonderful. Did you accept?"

"I did, Mom. It means I'll be leaving you. Will you be okay here?"

"I was here before you were born. I'll be fine. Besides, I'll have to come over to Jason's and show you how to set up the place." She laughed. Marge smiled and touched her mom's wrinkled hand.

⇒••⇐

The wedding day came and went without a hitch. The girls had made a great wedding dress and Marge's mom even made a tux coat for Jason. More people were there than Jason had thought would come. In fact, most of his high school class showed up. It'd been ten years since he had attended high school and most of the guys from his class had moved to St. Paul's or Chicago to get jobs. Of course some had gone on to college, some had married, and a couple even joined the army as lifers. It was good to see them again.

Everyone congratulated Jason and most were surprised that he'd found someone to marry him. Jason was not a really handsome man, sorta plain. But he was rugged and muscled and he'd been president of the FFA club two years in a row. Said he was gonna take over his father's farm. Everyone in class knew his only desire was to run the farm and stay in Minnesota. So when his dad died early, about age 57, Jason was ready. He'd just returned home from the Navy. His dad had probably waited for him to come back. He'd been diagnosed with cancer almost two years earlier but hadn't told anyone. Lucille, his wife, figured it out after a while and called ol' Doc Bean and scolded him for not telling her.

Jason had gone to 'Nam with the Navy, hadn't seen much action though. His MOS was gunner and there wasn't much happening on the high seas. He did patrol up the river a couple of times and the boat took fire from Charlie, but he said he never got a clear shot back. They had been instructed not to fire on the enemy unless fired on first. The rule seemed stupid. How the hell can you conduct a war by not shooting the enemy? But Jason obeyed orders and when he left he was an E-5, of which he was very proud.

So when Dad died, Jason stepped up to the plate and took over the farm. His mother expected as much and he really wanted to anyway. He bought some new milking equipment and inseminated some of cows that needed freshening with better sperm. It worked; his pounds of milk increased after four years and the new breeds had less mastitis and more cream. He'd also re-seeded the 80 acres of hay in a better broadleaf alfalfa, which not only helped production, but the extra hay sold for more, which gave him enough to up the grain count a little during the milking. All in all, Jason had made the little farm productive and profitable. He only had 93 head, which in that area was really small, but he was consistent, and Meadow Cream contracted to buy all his milk. It tested good and tasted sweet. They sent out the truck to pick up twice a week.

The guys tried to throw him a bachelor party but he said no to the idea of a naked girl and yes to some pizza and a couple of beers. Jay didn't drink much. He said he didn't need to relax, and he didn't need a lift. Occasionally he and Marge would go get some pizza and have a beer with it. Marge said it made the pizza taste better. Jay just kinda went along. All in all the wedding was great. They went to Minneapolis on their honeymoon and stayed with Joshua and Sarah for a week. Joshua was a cousin and was extremely kind to both Jay and Marge. They thanked him and even tried to give him a couple of hundred, but Joshua refused.

Marge moved in and set up house. She put new curtains on the windows downstairs and in the kitchen. Jason's mom was really good about letting her have the house. She had so many memories locked in the walls. But she knew her time, her queenship, had passed, and she quietly yielded to Marge. They became really good friends.

"Morning, hon. I've got to get that hay bailed up today. I'm already about two weeks late and the alfalfa's starting to bloom. I think we've got a good fourteen inches though, so I'm glad I let it sit a couple of extra weeks. Didn't think we'd have much rain this year, but obviously I was wrong. I'll get a good cut and we should be set for the winter."

"Okay, you want me to do the milking tomorrow? That'll give you the extra time you need to get the bails out. Might rain you know," Marge said with a smile.

"Want eggs or what?" she asked, standing next to the old white Vulcan stove.

"I'd rather have the what," Jay said, reaching out to pat her bottom. She sidestepped his advances and opened the fridge. Lillian came in and asked if there was any coffee ready.

"Yep, Mom, I think there might be two brews goin' on this morning," Marge replied.

Jay perked up and looked at Marge with a curious eye. "What's that mean?"

"I'm three weeks late." Marge smiled and Lil hugged her.

The two grandmas paced outside the delivery room anxiously waiting. The doctor had invited Jason in to watch, but he'd declined.

"I've delivered many a calf, but I still don't think it's right for me to watch my wife deliver," Jason answered.

About an hour later the nurse stepped out of the door with a pink, very little human being all wrapped in a tiny blanket.

"You have a daughter, Jason," she said and handed the miniature bundle to him. He looked at the tiny child with its eyes still closed and its body trembling.

"Wow. She's beautiful." He started to hand the baby back to the nurse, but both grandmothers swiftly intervened and each took the child for a few seconds until the nurse quietly ask for the child back.

"Can I see Marge now?" Jason asked.

"Of course," the nurse said, smiling.

"I'm going to call her Golden Fern. Golden Fern Bradley. Is that okay, honey?" Marge asked in a soft, slightly pleading voice.

"It seems a little strange, how come?" Jason answered.

"Don't you remember where we were when she was conceived?"

Jason looked puzzled. "Sorry, I don't."

"Last fall we went to the hills up by the old waterfall. I was looking at a beautiful fern that had turned golden. You know that almost never happens. It was so really, really lovely. I called you over and showed it to you. Well, you know the rest." Marge smiled. "I think she is like the fern, full of promise and beauty. She is so singular and so wonderful."

Jason smiled. "In that case, I think it's a good name."

⇾•⇽

Golden grew like a weed. Summers floated by with swimming, camping, horseback riding, hiking, and FFA projects. And Goldie grew, and grew, and grew. She was an excellent student. Almost straight-A. She was a great worker. Jay said she could milk faster and better than he. She never turned down a job and didn't often grumble.

The years came and went like watching a sped-up film of a blooming flower. First a bud, then a leaf, and then a bloom. Here and there a family vacation, a fishing trip, Jason even took Goldie hunting a couple of times, but the passing of time is always relentless. Now Jason and Marge looked out the back porch window at Goldie riding tall on her mare. There she was, almost a woman.

"When the summer ends, she'll start her last year of high school," Marge said with some melancholy and hesitancy.

"Has she decided what she wants to do when she graduates?" Jason asked with an edge on his voice and hoping Marge hadn't noticed.

"She doesn't think she wants to go to college."

Jason was relieved inside, and a little disappointed. He'd love to see her get a degree and get the experience of school away from home, but he loved her and she was so very good on the farm. Maybe she would stay.

"I could sure use her here," he said.

"Jay, she's a woman now. I'm not sure how long she'll want to stay after she graduates."

"Well, I'm not worrying about that yet. She's still got a year to finish and a couple more to make up her mind if she wants. I don't think she'll want to marry right off. She hasn't even got a boyfriend."

"Every woman sooner or later looks for a companion. I was slow, but she may need one sooner. You never know."

The evening came and supper was good. Goldie asked if her friend June could come over for a couple of hours.

"Sure," Mom said.

June came over and they huddled in Goldie's bedroom.

After an hour, Goldie came into the living room smiling.

"Mom, can June and me go up to the north forest by the old falls tomorrow?"

"There's nothing up there 'cept the old falls, sweetheart," Marge answered with her eyebrows slightly raised.

"Yeah, but I haven't been there since I was ten. Come on, Maw, we'll be careful."

"So what ya gonna do, camp out overnight? You know it's three quarters of a day's ride just to get there?" Jay asked as he turned the front page of the newspaper.

"We'll be all right, Dad, June's a good rider an' I'll take the Winchester."

"Okay, but take some extra food and drink. An I wanna see ya back here Thursday before sunset." Jay trusted Goldie implicitly. She had never let him down.

"Thanks, Dad. You're the greatest!" Goldie ran over and kissed her mom and ran back upstairs. Jay looked up at Marge and was about to say something when Goldie's head came around the kitchen door with her cheek pressed against the faded yellow door jam.

"May I be excused?"

Marge smiled. "Thank you for remembering. Of course you may."

III

WENDY AND THE WINCHESTER

"Let's stop for some lunch. We've only got four or five miles left to get there," Goldie said as her horse whinnied and turned its head to see the other horse. "There's a clearing up the trail a ways. I think it's an old park." Goldie was clearly the leader of the two and she was sorta in charge of where and when they would stop for lunch.

"Okay," June said. "What'd you bring for lunch?"

"I think Mom made me some ham sandwiches. I put in a couple of sodas and some leftover chicken. Dad made me take some jerky and some water. And I also brought some really good stuff for dinner later."

They rode for almost half an hour further without saying much. The forest was beautiful, filled with white pine and a whole variety of other trees and plant life. There were squirrels and birds and lots of invisible animals. The girls could hear a stream gurgling a few yards away, and the quiet peace was so soothing that neither wanted to disrupt it. As they came around the bend in the dirt road, Goldie was surprised to see an RV parked in the cleared area. Her first instinct was to go around the area unnoticed and avoid any contact with whomever it was parking or camping there.

"I think this is a really stupid idea, Dad." It was a girl's voice coming from the other side of the old park.

"You need to give it a chance, Wendy. You're always complaining that in your 17 years of life, I haven't spent much time with you. Now's your chance. We've gotta be here for my business till late Friday so I thought we'd get to know each other a little better."

"Why can't we stay at the motel like real people?"

"Believe me, honey, the motel is probably worse than here. You saw the town, there isn't much there."

Goldie rode up to the area where Wendy and her father were trying to set up a tent. It was a pretty big tent for two people; it looked like it was built for four or five.

She rode up to where the city-dressed blond teenager was standing.

"Hi, I'm Golden and this is June," she said from horseback. "We been out ridin' an' heard you over here. We don't see many people at this campsite anymore. The state doesn't take care of it like they used to. And you're right," she said to the man who had come over to his daughter's side. "Most folks wouldn't stay in Angora either. The only motel there is pretty old. I think you'll really like it here. The ol' dark river has a falls a couple of miles up that are really beautiful."

"Thanks," the father said. "Maybe you could give us a hand putting up this tent. I haven't done one for quite a while."

Goldie and June climbed off their mounts and tied them to a couple of bushes. Wendy looked curiously at Golden's saddle. It was made of deep brown tanned leather, which had been tooled with leaves and flowers and had silver buckles. Golden's name was stamped out in ornate lettering down both stirrup strips. The reins were light tanned leather woven into a tight circle and tied to a silver decorated bit. On the back of the saddle seat was more tooled leatherwork and in the center was what appeared to be a well-padded swayed lighter leather seat.

"Wow! Who made the saddle for you?" Wendy asked.

"My dad did most of it. He got the base from an ol' guy who uses only mesquite root. He tries to cut it out of a single piece. Usually he can't find one big enough, but when he does he's really careful. Then adds the horn and sometimes the back piece."

Wendy had no idea what she had just been told. But she was impressed.

"It must have taken weeks to do," she said.

Goldie smiled. "Months actually."

Wendy was wearing a pair of flowered short pants and a pink and green top that came only half way down to her belly button. The blouse was sleeveless and dipped down in the front to show she had breasts. Her shoes were Birkenstock sandals. Her hair looked to Goldie like she hadn't brushed it or at least it had been messed up by the wind in the van.

"June, you grab the back pole and I'll get the front one, then we can stake the sides one at a time." Goldie was used to getting things done and didn't even think she might be offending Wendy or her father by just taking over. He had asked for help, and she was giving it.

"Thanks for helping," the father said as he grabbed a support pole at the front right side of the tent. "We're gonna set up and drive back into Angora to get something to eat. If you wanna come you're welcome. I'll treat," the father said and then wondered if he'd gone too far.

"I've got enough for all of us in my saddle pack if you'd like to try some local cooking," Golden replied.

Her mom had taught her well. She was always gracious and even though she wasn't really sure she had enough, she figured it'd be a good chance to show these guys how well prepared people are in Minnesota.

"Why don't you go back to town, Dad, and I'll stay here and visit."

Wendy really liked Golden; for some reason they had hit it off right away. She didn't know why. Sometimes people stick to you. Like you've known them before, or like you share something intangible, some kind of mysterious bond, which leads you to like someone without knowing anything about them.

"You sure you'll be alright?" Dad had left Wendy alone most of the time in San Clemente, so it wasn't a different idea. And these girls seemed really nice. He figured it'd be okay.

"Yeah, I can get to know about Minnesota people," Wendy remarked as though Minnesota was another country.

"Okay," Wendy's father said, "I'll only be gone for an hour or so."

The father drove out the dirt road to state 22 and east to Angora. Wendy and Golden and June became immediately comfortable with each other and started to compare notes. Golden listened, wide eyed at the things they did in California schools. What they were allowed to wear, what the kids did on dates, at the football games, at the dances. She wondered at how Wendy talked about her father. About her divorced mother, and about her freedom. She didn't have to milk, feed cattle, clean up a barn, or even show her dad her homework. As Wendy talked on about life for kids in California, Golden began to feel like she had not been given enough freedom. Enough playtime or time to do the things that kids do. It wasn't that she didn't know most of the things Wendy was talking about, it was just that Wendy had really lived it. It was not in a movie or a book; she was living proof that those things, which Golden had read and seen, were true. The thought took on a life of its own. In her heart Goldie was envious. She walked over to her horse and opened one of the saddlebags, pulled out a big piece of elk jerky, and brought it over to the girls who were sitting on the fold-up lawn chairs brought by Wendy.

"Want some elk jerky?" she asked.

"What's it taste like?" Wendy asked.

"It's great! My dad shoots an elk every year and we eat roasts, steaks, hamburger, and ribs from it. We also make jerky, which is really good, especially when you're on a tip or out in the wild." Golden was trying to make Wendy think she knew all about the woods and was a pro at survival.

"Okay, I'll try it."

Golden tore off the top corner of the sheet of jerky and handed it to June, who then gave the sheet to Wendy who tore off a little piece just like a pro and put it into her mouth.

Wendy smiled. "It's actually pretty good. I buy jerky at the convenience store. But this tastes better."

They had been chewing on the jerky and drinking some cans of soda for about ten minutes when Wendy got up and walked over to behind the tent.

"Where ya going?" June asked.

"Oh, I thought I heard something over here and I figured I'd go see what it was."

She walked to the corner of the backside of the tent. As Golden looked up she saw Wendy, wide eyed and mouth open, backing slowly away from the tent. Less than five feet from her, crouched and snarling, came a huge yellow mountain lion. As she backed away the cat pressed forward. It was crouched and looked mad. Neither Wendy nor the cat took their eyes off the other. Wendy's skin was white and she was breathing in a way that let Goldie and June know that she was too frightened even to utter a cry for help. Out from behind the tent next came a little cub with an old chewed-on rawhide dog bone in its mouth.

Instinctively Goldie inched toward her mare. Reaching up, she pulled the Winchester out of the saddle holster. The cat had stopped. Wendy had backed up against a large boulder and could back no more. The cat crouched, curling its claws. Goldie knew it was going to jump. She quickly jacketed a round into the rifle. The sound of the weapon loading made the cat first turn to Goldie and snarl and then leap, claws out, mouth open wide, showing its white glistening fangs dripping with saliva. Goldie pulled off a round. She hadn't time to aim, or even to squeeze off the trigger like Jason had taught her. She even closed her eyes for an instant. The heavy cat crashed against Wendy. June screamed and Golden jacketed another round into the Winchester. The cat fell to the ground on top of Wendy. Goldie ran to the cat and rolled it off Wendy. As she rolled the cat it jerked. Goldie was startled by the twitch and put another round into its head. Both girls started looking over Wendy for bites, claw marks, or other injury. The cub scrambled off into the woods, squealing every 20 yards or so. Wendy blinked and Goldie hugged her.

"I wasn't sure you were alive," she whispered.

Wendy didn't answer; she looked at the dead cat lying beside her and started to cry.

It was almost eleven thirty at night when Golden rode into her yard. She didn't un-saddle her mare, but walked straight into the house. Mom and Dad were still up, which was very unusual. They were talking. Maybe just worrying about their daughter.

Jay usually got to bed early because he had to rise at 4:30 a.m. to get the cows milked.

"What ya doing home today?" Marge asked, surprised to see her.

"Oh, Mom!" Goldie started to tell the story and started to cry. She rehearsed the events of the day and ended with, "I brought the cat home, Dad. He's tied to the horse. Can you help me get him down? It took three of us to put him up there."

Jason walked out with a lantern to the horse tied at the barn. He looked at the cat, lifted his left front leg and saw a hole, a perfect shot through the heart.

"Too bad ya shot it in the head too, I'd a mounted it. Not much need, ya got her the first time." Jay tried to lift the cat down but it was too heavy even for him. He pulled on the leg and it flopped down to the ground. He tied it to the horse and dragged it into the barn where he used the pulley to lift the cat up. Goldie didn't want to watch it being gutted. She had seen lots of elk and deer and even a bear being done, but this cat was different. She didn't want to watch or help. Jay said it was all right and sent her into the house to get something to eat.

Morning time brought some unexpected guests. Goldie was up early and out to round up the milkers. She used Chase, the dog. It was mostly an Australian sheep dog, maybe some Cocker or something else in it. Kinda small, but really great at getting the cows into the milking yard. Once Goldie had put them in, closed the gate, and made sure there was enough grain mix in the feeder bin, she headed back in for some breakfast. The corral and milking barn were about 200 yards from the house, still too close for Marge who said the wind sometimes blew northwest and the smell made it tough to eat. But most of the time the wind blew southeast or northeast so it was no problem.

Goldie walked around the corner of the house. She was startled to see four or five guys with cameras and two ladies and a guy with a microphone.

"We heard you saved a life yesterday," the first reporter said as she stepped up on the cement stairway leading to the kitchen.

"Mom!" Goldie yelled, looking in wonderment at the little crowd of people around her.

Marge came to the back screen door and stepped out.

"Where is the lion?" one reporter asked.

"Can we photograph it?" another asked.

"It's hanging in the barn. Dad gutted it last night," Goldie heard herself say.

The reporters rushed to the barn. Goldie turned to her mom. "Why are they hurrying, it's not going anywhere now?"

"It's just the way they are, honey."

Golden and Marge walked out to the barn. They opened the door and were surprised at the reaction of the news people.

"Look at the size of that cat!" one of the reporters shouted.

"My God!" the woman interviewer exclaimed, "how did you get it home?"

"June and I and Wendy's dad threw it up on the horse," Goldie calmly explained.

The interviews and questions lasted most of an hour and they finally left. The reporters from the Minneapolis newspaper were going to release it nationally and the TV people were just going to carry it as a human-interest story. A couple of local papers were going to publish it as a "local hero" item.

"It wasn't that big a thing," Golden said as she finally sat down for some breakfast. You could hear Jay taking off his boots on the back porch. Marge smiled as Jay came in and said, "We have a hero in our house, honey."

"I know. Thanks for doing the right thing, sweetheart," Jay said and smiled.

"That was a damn big cat. And your shootin' couldn't a been any better."

They were finishing up breakfast late, about 8:30, when a knock on the front door interrupted Jay's outline of the day's activities. He also was asking if Goldie wanted to take and have a taxidermist tan the hide or if she wanted to do it herself. Jay had tanned up a couple of dear and elk pelts. It always made the entire yard and house stink for a week or more. So Goldie wanted to pay to have it done.

"I'll get it, Mom," Golden said as she left the table. She opened the door, sort of expecting to see another reporter.

"Hi, I just wanted to thank you for saving my life." Wendy and her father stood at the door. She looked better. And so did her dad. They had left camp and gone to the hotel to spend the night without even packing up the tent.

"Oh!" Goldie squeaked out, surprised to see them there. "Come on in."

"David Noble," Wendy's dad said, extending his hand to Jay who had just come from the living room to the front door. "I'm so very grateful to your daughter, and to you for teaching her to shoot like that. She saved my Wendy's life. If you want or need anything, just let me know."

"No thanks," Jay answered. "This is my wife Marge. We're just happy Goldie was there. We figure you must a set up your tent near the lion's den."

Marge had entered the room from the kitchen and was looking over Wendy and Dave with a curious eye.

"Where you folks from?" she asked.

"San Clemente, California," Wendy said with some pride in her voice. She was wondering if these people even knew where that was.

"Oh, how nice. I've been there a couple of times," Marge responded. Her voice hinted she might not have really ever been to California let alone San Clemente. But she knew President Nixon was from there, or at least had a house there, so she felt safe saying it.

"Would you like some coffee or breakfast or a roll or anything?" Marge asked, changing the subject as gracefully as she could.

"Yes, thanks," David said.

"Can we go outside and talk?" Wendy asked, smiling at Goldie.

"Yeah, you two go on outside and visit," David said without even considering what Goldie's parents might want.

The girls talked and walked around the farm. Goldie told Wendy about the reporters and Wendy confessed she had told the story eight or ten times at the hospital and to some reporters there and again at her motel room. She said her shoulder still hurt but except for a little bruising on her butt, she was okay. They went in to see the cat hanging from the ceiling beam in the barn.

"Wow! It's even bigger than I remember!" Wendy said, gasping a little.

"Why don't you come to California and stay with me for a while?"

"I've got my last year in high school to do first," Goldie answered. "But I'd really love to come." She was a little unsure if she meant it. She had never been out of the state for more than a day, let alone all the way across the country.

"I could show you how we do things there. Some real neat things. And the boys are awesome."

Goldie had become more interested in boys in the last few months. Not that she had a steady boyfriend, but a couple of the guys in school looked good. She now and then did some daydreaming about dates and even some about being married and having children. She thought she'd change things if she were the mom. She wouldn't make her daughters work. Of course she knew Jay really wanted a son, he needed someone to take over the farm and she sure wasn't gonna do that. It would be neat to see the ocean and to date real men. Her thoughts were interrupted by Wendy handing her a card with her name and phone number and address on it.

"It's my business card," she explained. "All the real kids have one. It makes it soo easy to give out your number an' stuff. It's even got my e-mail on it."

"Wow, that's really cool. I've done some surfing on the net at school, but we don't have a computer here at home, so I really don't know much about 'em."

"Come and stay with me for a couple of weeks and I'll show you some really awesome stuff."

They walked and talked for at least a couple of hours. They were heading back to the house to see what was happening there when the back porch door opened.

"Wendy, come on, honey, we've got to get going," Dave was calling off the back porch as though he couldn't see them coming.

"That's just like my dad, does it when he wants something from me!" Goldie said with a giggle.

"Yeah, I think parents are all alike. Even in Hicksville."

※

The summer ended too soon. School was different this year. Goldie's mind drifted more than it had ever done. She thought a lot about Wendy, all the things she had told her about the "real life." She wasn't as attentive as before. She wasn't interested anymore in what happened at Gettysburg. She was in line for the valedictorian, but somehow that didn't seem to matter so much anymore. Golden had thought about going to college. There were a couple that had written her letters and even a couple that said they had a scholarship for her. She had taken the SATs last spring and scored very high. Jay wasn't that enthusiastic about her going to college either.

"I'd give it a couple of years," he said. "If you haven't found a guy or settled on something local, then you could consider it." Deep in his heart he didn't want to lose his little girl. He had come to love her profoundly and thought she'd be his friend and daughter the rest of his life. Maybe she and her husband would take over the farm when he got too old to work. There was some acreage on the northwest side and he'd help her build a good house there. He had a little money stashed away and didn't figure on spending it anywhere. *What the heck did she need a degree for anyway? Honest folk live and love and work the earth. There is nothing better than seeing a crop come in or having the highest cream count in the county. Nothing better than fresh eggs and bacon from your own smoked pig with a glass of really cold milk for breakfast. Most of those college guys are just chasing the bucks,* he thought, *and for what? What'll they have in the end, green paper? No, life is about giving. Giving to your wife and kids, giving food to the world, even giving thanks to your God.*

"Sweetheart, don't you think you've got enough gravy?" Marge brought him back from his thoughts. He'd instinctively taken the gravy and was pouring it onto his mashed potatoes.

"Sorry, I got thinking, or stopped thinking, or something."

"You ever been to California?" Goldie asked as nonchalantly as she could.

"Yeah, I was there in the Navy. Was at San Diego and San Francisco a couple of times. I used to get extra leave 'cause I'd sell my cigarettes to guys in exchange for leave time. They'd cover my shift and I'd give 'em a carton. It was a great deal, I'd pick up cartons from the supply for two bucks and sell them when the guys were out of smokes and supply was out too. Yeah, I've seen California. Not much to it really. A lot of hype if ya ask me."

"Wendy says there are a million things to do there. She says you can go to the ocean, or to Disneyland or Knots Berry Farm or to Magic Mountain. You can see Hollywood and go to their theme park. You can even go see sea life in San Diego. She says there are millions of places to go dancing and great places to eat. She says the schools there are better than ours and there are lots of show houses. She said she has been to Disneyland at least ten times. Maybe you can take me when I graduate. I'd really like that."

Marge answered a little excited too. "I think it would be great, Jay."

"Okay, we'll see. If this crop is as good as I think it'll be, and if my poundage goes up, then we'll go. I'll have to see if that kid Jeffery can do the milking for a week. I'll sell the first fifty tons of hay, the rest of it I'll keep."

Dinner ended, and Goldie went out and cleaned up the cow manure. She put it into a bin where Jay loaded it into a spreader and put it on the fields in the late fall so it'd have time to break down and soak in and fertilize the alfalfa. She didn't mind the smell, and Dad had a little tractor with a scoop on the front that she used to pick up the manure. The holding area was all concreted up so it was easy to clean. After the clean up, she showered and went upstairs to do her homework.

※·※

Goldie's relationship with Grandma was really good. Over the years she and Grandma had had some great talks. Grandma understood things that Mom never seemed to get. She knew about boys for example. Mom didn't have a clue. They had discussed

Jeffery's butt at great length. Grandma said it was from riding horses a lot. Goldie thought he had just inherited it. But in either case they both thought it was really cute. Goldie had even confessed that she liked the way he walked. She had had a crush on him for half her life.

Grandma was sitting on the bed when Goldie came back in the bedroom from the shower.

"Ya know," Grandma said, "sometimes things are a matter of perspective. You might see a bail of green broadleaf, and I might see a bundle of weeds."

"I don't get it, Grandma, hay is hay."

"Well, Wendy might see life from the point of view of a young girl wanting to see it all and experience it all. She might be willing to take some chances, do some things that another girl would walk away from."

"I don't want to walk away from any experiences. I want to see what life's really about. I can't do that here, Grandma. I'd never see the ocean, and the boys here are really drab. If I could go there, only for a few weeks, I'd get to see what real people do. Maybe even date some California guys. Oh, Grandma, Mom and Dad have lived their life. It's my turn, it's my time, and I really, really, really want to see what this world has to offer."

Lillian looked deeply into Goldie's eyes for what seemed an eternity.

"You can have anything you want, Golden. Just remember there's always a price to pay. Nothing is free. If you want money you give your time and sometimes your soul, but you get money. If you want to explore, you have to buy it with not only your time but also your future. I love you, Golden, you are young, so let me whisper in your ear this truth. Nothing is free. Try to evaluate the price of an item before you buy it."

Golden wasn't sure she understood what Grandma had said. But she did know that Lillian loved her and was honestly worried about her. The subject was changed by Goldie and they spent another hour and a half talking about the prom and who she thought would ask her to go. It was her senior prom and so she was going to be really picky this time. Last year she had gone with Kim and he was very nice but a dud. She had wanted to go with Jeffery but he didn't go at all. He said his mom had some chores for him, but Goldie thought he was just scared. This year she had talked with him in the hall by the lockers and had suggested they might go to the prom together. He was genuinely surprised, but said he thought it would be great. Grandma left and Goldie finished her homework. It was boring and mostly stuff she had already learned the year before. She lay back on the down pillow Grandma had made for her and closed her eyes. She could see California, the beach, Disneyland, the boys, even Hollywood.

"Goodnight, sweetheart. I'm turning off the light now," Goldie's mom's voice interrupted her daydreaming. "Did you say your prayers?"

"Yeah, Mom," she responded and then realized she had not. Mom was gone and Goldie's first thought was that she should get up and go tell her mom she had lied.

How funny, she thought, *I still think I need to tell Mom everything. I know I'm too old for that now. But I still have those urges. It's really silly, I can decide for myself if I need to pray or not.*

⇸•⇷

School days went by slowly. Goldie got a letter from Wendy a week before Thanksgiving and she answered the same day. She was glad to get the letter. She had lost Wendy's address and so when the letter came it seemed God sent. They began to write each other every week, sometimes twice a week. Wendy would describe different places in California she promised to show Goldie when she came. Goldie really liked the birds that came to Capistrano every year. She loved the rugged cliffs next to the ocean in Northern California and Oregon. She thought Wendy's house was kind of funny though. Wendy had sent her a couple of pictures of the house on Polaroid. It was up on a hill and you could see the ocean from the second-floor porch. But it didn't have any property and no trees. It did have a chain-link fence. It had a big garage and a nice front lawn but for as big as it was and as nice as Wendy's room was, it somehow didn't seem like a home, just a house.

Wendy said her dad was gone most of the time. Her mom had divorced her dad several years before and she didn't see much of her mom. Sometimes her mom would call, but they'd only talk for a few minutes. Wendy really didn't know her mom very well. Since the divorce, she had never even gone to her mom's house to stay overnight. Mom lived clear up in Redding or somewhere up there. So Wendy mostly had the house in San Clemente to herself. She cooked her own dinners most of the time and went where she wanted. Her dad had given her a little blue Mazda, not much of a car, she said, but it was okay for riding around town or even going up to LA to see a concert. Wendy said she had lots of girl friends and lots of boys, none of which were really friends.

"Boys only want one thing," she said, "sex. That's it. Take care of that and you can get what you want."

It seemed weird to Golden. She had seen the horses pro-creating and the dog. The cows were always inseminated by dad, but she knew they did the same thing. She didn't yet understand what excitements that act had. Yet somewhere deep inside her she wanted to experience it. She knew it must be good.

School worsened. They did a Thanksgiving play. It was pretty good. Goldie didn't do anything in the play except for making and painting some of the backdrops. She couldn't spare the time. Dad seemed to be giving her more work around the farm and Mom was trying to teach her more about cooking anything that wasn't a rock. Homework seemed to be redundant and stupid, but she continued to do it. Some nights she didn't get to sleep until two in the morning.

They were in the kitchen scrounging around for something to cook for dinner when Mom got mad and told her she shouldn't stay up so late. It made her sluggish and sloppy. Golden wasn't sure why Mom had all of the sudden gotten upset. Usually Marge would step into the room and say goodnight and turn out the light. Golden would wait for five or ten minutes and then turn the light back on and finish her homework. For some reason Mom wasn't going straight to bed after her goodnight anymore; she'd stay up for a while. Golden could hear her walking past the door sometimes after midnight.

Goldie listened to Mom scold her and tell her she had to start doing better. Then she responded in a way that surprised even herself as she spoke.

"I don't know how to do better, Mom. You make me cook supper half the time and the other half I'm out with Dad checking for mastitis or cleaning up cow crap. I don't have any time left for homework or even for some personal things I'd like to be doing. I don't know where I'm going to go when I graduate and I don't know what I'll be doing. It's all coming so fast and I'm not ready!" She ran away crying.

Marge understood well what Golden was saying. She also had graduated from high school and worked around the valley in a sort of listless empty way, waiting for something. So when Jay finally came home from the Navy, she was glad to go out with him. She had gotten lots of offers for dates but most of the time she just didn't want to go. Jay was different. He seemed more mature. He was always very polite and considerate. He had said more than once to her that he knew he wasn't the most handsome guy in the world, but inside he was John Wayne, steady as a rock. Marge teased Jay about that for years to come. When things on the farm went wrong or when he did something stupid, she'd say his rock was cracking. It became their private joke. Sort of their inside password. Even Goldie had become aware of it when she was about ten and sometimes used it with her dad. It wasn't the same for Jay, but he would smile and brush it off.

Now Marge was faced with explaining to Goldie how to find herself after high school. She thought if she'd teach her to cook and give her the opportunity to prepare meals and keep her busy she'd discover if that was what she wanted in life. It didn't seem to be working. Marge sensed that Golden didn't want to learn to cook. It seemed strange because she had helped make cookies and lunches and dinners for more than ten years. Marge wondered if Goldie was learning to be rebellious from that Wendy in California. She had found a couple of Wendy's letters in Goldie's room when she was gathering laundry and read them. They were pleasant enough but carried a sublineal suggestion that Goldie's parents were old-fashioned and that she was living in a not very modern world. Perhaps Golden believed that California was the "real" world. Marge didn't know; perhaps she was just imagining this out of fear that Goldie would leave home when she finished high school. She shook her head slowly. *She will only be eighteen when she graduates; so very young. In some ways Jay's right. Why did she need to go off to college for four years? What's the final benefit? Maybe I'm just being old-fashioned. Maybe I'm worried about the empty nest syndrome*, she thought.

Her thoughts were interrupted by Goldie brushing against her arm. She turned to Goldie and smiled. "Thanks for coming back down. I know it's coming fast, sweetheart, life never slows down for anyone. Days come and go like waves in the mountain stream. New ones follow the ones that disappear. They never stop, and they take you with them for an instant or two, then you're gone."

"Oh, Mom, that's one of the dumbest things you've ever said." She turned and walked out of the kitchen again. Then she stopped and returned.

"What we makin' tonight, Mom?"

"Well, you suddenly seem happier than you were a few minutes ago. What's up?"

"Oh, nothing really, I just realized that you're right. I do need to make the most of my moment because it will be gone soon enough. And I'm going too!"

Marge didn't quite understand the last quip, but she figured it meant that Goldie was going to make the most of her time.

Dinner went well. Golden cooked stuffed pork chops, something they'd never had. She learned the recipe in a home economics class at school. Jay was very pleased.

"This is probably the best meal I've had for ten years," he said, winking at Marge.

"Ya know, I think I should learn to do the things Mom does. I know I'll need it someday. Even if I never marry, I'll need it for myself."

"You'll marry, honey, just don't be in a hurry. There's lots of time." Marge took Golden's hand and softly rubbed the back of it with her thumb.

The rest of the evening went well. Goldie sat on the front porch and swung. The night had the hint of autumn in the air. Leaves were starting to fall. The sky was clear and the smell of fresh-cut hay floated across the valley. It was the last cut of the season. She could hear an owl across the yard. In the past it had been an annoyance to her, sometimes keeping her up at night. But it seemed pleasant now. Life here was not so bad.

"I can live here. I can find a place."

IV

The Prom

    There's something about the senior prom. It's when you've arrived at the top. You've done your twelve years and you are a senior. More than that, you have learned enough about the world to make your own decisions. You are going to graduate and leave school behind and you can flaunt it to the freshmen, sophomores, and juniors. What a great feeling. Golden felt exceptionally good that afternoon. It was the last day of school before the Thanksgiving break and the day of the prom. Plus she was going to the prom with Jeffery. Two weeks before the prom and after a giant hint at the locker, Jeffery formally asked her if she would like to go to the prom with him. He was as excited as she.

    Jeffery was the son of the county veterinarian, Doc Davidson. He was a great vet. He would come out in the middle of the night and never minded staying to help deliver or even help clean up. He'd never charge for his time more than what he did as a vet. The "doc" would willingly come and help with the delivery of kittens if there was some problem that parents or neighbors couldn't solve. He was a great vet and a good friend to most of the people in the county.

Jeffery was quiet and intelligent. He was going to follow in his father's footsteps and become a veterinarian. He did well in school and was one of the other students being considered for the valedictorian. There would be four so it really wasn't a competitive thing between Goldie and Jeff. A little shy, he was afraid to say that he had been in love with Goldie since the fifth grade but had only let her know in the last few months. Over the years they had gone to parties together and out on four or five dates. He had even kissed her goodnight a couple of times. One night, a couple of weeks into the senior year, Jeffery had told Golden how he felt about her and she was very glad. She told Marge what he had said to her. Marge just smiled and said it was good that Goldie was so pretty that the boys were in love with her. She didn't take it too seriously. But Goldie thought a lot about it. So when he was slow to ask her to the senior prom, she nudged him on. He confessed he wanted to ask, but the prom was so important he didn't know if she wanted to go with someone else, like Richard, the football quarterback. She laughed that teasing kind of laugh that nobody but another girl understands and said she had thought about going with Richard. But she just had to turn him down. She giggled and said, "Where would I have been if you hadn't asked me? I already turned down the best date in the school." Jeff blushed and asked what time she wanted him to pick her up.

"Do you want to go to dinner before or after the dance?" he ventured.

"You never go before! How can you explain staying up really late if you go to dinner first?" Golden smiled. "I've got to get to class." And off she went.

An old, black 1949 Cadillac pulled into the backyard of Golden's home. It was a beautiful restored old limo with all the original emblems on the trunk, the hood, and even the Cadillac symbols on each of the hubcaps. It had been upholstered in the original type and color of cloth and the wood window frames and panels had all been taken out and refinished. The transmission was the newest thing in its time, a hydromantic that was run by oil. The windows were automatic and were raised and lowered by hydraulic fluid, not electric motors. The tires had white walls about four inches wide and were like the ones that came with the car when it was new. All in all the car was spectacular.

Out of the car stepped Jeffery. He was dressed in a fine tuxedo with a bow tie and tails. His shoes were shinny as a new penny and had little leather bells on the end of each lace. His hair was combed back in the '40s style and he had on thin wire-rimmed glasses. In his left hand was a blue box with a white ribbon and a fluffy bow. In his right hand was an orchid bouquet.

He closed the car door; it didn't make the same sound closing car doors do today. It was quieter and heaver. It was the sound of something solid, sure, and well built. Jeff also felt that way that evening. He had gained new self-confidence. Part of it was the realization that Goldie really did care for him and part of it was he realized that he was worth caring for. Some people come to the conclusion that they are worth caring for early and some take more time. Some never figure it out. But Jeffery had. He knew he had something to offer and he was there offering it.

Golden was watching from her window upstairs, and Jay and Marge were watching from the living room window. Jeff saw them but played like he didn't. He walked up to the front porch. The grass was growing in between the stones because no one ever went to the house that way. They always used the kitchen entrance. Even guests who knew the family would come to the kitchen. But Jeff was making a statement; he was taking Golden out on a very special date and he was going to do it right. He knocked on the door and Marge told Jay to wait a second. He did and Jeff knocked again, just three times, softly but firmly. Jay answered the door.

"Hi, Jeff, she'll be right down. I think she's still putting on some makeup or something."

It wasn't that at all, of course. Marge had worked three weeks to make the blue satin gown. It had a blue base and was covered around the bottom with a lace that was a lighter blue. It came down over the shoulder just an inch an a half and had a linen leaf coming off each shoulder and tapering back as it came down over her breasts. The linen leaf was embroidered and laced with white embroidered designs that dipped almost half way down the front, exposing what Jay thought was a little too much breast.

Jay was more than surprised when Golden walked down the stairs. She was beautiful. She was certainly a woman and walked with poise and self-confidence that neither Jay nor Marge had noticed in the past. She had on heals, not spikes, but still about an inch high. They were wide at the bottom and Goldie negotiated walking with them as though she had grown up wearing only heels. She came down into the living room.

"Wow, Jeff, where did you get the car?" she burst out before regaining her composure.

"It's my dad's. He keeps it locked up 'cept for special occasions. I was telling him about tonight and he handed me the keys. Didn't say anything, just handed me the keys. Wait'll you ride in it. It's really great."

Marge came into the living room with a camera in hand.

"Okay, you guys, let me take a couple of pictures. Jeff, let me get one of you giving her the corsage."

Jeff pulled out the long pin in the back of the corsage and handed it to Goldie. She didn't take it, she just stepped closer to him and said, "You pin it right here," and she pointed to a place on her left side just above her breast. Jeff was pretty nervous. He didn't want to stick her with the pin and he didn't want to put his hand into the top of her dress. He reached out with the corsage and put it onto the embroidered leaf covering up near Golden's shoulder. Before he could pin it Goldie said, "Don't pin it there. I'll hit it every time I turn my head." She smiled.

"I can't do it, would you?" Jeff said, turning to Marge.

Marge had already gotten several pictures of Jeff's embracement and his attempt to pin the corsage and so the fun of the moment was over. She pinned the corsage onto her daughter and put her arm around Jeff.

"We don't know where you planned to go to dinner," Marge continued, "but we thought if you'd like you could go to the park at Lyndon Grove and we'd present you with a great dinner in the moonlight."

"I don't know, Mom, we kinda wanted to be alone."

"No!" Jeff interrupted. "I can't think of anything better. After we eat we can go for a ride."

"Okay. Sure, Mom, that sounds really good," Goldie added, still not convinced.

Lillian came across the living room and kissed Golden on the cheek. She whispered in her ear, "This is your night, sweetheart, yours alone. Make it count." She stepped away and said in a louder voice, "I'm making the dessert," at which everyone laughed. She always made the dessert.

"Okay, let me take some more pictures and then you can go." Marge took eight or ten pictures of Golden and six or seven of Jeff. She then went to the closet and took out a wrap that was hand woven and made by her mother and wrapped it around Goldie's shoulders. Jay stepped out on the porch with Jeff and said, "Please take care of her. She's innocent and vulnerable."

"I will, Mr. Bradley," Jeffery responded with a somberness that seemed appropriate for vows at a Mason temple ceremony.

The couple walked out the front doorway. It had become almost dark, more like late dusk, and Lillian turned on the porch light as they stepped down from the five-step old cement porch. The car was as great as Jeff had said. It had a smell to it that was enchanting. It was some remnant of the varnish smell that Jeff's father had put on the old wood after carefully removing each peace and sanding it and refinishing it. It was a Danish rubbing oil, which he had hand rubbed into the old wood. The smell of the upholstery wasn't new but it was the kind of smell you get when it hasn't been used. Once it was new, but now it was just unused. The engine and oil smelled different. Not unpleasant, just different. It was a good smell.

Golden sat up front and slid over next to Jeff. There were no seat belts so she snuggled up next to him. They drove to the school and got there at about 7:30. The prom had started at seven but only a few kids came right on time. Mostly the girls who had decorated it and those assigned to get the refreshments ready.

The decorations at the dance were gold and green. The girls gathered around Goldie and admired her dress and wrap.

"Where'd you get that dress?" asked one of her classmates.

Actually, my mom made it," Golden answered.

"Man! I wish my mom could sew like that. It really is gorgeous. I see you finally got Jeffery Davidson to take you out."

"It's about time," chirped up another girl.

The prom was great. Golden was asked to dance by more guys than she ever thought possible. She would excuse herself politely from Jeffery and go dance with whoever asked. Jeff wasn't long to catch on. He would ask her to dance with him during the dance so the next one was taken. Goldie was glad. It showed her that he was a little jealous and that excited her in a way she wasn't familiar with.

At the intermission of the dance the principal got up and announced that the judges had come to a decision on who the king and queen of this year's prom would be. Stillness took over the group. Those who knew they didn't have a chance were either guessing who it was going to be or making wise cracks about how stupid the ceremony was.

"This year's king and queen are...Jeffery Davidson and Golden Fern Bradley."

The kids all applauded and the band, mostly sophomores who weren't invited to the senior prom, played the "Miss America" song. Jeff and Golden walked up the stairs to the stage where the principal, vice principal, and Miss Hawthorn, an English teacher in charge of school events, were waiting. Hawthorn crowned Golden and the principal crowned Jeffery. They got some free tickets to dinner at the Angora Dinner and a free stay-home-from-school day pass, a McDonald's lunch pass, and Golden got a beautiful bouquet of roses. Everyone clapped and the band played "Moon River" to which they danced alone on the floor for the first half and then students joined in and soon the floor was filled.

"I can't believe they made me queen!" Golden said as they walked off the floor over to the refreshments. "I never thought this could happen to me."

Jeff handed her some red punch, which had too much sugar in it. It was a combination of red Kool-Aid and Seven Up. Goldie walked silently over and sat down in the special seats made for the prom king and queen.

"Maybe I am someone special. Maybe I am better than this valley, better than a dairy farmer, better than all this," she thought half way out loud.

"It's ten to ten," Jeff interrupted. "I told your dad we'd meet him at ten thirty for dinner."

"Okay, go tell the principal we've got to be going."

It didn't matter much. The dance ended at eleven anyway. Jeff went over and told principal Gurley they were leaving. Gurley stood up and walked to the mic and congratulated them again and told the crowd they were leaving.

"I'll bet I know where you're going!" Kristine said as they walked out.

"She's so stupid," Goldie said to Jeff then turning to Kristine she remarked, "Just because you're the class lover doesn't mean the rest of us are."

Goldie grabbed Jeffery's arm and pulled herself close to him. It felt good to leave with him. They drove up to Lyndon Grove without saying much but small talk. Although it seemed more than that. It seemed that Jeff had finally changed. He was more assertive and more grown up than she had ever noticed before.

The grove was lit with what seemed to be a hundred Coleman lanterns. The picnic table was covered with Grandma's fine white linen tablecloth. On the table were crystal wine glasses and five covered dishes. There was also a bottle of chilled cider. The kind that is not fermented but comes in the dark green bottle and looks like an expensive champagne. The cork was not off the bottle but it was loosened and the silver wrapper was torn away from the top. The plates were fine china with a gold trim around the outside and a gold ring around the inside. Marge came up to the car dressed in a black dress with white trim.

"This way to your table, madam," Marge said in a voice that was trying to imitate a British hostess. Jason was at the table with a white towel hanging over his arm and a black suit coat covering his white church shirt. Goldie and Jeffery walked to the table where they were seated on the picnic bench. The bench had been covered with a heavy cloth, probably a bedspread, which had been carefully folded lengthwise until it fit over the bench just exactly. Grandma had tied a wool blanket under the linen tablecloth so it would not move when they were eating and maybe leaning on it. Then put her hand crocheted linen tablecloth over the top.

Dinner was exquisite. The steaks were half-inch thick and done to perfection. The bottle of cider was delicious and the corn and potatoes were baked just right. The salad was perfect and Marge had made wonderful garlic dressing. Goldie worried a little about the garlic but it was so good she couldn't help but smile and thank Mom for it. Dessert was a chocolate moose, which Grandma had never made at home. It was too rich for Goldie; still she couldn't help eating every bite. Jeffery said he had never had such a meal. That it was the greatest dinner he had ever had and he didn't know how they had made all this great food so fast and so well.

The evening got cold but Jeffery was prepared. He walked to the Cadillac and got a warm wool coat for Goldie and one for himself. Goldie asked Mom and Dad if they could stay out a little longer and they said yes. They got into the Cad and left.

The limousine had a great heater and Jeff turned it on as they drove out onto old Highway 22. They drove west for about three or four miles until they came to Highway 5, they then drove south to another campground where Jeff pulled in. Golden was a little afraid. Not that Jeff would hurt her or even do anything without her consent, but afraid that she would give her consent. He put his hand into the pocket of his coat and left it there. Goldie didn't know if he was holding on to something or just cold. He cleared his throat.

"Goldie, I love you. I think you love me. Life is passing us by and we need to make the most of our time. I know there a lot of guys who would like to have been with you tonight, but we are meant for each other. You know, I have a scholarship to Minnesota University in Minneapolis and if I do well there, my dad says I can get into his vet school and finish my doctorate degree in five years or less."

Goldie listened, sincerely interested, but wondering if this was some kind of preface to him asking her to make love.

"So," he continued, "I think where we live is one of the most beautiful places on this earth. We do well here and I believe that you and I can make a difference both in our town and county and is some ways in the world. What I'm trying to say, not very well, is…will you marry me, Golden?"

He pulled his hand out of his pocket and opened it. There in the middle of his palm was a diamond ring. Not just any diamond ring but what looked to be at least a full carat set in some other black stones. It was very, very beautiful.

Golden was very surprised. She stammered, "I do love you, Jeff. You and I have been not only great friends for years but I have come to care for you and yes even to love you in this past year. Let me think about it. It's the most important question that has ever been asked of me." She slid over and put her head on Jeffery's shoulder. She took the ring and looked at it. It seemed so great, so really perfect. He took the ring from her and slid it onto her finger. It fit perfectly. She didn't say anything, just reached over with her right arm and hugged him. His hand slid down her head, neck, and over her shoulder onto her upper arm. He pulled her even closer to him and they just held each other for what seemed to be an eternity.

"Oh, crap, it's almost one o'clock!" Jeff said. He put the car in gear, which had been running for the last half hour to keep the heater going. He kissed Goldie again and drove out of the empty park.

Goldie came in the back door. Jeff walked her to the kitchen door and passionately kissed her. In some ways Goldie was disappointed. She had wanted Jeff to at least make out with her. She had decided before the prom not to give herself completely to him, but she wanted to say "no" at least a couple of times. But Jeff was a complete gentleman.

Mom was still up. She didn't say anything to Golden as she entered, but was sitting by the fireplace reading or at least pretending to read. Golden came in and said she was tired and was going to bed. As she turned to go upstairs to her room, Mom said, "How are you?" in a voice that seemed to be asking, "Well what happened?"

"I'll tell you all about it tomorrow, Mom," Goldie said quietly as she walked up the stairs.

Marge had noticed the ring on her finger. She wasn't surprised John had told her and Jay at the restaurant that he thought Jeff was in love with their daughter. They all chatted and smiled about it, but there was the undercurrent that Jeff was pretty serious.

Marge followed suit and went upstairs and climbed in bed. Jay wasn't asleep. He rolled over and said, "So?"

"Well, honey, she said she was very tired, but she had a ring on her hand."

"What kind of ring?" Jay asked in a mildly accusing voice.

"An engagement ring."

"She's too damn young to be getting married."

"I don't think it'll be tomorrow, honey. We'll find out in the morning at breakfast."

Jay grumbled in non-words, kissed Marge, and went to sleep.

Goldie was up at four thirty and out with the dog getting the cows in. Jason was in the shed getting the milkers ready. He looked up and saw the cows standing in the holding pen and smiled. *She's sure dependable*, he thought.

"Well, how'd it go last night?" he shouted across the milking barn to the stall where Goldie was now closing the gate with all the cows in. She didn't answer. She was busy with the cows. The cows were so used to being milked they even lined up in order to go into the milking stalls. After each one was milked, it was shooed out the front of the milking stall and into the field and the next in line came in and walked into the stall. The steel gate stopped it from going past the port where it had to stand. Dad had finished the milking and started the clean up.

Golden came into the milk house and smiled. She walked over to where Dad was spraying down the floor.

"I'll tell ya," she said and then walked over and turned off the grain feeder.

"He asked me to marry him, Dad."

"You think you're ready for marriage?"

"We've got some time. Finish school and the summer. But next fall he'll be going to the university in Minneapolis. I would be going with him. It's close and we'd come home for the summers but it's four years of being away from you and Mom and here. I don't know how you'd get the farming and milking done without me. Then we'd go to vet school. I'm not sure where that is, but he said he could do it in five years or so. Then we'd come back here. I don't know if I'm ready. I don't know if I'll be ready by next fall. I don't know if I want to spend the rest of my life here in the valley. And I don't even know if I love him that much."

With that she said she was going to go get some breakfast and go back to bed. It was Saturday. Jay didn't answer. He didn't have much of a chance to answer, but even if he could he didn't know exactly what to say.

"Okay, honey," he said mostly to himself as she walked across the yard to the house.

When Golden got into the house, Mom was up fixing some pancakes. The pancake breakfast included eggs, bacon, sausage, cold milk, and coffee. It was always too much for Goldie to eat but Mom still filled her plate with three pancakes, an egg on top, two sausages, and two thick strips of bacon. She put real butter on the pancakes, a square on each one, and poured real Vermont maple syrup all over the eggs, pancakes, and meat.

"Well, tell me everything!" Mom almost couldn't hold herself back.

"He asked me to marry him, Mom. Dad said he didn't know if I was ready for marriage. And I said I didn't know either."

"You're never ready, sweetheart, you learn as you go. You get new challenges and new realizations every day. You give, you take, you love, and you work. That's all there is to life. You hope you leave more than you took. I think we have. You are much more than either of us; you are the product of two lesser people. Your father's and my life have been extremely blessed and great, just great mostly because we had you."

"Oh, Mom, I have always admired you and Dad. You love each other so much and you're so very giving. I just don't know if I can be that way. I don't know if I want to stay in this valley the rest of my life."

"Where else would you go? Life is not any different wherever you are. You are the thing that makes it go, you are the center of your universe. Life here could be as new and exciting as anyplace else on earth, but you have to make it that way. Jeffery will get through school, he will make good money, and more importantly, he will love you and give you children you can teach and raise."

"I'm not sure I love him that much. I do love him, but we don't know each other very well."

"I dated your father for several years, but I never knew him until we were married. You think about it, sweetheart. You have time."

"I didn't say yes, Mom. I only took the ring because he put it on my finger."

"Let me see it."

Golden slowly and carefully took off the ring and gave it to her mother.

"No, Goldie, you never take off the ring, you hold up your hand and show it that way."

"Oh, Mom, that's silly."

"I know, but that's how it should be done." Marge held the ring up in the air above her head and looked at it in the light. Not that she knew how to see a flaw, or even know the difference between a cubic zirconium and the real diamond, but she went through the motions anyway.

"Wow! It must be more than a half a carat," she said sincerely, admiring the stone.

"It looks bigger today than it did last night. Maybe 'cause I was excited and scared at the same time, I don't think I looked at it very closely," Golden said and smiled, feeling a little important to have gotten such a big and expensive ring.

Jay came in and sat down in his regular place at the table's end next to the wall.

"Got some mud, Mom?" he asked, smiling and winking at Golden.

Goldie repeated the events of the night to Dad. He didn't say much, just smiled and told Golden she could do whatever she wanted. Maybe she could wait until he came home from college. Then upon reconsideration, he said, "No, most men won't wait. College is full of young and beautiful girls. If you decide he's the one for you, you should marry him before you go to MSU."

V

Time to Cast Away Stones

Thanksgiving was great. Jeffery and his mom and dad and three sisters came. Jeanine, Marge's mom, came, Uncle Bowman came, and of course Grandma Lillian cooked the sweet potatoes and Mom cooked one really large turkey and one ten-pound cured ham. Jeff's mom brought some wonderful lemon pies and mincemeat pies and cherry pies made from her canned pie cherries. She also brought twenty fresh sweet corn on the cobs and enough potatoes to store for the winter.

The ladies, including Golden, cooked in the kitchen from 7:30 in the morning until almost two in the afternoon. They all talked and congratulated Goldie. They discussed who was going to make the wedding dress and who was going to get the flowers and where they were going to be married. They all agreed that the Lutheran minister would do the ceremony. Jeff went to the same church with his dad so there was really no conflict there. Everyone in the room asked when at least five or six times. Goldie was tired of answering that she didn't know, and even once she had said she wasn't sure she would accept the proposal. But everyone ignored her and went merrily on, talking and planning.

Finally it was ready. The table, which was outside under the giant old poplar tree, was set and all the food was brought out. Jay had put four small card tables around the table to put food on so the guests could finish passing around the potatoes or other foods and, when done, place them off the table. He put the desserts and whipped cream, not the store-bought stuff but real cream milked that morning, on the kitchen table, which he and Jeff had hauled out earlier that morning.

Jason sat at the end of the table and when everyone had sat down he rose and spoke. You could see pride in his eyes.

"I am so very thankful at this time in my life for having been given a beautiful daughter. She is my life. We welcome the Davidsons to our meal and all the other family members. I guess I'll say grace, Marge makes me say it every year," he said sort of under his breath, but so everyone could hear. Everyone chuckled a little and bowed their heads. It was a short prayer, but to the point. Jay thanked God for the food, for blessing the crop that year, and asked him to bless everyone. He then quickly added, almost as an afterthought, that the lord should bless his daughter's marriage.

⇾•⇽

School started again and the whole high school was already buzzing about the marriage. Some, like Goldie's English teacher, thought it was foolish. She wanted Golden to go to college and make something of herself. Principal Gourley called her in, out of class, and asked her if marriage was what she really wanted. He said she was clearly gifted and that she could choose her career and life path. Goldie thought a lot about what each proponent had said. Both sides seemed good. On the one hand where else could she go that would be as beautiful as the valley? After all, her mom was right, wasn't giving and having children the real objective in life? On the other hand she really wanted to see the world. She really did think she could contribute in ways other than making babies.

The congratulations faded as the weeks went by. Goldie and Jeff were seeing a lot of each other now. They went out twice a week and sometimes more. They ate lunch together in the cafeteria and Jeff occasionally would take her home in his mom's car when he had it. They would stop and kiss and Goldie would ask questions. Jeff would answer as though he was older and wiser. They parked and made out sometimes. Jeff never went too far. Even though Goldie had thought he should try so she could say "No."

She was learning to love Jeff. He had a multitude of qualities and he really loved her. He continuously sent gifts. His mother would make and send candy and flowers in Jeff's name. Golden had never in her life been given so much attention. As the weeks passed, she bathed in the attention like a hippo rolling in a drying mud hole, happy but wishing for more. Perhaps not more of the same, but something different. Something not yet said, something she thought was missing.

⇾•⇽

Christmas came and Jay took Golden and Jeff up into the mountains for his annual tree cut. He let Jeff pick the tree and cut it. Golden thought that was a real show of confidence. Jay had waited until she was twelve years old before he let her pick the tree. Marge went with them and stayed busy chatting about how much snow there was and how it had come early this year. She occasionally asked Jeff about what his mother was doing for Christmas. Jeff said friends and family were coming for the Christmas day present opening and for the goose dinner afterward. He had invited Golden but she said she would rather spend her last family Christmas at home. They made plans to get together on Christmas Eve and again on Christmas day.

Jeff said he had picked out a great present for Goldie. He knew she'd love it. Goldie hadn't found a gift yet for Jeff and was worried about it. She had saved about four hundred dollars, but wanted to keep it for acquiring some things, which were personal. Things like makeup and bras and other very personal items. She wondered what it would be like if Jeff knew about her period. She wondered if he wanted to wait to have children and if so what should she take to prevent conception. She thought about sleeping in the same bed with him. It seemed strange; she had never slept with anyone except her mom on occasion. She kept picturing in her mind her mare and Jay's stud. How they had sexual intercourse. She wondered if that was the way she and Jeff would do it. She couldn't imagine how it could feel good. But she knew it did. Some of the girls at school had given away their virginity in exchange for attention, love, gifts, or fun. Most of them said it was great. Some said it wasn't worth it. But most said it was great.

They brought the tree down in Dad's old Ford F150. It was about a '56 but he had rebuilt the engine a couple of times and modified the tires and put on heavier springs and shocks.

Both families spent the night decorating it and Mom, as was the household tradition, put the star on the top. Mom served a roast goose for dinner afterward. It wasn't the full-fledged Christmas goose with all the trimmings but it was very well done and Golden thought she couldn't remember when they had that nice a dinner on a "Tree Day." After dinner, Jay put a couple of 33 &1/3 records on his old stereo and he and Marge danced in the living room. After a couple of dances they invited Jeff and Goldie to dance. The music was some old Bing Crosby Christmas stuff, but it was nice to dance to. Goldie felt good inside for the first time. It was going to be okay after all. She did love Jeff and she knew that Dad would give her ten acres on beautiful tree-covered land and help them build a house on it. What else was there anyway?

They danced for a half an hour and Jay went into the kitchen and brought out a bottle of champagne. He never drank so Goldie was surprised to see him come into the living room with it in a silver bowl filled with ice. Grandma followed with some crystal champagne glasses and everyone became silent. She poured about a half a glass of champagne into each goblet. Jay stood up.

"You give kids their life, you teach them and you feed them. I guess you never realize they will become adults. You know it but you don't realize it. I'm thankful you are becoming such a good adult, Goldie. May God bless you and your husband-to-be."

Goldie drank it and thought it tasted kinda funny. They spent the next hour talking and visiting. Golden thought it seemed strange to be included in adult circles now. She didn't think she had changed, but she was being treated differently. Her mom included her in some mild gossip about one of the church member's babies and made an off-color comment about one of the single sisters. Golden was a little confused; perhaps it was the alcohol. Jeff and his parents said their goodnights and Golden went upstairs to bed without saying much to her parents.

Christmas was great. Jeff gave her a pearl necklace, which had the some kind of black stone in between each pearl. The pearls were a pale pink. Jeff said that they were really rare, suggesting that they were very expensive too. Jeff's mom gave her a sweater and a blouse. His dad gave her a silver brush set for her hair. It had a silver mirror and comb and two brushes and came in a silver box with what looked like swede leather in the lining.

Dad had offered to help her buy a present for Jeff. He knew she only had four or five hundred dollars and was saving it. So he paid half of the price for a saddle and spent about two weeks tooling it for Jeff. It was magnificent. Goldie thought he had done a better job than he did even for her. He hadn't built it, but he did spend most of the previous two weeks tooling the leather and getting it finished for Christmas. Everyone in both families oo'd and ahh'd about how beautiful it was. The basic saddle cost almost five hundred dollars so Goldie thought she had done more than was expected of her. You couldn't buy that kind of workmanship anywhere. A less worked but similar saddle would cost at least a thousand dollars.

Mom gave her a beautiful green dress. It wasn't formal, but probably too good to wear to school. It looked great. It came down to her knees and was pleated. She thought she'd wear it to dinner. Maybe to church. Dad gave her some money. He said she'd need it for personal things. She hugged him and kissed him but didn't open it up until she got into her room. She picked up the wrappers off the floor and vacuumed up. Mom and Grandma had dinner almost ready and Mom's brothers were on their way. Dad's first cousin and sister had come the night before and were in town looking around. Golden went up to her room and sat on her bed. She opened her father's envelope and was surprised to find five hundred dollars in it.

"I wonder if he's glad to be getting rid of me, or if he is inviting me to be sure to take the land on the upper wooded corner?" she mused. "No, I know he isn't glad to get rid of me. Who else would clean up the dung?" She smiled and went back downstairs. Jay was sitting in the living room and she went to him and hugged him.

"I love you, Dad. Thanks for the money."

Dinner was great. Grandma made the greatest gravy in the world. Goldie helped and this time Grandma showed her carefully each step. She knew it from ten Christmases before but she patiently listened to Lillian and did exactly what she was told. It was the same with the goose the night before; Mom explained carefully every seasoning, how to clean, dress, and prepare the goose for the morrow's baking. Pie crusts were no problem and Golden made up ten of them without much instruction or help from either Mom or Grandma. She always made peach pie for Uncle Paul. He loved peach and claimed to be an expert in judging peach pies.

"Only the finest ingredients can be used. Not too much sugar, not too thick a crust, and only the best peaches, tree ripened and naturally sweet, make the perfect peach pie," he'd say. He said it every year and every year after dinner, he'd say that that was the best peach pie he'd ever tasted. Goldie smiled to herself. *Paul lives okay. He hasn't traveled much and he makes good money. He teaches at the university in Denver and is tenured. He loves his wife and they have four kids. Mostly brats*, she thought in retrospect. But Linda, his wife, seems happy. She very seldom complains. She doesn't do much to help cook the Christmas dinner, but she does keep her kids out of the way. Last year Golden had to take them horseback riding. That was a nightmare! The youngest, Dillan, fell off the horse and refused to get back on. They were about a mile out and so Goldie had to put him on her horse and lead his mare back to the house. He was nine years old and should have known better.

Jeff came over the next day and met all her extended family and she had to go to his house and meet his. They were good people, although some were a little snooty. She defended her father's lack of education by pointing to his cousin Paul who had a PhD. She was carefully examined from head to toe by Jeffery's grandmother who after ten minutes snorted and said, "Welcome to the family, sweetie."

After it was all over she and Jeff sat on the porch swing and talked as they rocked back and forth.

"Is this what you really want to do, Jeff?" she asked, partly exposing an internal fear of her own and partly in sincerity making sure he wasn't just doing what was expected of him.

"I know, sometimes I have doubts too," he answered. Goldie was surprised to hear that coming from him.

"But where could I go and find a girl as wonderful and beautiful as you? We can make life a great adventure for you and me. So to answer your question, yes, this is really what I want. How about you?"

"I wish I were as sure as you. I do love you, Jeff, I just don't know if I'm ready for marriage. It seems like I'm skipping a step. Losing your after high school freedom and trading it in for security. I don't know, maybe I've just got the pre-wedding jitters. But don't you want to go explore? To find out about this world, to find out what's out there? Don't you want to travel and see, to discover, to run without having to wake up and prep the cows or to go fix the sick ones? Are you okay with just doing what your father did? I don't know, Jeff, I just don't know." With that she started to cry.

Jeff pulled her close to him and held her but didn't say anything for about five minutes. Then he took her face into his hands and turned her to his. He looked her straight in the eyes and said, "I've thought about all those things. But I figure we can do them together. School will have summer breaks, and we can travel, we can explore, we can go and learn together. Golden, I love you and I don't think you'll find anything out there you don't have right here."

Goldie didn't answer; she just smiled and hugged Jeff harder than she had ever hugged him before. They kissed goodnight and she drove herself home in her dad's truck.

School started again on the 8th of January. Golden found it worse than before.

She had written Wendy and told her about the proposal. Wendy wrote back and said she had been proposed to at least eleven times. She said it was nothing. Most of the guys who proposed to her just wanted sex. Goldie didn't think her case was the same. She believed Jeff loved her and thought she loved Jeff. They corresponded back and forth, each giving their defenses for their opinion. In addition Wendy always inserted a tale about what happened to her in class or on the beach or at a party. Golden thought a lot about that. She thought both negatively and positively. It seemed so shallow, so hollow, and so very empty and yet Wendy was so free. She was having so much fun. She was getting as much attention as Golden, only from lots of people. Wendy could go where she wanted to when she wanted to and do what she wanted to.

She seemed to have the one thing that Golden did not have and deep inside longed for: personal freedom. Golden got up every morning at four thirty and rounded up the cows. She cleaned the stalls and the holding area out every night after school. She continued to do her homework, but inside there was a gnawing. What if all this was a lie? What if it was just parents and other adults trying to keep you in an out-of-the-way place? Trying to perpetuate their old philosophies, their old ideas and their own wants and needs on to her. What if there really was happiness bigger and better out there? All her life Golden had been a straight arrow. She had served, she had worked, she had studied, and for what? To get married and settle down in the same town her parents live in? To live life as the wife of a country veterinarian? Although it didn't seem so bad. Jeff certainly loved her and what else was there out there? Another house somewhere else. Another yard, another man to have children with? And one thing Golden knew more than anything else: her parents loved her. She thought they would go along with anything she decided. They would let her be herself and find herself. Even Jeff said he would take her to California if she wanted. So what's the big deal? Still, going with Jeff meant she'd have to go where he wanted and do what he wanted to do, at least mostly.

The weeks passed by. In late February, Wendy wrote again and said that she thought the ocean would be warm enough to swim in by late March or early April. She said she had found the "perfect" swimsuit for Golden. A two-piece that would show off her "finer parts." She said the diehard surfers were still at the beach but most people weren't going out until it got a little warmer. She told about a party with her girlfriends. It was a sleepover and they all snuck out the bedroom window and went down to the beach late at night where they built a big bonfire. It was really fun. She said she missed school the next day. She wasn't doing well in school. She said her grades were horrible and the teachers didn't like her.

"Except, of course, some of the men teachers who look longingly at me."

She said her dad didn't care if she went to school or not. He said she was beautiful and could take good care of herself. Wendy repeated her dislike for school a dozen times in the letter. She concluded by saying she'd probably quit. Golden was agreeing, in part. She didn't really see the value of school. Most of the classes were repetition of what she had learned a year or two or five ago. And even the new stuff didn't seem to have much application to what she was doing or even would be doing. Of course school was important in lots of other ways. To get a job you needed a high school diploma and, of course, to get into college you had to have one. Also, she needed to be a high school graduate if she was going to be married to a doctor of veterinarian medicine. Not just because he would expect it, but socially it would be a must.

Golden sighed. "No one seems to care about your high school degree in California," she said as though talking to someone else sitting there.

Jeff came or called almost every day now. He was attentive and very kind. He always talked about how much he had grown to love her. Goldie was feeling pressured. Her mom and dad talked a lot about the wedding. They would ask her at least once a week if she and Jeff had set a date. Jeff had tried to set a date a couple of times but Goldie kept saying she'd have to check. She was feeling more and more trapped. Less and less able to see why she should marry and settle down at nineteen. Jeff had proposed the wedding date should be in late August, which would be after her nineteenth birthday but before school started in Minneapolis.

"That sounds really good," she had responded without much internal conviction.

"Mom and Dad have really been bugging me about the date. They'll be glad at least to get a general idea. Grandma's already started making my dress." She smiled and kissed Jeff.

"I really do love you, Jeff," she said mostly to herself.

VI

To California

It was the fifteenth of March. Goldie had just gotten a letter from Wendy. She was going to drop out of school. She said she had had it with the "chauvinistic teachers" and the stupid third grade rules they put on you. She said she had a job working as a mail clerk for a company in San Clemente and it paid pretty good. The letter invited Golden to come and spend spring vacation with her at the beach. Wendy said she'd send her some money to fly out if Goldie could afford to fly back.

Spring vacation for Golden didn't start until early April or the weekend of Easter, whichever came first. This year it came on April 5. She read the letter over and over. In class the teacher asked her what she was reading and if she would like to share it with the class. After third period the principal came and got her out of class and took her to his office.

"Golden, you're attentiveness has dropped notably in the past couple of months. I know you are planning on getting married, but unless you improve you'll lose your chance for the valedictorian seat. Mrs. Meyers says she'll have to give you a 'B' if you don't make up two reports and turn in some missing homework. You are a great student and a great asset to our campus. I've known your father for 40 years. You are a splendid example of what hard work and intelligence can do. Please don't drop the ball now, Goldie, everyone is counting on you. Especially me and the faculty members."

Golden left the principal's office. She slowly walked to her locker where she opened it and took fourth period books out. She tucked them under her arm and walked into the room with her head cocked a little sideways.

So what? she thought. *What is this thing about giving a speech to another 160 graduating classmates? Will they remember? Will they even care? Do I care? Ten years from now when most of them are cleaning house and dirty diapers, will they remember that I said we should stretch, reach for our dreams? That we can make a difference? I doubt it. In fact I doubt that Mr. Gourley can even give the names of valedictorian graduating speakers for the past ten years, let alone what they said.*

Jeff drove her home in silence that day. She kissed him as he opened the door of the car and scooted over by him as they drove home, but she didn't say much, just thought.

Golden didn't eat much that night and after the dishes were done she went up to her room and re-read the letter from Wendy.

I wonder if she does the dishes every night, she thought. *How silly, what does it matter?*

She went to her drawer and looked at her clothes. She pulled open the silver brush and mirror box and took out her dad's Christmas gift. She sat on the bed and re-counted the money three or four times. She shook her head.

"I'm going!" she said out loud. "I'm going to go spend spring break in California, and I may not come back."

The decision was more than radical for Golden; it was monumental. It meant changing her life. It meant leaving, going away like she had never done before. But it meant freedom.

The next day Goldie skipped school. She went to the bank and withdrew her savings. All total she had about five hundred dollars plus five hundred from her dad, plus another two hundred in Christmas gifts from other family members. Plenty to fly out to San Clemente and live for a month or two, but that would leave her short, so she decided to take the bus because when she checked with the station she could get to Los Angles for less than a hundred dollars. The flight was four hundred and fifty dollars.

Besides, she thought, *I'd love to see this country from a bus*. Also the bus would take her four suitcases and the airlines would only take two.

One of the problems was getting to the bus station. The bus left at 6:15 a.m. two days a week and she didn't want to be leaving right while her dad was out milking. She decided to borrow the car from Dad on the pretext that she needed to go see Jeff and get some things arranged. Golden decided not to tell her parents but instead write them a note. It turned out to be more like a letter. She called Melissa, one of her girlfriends who told her at least a dozen times not to get married. Melissa had said she should do anything to avoid it. That it was the worst mistake in her life. Melissa was pleased to hear from her. Golden talked in a quiet subdued voice.

"Can you pick me up in the morning at about four on the road in front of my house?" she asked.

"Sure," Melissa answered. "What's up?"

"I've decided to take your advice. I'm going on a vacation to California and I don't think I'm going to marry Jeff."

"Way to go, girl! There are plenty of men out there, you go get 'em."

They talked for another ten minutes and Golden said good-bye.

After dinner and the dishes Golden told her dad she had to go see Jeff and asked to borrow the car. He said of course and went in to take a shower and get ready for bed.

Golden went up to her room and carefully packed her most valuable clothes and some pictures and some keepsakes. She still wasn't sure if she was going to stay in California or come back home in a couple of months. She would at least stay until Jeff got off to school.

She sat down at her desk and began to write two letters, one to Jeff and another to her mom. In the letter to Mom she said she had thought a lot about the marriage and about staying in Minnesota. She said she wasn't ready to do either.

Dear Mom and Dad,

I knew you wouldn't or possibly couldn't understand my decision to leave. But I can't stay. It's not just that I can't marry Jeff. He's good to me and I do love him, but the thought that that's all there is to life scares me. I really want to see the world or at least the U.S. I would like to know about other people and why they do what they do. I really need to find my place in this world and especially in my relationships. I love you, but I just can't marry Jeff and I can't stay here either. In the first place there's the social thing of bowing out of all the plans that have been made for us. Secondly there's what's left after I tell everyone that I am not going to marry the best catch in the valley. What would I do? Go out on dates? No, I can't think of anyone else to date. Jeff loves me and it would not be good for him to know I was going out with other guys.

I don't know, Mom. It seems like I'm trapped. So I'm going to go to California. I've taken all the letters Wendy has written to me so you won't have her address. I'll call you after I get there and let you know I'm all right. I would like to come home in November or so, after Jeff's in college and everything has settled down. I thought about keeping the ring, I think I earned it, but Jeff will probably need the money for school. I don't think he's paid for it yet and it would be dishonest to keep it and have him paying while he's in school. So it's wrapped in some tissue paper in my top drawer. Please give it back to him.

I love you, Mom and Dad, but I just have to do this. I'm sorry I won't be finishing school. I know I only lack a couple of months, but I just can't stay here in this situation. Tell Principal Gourley he was right, I didn't have the guts to finish it out.

Love,
Goldie

The letter she wrote to Jeff was simple. It said:

I love you but I can't marry you. I need to see the world and I need to find myself. I have given Mom your ring; you can get it from her. This isn't about you, Jeff. You are and have been wonderful to me. You are great and I know you'll find someone else in college. Perhaps someone who shares your interest in staying in Angora.

Take care,
Golden

It was eight thirty and Golden knew that her mom and dad were in bed. She stepped out of the door and looked down the hall. She walked downstairs and checked to make sure Grandma wasn't up and around. The coast was clear. She grabbed two suitcases, careful to close the door tightly behind her, and walked down the stairs. She got out to the truck and put the bags in the back. Coming back in, she met

Grandma, who was standing on the front porch. Golden wasn't sure how much she saw.

"Hi, Grandma, how you doing tonight?"

"Sweetheart, I love you and will miss you. But you must do what your heart tells you. Are you going to be gone a long time?"

"Probably three or four months. Just until Jeff gets into college in St. Petersburg."

"I suspect a little longer," Grandma said and turned and walked back into the house.

Golden went back upstairs and got the other two suitcases and her purse and another shoulder bag. She walked as quietly down the stairs as she could and went out to the truck and put the rest of the things except for her purse in the back. She didn't return even to close the door. She drove to the bus station in Chisholm. The station manager didn't know her there and wouldn't be asking any questions. She purchased the ticket. It would take her to Grand Rapids and then across Highway 2 to Grand Forks, North Dakota. From there she would go south to Fargo and across North Dakota on Interstate 94.

Golden returned later than she had figured. It was after one in the morning when she got back. She had driven past Jeff's house one last time and wondered if she was doing the best thing for her. Not the "right thing" but the best thing for her personally. She had never been selfish before in her life. She had always given and shared. She wasn't sure if there was a right or wrong thing to be done here. Except for hurting her mom and dad by leaving, she didn't think she was doing either right or wrong. There are so many ramifications to choices; what's right for one could well be wrong for almost everyone else.

Her determination increased as she saw his house disappearing in the rearview mirror of the truck. She turned off the engine a couple hundred yards from the house and coasted into the yard. She left the key in the ignition where it usually stayed and stepped out of the truck, walked over to the front porch, and sat on the steps. The night was beautiful, skies were clear, and the stars were sparkling. The moon was almost full. She looked at it and thought Daddy always called that the "harvest moon" in the fall when he was making his last cut or finishing picking the garden vegetables for Mom to can. *I guess now it's the late winter moon.* Spring didn't break until March 21. Only a couple of weeks ago. But it was already warm. Some years it stayed cold until late June. Not this year; this year, besides the lilacs, some tulips and other flowers were coming up and blooming.

This is the most beautiful place I have ever been. Clear air and beautiful country, she thought as she leaned back against the paint-pealed post, which held up the porch roof. Golden closed her eyes. In an instant she started; she looked at her watch and it was ten to four. She stood up and started to walk down the long dirt driveway. She got only a few steps when she realized she had forgotten her purse. She turned and ran to the porch, maybe fearing that at this last minute she'd change her mind or that Grandma had woken Mom and told her she was going. She wasn't sure but she grabbed her purse and ran. She wasn't sure whether she was running from home or to a new life. She wasn't sure about anything except she had made the decision and was facing a scary new future.

Melissa showed up at about quarter after four. Goldie hoped into her '88 Pontiac quickly.

"Let's go!" she said. "My dad's gonna be up in five minutes."

They drove off and when Golden told Melissa that she had to go to Chisholm, she replied that she didn't have enough gas. Goldie said she'd pay to fill her up. So they went to Angora where there was the station that stayed open all night. Goldie could never figure out why. No one bought gas after ten or eleven. Goldie kept a low profile and didn't think the attendant saw her. She gave Melissa twenty dollars for gas, which filled the tank and left her with enough to buy a couple of cookies and candy bar.

Melissa was sworn to secrecy and promised she'd not tell anyone, not even at school, where she had taken Golden. They arrived at the station just before five.

"You have a great one, girl!" Melissa said with sincerity and a tinge of jealousy.

Golden got out and went into the station. It was empty except for a middle-aged woman with two children. One, maybe three years old, sitting on her lap and the other, about five, playing on the floor. She went to the ticket clerk and reaffirmed her ticket.

"How long does it take to get to Los Angeles?" she asked.

"About four and a half days," he said, not even looking up at who was asking. "I can check the exact time of arrival, but usually something happens or the passenger changes or stays over somewhere so there's really no point."

"Thank you," Golden said without even noting she had said it. It was a matter of habit. A matter of years of saying it at home. She went over and sat across and three seats up from the woman.

The hiss of air from brakes of the bus startled Golden awake. She had fallen asleep again. The clerk spoke over the microphone as though there were more than just the two people waiting at the station.

"This is bus 93 going to Grand Rapids, Bemidji, and on to Grand Forks, North Dakota. Have your tickets in hand as you board the bus," the speaker squealed.

The door swung open and Golden could see the little pipe rails, which led to each parking stall for the busses. There was only one bus there and the driver looked tired. She wondered if he had been driving all night or if he just started.

He'll probably get better when the sun comes up in an hour, she thought.

The bus was mostly empty. There was a hippie type lying down on the back seat. He looked like he may have been playing the guitar that was lying in a banged-up case next to him on the floor. Perhaps he played for some club or group or something. Up from him on the left side of the bus, across from Golden, sat another woman. She was quite large and had in front of her two kids and one lying on her lap. She was an Afro-American and Golden stared for a few minutes.

There was only one person of her race in the school at Angora. He was a junior so Goldie didn't know him very well. The woman was half asleep and half awake but when she caught Goldie's eye she smiled. Golden smiled back and thought she might be someone to talk with in the morning.

Goldie went to the middle of the bus on the right side and sat down. She tucked her purse tightly under her right arm and closed her eyes. She tilted the seat back and lay across the two seats putting her legs up on the second seat. She was wearing the pants she had worn when she shot the mountain lion. They were comfortable and somehow gave her the courage to go see Wendy. The seat wasn't comfortable but she knew she'd be that way for four or five days so she just ignored the discomfort and closed her eyes.

The bus pulled into Grand Rapids in about an hour and four more people boarded.

An older man with thin, graying hair and an old plaid trench coat climbed aboard. He was carrying a plastic-coated wire box in which there was a small Cocker. The dog was very uncomfortable in the box and whined every few seconds. At first Golden thought, *Oh no, that stupid dog will annoy me for the next four days*. But in an instant she reconsidered and thought she might get to be friends with the man and the dog. His face was wrinkled, especially around his eyes. It gave Golden the impression that the man had smiled a lot during his lifetime. He sat across from her and in front of the lady with the three children. When he sat he went next to the window and put the dog on the seat next to him and not on the floor, then tilted up the little wire house and said, "It's okay, pup. I'll keep you as comfortable as I can for the trip." His eyes seemed to moisten a little and he said it so sincerely that Goldie thought he was talking to a person rather than a dog. His pants were green, old, and unpressed and the old brown belt had been punched twice with a knife to make a new hold for the buckle tongue.

He has lost weight, she thought. He had taken off his coat and placed it carefully in the upper rack, folding it in an exact manner and then putting it in so the collar was toward the wall and the bottom was out. He had taken about two minutes to do it and yet to look at the coat, it seemed like one that you'd throw away for wear. The old man looked across the aisle at Golden. He smiled and his whole face seemed to express love and lack of care for the complexities and sorrows of the world. Goldie would normally feel a little uncomfortable if an old man smiled at her, but not this time. She felt warm and assured that this man had a genuine kindness within.

"Hi," she said, listening to herself speak as though an outside observer.

"Well, good morning," he responded in the same kind of voice and sincerity that he had spoken to his dog with. Golden looked at him a little puzzled and then looked away and laid back in her seat and closed her eyes.

A young couple got on the bus in Grand Rapids. Probably about 18 years old, but clearly together. The girl was wearing a wedding band without any engagement ring. It was just a gold band with some decoration around it to make it appear more feminine. The guy didn't have a ring on, but he held her hand as they walked back three seats behind Goldie and sat down. She giggled a couple of times and Golden thought about the times when Jeff would make her giggle. It was a different kind of giggle she was doing. Hers seemed more childish. Perhaps because Golden didn't want to think of herself as a giggly little kid in love. She would rather imagine herself as mature, experienced, and level headed. After all, that's why she wasn't going to marry Jeff, because she didn't want to giggle now and cry for the next twenty years.

A businessman also got on in Grand Rapids. He probably wasn't a real businessman from St. Paul or any big city. No, but he did have a briefcase and a pretty nice suit. Although his tie was loosened a little, his shoes were shined and his hat was brushed. The hat appeared to be one out of the forties. It was felt with a leather band

and looked like something a detective might wear. His briefcase was sort of old and his face seemed to have lost its luster. He smiled and his smile seemed hollow. Like there was nothing left behind it to make it real. The way he smiled and greeted everyone as he walked down the aisle made Goldie believe he was some kind of a salesman. He walked down the aisle of the bus to the back and turned and came back up and sat on the right side of the bus in the second seat from the front. He opened up the newspaper and turned to the classified section, reached into his shirt pocket and took out a pair of thin gold-rimmed glasses and began to read. Goldie thought he probably didn't have a car and probably not a job either. Maybe he was just looking to better himself.

The bus backed out of the stall like in Chisholm. It came very close to the wall and Golden thought they might hit it, but at the exact moment of impact the bus stopped and inched forward until it had cleared the overhead awning post and pulled out into a sort of alleyway that led to the street. He turned onto the street and out of town to Highway Two. The bus stopped for about ten minutes in a little town about twenty minutes out and got a couple of boxes and then got right back on the road. About an hour and forty-five minutes later the bus driver pulled into a gas station restaurant just outside of Bemidji, Minnesota. As he pulled in he announced over the intercom that the bus was stopping for forty-five minutes for breakfast. Everyone had to get off the bus even if they were not eating. It was about five to nine and Golden was hungry.

She walked into the restaurant and sat down in a booth by the window. She could see the bus and the station. It wasn't really busy but there were a few cars coming and getting gas. A couple of drivers and their companions came into the restaurant and sat down.

As Golden looked at the menu, she thought about the pancakes her mom made. She knew that these wouldn't be nearly as good. She looked up to see where the waitress was. The woman with the three kids was walking between the tables holding one of the kids and dragging one of the others while the third one was waddling behind. He seemed to have a dirty diaper because the front of his pants were wet and the back seemed to bulge more than just what a diaper would cause. The woman looked at Golden and smiled.

"Looks like you could use some help," Golden said, standing up. The woman smiled more broadly and walked over to Goldie's table.

"Yeah, could you watch these two while I go change this one?" she said, pointing to the little one trailing in behind. Golden sat the kids down across the table from her and said, "Would you like some chocolate milk?"

To which the little girl who appeared to be about five or six said, "Oh yes, ma'am. We'd love some!" She spoke in perfect English and was very polite.

Golden smiled. She was beautiful. Turning to the other little girl, who appeared to be about four, Golden asked, "Is that okay with you? Would you like some chocolate milk too?"

"Yes, thank you," came the response. Both girls sat quietly and stared at Golden and waited patiently.

The waitress came before the children's mother had returned so Golden ordered two chocolate milks for them. She figured she'd pay for it. Their mom came out of the restroom and immediately the older girl stood up, stepped out of the booth, and waited for her mother. Mom came and sat down in between the two girls and put the little, maybe one-and-a-half-year-old boy on the seat next to Golden.

"Where ya going?" she asked.

"I'm going to San Clemente, California. I got the girls a couple of chocolate milks. I hope that's okay."

"Sure it is. They love chocolate. My name is Zada. I'm going to San Francisco. I hope to meet my mom there. She's got a place there for the kids and I. I hope. I sent her a letter a couple of months ago, asking if we could come and stay with her. My husband drinks a lot and had become more and more abusive. I didn't mind so much. He'd come home from the bar and accuse me of having an affair and then beat me. But he started in on the kids a couple months ago. I talked with him and he would apologize and cry, but then he'd do it again. I wanted to go see a marriage counselor but he kept saying they wouldn't understand him. That his case was different and how could they know how much he loved me if they knew that occasionally he hit me. It got better for a few weeks, he stopped beating the kids and me, but he still yelled at all of us and still drank way too much. I stayed hoping that if he'd stop hitting us maybe he'd learn to love the kids and not yell at them. So we didn't go, but things got bad again. He slapped little Joey so badly that it broke his jaw. So I just got all the money out of the bank and took a cab to the bus station and here we are. Now we're hoping Mom'll still have us."

Goldie smiled. She was surprised the woman would tell her all of that personal information. But she liked her. She appeared to be only twenty-two or three. Her hair was pulled back on each side and had two red ribbons tying off the short ponytails. She had some early wrinkles on her forehead and in the corners of her eyes, but she was pretty. In spite of the fact that she was heavy, she was, Goldie thought, quite attractive.

The waitress reappeared and Golden ordered a couple of eggs with some sausage. She got a glass of milk with it but didn't drink it after one taste. It tasted like water. No cream and no body. Dad had always said that the cream in milk was really good for you. He said the heart people were full of bull. Zada ordered pancakes for the kids and just a cup of coffee for herself. Goldie told her not to order the milk; she'd give hers to the kids.

"So why are you going to San Clemente?" Zada asked after the waitress had left.

"It's a long story," Golden said, not wanting to expose herself to a stranger.

"Oh, I'm sorry if I was prying. It's just that we've got a long trip and I don't very often get a chance to talk to another adult. I'm usually with the kids all day."

"It's okay, you're not prying. I'm just very tired of life as it has been and am hoping to change all that by going to California."

Zada mused a little at that and then said, "I know they say you can't run away from your problems, but sometimes it's the only thing you can do. The problem won't change and you can't change it, so all there is left is to leave."

"I know what you mean," Goldie said. "I just ran out of solutions too. My boyfriend wanted to marry me and my folks were excited about that but I wanted to do more than marry and settle down in the same town I had lived in for eighteen years. You know, I have never seen the ocean. Never. I have never gone to a movie place where the screen is bigger than eight feet square. There are so many things I don't know about, and there I was trapped, unable to seek and discover the millions of things I wanted to see. Unable to find myself. You know what I mean?"

"I do," Zada affirmed. The breakfast came and Zada spent most of her time feeding the children. They talked in between bites; Zada would give the kids a bite and then take one for herself. Goldie helped with the baby boy whose name was Chad. He ate well. Goldie thought it strange that he wasn't yet potty trained. At the meal's end the waitress brought out a bill and both the girls explained almost simultaneously that they needed separate bills. The chocolate milk ended up being on Zada's bill. She paid it and didn't say anything about it. About five minutes before they finished eating, the driver stepped into the restaurant and announced the bus was leaving in five minutes.

On the bus the girls talked for about an hour about Zada's husband and men in general. Then Golden finally began to tell her story and Zada listened carefully for almost an hour and a half. When she finished, Goldie was a little embarrassed; she was talking and telling so much that she hadn't given Zada a chance to speak or even respond.

Just as she finished the driver announced that they were coming into Grand Forks, North Dakota. The bus had stopped a couple of times at little towns and picked up a couple of people at each stop. As they crossed the river, Goldie turned and looked out her window. The river was beautiful and once again she reconsidered what she had just done. The river reminded her of the river behind her house. It wasn't really a big river, but Dad fished there often and always brought home some trout. The driver announced that they would lay over in Grand Forks for two hours. Zada had some friends in town and said she was going to call them. Golden went to the snack bar and ordered some french fries. When they came she was disappointed. They weren't crisp like the ones Mom made. They certainly weren't made from fresh potatoes. Goldie hoped they were not from frozen pre-cut potatoes. She sat at the stool and ate the fries, dipping into the ketchup and mayonnaise and sprinkling a little salt on the fry pile after she had eaten the top ones.

"Mind if I have a seat?"

She looked up and standing next to the stool by her was the old man on the bus. Goldie smiled and said, "Sure." She was comfortable with him even though she didn't know anything about him. Maybe because he was old or maybe because he had a look of wisdom and age. He was carrying the little dog cage. The dog seemed to be asleep.

"Want some french fries?" she asked, trying to think of something to say.

"Sure," he said, surprising her a little.

"Where ya going?" he asked.

"I'm going to San Clemente, California. Where you headed?"

"I'm going all the way to Los Angeles. My boy is there and he needs some help."

"I guess we all need help sometimes," Goldie replied, not sure if she should be that presumptuous.

"Yes we do. Sometimes we need help and don't know we need it." He looked into Goldie's eyes for what seemed to be an eternity and finally she looked away. She didn't turn her head, just shifted her eyes. She thought he might see too much. He took a french fry and dipped it in the ketchup.

"Good fries," he said, and then added, "Probably not as good as you get at home, though."

"You're right there. Mom made the best fries in the world. They were always golden brown, not pale like these, and they are cut by hand from fresh potatoes. She deep-fried them in peanut oil. Bet ya didn't know that. I don't know anybody who fries their french fries in peanut oil but Mom."

"Oh, yeah, I've eaten fries done in peanut oil. I've also had fresh catfish fried in peanut oil. Nothing like it. It tastes great and it's great for you too. You wouldn't be from Angora area, would you?" he asked, looking not only at her eyes but at her face and hands as well.

"How did you know?"

"I used to help an old dairy farmer up there. He'd have me do the milkin' while he was out cuttin' hay. He had a big herd for his day, about a hundred head. His wife made the best fries I ever tasted. I think his name was Josiah Bradley. My name is Jackson. What's yours?"

"Golden. Golden Bradley, and I think the man you worked for is my grandfather. I never got to meet him; he died when my dad was only about twenty-two, before he married my mom," Goldie said, finding pleasure in meeting someone who actually knew her grandfather.

"Yup, I'd been working mostly corn during the summer, but I could always count on a few extra bucks and great meals when the last cuttin' time came. Your grandpa was a great man. He believed and practiced sharing and helping. Never wanted to get rich, just do what he thought might contribute to the world. Leave more than he took sort of thing. I knew your dad a little. He was a young squirt when I was there. He was a good worker though. Always did what Josh asked of him and I don't remember hearing him complain or grumble ever. Tell him ol' Jackson said hi. Not sure he'll remember, but tell him anyway."

"I won't be seeing him for a while," Goldie said, leaving open the obvious question.

"You'll miss them and call them in a couple of weeks," he said matter-of-fact as if he was talking about the fries. "We got a lot of miles and some time left. Let's talk when you get a chance." With that he stood and excused himself and went over into the men's restroom.

"Okay," Goldie said with no apprehension at all left in her.

It was good for Goldie to get to know some of the people she was riding with. So far everyone had been nice and she had even made a new friend in Zada. The old man seemed very kind and somehow he conveyed wisdom. Goldie liked him too; he had a connection with her through her grandfather. It was thin and yet Goldie liked hanging on to it as though she was somehow staying connected with her family. In a way, it was apologizing while still maintaining her decision to not stay and not to marry.

She grabbed a soda and went and sat in the terminal.

VII

INTO TOMORROW

From Grand Forks the bus went south to Fargo. It stopped twice and picked up two more people at the first stop and some boxes at the second. It was three p.m. when they finally got into Fargo and Goldie thought the bus had to be the slowest form of transportation on the planet. Her dad could make Fargo in less than four hours. Goldie had slept most of the way since Grand Forks. The bus stopped at Fargo for twenty minutes. She was glad of that. They arrived in Jamestown at about a quarter to six. Golden and Zada talked on and off during the drive. Zada asked Golden to watch the kids while she slept. So Golden told the Jack in the Beanstalk story. They had never heard it, which delighted Golden. The guitarist was awake now and sitting up, listening. Every five or ten minutes during the story he would say something he thought was cute or clever to add to the story. Generally it was in poor taste. When Goldie got to the part where Jack wakes up and sees the giant beanstalk, the guitarist said, "All Jacks have beanstalks, some are just bigger than others." Goldie wasn't sure she got it, but he said it in a way that was suggestive and she didn't like it.

When Zada woke up Goldie was telling the kids the Cinderella story, which the children had heard before but all wanted to hear again. Zada interrupted and offered the kids some cookies and punch. The driver announced that they were stopping for a dinner break and that they would be in Jamestown for forty-five minutes.

The hippie got up with his guitar as the bus was pulling into the stall and walked to the front. As he passed Golden he stopped, turned to her and said, "I'm getting off here. If you want to rest from your travels, you can come and stay a couple of days with me. I've got a little apartment in town here. I think we'd be great together."

Goldie didn't answer him, she just looked away. He smiled and walked up to the front of the bus. The door wasn't open yet but he stepped in the stairwell and leaned against the support. The driver told him to stay behind the yellow line until the bus was completely stopped and he had opened the door. The hippie grumbled and stepped back of the yellow line. The bus driver then opened the door.

"Thanks for riding Greyhound," he said as the guitarist stepped down the stairs of the bus. The hippie stopped after taking a couple of steps, turned, and gave the driver the finger. Goldie wondered how he had become so rude. Maybe he'd lost a loved one.

Goldie wasn't hungry. She hadn't sat so much or for so long in her life. She stood up and stretched. She asked Zada if she needed help feeding the kids. Zada answered, "Only if you want to."

They sat and talked intermittently while Zada went back and forth getting food for the kids and Goldie tended and helped the little ones eat. Zada seemed so content with her kids in spite of her circumstances. Goldie thought it funny. *How can someone be happy when they've lost their husband and have three kids to raise alone?* Her thoughts turned inward and she realized that she too lived with conflicts. Maybe that's the nature of all mankind, conflicts and change. She hoped California would be all that she wished for.

The bus driver announced over the PA that the bus was leaving in five minutes. Goldie helped Zada carry the little one onto the bus and get him seated. Four or five new people came onto the bus. Goldie put her carrying case on the seat next to her so no one would sit by her. She stared out the window for the next two hours. The bus rolled along in a seemingly endless stream of farms and woods and little towns. It was about nine o'clock. Golden got up and walked to the back of the bus to use the restroom. It was surprisingly clean. And it didn't smell badly either. She was pleased. She had been told by Melissa that bus restrooms were horrible and never to go in there.

Walking back down the narrow aisle toward her seat she saw the gray-black curly hair of a man sitting in the seat where her handbag had been left. She approached the man and was about to tell him that she didn't want to share her seat, that there was plenty of empty seats left on the bus. As she stepped up to the seat the man turned and smiled. It was Jackson.

"Oh, hi Mr. Jackson, I didn't know it was you."

"Jackson is my first name, most folks think like you, but they'd be mistaken. Mind if I sit here a spell?"

"No, I can't sleep anyway."

They talked for fifteen or twenty minutes. Goldie told Jackson about her mom and dad and their marriage. Jackson listened and then asked.

"So yer dad married Marge? She was sure a sweet pretty thing when I last saw her. Good choice. I know they were dating for about three or four years but he didn't seem to want to commit."

"Oh, Mom finally got him. She did it her way. She always does things like that, sorta slow but very deliberate."

"Why'd ya run away?" Jackson abruptly asked.

"I didn't really run away," she answered. "I love my parents but I just wasn't ready to settle in a small town and not see the world. I just didn't tell them I was leaving."

Jackson smiled. "Ya have friends or someone to stay with when you get to San Clemente?"

"Yes, I met a girl who invited me to come and stay at her place. She and I hit it off really quickly and I think we'll really have fun together in California."

"Fun is great, but you're going to need to eat. Made any plans for living while you're having fun?"

"Wendy says it's easy to get a job in California. She says there's lots of companies hiring all the time. I won't make a lot at first, but one thing I know is that I'm a hard worker and I'll do okay in that area. What I'm really worried about is boys. I've only dated a few guys and one of them asked me to marry him. It makes me pretty nervous thinking I'm gonna be going out with different guys. Dad says that most guys don't have the same moral training that I do. Wendy says that they are all the same: they only want sex. So I don't know, I don't think I want to start having sex with lots of different men."

"Sometimes what we want and what we do is opposite. It depends on how much you want something whether you really do it or give into the pressures of society. One of the problems is that most of us don't anticipate our interaction with others until we are there doing it. That can lead to trouble," Jackson said with a quiet voice.

Goldie wasn't sure she understood all of what he was saying. But she knew at that instant she really was going to like Jackson. He had a twinkle in his eye and softness in his voice that seemed to scream wisdom. He never attacked and never accused. He just said what he thought without presumption and without guile.

They talked until one in the morning, sharing feelings and life experiences. Golden had more experiences than she realized. Somehow Jackson brought out in her new self-confidence and a new realization that she was ready for her new life. He was so easy to talk with and so very wise. She had not known any Afro-Americans before her bus trip, but now she was friends with two. Zada was not the same as Jackson. Jackson had some depth. He had wisdom and love. Yes, that was it; he had love. He didn't care about what you had done, he didn't try to correct or turn you around, and he just listened and shared his feelings with you. Even her father never did that so very earnestly. Jackson seemed to be filled with love. Unconditional love.

He got up and walked forward a couple of seats and pulled down his plaid overcoat, talked to the dog for a couple of seconds, and went to sleep. Goldie was tired too. She drifted off in a few minutes.

While she slept she dreamt. It was a funny and strange dream. They, she and Wendy, and a couple of men were standing in an open field. You could see the ocean down below the hill and could hear the surf crashing against the face of the cliff. Seagulls were squawking overhead, and out in the water you could make out the outline of a couple of boats. The field was half green, cultivated with what looked like chilies or some other low-growing plant. The other half was barren, not plowed, and cracked with lack of water and wind. They were standing near the dividing line. Goldie was in the green area and the men were in the barren field. Wendy was walking back and forth talking first to the men and then to Golden. The earth began to tremble. Goldie looked across the field behind the men and could see the earth moving like a sea. The ground would swell up and the great swell was moving toward them. She didn't think of her own safety, but she knew that if the men didn't move they would be killed. She ran to one of them and grabbed him by the arm and pulled him to the cliff. They slid down the steep wall to the beach. Above, the earth rose and fell like a surf and passed onward, diminishing in the distance until it was gone. The man held her in his arms and said thank you. He had beautiful brown eyes and was very strong. But as he said thank you he began to wrap her in what appeared to be wide, silver boxing tape. The tape covered first her arms and then her legs and then her upper body. Soon she was completely wrapped in tape like a mummy except for her face. He came to her and kissed her on the lips. A passionate kiss, which seemed to last for an hour. Then he picked her up and tossed her into the sea.

She awoke with a start and looked at her watch. It was five thirty in the morning and the sky was a pale gray. The pre-dawn light cast faint shadows through the bus, and as the bus turned on the windy road she could see dawn breaking in the east. She shook her head and tried to go back to sleep but could not. The dream haunted her. The morning light now appeared and turned the clouds a pale pink. *It's a different pink than the sunset. It seems milder, softer and quieter. The start of a new day, a new beginning....* Like Jackson said, "Every day we get a chance to start over. We get a chance to fix our mistakes and follow our dreams."

It was about 7:30 when the bus driver announced that they were stopping in Billings, Montana. Fifteen minutes later they pulled into a bus stop with a dilapidated overhang. As the bus stopped, the driver said they were changing drivers and fueling the bus and they'd be there for about 45 minutes.

Billings seemed like a funny place to make a town. Golden didn't see much farmland and not a lot of trees. At least not a tenth of the trees she was used to seeing in Angora. She walked alone over to the restaurant. It was next door to the bus station. The prices of food were more than she thought she should have to pay. Maybe she could find a better place in town. She got up and left without ordering or even speaking to the waitress. She smiled at the hostess as she left but the hostess/cashier didn't smile back.

As she walked down the street she saw a couple of trucks pass. One was filled with manure. She figured they were going to fertilize a field early enough to get a good cut in a couple of months. There was no snow on the ground but it was cold and she thought it was a little late to be putting down dung. She looked at the mountains surrounding the town. They were sharp, jagged mountains. Not round and smooth like the ones at home. No, these mountains were rugged and harsh, some with pine and some without. There was snow on the mountaintops and signs that some had fallen in town, but there was no fresh snow in town now.

"Home cooking" was the sign at the top of the restaurant, a little hole in the wall about half way up the main street. As she stepped in she could smell the coffee and eggs cooking. It smelled good and brought her back to the mornings she got up and rounded up the cows. There was an empty booth against the wall on the right and because no one greeted her at the door, she went over and sat down. A couple of minutes passed by and the waitress, a thin dishpan blond about thirty-two, came to the table and said, "What'll it be, sweetheart?"

To Goldie, that seemed a little familiar. Maybe that's how they did things out west. She squirmed inside and then said, "How's your pancakes and eggs?"

"Pretty good. Ya have to get the eggs over well or the cook will give 'em to you raw."

"Okay, can you put some bacon with the eggs too?"

"Sure, honey, want any coffee or something to drink?"

"Yes, thanks. Coffee." Goldie didn't drink much coffee. She didn't like the taste and it made her head sometimes buzz. She thought people became dependent on caffeine. Her dad certainly had.

The waitress walked away, leaving a glass of water on the table and some silverware with a paper napkin. As she passed a guy sitting at the table across from Goldie, she swatted him with the table wiping cloth she had in her hand. He seemed like a real cowboy. Not like the cowboys Goldie had known at home; this guy had one of those white felt hats with a tall top, and the rim was curled in a very specific way. The leather band around the center was stained with sweat, as was the hat in that part. When the guy stood up, he had on chaps and spurs. Some levies on under the chaps and a long-sleeved checkered wool shirt. He reached out and grabbed the apron of the waitress, but she pulled away and continued walking without so much as acknowledging his presence. He picked up his bill and walked toward the cash register, leaving a dollar bill on the table as a tip.

"Isn't it a little early to be range riding?" Goldie asked as the waitress brought her plate out.

"Not around here, honey, we get the cattle out to pasture early in March."

"What if it snows again?" Goldie asked.

"It don't snow that deep here, at least not after February or early March. Where you from?"

"Minnesota."

"Get a lot of snow there?" the waitress asked.

"Oh yes, two weeks ago we had a couple of feet."

"Can I get anything else for you?" the waitress asked, seeing one of the patrons raise their cup of coffee in the air.

"No thanks."

Breakfast was all right. Golden was already feeling different. Not about leaving, but about herself. Somehow she felt more grown up. It was surprising to her.

How can a person change in two days? she thought. But she had. She was seeing life differently, people differently than she had before. The salesman who boarded the bus in Grand Rapids somehow held the answer, he had probably spent his life selling, maybe because he had a wife to support or maybe because he loved to do it, but now life had changed. He seemed spent, he seemed to have changed, and yet even with the change he still looked for jobs in the only field he knew; he still was a salesman. He would die selling. Maybe not products but himself, or his grandkids, or his church or something, anything. So for Golden there was the question more clearly put: "What do I want to become, what am I now, or should I live for something else? Should I seek out more life? I think that's what I want to do. It's what I'm going to do."

She boarded the bus early. Only a couple of people were on it waiting for the new driver. There wasn't any security; anyone could just get onto the bus. Golden thought it okay, though; after all, who wants to hijack a bus? Or even steal the things on the bus? Most of the people there were pretty low on money and personal valuables.

The depot announced over the PA system that the bus was leaving at 8:20 a.m. At about 8:15 the bus driver got on and checked the tickets of everyone on the bus. He was the first driver to do that and Goldie thought it was more a money thing than a security thing.

The bus rolled westward. It was an express bus so it didn't stop at every town along the way, possibly because there weren't a lot of towns in Montana. It took about three hours to get to Helena and then they turned south and picked up Highway 12, which went to Coeur d'Alene, Idaho. The country was beautiful. Golden felt comfortable as she drove into the forests. The mountains were rugged and stunning. She pulled the wool blanket she had brought with her over her shoulders and snuggled against the window, staring out at the scenery. There was an empty train track that ran along a rugged river, which was twisting and turning along the valley below the road. She could hear a train whistle in the distance and she wondered if it was coming or going. Soon she could see the five-engine train climbing up the mountain; it was pulling cars filled with coal.

I wonder what they use all that coal for? she thought. But before she could consider the answer, she felt a tug on the blanket covering her. She turned to look and there standing in the aisle was ol' Jackson.

"Good morning, may I sit by you?"

"Sure."

"How'd ya sleep?"

"Okay. Not great, it's hard to sleep when you've got so many thoughts racing through your head. I keep wondering if I did the right thing and what will happen to me. I wonder if I'll go back in a couple of months or if I'll stay."

"It's a quick way to grow up," he said in a voice that seemed to carry a million other nuances and suggestions.

"I'm not sure I want to grow up. What's so great about being an adult? All my parents ever did was work the farm and go to dinner together every week or two."

"They raised you. That was probably their greatest accomplishment. You are a beautiful, brilliant young lady."

"Thank you, Jackson. I don't think I could have made it without you. You have been a true friend."

"I see in you lots of conflicts, Golden, but they are manageable. You can make a difference. In fact you already have. You have served and loved and given to everyone you have known. I think you need to call Mom and Dad when you get to San Clemente and tell them where you are and that you're all right. Tell them that you love them and that you weren't running away from them, just from yourself."

"How can I run from myself? I'm always here with me."

"Maybe you can't. Perhaps you only needed a break from circumstances and people. Take the break, but remember where your roots are. That's important. Don't abandon your source of life. Don't run away from the things that made you you."

The hours passed by as they sat and talked, mostly about Golden. She felt a little selfish in talking only about herself and her problems. But Jackson seemed so very sincerely interested and he was so wise. He understood her and her motivations like no one ever before had. He seemed to love her unconditionally and express only helpful thoughts and concern for her. He was like her dad, only better at talking, better at understanding, and better at knowing her feelings. Golden began to love the old man even though she had only known him for a couple of days.

In Coeur d'Alene, Idaho, the bus stopped for three hours. It was a little late getting in and Goldie was hungry. She also felt very dirty. She took a cab to the YWCA building and took a shower. She then picked up a pizza at a little pizza place across from the lake, ate it, and walked along the shore. There was a park on the northwest side that she walked through and watched the birds and the waves splash against the shoreline. There was not much activity on the lake. It was about 8 p.m. and the water was cold. The bus was leaving at 9:15 so she had an hour or so to get back.

As she walked she saw a group of shorthaired blond guys sitting at a table in the park. They were drinking some foreign drink; it looked like dark beer. She stopped to look. One of the young men stood up and walked toward her. Her heart jumped a little. She didn't know the man, but she was in a public park, so she assumed it would be okay.

"Hi, you from around here?" he asked.

"No, I'm from Minnesota."

"What brings you all the way out to Idaho?"

"I'm going to San Clemente, California, to see a friend," she said, wondering if she should tell a stranger where she was going or from where she had come.

"Ya on the bus?"

"Yes, I'm traveling with my dad," Golden answered, hoping that that might deter any thoughts of aggression the boy may have.

He was dressed in khaki pants and a light brown shirt that looked like it belonged on a security guard. His hair was cut short and he was clean-shaven. He wore black boots that came up to the middle of his calf and his belt was plain except for a funny buckle. He spoke well without an accent and yet seemed to be dressed like a tourist from another country. Golden couldn't quite figure him out. Perhaps kids dressed like that in Idaho.

"I think you dress funny," she said, finding her words a little strange even to her.

"You wanna come over and have a beer with us?" he asked.

"No, thanks, I'm still a minor and am not allowed to drink. I'm only 18," she answered without guile.

"My God, an honest woman. Most girls your age would lie and finagle just to get a drink of our beer." His voice had changed; it had become less accusing and more sincere. He was surprised to find someone so refreshingly honest.

"Okay," she said, "I'll come over and talk, but I have to go in a couple of minutes, I've got to catch the bus," she said, forgetting that she had said her father was waiting for her. She walked over to the park table where the others were sitting and standing. There were five in all and the first boy introduced them to her. Golden thought that some of them had strange names like Hans, Adolph, and Rolf, but the boy who came to talk with her said his name was Michael. That was okay. She told them her name was Golden, Golden Fern, and that she was from Minnesota.

"Are you really a blond?" Hans asked.

"If you mean do I dye my hair, no, not yet. I live on a dairy farm and don't have much time for dyeing my hair," she answered, not knowing whether he liked dyed hair or not.

"That's good," two or three of the boys chided in at the same time.

Michael stood up and said, "She said I dress funny," at which all the boys laughed. Adolph put his dark beer down and stood up, walking around the cement park bench. He got close to Golden and said, "You ever heard of skinheads?"

"I don't think so, is it a club or something?" she answered, then instinctively looked at each of the heads of the boys to see if they were shaven. None were. They all had short light hair but none had shaven heads.

"No, it is a group of patriotic Americans who want to protect the people from the tyranny and the destruction of their rights as a free people by the oppressors in Washington. It's a group of people dedicated to making this country a great and decent place to live."

Golden was a little surprised at the answer. What could these guys possible do to change the country or the government? What could they do to make things better?

"I agree that we need change. I live on a farm in Minnesota and nobody cares if my dad makes it or not. No one cares when his milk production falls or one of his cows gets mastitis. It's not just that, because we live in a very small town, nobody ever pays attention to us. My dad says it's because we don't represent a significant money source."

"That's exactly what I'm talking about. It's all money to those mongers in Washington. They aren't representing the people; they are representing themselves. The more they can put into their pockets, the happier they are, and to hell with the free people of America."

Adolph shook his head side to side and walked back around the table and sat down. He took another sip of his beer and sighed.

Michael offered Golden some potato chips. They were a little different than those she had in Minnesota. They were thicker and wrinklier but they tasted good.

"One of the things that has really damaged our country and our freedoms is the darker people, if you know what I mean. They should have shipped them back to Africa. You know that they are dumber than real people and most of them are lazy and thieves. Just turn your back and they'll take everything they can get from you. This whole civil rights thing is just a rouse; it's a lie. They don't want to give us civil rights; they want to train the blacks to kill off the people who oppose their totalitarian form of government. So they give them civil rights and induct them into the army. They give them all our hard-earned money in welfare checks so they can then control them. It's a conspiracy."

Golden was offended by the generalization and by the regard these guys had for people she had just come to know and love. She thought of Jackson; he probably wouldn't accept a welfare check. And Zada, who else needed the money more? She loved her kids and needed to raise them.

"If I were in the same spot, I'd certainly use the help of the country. I'd accept welfare," she said and turned away from the boys toward the sidewalk. "I have to be going now," she continued. Her voice had the sound of the strength of her own conviction. She started to walk away. Michael reached over and grabbed her harm.

"You know we could take you to a place where you could learn about those people and about the Jews and others. Where you would see that we are right. You're a victim of the propaganda that the government officials puts on us."

"I am going to miss my bus," she replied and pulled her arm away from his grasp.

Michael put his hand on her right shoulder and stopped her from walking away.

"We could teach you great things."

"You could teach us some things too," the third boy said, snickering and looking at Golden's beauty. "We need to perpetuate our race and you have the perfect body for it."

Golden was not so naive that she didn't understand what they wanted. She became suddenly scared. This was going in a direction she did not want.

"I'm not going anywhere with you. My dad's probably looking for me right now."

"Bullshit. Your dad's not with you, you're alone," Adolph said, looking into her eyes.

Over the years working on the farm, Golden had learned to be strong and courageous; she had shown her personal courage dozens of times. Her mind flashed back to the mountain lion. At that moment, three of the boys grabbed her arms. One led while the other followed closely behind. They began forcing her toward the car that was parked in the lot about twenty yards away. As they got closer to the car, Goldie knew she was going to have to do something or she'd be in too deep to ever get out. Using the support of the two boys holding her arms, she kicked the lead boy in the groin. She kicked so hard it lifted the boy up off the ground and he fell forward, groaning in pain. She pulled her right arm away from the surprised Adolph and slugged the boy holding her left arm in the face. Surprised, he let go of her arm and grabbed his now bleeding nose. Michael, who was following closely, stepped forward just in time to get kicked in his groin too.

She turned to Adolph and said, "I said I was going to the bus stop," at which she began to run toward the street and away from the parking lot. The two downed boys were just getting up and Adolph and the hit boy gave chase. They caught Golden by the giant poplar just next to the sidewalk and grabbed her. She screamed, "Let go of me!"

Michael was the first to get there from the downed boys and he put his hand over her mouth. Golden bit his finger so hard it began to bleed. He jerked his hand away and slapped her in the face. She kicked toward him but he had anticipated the kick and stepped aside. The other boy had gotten there and said, "Let's take her to the compound and teach her how to treat a man." Golden screamed again.

The boys in unison lifted her up, crossed her legs, with the bloody-nosed boy holding them, and carried her toward the car. Michael pulled her hair and told her if she screamed again he'd punch her in the face so hard she would be able to see next Wednesday. She shut up. When they got to the car the first boy she kicked let go of her legs and opened the back door. That left only the bloody-nosed guy holding them. She bent her knees and pushed with all her might against the car with her legs. The action pushed Adolph and the other carrying boy to the ground together with Michael who was holding her head. She rolled over the boys and stood up. Michael grabbed her leg and she fell.

"I'm gonna beat the shit out of you!" Michael said as he doubled up his fist and cocked his arm. At that moment a police car pulled into the parking lot. Two officers stepped out of the car. The cop on the passenger side stepped out first, rather quickly, and flashing his light into the eyes of Michael, said, "What the hell is going on here?" Before Michael or any of the other boys could answer, the other officer had gotten out of the car and approached Goldie. "You okay, miss?" he asked.

"No, these guys were taking me someplace and I didn't want to go."

"That's bullshit," Michael said. "She was giving us the come-on, and then when you pulled up she suddenly changes her mind. She's a hooker and doesn't want to get booked."

Both officers looked carefully at Golden. She wasn't dressed like a street lady.

"What about that?" the first officer, turning to Goldie, asked.

"I'm not sure what a come-on is, but I most certainly am not a hooker. These guys said they'd take me to their compound and teach me how to treat a man. I was afraid and was trying to run away when you came."

Both cops smiled. "Where you from?" the driver asked.

"I'm from Minnesota. I'm traveling by bus to California to go visit a friend," she answered with some defiance.

"You got a bus ticket?" the second cop asked.

Goldie opened her purse and pulled out her ticket. The officer looked at it and turned to Michael who seemed to be the leader.

"You guys are in deep shit. I could charge you with kidnapping, attempted aggravated sexual assault, aggravated physical assault, and conspiracy to kidnap. To say nothing about you drinking as a minor in a public park." He turned to Golden and asked, "What do you want to do?"

"I've got to catch my bus. I can't miss my connection," she said, knowing it to be a lie.

"Okay," the second officer said. He turned to the boys and said, "If I find you guys doing anything, I mean anything that even hints of illegality, I'll arrest you and charge you myself." He turned to Golden and said, "You want a lift to the bus station?"

"Yes! Thank you," she replied, breathing a sigh of relief.

On the way over to the station the officer explained a little about the boys.

"These guys are two faced. They claim to honor the law, but we catch them breaking it all the time. We've tried to set them up for prosecution but they have a couple of attorneys who file a myriad of pleadings and petitions. It's usually not worth it to proceed. In this case, we might have gotten something. But the prosecutor who's mildly sympathetic towards the skinheads would probably plea bargain it down to a misdemeanor and let them off with probation. It'd cost the city twenty or thirty thousand to go through the motions and we'd really get nothing for it. So if you want to stay and press charges, I will certainly support you. You'd have to be here three or four weeks because the damn attorneys make motions to extend and change venue, and they just keep screwing with the system until we give up. Last time, we arrested a guy making an illegal u-turn. He had no driver's license and was probably an illegal alien. Time we got through he had filed five lawsuits against our department, the city, the detention center, and me. We finally had to drop the prosecution plans and let him off with a $150.00 fine."

Goldie got on the bus. She boarded only five minutes early. She walked back to her seat and sighed. *How funny*, she thought, feeling the ache in her head from the hair pulling and a sore arm from the struggle. Her face was red from the slap, but it left no bruise. Goldie thought out loud, "People who think they are so right that they can hurt others with impunity. I wonder if Miss Hawthorn was right. Do these people really believe that the means are justified by the end?" She pulled her sweater off her right shoulder and saw the fingerprints of Adolph bruised into her upper arm. It hurt a little, but she had been bruised many times before.

Maybe I should turn around and go home, she thought. *Maybe I don't know enough about this world to be out in it alone. I remember a little about the skinheads from school, but we never really studied them. Like almost everything else, we only talked about them without really telling the whole story. Well, now I know more than I did before. Perhaps life teaches you better than school. I don't know. I left without graduating. I left Mom and Dad without even saying thank you for all they did for me. I must really be stupid. I left home, a good life, a good man, and all for what? An adventure in California? So far, I don't have much to show for my decision.*

The bus driver got on and started the bus. Ol' Jackson climbed on the bus a couple of minutes later and walked down the aisle. His kind eyes caught Goldie's and he walked toward her with the determination of a shot arrow.

"What happened to you? You look like you've been hurt," he said. Jackson had the eyes of an eagle. He could see in her face and her clothes and her manner of sitting that she had had some kind of an encounter. Something was wrong. He knew by her innocence that she was not the cause of the problem but probably the victim.

Goldie's eyes filled with tears for the first time since she left home. Her lower lip quivered and she could only nod in the affirmative. Jackson sat down beside her and as the bus pulled out she began to tell him the whole story. As she spoke he reached around her shoulder and pulled her next to his chest. She began to cry softly. More like a weep against Jackson's chest. Her whole body shook and she spoke incoherently, sometimes inaudibly, shaking her head and crying. He held her for probably forty-five minutes. In between sobs he got the gist of the story.

What evil people, he thought. It wasn't really because they hated people of his race. No, it was because they wanted to force a beautiful young girl to go with them. It was because they felt so superior that they disregarded all but themselves. It was because they had cruelly injured Goldie. Not just physically, but they had taught her that there are people out there who are ruthless, who care for nothing but themselves or their cause. It didn't have to be that way. One has a right to his or her ideology, but not to impose it on others, especially by force. And Goldie, she would probably never regard people the same. For sure she would never look at someone who represented neo-Nazi movements the same. She stopped crying and fell asleep in his arms.

The bus pulled into Spokane a few minutes later. It stopped there for a half an hour and picked up ten or eleven people. The bus was now about three quarters full. It didn't matter anymore. Goldie was asleep on Jackson's shoulder and she would remain asleep for most of the trip across Washington.

She tried to roll over a couple of times but there was no place to go, so she settled again on Jackson's shoulder and fell fast asleep once more. The bus stopped to let off three people in Moses Lake then continued on Interstate 90 towards Seattle.

At about 5:40 a.m the bus pulled into Seattle. The driver came onto the speaker and told the passengers that anyone going on to San Francisco had to change buses. They needed to connect with the Express Southbound to San Francisco. It was going south on I-5 and would be leaving at 8:00 a.m. Jackson woke Goldie and told her they were going to change busses here. She seemed a little confused at first. She thought she was still home and it had all been a dream. In a couple of minutes she woke up and recognized where she was. She remembered the ticketing agent had told her she needed to change busses in Seattle.

As she was getting her handbag out of the upper holding area, Zada came and took her by the waist and hugged her.

"I'm sorry I was kinda eavesdropping. But are you okay?"

"Yeah, thanks, Zada, how are the kids?"

"The same, little rascals," and they both laughed quietly.

"We have a couple of hours here. Ya wanna go get a bite or something?"

"Can we invite Jackson?" she said, turning to find him standing next to her.

"'Course."

They all got a cab and went to see the Needle. It wasn't open, but they looked at it and admired the structure and beauty. There was a hamburger stand, which claimed to have the best burgers in Washington, a block or so away, so they went there and got some burgers for breakfast. The kids were all pretty good. The baby was still asleep and Goldie carried him from the cab to the restaurant.

The trip to San Francisco was good. She, Zada, and Jackson talked and laughed and mused. In San Francisco, Jackson was so kind. He didn't even express hatred or anger to the guys in Idaho. He only smiled and said he'd seen worse in his years of living in the south.

Zada got off the bus in San Francisco. She kissed Goldie good-bye and told her if she ever needed a place to stay to come to San Francisco and see her. She handed her a slip of paper with her address and a telephone number. The kids kissed her too and each dutifully thanked her for the food and ice cream she had given them. The little girl thanked her for telling the stories and said they were the best stories she had ever heard. Zada left and Goldie felt a feeling of missing her she had not felt before. It was like they had connected for such a short time and she wanted more. She wanted to be friends, to follow Zada and make sure she was okay.

The bus pulled out of the San Francisco station and Goldie thought she was losing a better friend than she had had in all her years of school. No one had listened and shared as much in twelve years as Zada had in three days.

How strange, Goldie thought. *If for nothing else than getting to know Zada and Jackson, this trip has been worth it.*

Jackson went back to the seat behind Goldie and told her to rest. She obediently complied and soon was fast asleep again. The trip from San Francisco to Los Angeles took most of the day. The bus stopped in about six or seven towns even though it was supposed to be an "express."

The bus finally arrived in Los Angeles. It was 10:00 p.m. Jackson woke her and said he was leaving. Goldie kissed him and wished him luck with his son. He again advised her to call her parents and said, "You know, Goldie, not everyone is like the guys that hurt you. The world is full of good people and people who love. Some people need something to hang on to, something to motivate them, something to explain the world, so they cling to an ideology that fits them or meets their personal needs. Most of us want to feel superior or better than our neighbor. That's all these guys were about, feeling superior. I wish you luck. Please remember who you are and where you are from. You can be proud that your father is a dairyman. He feeds people and gives them his love. Don't forget your roots."

With that he took his two bags and the exhausted little dog and walked out front and caught a cab.

There was a five-hour layover in LA. Goldie hated it and decided she would go for a walk and see the city. She started out the front door of station. There were a couple of panhandlers there and as she looked around she didn't like what she saw. It wasn't that the city wasn't beautiful; it was that she was unfamiliar with it and didn't know anyone there. Nor did she know how to get around. She turned and walked back down the stairs to the main lobby. There was a little restaurant still open there and she ate a hamburger. It wasn't bad. In fact it tasted good except they charged two fifty for it.

I hope it's not that expensive in the regular outside world to live here, she thought.

She finished eating about eleven and walked over to the main lobby again. There were eight or nine people there, sitting in the seats. Some were asleep and others were reading or talking. Goldie felt alone. More alone than she had felt up to this point. All of her life she had family. Even on the bus she had Zada and Jackson, but now, now she was alone. At first she was a little afraid. She thought about yesterday's encounter with the guys in the park.

"It's okay. I think they were really just boys. Just guys who wanted some love and didn't know how to get it. Maybe that's the nature of adulthood. You learn to live with and adjust to your needs. Humm."

The feeling of loneliness clung to her like an oily film you can't get off your hands. It made her afraid. It made her wish she had never come. She looked around the station for a phone and saw a set of them against the wall by the bathrooms. She started to walk over there. She figured she'd give her mom a call and tell her she was all right. She really needed to talk with someone. Someone who loved her and would understand what she was going through, someone who would ask her to come home, back to the farm and to her comfortable bed. Back to her friends and her mare. Even back to the stench of the cow dung. She stopped just short of the phones.

No, she thought. It's too soon to call Mom. I have to do this. I know I have to do this alone. She turned and walked over to the bench, which was against the wall next to a bunch of little storage boxes. You put fifty cents or a dollar into them and keep the key. Goldie figured that it was for people making a connection like her who didn't want to carry all their personal things with them but did want to go see the town. She thought she'd probably come back to LA with Wendy anyway so she wasn't too unhappy about not seeing the city right then. She curled up and fell asleep.

Sleepy-eyed she got on the southbound bus at about three a.m. It was late and some of the passengers were complaining. The bus was a "milk run" and would take three hours just to get to San Clemente. Goldie didn't mind. She found a seat and curled up against the window. The bus was almost full and a couple of times guys asked if the seat next to her was taken. She said yes, that her girlfriend was coming. The bus pulled out at three thirty with only a couple of seats empty. Goldie was glad she had one of them.

VIII

A New Life

The hiss of the air leaving the break system rang again in Golden's ears. She looked out the window and was surprised that she could see the ocean from the bus stop. She had seen it off and on during the trip down the coast on I-5, but now she was finally here. Here in San Clemente. The town looked like the thousands of other towns she had seen and stopped at on the long bus ride. It was a quarter to seven and she climbed off the bus. She remembered Zada who had gotten off in San Francisco and Jackson who got off at LA. They had been such good friends. She had learned a lot from both of them, especially Jackson. He had such wisdom and such kindness. Goldie wondered how he had gotten it; especially considering how he and others like him had been treated over the years. She thought it funny that you'd treat someone different because they had a different skin tone. *What if it was your haircut that was different?* she thought, *Or your clothes?* Come to think of it, people do treat you differently when you don't conform to their hair or dress styles. She walked up to the baggage claim counter and gave the man her tickets. He walked to the back where suitcases were stacked three or four high and in rows of ten or so. After a few minutes he came forward with two of Golden's bags.

"Here ya go," he said in flat, emotionless tones.

"I had four bags," Golden responded.

"Let me see the ticket," he asked.

"You already have them," Golden said a little impatiently

"Oh yeah, I forgot. Well, let's see. Yup, you did send four, but I can only find two. Can ya come back tomorrow at about ten in the morning. There'll be another bus from the east in then."

Goldie was too tired to argue. She grabbed one of the small carts and loaded her bags onto it and wheeled it back to the front of the station where there were some phones.

She dialed Wendy's number. She was getting excited, not only to see Wendy, but also to see the ocean and to see what California was really like. The phone rang at least ten times. Goldie thought maybe Wendy had gone to work or wasn't home but finally she answered.

"Hello?"

"Is this Wendy?" Golden asked, not knowing exactly what to say.

"Yeah, who's this?"

"It's me, Wendy, it's Golden!"

"Wow, where are you?"

"I'm at the bus station here in San Clemente. Can you come and get me?"

"Hell yes! Give me half an hour to get dressed, I was just getting up."

"Okay, I'll see you in a while," Goldie said, knowing she had probably woken her.

Wendy pulled up in what looked like a new Mazda convertible. It was an off color blue and had light tan leather seats and dashboard. The top was down and Wendy was dressed in a multi-colored open blouse and short pants. When she got out she had leather thongs on. Not just the average thong, but Airwalks or Nikes or some shoe that must have cost her a hundred dollars or so. She didn't walk toward Golden but sort of skipped. Not a skip really but a bouncy walk. She was sure pretty and she seemed so happy. Goldie thought she hadn't personally been that happy ever in her life. Maybe Wendy's happiness was contagious. She thought, *This is the place to be.* California, where all the "in" people were.

"They lost two of my bags," Goldie said with some frustration.

"Screw it, you need to get some other clothes anyway. What you're wearing is so out of it."

"I've got a little money but not a lot, Wendy, so I can't be buying a new wardrobe."

"We'll put it on my dad's credit card."

"Can I come back tomorrow to see if they found my bag?" Golden asked, unsure of what was okay to ask and what was not.

"Sure. If they've lost it we'll get the maximum insurance out of it," Wendy said flippantly.

Wendy's house was beautiful. It was two stories and on a hill above San Clemente. It overlooked the sea but didn't have any yard to speak of. It was white and irregular, that is, part of it stuck out over a patio and part of it was only one story. Still it was beautiful. Golden looked out to the sea for a minute or two and then Wendy interrupted and said, "Let's go in, okay?"

The downstairs was really beautiful too. It had a magnificent kitchen, which had a counter in the middle and two ovens, two microwaves, and one large stovetop with six cooking units on it. It had a refrigerator that had two doors on it and a sink with an electric dishwasher built right into the counter. The counter was done in black granite and lights hung down from a ten-foot-high ceiling above it. There was also a table in the corner of the kitchen that was surrounded by four leather-covered chairs. The table was glass and Golden wondered if it would break easily.

"Your bedroom is gonna be upstairs down the hall from mine. My dad sleeps downstairs in the master bedroom, but the upstairs is mine. Come on, I'll show you." Wendy carried one of the bags up the stairs and Golden carried the other plus her handbag and her purse. The stairs winded up in a coil. The second floor was up higher than the second floor Golden was used to. It was a lot higher than her house.

"You have your own bathroom. It extends off the bedroom. So just put your makeup and personal stuff there. Nobody will ever bother it. My dad never comes upstairs. Hell, he almost never comes home."

"Thank you, Wendy, thanks for taking me in. I think I'm gonna love California."

"It's nothing. We're friends. You saved my life, remember? It's the least I can do. And besides, I'm gonna teach you about real life. I'm gonna show you how to live!"

"Are you hungry?" Wendy asked.

"Yes, I got so I hated to eat at those bus stop places. The food was okay, but it wasn't real. It seemed so, so, pre-made."

"You're gonna love Wendy's then. It's one of the places I eat. I usually don't eat much 'cause boys'll take you out to dinner and stuff, so I just wait for that. But we've got plenty of food if you wanna cook."

"Thanks."

"You're probably tired. I know I'd be if I had to sit on a bus for four or five days."

"I am."

"Why don't you go up and take a shower and lie down for a couple of hours? I'll go get us some food and wake ya up this afternoon."

Golden thought of how nice a real bed would be and inside sighed with gratitude.

"What a great idea," she said.

So up to bed she went. The bed was pink with a canopy on the top and what appeared to be silk sheets. It had a nightstand and a flowered bedspread. The walls were papered with a cloth-like material that had flowers and bees and birds throughout, and of course it matched the spread perfectly. As Golden stood in the hot shower, she thought about home. She missed her mom and dad. But it was so nice here.

Wendy's dad must be really rich, she thought.

She snuggled down in the bed and fell asleep in five minutes.

"Hey, girl, wake up."

Golden opened her eyes to see Wendy looking down at her.

"It's seven o'clock. I let you sleep 'cause you seemed so tired, but we're going out tonight at nine and I thought you'd like to get ready."

"Out? Where and with whom? I don't know anybody," Goldie stammered, getting oriented.

"Just a couple of guys from San Diego. They are ocean life people or something. They are at the college there and I gave them a call. They'll be here at nine."

"Probably botanists. Or maybe biologists. What'd you tell them about me?" Goldie asked, a little resentful that she had not been consulted before committing to a blind date. Still, isn't that why she came to California, to see the world and to learn about other people and cultures?

"Just that you were really cute and that you'd come from Minnesota and was visiting for a while. You'll go out with David, and I'm going out with Bryan. Bryan is much more aggressive and I know how to handle him. David's okay and he'll leave you alone unless you tell him it's okay."

Goldie wasn't sure what she was talking about, but she was sure it had something to do with sex. She had stayed a virgin throughout high school and was determined not to give her body to anybody but the man she married. It was a romantic notion, but one she had been taught by her mother and she believed in it.

"You got makeup and stuff?" Wendy asked, knowing the answer was probably in the negative. She had never seen Goldie wear any makeup except for a little lipstick.

"I'm not sure. I've got some lipstick and I use it to pink up my cheeks a little. Other than that I don't really need anything."

Wendy thought, *That's probably true. She works outside and her skin is so dam smooth. You'd think it'd get rough and callused working with the cows and all.*

"Okay, that'll do for tonight, but later on I'll show you how to put on war paint. Dating is like going to war. You've got to be ready and dressed for the part. Speaking of dressing, I bought you a couple of dresses. I hope you like them. I picked them up at Macy's."

"How'd you know my size?" Goldie asked, knowing the answer.

"Honey, I know everybody's size. It's really important to keep up with those kinds of things."

"Well then, let's see 'em," Goldie said.

Wendy didn't go to a bag or box to get the dresses out; no, she went to her closet and returned with two dresses hanging on funny-looking hangers. They both were gorgeous. The dark blue one had some sparkles on the dress part and an open front with only straps over the shoulders. But it was really lovely.

"Look at these," Wendy said. "I'm gonna go get you the shoes I bought."

"You bought shoes too?"

"Yeah, you can't have a dress and wear the wrong shoes with it."

She returned with a pair of dark low-healed shoes. They were satin covered with a silver buckle on the front. Of course they matched the dress perfectly.

"Let me help you with your hair," Wendy said, implying that Golden didn't know a thing about dressing up.

"I'm pretty good at doing my hair. My mom taught me and she always looked beautiful."

"Yeah, but moms are moms. They don't know our fashions; they don't know our way of life."

Nine o'clock came and the boys were right on time. Wendy introduced David to Golden and he smiled. She thought he must like her because he took her hand and walked her out to the car.

"Where we going?" Golden asked.

"We are going to the Hyatt Ballroom in San Diego. The food there is exquisite and they play the best dancing music."

As they drove down the Interstate 5 freeway, Goldie asked a million questions. David and she were in the back seat and he told her about the swallows in San Juan Capistrano, about the Marine base in Oceanside, about the farmers, and about each town they went by. He told her about the sea and diving. He told her about the La Jolla reserve and offered to take her diving there.

"I've never seen so much variety in my whole life!" she explained. "How wonderful to have so much so close at hand."

The Hyatt was beautiful indeed. They entered and walked across the main floor and down the curly stairs to the lower floor where the ballroom was. Next to the ballroom was a restaurant. It opened into the ballroom where there were people dancing to a live orchestra. The restaurant was buffet style and at first Golden thought it was inappropriate to serve food that way in a stylish place, but when she entered she could see that there was a chief at four booths ready to prepare whatever food you'd like in that specialty. One with steaks and another with seafood, one for pastas and one even for salad; it was really marvelous.

Golden and Dave went first. Dave took her to each food stand and she ordered what she thought she'd like. Even the salad was prepared to your liking. It was wonderful. Golden had never seen or been treated like this in her entire life. California was going to be great. It was so new and so exciting. Golden was suddenly immersed in a world much to her liking.

As they were eating, Dave offered her a drink of champagne. "I'm too young," she repeated like a record playing off at the right cue. But then she thought, *Well, Dad did let me have some champagne last Christmas.* Golden smiled. "Well, yes, okay, on second thought I think I'll have one glass."

One turned into three and Golden realized that the alcohol was affecting her so she stopped. She thought about what her mother had told her, that guys sometimes get girls drunk so they can have their way with them. Goldie didn't think Dave was like that, but she didn't want to appear easy or stupid or out of control.

The night passed in new adventures and new sights. They danced what seemed like a hundred dances from the cha-cha to the swing to '60s rock to the closing song, which was taken from the Blue Danube. It was wonderful and Dave was gracious and kind. He was a perfect gentleman. On the way back Bryan drove and Dave and Goldie sat in the back seat. She instinctively snuggled up to him and laid her head on his shoulder. On the one hand she was tired and he was so warm. He held her like she had never been held before. In comparison, Jeff didn't really know how to hold a girl; he was young and inexperienced. But Dave, he knew. Goldie closed her eyes and her mind flashed back to her home in Minnesota. She saw herself riding her mare, Patches. She was a beautiful horse. *I don't suppose I'll get to ride much out here*, she thought. She pictured her farm and the holding stall always filled with manure. In most ways she was glad to be away from it. Life here was different. It sure was great. People treated you so well. *Men are great. I'm so glad I didn't marry Jeff*, she thought.

"Golden, Goldie. We're home." Dave was gently shaking her shoulder. Golden woke with a start.

"I'm sorry. I fell asleep. It must have been the champagne." She weakly smiled and realized she was now lying in Dave's lap. Dave smiled.

"I was hoping to get to know you a little better," he said.

Goldie wasn't sure what he meant, probably nothing. She had the bad habit of reading into statements more than was really there. She sat up and straightened her hair. Wendy and Bryan were not in the car.

"Where'd Wendy and Bryan go?" she asked.

"They went into the house. I told them I'd bring you in in a minute."

"Oh, okay, let's go on in," she said with some hesitancy.

They walked into the living room, which was dark except for the light in the kitchen. It cast its glow into the living room, making long shadows and giving Golden a sort of misty, melancholy feeling. Dave walked over to the big bay window, which overlooked the ocean about three miles away. The stars were out, but the sky was starting to lighten.

Wendy looked at her watch. "Geez, it's five o'clock."

The night was spent. They looked out at the sea and talked for ten or fifteen minutes about the sea and the stars and other trivia. Golden offered Dave some coffee.

"I was hoping for something more personal," Dave said.

"That's as personal as I can get right now," Wendy said, understanding exactly what Dave wanted.

"Okay," Dave said. "I spent a lot of money tonight and Wendy said you were really a kind girl."

"I am kind. I just got here and I don't know what your culture says, but mine says to get to know somebody before I get intimate with them."

"Wow, you're a pretty direct person," Dave said, realizing that she was not the country bumpkin that Wendy had described.

Goldie made some coffee for Dave and they talked for another forty-five minutes. Wendy and Bryan came down the stairs. She was in some jeans and a light blouse with no bra.

"Hi guys," Wendy said, smiling and holding onto the arm of Bryan.

"Hi," Dave said. "We've been down here talking and drinking coffee."

"Oh," said Wendy, understanding exactly what Dave was saying.

"Well, thank you guys for a wonderful night. It was great!" Wendy said, smiling and turning to Bryan.

"Yes, thank you. I don't think I have ever seen so much and had so much fun in my life," Golden said. "I'm sorry, but I'm really tired. It's almost six thirty and I'm gonna go and lie down for an hour or two."

With that, Golden turned to Dave and kissed him. It was a refreshing kiss. A clean, sweet, innocent kiss. She was really lovely, really beautiful, and really innocent. Golden turned and smiled to Wendy and walked upstairs to her room where she fell on the bed without disrobing and fell fast asleep.

❧•❧

The days and nights flew by. Wendy and Goldie went out on dates four and sometimes five times a week. Golden now had a drink or two with all her meals. She would kiss and hold and caress the men who took her out, but would not go to bed with any of them. Wendy argued with her on several occasions. Wendy would say that these men pay a lot and they expect to get something back. Goldie would argue that giving sex in exchange for dinner and/or gifts was equivalent to being a prostitute. She felt like that would be selling her body in exchange for dinner and gifts. She said she was worth more than that and she was holding out.

At the end of the first week Goldie called her mom. Marge cried and thanked her for calling. Jason was out in the barn but Marge begged Goldie to hold while she went and got Dad. They all talked for more than an hour. Goldie said she wasn't ready to come home yet, but that she loved them and would call every week from then on. She said she missed them and missed the farm. She even missed cleaning up and doing her other chores. Love vows were renewed and both Mom and Dad said they weren't mad at her. Mom asked several times if Goldie had enough money. She said she was running low but that she was going to find a job in a week or so. Jason mentioned that she wasn't going to graduate from high school and reiterated how important a high school education was. Goldie understood but said she just couldn't come back. It was already May and school was going to end in June. By September Jeff would be down in St. Paul going to school and maybe she would come back then. She wasn't sure. Mom said she'd send Goldie some money but Goldie said she knew they didn't have much and she didn't want to take from their savings. Mom said she could pick it up at the Western Union.

The next day Goldie went to the Western Union expecting to get a hundred dollars or so. Instead, they had sent her a thousand.

This is way too much! Goldie thought. *Way, way too much.*

She thought about sending back five or six hundred, but decided against it. It would probably worry Mom and Dad. So she cashed the check at the Wells Fargo bank and put the money in the inside pocked of her shoulder bag with what was left of her original money.

It was Friday and no one had asked them out. It was actually a relief for Golden. She asked Wendy if she'd like to go out to dinner together and talk. Wendy was almost gleeful.

"What a great idea. Even I get bored with men sometimes. Yeah, let's go out. You sure you can afford to treat?"

"Yeah, Mom sent me some money," Golden responded.

They dressed up in spite of the fact that they weren't going out with anyone except each other. Wendy knew of a really great restaurant just south of the *Queen Mary* boat right on the shoreline. It served the best and freshest fish in the state. They drove with the top down. The weather was getting warm and the sky was clear. The wind tossed their hair in all directions but neither girl cared. They were alone and didn't have to impress anyone.

The restaurant was crowded and they had to wait an hour before being seated. The host said usually they only accept reservations on Fridays and weekends, but that he'd try to find them a place. He did. It was great. It was right out on the veranda overlooking the ocean. You could hear the waves splashing against the rocks and smell the salty sea air. Golden ordered lobster. She had had some on her first date with Dave, who still called and took her out occasionally but not like the first night. Still, she remembered him very fondly. The lobster was served whole and on a huge plate. It didn't have any claws and

Goldie thought it was sort of a gyp because you didn't get to eat all that claw meat.

"Why'd they take the claws off?" she asked Wendy.

"You silly girl, these are Pacific lobsters, they don't have claws," Wendy responded and started to giggle. "You're still a country bumpkin."

"Am not!"

"Are too"

"Am not!"

Both girls started to laugh and couldn't stop until the waiter came and asked them to please be a little quieter as they were disturbing some of the other guests.

They quieted down, but every once in a while they'd look at each other and Wendy would say, "Are too!" to which they both would giggle again.

About half way through her lobster, Goldie reached out to take a drink of her Merlot wine and a man walking back to his table with a plate of salad bumped into her arm. The wine spilled on the tablecloth and onto the lobster.

"Oh, please excuse me!" the man who looked to be in about his middle or late twenties said.

"I should hope so!" Goldie replied. "You've ruined my dinner!"

"Please let me pay for it. I'll even buy you another lobster," he said in soft tones and in a very humble way.

"My name is Gregory Coleman." He extended his hand. Goldie didn't take it. She just signaled to the waiter to come. He came over right away and seeing the plate and the mess on the table quickly began to clean it up.

"Give her another dinner. I'll pay for both of them," Gregory said in an authoritative voice.

"Yes, sir," the waiter responded.

"May I sit with you?" Gregory asked.

Golden looked at Wendy. Wendy nodded in the affirmative.

He was a large muscular man with a short haircut and in a very expensive suit. He had evasive eyes but spoke with a calm assurance that reminded Golden of Jackson. He was also an African American. Instead of sitting next to Goldie, he sat across the table next to Wendy. She looked at him for what seemed to be an eternity and then looked at Golden. Golden wondered if Wendy was okay with people of different races.

"You're sure a big man," Wendy said, leaving Gregory to pick up on all the innuendoes involved in the statement.

"Yeah, I work out a little and my dad played football."

"What'd ya do for a living?" Wendy asked.

"You're gettin' kinda personal. But it's okay. I sell for Mercedes Benz. I'm the regional director so I get ta travel a lot."

"Where ya from?" Wendy asked

"I have an apartment just above Hollywood."

"I hate Hollywood. It's full of weirdoes."

Gregory laughed and his laugh seemed to Golden to be deep and sincere. He seemed to be a deep thinker and a really kind man.

Golden didn't finish her dinner, but ordered a to-go bag and took it home. She reluctantly gave Gregory her phone number, figuring that she could always tell him no if he called her up and asked her out. He paid for both Golden and Wendy's meals. He walked the girls out the their car and said goodnight. They drove home mostly in silence.

When they got home Wendy said she knew about black men, and Goldie needed to be careful. Most of 'em just want sex, she pointed out. Golden said that that was probably true of all men and Wendy laughed and agreed. They talked until about one a.m and then went to bed.

※

"Goldie, wake up; it's 11 o'clock in the morning. Guess who's on the phone?"

"Huh? Oh, good morning, Wendy. I guess I slept in."
"Well, guess who's on the phone?"
"I can't imagine. Who?"
"Greg."
"Oh, crap. Tell him I'm still asleep."
"I did, but he insisted on talking with you."
"Okay, gimme the phone." She took the phone, cleared her throat and said, "Hi."

On the other end was the man who had met the girls the night before at the restaurant. He was suave and very polite.

"Goldie, I just got tickets to a Rams game. I don't know if you like football, but they're on the forty, only a quarter of the way up. Would you like to go?"

"When's the game?" Goldie asked, still in her sleepy voice and not believing she really asked.

"This coming Friday. I'd love to have you there with me."

"Just the game?"

"No, I'll take you out to a nice dinner after. Maybe we can get to know each other."

"I'm not sure I want to get to know you, but yeah, sure, I'd love to go see the Rams. My dad'll kill me when I tell him," she said, knowing she wouldn't really tell her dad she had gone to a football game with a guy she had just met the night before.

Golden hung up the phone after making arrangements for the time of pick up and other details. She sat there in silence thinking of Jackson and Zada, both of whom had been real friends. She knew she loved Jackson and maybe Greg was like him. He sure seemed to be.

"Okay, girl, what'd ya do?" Wendy asked in her California valley girl talk.

"I told him I'd go to the Rams game with him Friday."

"You damn sure better get me and a guy a ticket too. I love the Rams. Call him back."

Golden faithfully did as she was asked and returned the call to

Greg. She said she couldn't go with him without taking some insurance along and so if he really wanted to go, he'd get some tickets for Wendy and a guy. Greg reluctantly agreed. He mentioned the cost and the improbably of getting more tickets, especially on the forty, but said he'd do it if he could.

Golden got up, showered, and got dressed. She didn't eat any breakfast. She told Wendy it was time for her to start looking for a job. She was running low on money and thought she'd laid around too much anyway. She wasn't really low on money, but she did have a need to get settled on her own.

"I still don't have a car, Wendy, and I can't get much done taking the bus and waiting for it at each stop. Could you drive me or let me take your car?" There was a subtle plea in her voice that Wendy hadn't heard before. Wendy thought, *I certainly owe her something, she saved my life and hasn't taken anything but food and a couple of clothes from me since she got here.*

"Yeah, sure, take the car, but please be back by five. I've got a great dinner planned. We're going for pizza. Take-out. We'll go up to the mountains, east of 395. I know a great place."

"Thanks, girl, you're great!" Golden was getting the hang of California communications.

Golden went to a couple of employment agencies and also made a list of jobs offered in the newspaper. She filled out four applications and did one test at the employment agency. It was a typing test, which she passed with an 85-words-per-minute score. The woman giving the test kept raving about the score, but Goldie thought she hadn't done up to her potential. In school she had done better a couple of times. She returned home and got there at ten after five. She apologized for her tardiness to which Wendy shrugged and said, "I didn't know it was five already. I've been watching TV and sleeping most of the day. I did get some laundry done. How was the job hunt?"

"Pretty good. I took a test and filled out four applications. Most of 'em wanted a resume. Let me use your computer and I'll make one up tonight."

"Ya know, you really don't have to go to work. I'd love to have you stay and play. My dad gets me all the food and gas I want. And you're beautiful, so you won't have any trouble getting anything you want or need from guys."

"I know. Thanks. You've really been a pal, but sooner or later I've got to make it on my own."

"Make it later," Wendy said and laughed. "Let's go eat and see if we can stir up some adventure."

"Okay, kid, but I'm pretty tired from looking for a job all day, so let's try to avoid men if possible."

"What, you kidding, that's what life is all about. It's not work; it's play. It's the chase and the kill. I don't think you get it, Goldie. Life is a game and a hunt, and you can either be the hunter or the hunted. Me, I'm gonna be the hunter. I'll take which men I want and leave the rest. And in the play I'll get what I want. Men are easy, Goldie, you give them what they want and they'll give you what you want."

"Well, I'm not willing to give what they want yet," Goldie said, a little slower than she usually speaks.

"Then pretty soon you'll run out of men who are willing to date you and who are willing to give you what you want and need."

"I know, Wendy, I'm just not ready yet."

Wendy laughed again and said, "Are you going in your job clothes or do you want to change?"

"Give me a minute and I'll change."

As Golden was coming down the stairs, the phone rang. It was Greg. He said he had made the arrangements and got the tickets. He said, "I even got them together!"

Golden was glad and internally breathed a sigh of relief.

"Okay, what time will you pick us up?"

"About four, the game starts at six. But we need to be there early," Greg answered.

"Sounds fun. I'll see you at four Friday." She hung up the phone and told Wendy she was going. Wendy was excited.

"I've only been to a couple of games and they were great!" she said.

The girls talked and giggled for the next hour and went out to get some pizza.

The evening went well. Of course, they did meet some boys who took them up to a cabin that Wendy's father had bought while he was still married to her mother. The cabin was east of Temecula. It was dusty and Wendy couldn't find anything to drink and very little to eat. They had brought the rest of the pizzas from dinner and some sodas, but Wendy was looking for some snack food. Something to sort of munch on. Goldie loved it. She thought it was great. She went exploring through the cabin and found some whiskey under the sink. It was a liter of tequila. They all drank until they were drunk except for Goldie. She had a couple of drinks and stopped. Golden still felt uncomfortable drinking, even though she usually had champagne or wine with dinner. She would only have one or two glasses. When guys wanted to keep her drinking she politely refused.

But she had changed. Somewhere in her heart she knew that she had grown up a little more. When she was a senior, she felt that there wasn't much more to learn about life or about the adult world. But now those ideas were changing. She was learning.

Maybe Wendy was right all along. Maybe all boys want is sex, she thought. That's how it seemed. Every boy she went out with tried to get her to put out. Goldie had stayed faithful to her promise to save herself until she met that perfect man. Some of the guys wouldn't re-date her. Some came back for seconds. Goldie was so very beautiful that most could not resist being with her. So it was with the guy she had brought to the cabin. He kept grabbing her and started kissing her. He was drunk and his breath smelled bad and his coordination was way off. Goldie thought he probably couldn't do it even if she was willing.

"Why the hell did you bring me up to this cabin if you didn't want some action?" he asked challengingly.

"Because I thought we could come and enjoy the night. Have some fun."

Golden could hear Wendy and the other boy in the loft. Somehow it seemed like a bad idea to go to bed with a guy you met three hours ago.

The night passed slowly. Wendy came down the steps about forty-five minutes later. Goldie suggested they play some games. But Wendy couldn't find any in the cabin. They talked for a little while. Goldie's guy fell asleep on the couch and snored loudly. Wendy said to wake him up, but Goldie didn't want to bother. She figured it'd save both of them some trouble.

"He's pretty grabby, so I'll just let him sleep."

Goldie's thoughts drifted back to Jackson and the trip over. Then she thought of Greg. He seemed so nice. He didn't grab her and didn't assume anything. Maybe the football game would be great. Maybe, just maybe, he'd be courteous and kind and considerate.

"I've got to get home, I've got things to do tomorrow," Wendy said to her date.

"Goldie, you got money for gas?" she asked, and then without giving her a chance to answer she turned to her date and said, "Let me give you my number. I really like you and hope you'll call me again."

The guy opened his wallet and took out a fifty-dollar bill and gave it to Wendy and said that it should pay for gas. Then he took out a pen and wrote down the number Wendy gave him. It wasn't really her number. Golden thought it was silly to offer if you didn't really intend to give out your phone number. But she knew that Wendy was manipulative. And she figured that fifty was cheap for what the guy got. Golden woke up her guy and sent him out with the first. Wendy locked up the cabin and got into her car. She put up the top and shivered. "Crap, I thought it'd be warm by now," she said without any emotion. Golden said she'd rather drive because Wendy had had a lot to drink. Wendy agreed and after going down the road for five minutes she was fast asleep.

Friday came and Golden got a call from GTE in Hollywood. They set up an interview for Monday. Goldie was elated. It was her first real promising interview for a first-time real job. That is if she got it. She went into Wendy's room and woke her up and told her. Wendy wasn't as excited as Goldie had hoped. Still, she was glad and said, "It's gonna be a long drive 'cause you're not moving from here. I can't live without you, girl. You keep me sane and safe."

Goldie smiled. She knew that Wendy loved her and that they were becoming the best of friends.

They went out to the Subway sandwich shop. Wendy had a meatball sandwich. Goldie could never figure out how she ate so much and still kept her waist so thin. She ordered a seafood sandwich and they both had sodas.

"Okay, girl, we go to football games in jeans. We go casual. You gotta open your blouse a button or two and wear tennis shoes," Wendy carefully instructed Golden.

"Okay," Golden replied, thinking she didn't want to unbutton her blouse.

Wendy knew Golden by now and laughed. "I know you. You'd button the top button if you could."

"No!" Goldie answered, realizing that she was probably right.

"Yes you would! But it's just a football game and all the men there come to see some hard hitting and some boobs. They'll watch the cheerleader girls or they'll watch you. So you gotta decide which you want."

Goldie thought about it for a couple of seconds as she took another bite of her sandwich.

"Okay, you're right, maybe this Greg guy is as nice as he seems. He sure is good looking and has a great body. I'll unbutton one, just one."

Wendy was delighted. She was getting Golden to loosen up a little. She was showing her how to live and how to be loved. It was great.

They finished their sandwiches and went home.

"It's lucky you're my size," Wendy said with a little sarcasm.

Actually Golden had a little bigger waist and longer legs. But Wendy's pants would fit her. A little too snugly for Golden's tastes, but they fit. They couldn't have exchanged blouses for their life. Wendy had a smaller upper body including her breast size. Goldie had larger breasts and in truth she was a prettier girl. That didn't matter to Goldie but occasionally Wendy was jealous when men would look at Goldie instead of her. Goldie thought it was Wendy's imagination, but Wendy knew. She really did know.

The doorbell rang at exactly three p.m. Wendy answered and said she wasn't expecting them until four or so.

"The crowd's gonna be really big, and we need a good place to park, so we'd better go now, unless you want to walk a mile to get there. Where's Golden?" Greg asked, looking around Wendy into the living room. Wendy did not invite him in but she too was looking around Greg to see her date. He was standing behind Greg. He was also Afro-American but he looked pretty handsome and was younger than Greg. She stepped around Greg and said hi. Wendy turned and yelled, "Come on, Goldie, we gotta get there so we don't have to walk five miles to the stadium."

Goldie appeared in less than five minutes. Greg was still standing outside the front door. Wendy still hadn't invited them into the house. He looked good and Wendy was right. He had on jeans and a plaid shirt that looked it came off a lumberjack. He was also wearing cowboy boots that were made of snake or lizard or some other reptile skin. They were light gray and Golden knew that must have been very expensive. To Wendy's surprise he was driving a Mercedes Benz. It looked like a new or nearly new model. The car was black with black leather interior. It had a great stereo and Greg played it with some soft country music. He told her a little more about himself on the ride north. He said he lived in Hollywood and lived alone. He had two brothers and no sisters. His mother kept pretty good track of him. He didn't own a house because he wasn't sure if he wanted to stay in LA. He admitted he grew up in Watts and didn't finish high school. Goldie laughed and admitted she hadn't either. He was surprised.

"You sound so well educated. I was sure you were a college student or even had a degree."

"No," she said, "I'm just a cowgirl."

"No kidding? You ride? Wow, I'd love to take you horseback riding. I know of a place in El Cajon where they rent horses out. They are pretty good animals and they let you go without a guide. We could go up the hill above El Centro; it's beautiful country and no roads."

"I'd love to go riding again!" Golden said enthusiastically.

"We could go next Wednesday. How about 2:30, I'll be free then."

"Great! You wanna come too?" she asked as she turned to see if Wendy was still standing behind her.

"No thanks, I don't like horses, they smell," Wendy answered and made a wrinkled nose gesture that made everyone laugh.

They got a parking spot and went into the stadium. It was huge. Goldie had never been in anything so big in her life. She was really glad that they had seats so close to the field. She could see everything. The game was exciting. It was tough, and the players were merciless. They were big men who seemed to live for the hit. Golden thought that the sport had become much more than what she had known in high school. Greg put his arm around her shoulder and it felt good. He didn't try anything sexual, just held her close to him. Of course when they made a touchdown or did something stupid, he'd be up and screaming. Occasionally his language was a little offensive, but never toward her, only to the refs, or the coach, or a player who he said faked an injury. The halftime entertainment was great. Greg went and got beer for everyone and when Golden refused he grumbled for a couple of seconds and then said, "Great, more for me!"

About half way through the halftime, a shabby-looking man came to the end of their row and signaled to Greg. The guy looked sort of funny in that he had on an expensive leather jacket, leather pants, and a large belt with a rodeo buckle and a little chain coming off the belt and going into his back pocket. Goldie figured it held his wallet. He had a tattoo on his neck and another on his forearm. She could only see it just above his wrist, but it was colored in yellow and red so she knew it must have gone up his arm. His hair was drawn in a ponytail and he was unshaven. He had pockmarks on his face, probably from bad acne as a youth. He kept looking around and as he signaled Greg, he'd also shift his head from side to side. His eyes were cloudy and his smile showed dirty teeth.

"Excuse me, Goldie, this is a business associate I've got to go see for a couple of minutes. I'll be right back."

Greg was gone for at least twenty minutes. The game had restarted and the Rams got the ball at the kickoff and were on the 35-yard line. Greg came back with some hot dogs and a soda for Golden. His friend had gone and gotten some more beer for Wendy and had returned just a minute before Greg. He scooted across the row to his seat.

"Sorry it took so long." His breath smelled like Sen-sens and his coat like sweet pipe smoke. Goldie figured he smoked a pipe and didn't want to offend her by smoking in her face. He put his arm around her and for most of the rest of the game held her. For the whole second half he didn't stand up and shout or swear or even yell at the refs. Golden was flattered. *He likes me enough to stay with me and hold me in preference to the game*, she thought.

The game ended and they went out to dinner. It was great. They went to North Hollywood to a small Italian restaurant where Goldie saw one of the Jackson sisters with a couple of other girls. They had some security around them so Goldie didn't go talk to her. She probably wouldn't have anyway, but the guards cinched it.

After dinner, they drove to Northern Hollywood where Greg suggested that Wendy and her date disembark. He had a new Corvette parked in the driveway and Wendy was all too eager to go for a ride in it. Goldie didn't want to be alone with Greg just yet, but the decision was made without regard to her. As they drove away, Greg sighed and turned to Goldie.

"Glad we got rid of them. Now where would you like to go?"

"I don't know the area very well, so take us where you'd like to go," she answered.

"Okay, let's go to a beach I know."

They drove north for about a half an hour. Then turning off the road and down a winding dirt road, they came to a beach that was obviously not maintained by the state. It had driftwood and kelp and large stones in the sand. Still, it was beautiful. The moon had risen and the sea was calm. The tide was out and the beach seemed like an empty cove where no one had ever been. The sand glistened in the moonlight and the water smelled good. It smelled sweet and salty at the same time. Even the foam of the ocean was beautiful. Greg walked back to the car, opened the trunk, and pulled out a couple of big blankets, a shovel, and one of those old milk delivery cartons full of wood and a bag of barbeque briquettes. He walked over to the cliff where the rock hung over the sand and a small indentation in the rock made for a perfect place to put the blankets. Then he dug a little hole in the sand and walked around and got some rocks to place around the hole. He put the wood and briquettes in the hole and lit the fire.

"Go gather some wood and we'll make this fire blaze!" he shouted to Goldie who had walked down the beach to where it curved around the stone mountain tongue and the beach disappeared into the sea.

She gathered an armful of dry wood branches, which had washed ashore during high tide and dried in the sun. As she came back Greg was coming from his car with a black pot. It looked like a witch's cauldron only not as big. She giggled.

"What ya gonna do with that? Make a brew?"

"No, my beautiful girl, we are gonna cook some clams."

Goldie had never gone clam hunting and didn't know a thing about it. But this was the perfect beach for it. In ten minutes Greg had dug up ten clams and was still digging for more. Soon they had about twenty clams and he brought them over to the pot, which had been put on the fire by Golden in obedience to Greg's instructions. She had filled it with some water in a little tide pool, which Greg said made the perfect water to cook the clams. He went to the tide pool, rinsed off the shells, and dropped them into the pot.

"You've never tasted anything good until you've tasted this," he said as he walked back to the car and brought back a six-pack of beer and some sauce for the clams.

Goldie didn't usually like beer. She had only drank it once or twice before and she just didn't like the taste. But when he gave her a bottle, it was different. He said it was German beer and was really good. She thought it was okay, but when she ate it with the clams, it was actually a pretty good combination. He had brought a little yellow plastic lemon bottle and a couple of other spices. He was a great cook and Golden really enjoyed the time, the place, the company, and the food.

The moon moved across the sky in a magical sort of way. Greg was strong and beautiful. They swam. At first Goldie didn't want to go in, but Greg took off his clothes and jumped into the water. Goldie followed, taking off her clothes too. He held her in the surf and she couldn't resist his embrace. He was so very good to her. So gentle and so very understanding. She told him about her home and Jeff and everything. He listened and understood.

When they got out of the water he held her and they walked over to the fire. She covered herself in the blanket and he gently uncovered her. The night was now passing so slowly. Everything he did excited her; every place he touched her was new and thrilling. She touched him, and they made love.

❧❦

The morning light awoke Golden. She looked next to her to see Greg still asleep. He snored a little.

That's okay, she thought, *my dad snores a lot.*

She quickly got dressed and began taking things back to the car. They had drunk two six packs. Her head hurt. She read the carton as she took it back to the car; it wasn't beer, it was ale. Goldie didn't quite know the difference, but she felt it in her head. It ached and her vision was blurred and the sound of the sea seemed too loud. She had just finished putting the empty bottles into the car and emptying the pot and carrying it over to the trunk when Greg woke up.

"What time is it?" he asked.

Golden looked at her watch and said, "It's almost eight thirty."

"Shit. I have a really important appointment at nine. We'll never get there in time!"

He ran naked to the car and grabbed his cell phone.

"Go get the blankets," he said in a neutral voice.

As Golden left she could hear him swearing and sometimes defending himself on the phone. *What a strange way to do business,* she thought. *Maybe that's how it's done here in California.*

The drive home was too silent. Finally Golden took the courage to speak up.

"Last night was the most wonderful time I have ever had in my life!" she said hesitantly. She wasn't sure whether it was just another thing for him or rather he really meant what he had said, that he loved her and she was destined to be with him forever. Moonlight sometimes makes you say things you regret. She hoped with all her heart he had meant it.

"It was the greatest and most wonderful time of my life too. I have never been so much in love, Goldie. Please know that I took you only because I love you."

His words rang true in her heart and she reached over and hugged him.

"Don't make me stop the car," he said playfully. Then his mood changed and he continued. "I've got to meet a couple of guys this morning. Can you drop me off and give me 'til twoish and pick me up?"

"Sure, tell me where." She smiled at him.

"I need to go to Hollywood and see the phone company anyway. The woman I spoke with didn't make a specific time appointment but she said come in today, so I'll go do that. I think she liked my scores and we talked for almost half an hour. She probably just wants to interview me in person without making any commitment or anything."

It was nice driving a new Mercedes. Goldie didn't have much time. She had to go all the way back to San Clemente, take a shower, and change clothes. Traffic was horrible but she didn't mind. She hummed one of her dad's favorite tunes, "Blueberry Hill," but changed the words in her mind to "on the sandy beach." She felt changed, new, grown up and in love.

I'm glad I waited for the right man. He's so great and so very right for me!

She thought about telling Wendy and at first decided not to. It was so different with Wendy; she did it just for fun. Sometimes she did it just to pay for her date or to get things she needed. Goldie thought it was sorta like being a prostitute. She remembered what Zada had said, that all women were in reality prostitutes because they traded their bodies first for themselves and later for their children.

"If ya don't give a man sex, he'll get it somewhere else," Zada said.

"I don't believe that," Goldie said out loud as she pulled into the driveway of Wendy's house.

"Oh crap, you got his car," Wendy said. She was up and came to the door when she heard a car pull into the driveway. Goldie saw the red Corvette parked next to the garage.

"I see you've still got the Vette," Goldie responded.

"Yeah, but the guy's here with it. Okay, girl, where the hell were you last night?"

They went into the living room and sat on the couch. Goldie spilled her guts. She couldn't help herself. She told Wendy everything. Wendy was better than Goldie thought she'd be. She understood. She was excited about Goldie being in love. She asked her to repeat the part about being destined to be together forever. They talked for almost an hour.

"Crap, it's ten after twelve, I've got to go."

Goldie ran upstairs and put on some clothes. She didn't shower but washed herself with a damp washrag and brushed her hair and put a clip in it to hold it in place. Ryan was up and running around in his shorts. She wondered how much of the conversation he had heard. As she came down the stairs, Wendy walked over and took hold of her hand as she came to the last step.

"What are you gonna tell your dad? You know how he is about colored people." Golden had told Wendy all about home and her parents and her life. Wendy's words hit Golden like slap in the face.

"Wow! I forgot about that. I think I'll wait and see if Greg really wants to spend his life with me. If he asks me to marry him then I'll have to tell my parents." With that, she ran out to the car and took off.

⋙•⋘

The interview went great. Anna, Ms. Anna LaSterna, offered her a job. It was as an operator trainee on probation. The job offer had some provisions; she had to finish high school or get her GED. And she had to come to work there in Hollywood. But it was a job. It was her first real job. How could life get any better?

"Yesterday I fell in love, today I'm getting a job. Not just a job at a Burger King, no, but a job at GTE. I'm gonna be a telephone operator!"

She got to Wiltshire and 110 at 2:45. She was a little late and worried that Greg had gotten a ride back to work or taken a cab. It was a sleazy part of town and Goldie wondered why Greg wasn't doing business at the Mercedes company. But he had said he traveled around the whole state to supervise sales people and solve problems. Maybe this was one of those problems. She sat on the corner under the freeway where he had said to wait for him. Some of the people walking past stared at her and others smiled. She looked out of place and felt a little conspicuous.

Greg showed up at five to three, got in the passenger's side, and said, "Hi, honey, sorry I'm late. I had to take care of a really big complaint. Thanks for waiting. You sure look good. Wanna have some lunch?"

Goldie was relieved that he didn't know she had just arrived a few minutes earlier. She was happy that he was so nice. She leaned over and kissed him. He pulled her to him and held her tightly for what seemed to be an hour. It was really only a couple of seconds, but to Goldie it was more evidence that he really did love her and that he was the man of her dreams.

"How did you change clothes?" she asked, noticing he had on a different suit top, shirt, and tie.

"I got a ride over to the apartment from my client. We needed to drive his 620D anyway so he could show me what it was doing. Wanna get some lunch?"

Goldie was hungry and so she almost shouted yes. At lunch she told Greg about her job offer and that she had to live in or near Hollywood. She said she was gonna have to get a little car. Not anything fancy like his, but something to get to work and back. She said she'd probably commute from San Clemente for the first month but as soon as she got paid she'd find a little apartment and move in. Some of the telling was to prompt Greg to offer his place or to at least see if he intended to stay with her or she with him. Goldie didn't want to move in with him. No, her parents would never allow that, but maybe, just maybe… No, on second thought, she wasn't going to even think of moving in with him, let alone marriage. It was too soon. And yet he loved her and she him. They had made love on the beach and he did promise to keep her forever. Or that they'd be together forever. Surely that could only mean marriage. Her thoughts were interrupted by the waitress who brought her a ruben; she loved rubens with extra sauerkraut. It was delicious.

Greg talked about business but she wasn't listening. She watched him. His hands were really big. There was so much she hadn't noticed before. His mouth was beautiful. His face was clear and, except for a scar on his right cheek, unmarred. His eyes were clear and dark brown. They didn't stay looking at any one thing for very long. He seemed to scan the area and noticed everything. Anyone who walked into the restaurant he looked at and evaluated. *He must be really intelligent*, she thought. His shoulders were broad and muscular, his legs were strong, and she knew the rest of him was magnificent. She loved his dark skin. It almost glistened in the night light and seemed so magnificently designed. She was so pale and he was so dark and strong. What a difference! She wondered how the whole thing had happened so fast.

"When do you start?" he asked. The question startled Goldie who had wandered off in her own world.

"Oh. Oh, I start Monday," she answered and smiled again.

"You're sure smiling a lot," he said with some clear satisfaction.

"It's because I was just looking at you and I find you really handsome."

"Well, while you're finding me handsome, could you pass me the mustard? I'd like to finish my burger." They both laughed and he ate while she talked about nothing important but implying how happy she was with him and even with herself.

IX

THE JOB

    Wendy had been such a friend. She had given Golden her years of experience in California and tons of great advice. She had given her a home and food and had lent her the car and mostly she had given love without question. Goldie had been working for three weeks now and had just found a place to move into. She was getting a paycheck tomorrow and they were going to go put down some money and start moving. It wasn't like Golden had a lot to move. But Wendy had given her a little dresser and some clothes. She had acquired lots of new clothes over the time she had spent with Wendy.
    Goldie had called her parents and told them about her job and how excited she was with it. She had also told them a little about Greg. She left out the part about his race and their night together. Her dad was pretty prejudiced in some areas and she wanted them to meet him first. Greg had helped her in a million ways. He had even given her some money to help her buy her first car. He didn't approve of what she came home with, but when she gave him that lost puppy dog

look, he laughed and said it was great. The car was old, a 1976, but it had a rebuilt engine and everything on it worked well. It was a two-door Datsun, green and white with new tires, and the interior was immaculate. No tears in the seats and not even a crack in the dashboard. It was a stick shift, which Goldie loved because her dad's truck was a stick and she loved to drive it. The car reminded her of Dad. Old but great; it always started and got really good gas mileage. Dad was like that; he got up every morning no matter what the weather and worked until night. The weather here in California was great. Not tons of snow or freezing temperatures. Yet she missed home. Greg would console her, but inside she knew she had become an adult with responsibilities and that she would probably never go home again to stay, at least not as a child.

⇒•⇐

Greg's sexual appetite was insatiable; he wanted to make love every day. Goldie had decided she really loved him and would accommodate him as much as she could. It was hard to find a place and she was very particular about privacy. Not Greg, he didn't care where, he just wanted her in his arms, he said. He never was as kind as when they were on the beach, but Goldie knew he was very busy in his job. They'd meet for dinner three or four times a week but often he had to leave in the middle of dinner to go take care of a client. Sometimes he'd get back and sometimes he wouldn't. But he'd always call and tell her he got tied up. She had gotten a cell phone from the company for almost nothing and so he could call her at any time. Goldie at first thought it funny that he did so much business at night, but she figured that that's how business was done in LA. Sometimes she'd see him drive past her work on Wiltshire. Occasionally he'd be with a young woman, which would make Goldie mad and jealous. But when they met for dinner Greg would explain this or that problem the woman had and how he had to help her.

"It's just business, honey. I really only love you."

One great thing had happened. Goldie, who now called her parents at least weekly, had received a call from Mom. Mom told her that she talked with the high school and that after review of her credits and talking with her teachers they were going to give her high school diploma. The teachers said that when her grades were averaged in she would pass their classes even though she had not taken the last two or three tests. Mom was sending her the diploma in the mail with something special to reward her for finishing high school. With the diploma Goldie could go from temporary employee to permanent. It was a big step for her. She was glad it had worked out this way. Now she could show Greg she did have a degree. That made her feel good inside too.

Mom and Dad wanted really badly to come and visit but said they'd have to wait until next summer. It was impossible to get someone to take over the farm in the fall because all the kids were in school and most of the adults had their own jobs. Goldie thought about Jackson; he'd do it. She missed him and even though they had only been friends for a couple of days, still she loved him. He seemed so very wise. And he cared about her and her struggle with life. On the phone she spoke about meeting Jackson on the bus and how he knew Grandpa. She spoke glowingly about him and said he was a real help in her transition from home to the "real world." Jason laughed.

"So you think California is the real world? I think it's a madhouse of people coming and going and not knowing where they're from or to where they're headed."

They both laughed. It was good to hear Dad's voice. He seemed to have grown up since she left. He knew lots about California and about work. Everything she told him about work, he'd have a story or an experience that was like it. Occasionally he would barb her and ask when she was coming home to take over the farm. She could bring her boyfriend and see if he was a real man or just show and tell.

Jason was a little insensitive about personal things and would directly ask Goldie if she was sleeping with Greg. Goldie lied. She just couldn't tell Dad she was sleeping with someone. He didn't really believe her but accepted her answer and internally accepted her right to choose. In any case, Jason thought the measure of a man was whether he was willing to work and to sacrifice his personal time in exchange for the good things in life like a wife, love, a home, and all that accompanies it. Goldie knew that Greg wasn't exactly like that. He was a good worker, he always spent time working on or off the job, and he was very protective of his work. He still hadn't told Goldie where his head office was and instructed her very specifically never to call him at work. He had given her his cell phone number but it was busy most of the time. He seemed to think that he didn't need to sacrifice himself in exchange for love. He seemed to figure love was his right.

Jason, Marge, and Golden talked on the phone for almost an hour. Finally Jason said he had some cleaning to do. It was sort of a subliminal implication that if she were home she would already have the holding pen cleaned and he wouldn't have to be there; he could be in the field cutting hay or loading the feeding bin with grain or inseminating the cows that needed to be freshened or one of a million other things that needed to be done. To say nothing about painting the house for Marge or fixing the stupid TV antenna or even tiling the bathroom floor that had worn down to the wood just in front of the mirror. So Jason in his usual abrupt manner said he had to go back to work. He wished Goldie well and told her he loved her. He said he and Mom would come out next summer for sure and to please keep in touch with them. After all, he said, she did work for the telephone company and could call almost any time she wanted.

In a final note he wished Greg well and said he was anxious to meet him. Goldie cringed at the thought. But she loved her dad and knew he would accept anything she decided. She did love Greg and it didn't matter his color or his background. He was good to her and he understood her. Even though he was not as patient as she had hoped, certainly not as patient as Jackson. Still he loved her. There were times when his eyes were not as clear, times when his voice slurred and his step was not sure. Goldie thought he might be drinking a little too much. He had so much to worry about at work and he worked so hard that she thought it was okay occasionally to get a little sauced. Even she was now drinking almost every time they had dinner. She had gotten completely drunk on one occasion and didn't like it. She didn't like losing control and didn't like the hangover she had the next morning. Wendy said she'd get used to it and that drinking was a part of being an adult. Goldie wasn't so sure.

"Why did you have to feel like shit to be an adult?" she asked.

Her new apartment was fresh and she had decorated it well. At least to her it was decorated well. Wendy said it looked like a farmhouse and advised her to update it. Golden wanted it to feel like home. Not like her home in Minnesota, but like the place where she would like to live for a while and spend her home life. Comfortable and quiet. She only had one bedroom and a little kitchen, but the price was great and she quickly adopted the place to be her own. Greg said he liked it and it was only temporary anyway. She thought he meant that he was going to propose to her; at least that's what she hoped.

Two more weeks passed. Greg came over to dinner. Goldie had promised to cook him a real homemade meal. She finally had enough money to get the kind of groceries that she needed to make a real meal. She had been paid just the day before and had gone out shopping. Greg came over often. Usually he just stayed for an hour or so. He always wanted to make love. She wanted to talk and to tell him about work and about her mom and dad and about her farm in Minnesota. She wanted to know more about him and his childhood and his parents and where he lived. He still hadn't invited her to his apartment. He said it was a mess and would just have to clean it up before he had someone as beautiful and great as her enter his humble chambers. He never seemed to have time to clean it up.

At least two or three nights a week he'd sleep over at Goldie's place. She had to leave for work at six thirty to get there before eight so she'd get up at five. Not an unusual time for her. In fact she was relieved she didn't have to get up at four. It seemed like she got an extra hour or two of sleep. But she'd leave him to fix his own breakfast. He'd complain that she should be fixing him breakfast. That was woman's work and he didn't know how to cook. Goldie would apologize and kiss him and leave for work anyway.

⇒•⇐

Ms. LaSterna really liked Goldie. She was great with people and solved lots of complaints and took care of tons of information. She handled almost twice the calls in one day that the other operators did and they never got a complaint from a customer. Not only was she a great operator, but also before work she'd type up notes for the management, which included complaints by customers about other operators and information needed for the callers. After work she'd make notes to ask management and do lists for herself for the next day.

She always came to work dressed well and didn't spend too much time in the restroom putting on makeup or refreshing her lipstick or at the coffee pot. She wore conservative clothes and never swore or got mad at the customers or at other operators. In Ms. LaSterna's opinion she was almost the perfect employee.

This morning Goldie was a little sick; she had an upset stomach.

She had to leave her post a couple of times and went to the restroom and threw up.

"You okay?" Maria would ask.

"Yeah, I must have eaten something last night that didn't agree with me. Greg brought us over some baked clams in a kind of remembrance of the night we first went out."

"All right, but if you're ill, you can go home. You do have sick leave coming and I want you to feel good. You're one of the best girls I have and I don't want to lose you."

"Thanks, Maria. You're such a great boss and friend."

"Come into my office, Goldie. I would like to talk with you for a couple of minutes," Maria said.

Goldie was a little afraid. What had she done? She walked into the small cubicle that Maria called an office and sat across the desk from her.

"Goldie, you are a great employee, you have the right stuff to make a really good manager. I was going to send in a request for a promotion in a week or two, but I was informed that they are having the school next week in San Diego. We had one of the night supervisors quit last week and I was thinking of putting you into that slot. It's an assistant manager and you'd still have to be on the line and work the switchboard, but we'd give you mostly international calls and you could do the paperwork and counsel the girls. I'm sorry it's such a short notice, but I'm left with trying to replace Sandra, and you're the best choice I have."

"How long is the school?"

"It's two weeks, but you can come home on weekends."

"I'd love to do it, Maria. I feel a little inadequate I'm so young, but if you think I can then I know I can."

"Good, one week from Monday be at the San Diego school at 9:00 a.m."

With that, Ms. LaSterna gave Goldie a map showing how to get to the school and the name of the instructor and a check for expenses.

The motel room was pre-paid and she could eat lunch in the work cafeteria. For the other meals she could go where she wanted. The check wasn't for much, twenty-five dollars a day for food and ten dollars a day for gas and incidentals. Still it was for her and she was excited.

That night Greg was in one of his rotten moods. Every once in a while he was moody and cross with Goldie. She understood how stressful work could be. Hers was sometimes very stressful too and so she understood. After all, Greg was a manager and he probably had a lot more responsibility than her, so she would feed him and make love to him and tell him he was great. They didn't go out much anymore. Greg loved her cooking and would tell her he'd much rather stay home and have two of her meals. One she cooked and the other she was born with. Sometimes his lovemaking was just short of her expectations, and to Goldie, sort of empty. He didn't seem concerned with her or with her happiness or satisfaction, just his own. But there were other times, times when he showed love and tenderness, times when all his attention was on her and he met her every dream. All in all, he was great.

No one is perfect, certainly not me! Goldie thought. *So why should I expect Greg to be like my dad? He's good most of the time and those times when he's not, I'll just have to take it as it comes. Mom said that men have different natures than we do. They do things differently. Still it seems funny that he doesn't want me involved with his work. But come to think of it, I've never taken him to my work either. I guess the door swings both ways. I think I'll invite him to the office party next week. He'll love it.* Her thoughts drifted to work. She really loved her place of work. Her boss was good and the work was easy.

It was after eight when Greg finally got to her apartment. He was grumpy again and disheveled. He had taken off his tie and suit coat and was wearing a black turtleneck sweater. The knees in his pants were dirty like he had been kneeling in the dirt or on the sidewalk. Goldie mentioned it in passing and Greg growled that he had to kneel down and look at a car. She had fixed fish for dinner but it had gotten dry because Goldie kept it hot waiting for him. Greg complained that it tasted like "shit" and suggested they go out for dinner. Golden was delighted.

"Where we going?" she asked.

"Wherever you want. You're paying."

Goldie had some money in the bank and she still had the stash her mother had sent her. At least most of it. Greg frequently got her to pay when they went out lately. She didn't like it because she had been raised with the concept of gender roles and because they weren't married and she thought he should still be trying to win her heart. But it would be nice to go out. They seldom did it anymore so she gladly accepted. They went out to his car but it was not the Mercedes she was used to. Instead it was a yellow and white Camero. It looked like about an '86 or so.

"Where's your Mercedes?" she asked.

"It's broken. They have it in the garage trying to fix it. This is a loaner."

Greg had borrowed the Datsun two weeks before when the Mercedes had broken down and had wrecked it. It was insured and Goldie was still waiting for the insurance company to send her some money for it. They had said that it wasn't worth what she had paid for it, but she kept insisting they give her enough to pay it off and get a new car of equal value. So far they hadn't budged. One of their arguments was that the accident was Greg's fault and so they had to pay off the other guy's car too. They gave her notice that her insurance was going to be canceled. She was really mad about that. *Accidents happen*, she figured, *and that's why we get insurance. So what's the big deal?* Greg had explained that he had looked down at some papers lying on the front seat and had accidentally steered into the oncoming traffic. He admitted it was stupid, but it happened. Goldie didn't care. She loved Greg and the car was replaceable.

"I found you a great car," Greg blurted out "It's great on gas mileage and it's cheep. It runs well and I thought we'd go take a look at it after dinner."

"Thanks, honey, I've really been hating riding the bus to work. What kind of car is it?"

"It's a VW. It runs well and is perfect for this part of the country. The guy only wants eleven hundred for it, which is a steal."

Goldie agreed. She knew that Greg knew about cars and their value and if he thought eleven hundred was a great price, she knew that it was.

"What year is it?" she excitedly asked.

"It's about a '75 or so. You know, they all look alike. But it has a great paint job and the interior is good. The seller says it runs like a jewel."

"I don't have that much money, Greg. Will he take payments?"

"How much you got?"

"I think I can come up with about 850 or so."

"Yeah, I know the guy, he'll take that as a down and you can make payments for the rest."

"Okay. After dinner let's go look at it," Goldie said with a tinge of hesitancy.

They settled on Black Angus steaks. Goldie wasn't so excited when Greg picked it. But she liked steak and he seemed in a dark mood so she wanted him to feel good. She was feeling all right now, but ate cautiously because of her earlier illness. She didn't want it to come back and so she didn't have anything to drink. They met some friends of Greg's at the restaurant, which seemed funny to Goldie, because they acted as if they were waiting for him and that Greg had planned to meet them there. Why had he said she could pick where they were going to eat if he had made arrangements to meet friends at a specific restaurant? It didn't matter. They were nice and the girl whose name was "Honey" was real sincere and interested in Goldie and her work. The guys talked business most of the night. Although it wasn't always about cars, Goldie didn't notice it much. At first Greg made reference to the car and the delivery date and location. But every once in a while he would say the "stuff" in place of the car. Maybe he was referring to accessories. Goldie couldn't figure it out.

About half way through dinner Goldie invited Greg to come to her office party.

"We're having it on the first of June. Can you make arrangements to come?"

Goldie really wanted Greg to come to her office and see what a great job she was doing. She also thought that if she brought him to her office, then he'd invite her to his and she could meet some of his co-workers and others of whom he had spoken.

"I'd love to," he answered. "Thanks for the advance warning. I'll make arrangements to take some time off work."

The rest of the dinner went well. Greg went off with Aaron and talked for twenty or thirty minutes just as the check came. Goldie asked Honey if Aaron or she was paying for their dinner, to which Honey answered that she thought Greg was paying for dinner as he had invited them. Goldie knew better than to go interrupt Greg when he was having one of his meetings. So she reluctantly paid the bill, which, with drinks and all, exceeded one hundred and fifty dollars. That was a pretty expensive going out for dinner.

They said their good-byes and parted ways. Greg, when they got into the car, profoundly apologized.

"I didn't remember I had invited them to dinner until we were out looking and I saw the Black Angus sign and remembered. I'm really sorry. Did you end up paying for their meal too?"

"Yeah, and I don't have enough money to be doing that, honey, especially if we're going to get me that VW."

"No problem, Aaron paid me some money he owed me so I'll pay the difference on the car."

Goldie was elated. Sometimes Greg was so short and other times he seemed so very self-confident and giving. She never knew. But it was okay; she was glad Greg was going to help her with the car. She thanked him and gave him a kiss and a hug.

They went across town and test drove the car. It ran very well and even though it smelled a little like fresh-cut hay, it looked clean and had good tires. Goldie said she'd take the car if the guy would take a thousand for it. He didn't hesitate, he said sure, and they exchanged money. Goldie wrote him a check for seven hundred and fifty and Greg reached into his pocket and pulled out a large wad of bills. It looked like they were all hundreds. He peeled off three and asked for the fifty change. The guy said he didn't have it on him but would get it back to Greg on the morrow, Greg responded by reaching over and taking one of the hundreds out of his hand and saying, "We bought if for 950."

The man stammered a little, but nodded and they left, Goldie driving the VW and Greg in his Camaro. Before they departed Greg said he had some business to do and would see her tomorrow. Goldie went home and flopped into bed. She was tired and the day had been both great and bad. Greg had been so very nice in paying for the part of the car. But why was he carrying so much money? It was probably a payment for a car or something and he took out his commission to pay for her VW. That was the man she loved. Giving and caring and thoughtful. She fell asleep thinking of Greg. He was certainly hard to understand. One moment great and the next mean and belittling. But all in all he was really good to her and she loved him.

❖

The alarm rang and music started to play. Goldie had set a little alarm clock by her bedside on the night stand and also put a radio there, which came on and played cowboy music at six. She turned and pushed the button down on the clock and sat up. No sooner had she sat up than her stomach turned.

"Ugh," she said out loud, "I've still got the flu." She got dressed and put on what little makeup she kept in the bathroom. Thought about a little breakfast but was repulsed by the thought. Before she left for work she went to the bathroom and tried to throw up once but there was very little left from dinner and no breakfast. She hated the dry heaves. Work was great and Goldie took great care, not to mention she wasn't feeling well. She got a glass of water from the cooler, something she never did, and put it on her desk. It was a desk she shared with other operators but it had a space for Greg's picture and a picture of her mom and dad. She had a special telephone number that no one outside the company was allowed to call her on, but she had given it to Wendy. At about two thirty in the afternoon, Wendy did call.

"Hi girl, how's work treating ya?" Wendy asked.

"It's great! I love it here."

"That's so much like you. You're an idiot. You're not supposed to like work; you're supposed to hate it. Can't you get it right?" Wendy responded, laughing.

"Hey, how 'bout I come up and see you tonight?"

"That'd be great! I really miss you."

"Okay, I'll be at your apartment at about fiveish."

"Great! I can't wait to see ya. I've been feeling a little down and you'll do me good!"

Wendy started to continue the conversation, but Goldie had to go.

It was almost five thirty when Wendy finally showed. She was dressed in a mini skirt and a little sweater with no bra. Her belly button was showing and she was wearing sandals. She was as cute as ever and bubbly and full of life. They decided to go get some pizza and Goldie insisted they take her Volkswagen. Wendy actually liked it and said it was great for Goldie. She said it smelled like pot. Goldie said she didn't think so; it smelled more like the owner worked on a farm or something.

"I can't believe you're still so naïve," Wendy said jokingly.

"I just believe in people. I think most of 'em are good and most don't think like you."

"Hey, girl, this pizza is great! How come you haven't eaten your usual five or six pieces?"

"I dunno, I'm just not feeling well."

"Like what? You got a cold, the flu, stomach cramps, what?"

"Mostly in the morning. I think I've got the stomach flu. I keep throwing up and sometimes I'm dizzy and nauseous."

"Stop the train. When did you have your last period?" Wendy's eyes widened.

"It's been a month and a half. But sometimes I go two months. I'm not very regular."

"The hell you say. You need to go see a doctor or get a home kit!"

"I just don't think I'm pregnant. I've been real careful not to let Greg make love to me when I ovulate."

"That's it? That's how you control pregnancy? You're an idiot! Honey, the rhythm method doesn't work. You need pills, 'cause most guys don't want to wear condoms. You gotta get with the program. Crap, you're probably pregnant. I know of a good doctor down in Tijuana who'll do you a really great abortion for less than three hundred bucks."

"Wendy, I don't think I could have an abortion. Especially without asking Greg."

"What, you think he's gonna be willing to take care of the kid? Hell no. Those guys are great lovers but not many of 'em want to raise kids!"

"Greg's different. He loves me, and if I am pregnant, he'll take care of the baby and me. I think he'll ask me to marry him. I love him and I know we'll live happily ever after!"

"Man, have you got it bad. You think love has anything to do with it? Let me tell ya, sister, it doesn't! I was in love like you with my first guy. He dumped me and told me that I was just a piece of ass and not a very good one at that! So I determined to get smart and I realized just how pathetic this world is and how I was gonna get what I wanted without having to suffer. So I don't fall in love with the guys I go with.

They want me and they pay my price. You think I'm a hooker, well so be it. I don't walk the streets and I don't go to jail, but yes, yes, I get paid for putting out and so do you. You don't think you're getting paid? Ha! He helps pay for your VW, he buys you groceries, he helped you move into your apartment and bought you some furniture. He compliments you and takes you to dinner. What do you think that's for? If you didn't put out, I know he'd be gone tomorrow. So think about it. We all put out for goods. I'm just a little more honest than you about it."

    Goldie was offended and a little hurt by Wendy's words and yet they rang true. Maybe in at least one sense she was right. It didn't matter. She wasn't sure she was pregnant anyway and she did believe that Greg would marry her. They spent the rest of the evening shopping and talking. Wendy talked about guys and about her father who went to the doctor and was told that he was diabetic. He was really upset about it and came home drunk. Wendy said he never came home drunk, he left that to her mom.

    They went to the mall and bought some disks and a ghetto player. Golden didn't have any good music in her house and she didn't have a CD player or even a tape player to listen to. She did have her clock radio and said it was great but Wendy said she needed something to give her internal peace, so she bought the CD player and gave it and five disks to Goldie. When they got home there was a note on the table; it was from Greg. He chastised her for not being home and not having made him dinner. He ended the note with "I miss you and love you," which made everything else all right. She had, of course, given him the key and he came and went lots of times when she was at work. Sometimes she'd have to clean up the cigarettes and glasses left by Greg when he took people to the apartment to "close a deal." Goldie didn't mind. She was glad to help and he said it saved him going back to the office and allowed him to get more personal with his clients.

X

The Fight

It had been a week since Goldie had seen Wendy. Things had been going well at work. Goldie had been accepted full time since she had produced her high school transcript and she had been promoted. She was a "temporary" assistant manager now and would get the official title after she finished school in San Diego. The girls liked her and instinctively did as she asked. She was well organized and followed around both Maria and the floor supervisor for training when calls weren't really busy.

She was about to leave work when she got a call from the doctor's office. He confirmed she was in fact pregnant and was at least six weeks along. Greg had promised to come over tonight and have dinner and spend the night. She was excited and a little scared. It was Tuesday and she was scheduled to be off Saturday and Sunday. That was unusual for her. It was probably in preparation for her trip to San Diego this coming Monday. She had decided to tell Greg about the pregnancy tonight. She hoped he'd ask her to marry him, but even if he didn't she knew she had to tell him. He was the father and had a right to know. She felt so young and so very unready for a child, but that was how life treated you. You had to work through problems. "Face them and beat them!" her father would say.

Wow, as I get older it gets easier to see what a great man my dad is, Goldie thought.

Goldie knew not to put on the steak until she saw the whites of his eyes. She had put dinner on before when he called and he ended up showing up after two or three hours. So when the door opened and Greg stepped in, she ran to him, hugged and kissed him, and told him to sit down on the couch, that the steaks would be done in ten minutes.

He had been drinking, she could smell it on his breath, and he seemed a little grumpy, so she thought she'd wait until after dinner to talk to him about her pregnancy. She felt good about it and she knew it had to be done. She was scared, excited, and hopeful all at the same time.

Dinner went well. He loved the steak and she had made him a salad with avocado and shrimp. He said it was delicious. She served him some expensive wine, a Monet, which he guzzled down. He said it was great but he preferred a good Bud. Golden had also made a great peach cobbler. It was so good that Greg had three servings. After dinner he finished the wine and downed four beers. Greg got up, sighed, patted his stomach, and sat on the couch. He demanded another beer and reached over to turn on the TV with the remote, but Goldie took it and set it aside and said, "Sweetheart, I need to talk with you for a few minutes before we watch television."

"Can't it wait? You know I want to watch the game, it's really important to me."

"So is what I have to say. Please." She looked longingly into his eyes and took his hand in hers.

"Okay, but make it as brief as possible."

She took a deep breath. "Honey, I'm pregnant."

He carefully set his beer down on the armrest of the couch and turned and looked her directly in the eye. His look was not like anything she had seen before. It was angry.

"You think I'm the father?" he said loudly, pointing to his chest.

"Of course you are, I have never made love with anybody else. Ever!"

Greg stood up and walked around the couch.

"I've seen you walking around at work with your tight ass and smiling at the men there. You think I'm stupid?"

"I just do my job. Incidentally I was promoted today and they are going to send me to a school in San Diego for the next two weeks," she said, trying to divert an argument.

"Oh, so now you're going down to San Diego where I can't keep an eye on you and spend God knows how long there with more men."

"The doctor called me today and told me I was about six weeks along."

"Yeah, well, you won't make seven. You're getting an abortion."

"Why? I know you'd love to have children, you've told me and I'm a good mother. Even you have said that you know that I'd be a great mom. I know it'll be hard, but we can make it work."

There, I've said it, she thought. *I even suggested we marry. I don't know what else I can do.*

Greg got close up to Goldie. His face had changed color; he was mad. But Goldie stood her ground. She got close to his face and stared right back at him.

"Damn you!" he said and pushed her down onto the couch with such force that she literaly flew over the arm rest, her legs hitting them as she fell. He was clenching his fist and she was scared. He leaned over the couch, supporting his weight on the back of the couch, and bent down to her face.

"I'm not having children with you! Not now, not ever! My God, woman, are you stupid? We are just lovers. Just lovers, don't you get it? You really are from another planet, you stupid bitch!"

Goldie couldn't believe what she was hearing. She thought he loved her. She thought he wanted to marry her. What was happening? He stepped back from the couch and took a step toward the kitchen. She stood up from the couch and walked toward him. He turned and she stepped another foot toward him. She leaned to him and got close to Greg's face.

"But you said you loved me, you said you loved me more than any other person you had ever known, you said…"

Without warning, Greg slapped her across the face. His hand seemed huge as it came at her. It knocked her down and half way across the room. As she fell she hit the coffee table. She screamed only once and then tightened up her face and got up again.

Goldie certainly wasn't a wimp. She had faced fights before and she didn't run. She stood up and ran at him. She grabbed his hair and face with her fingernails and clawed deeply. She screamed into his face, "Don't you ever hit me, don't you ever hi…"

He slapped her again and grabbing the hand, which was pulling his hair, he twisted it backwards and pushed her away with a force she hadn't ever known before. Her dad was strong. He worked all day every day. She had seen him lift huge tree stumps and move equipment that would take three other men to do, but he had never hit her, never in 18 years had he hit her. She didn't realize the brute strength of a man. When he slapped her, she fell backwards and slid across the floor and hit her head on the corner beam that supported the kitchen arch.

The hit made her dizzy. She grasped the beam and started to stand up. Greg was on her like white on rice.

"Stay the fuck down!" he shouted, pushing her in the chest down to the floor again.

She had lost this battle. He was bigger and stronger and was standing over her with his fist doubled and rocking it inches away from her head.

"Get out of my house!" she said defiantly but quietly.

"You stupid bitch, you *will* have an abortion." He turned and walked out of the house.

Goldie got up slowly; she was hurting. She staggered over to the couch, which was tipped over and lying cockeyed on the floor. She collapsed, falling onto the backrest part of the couch and becoming unconscious.

In an hour or so she woke up and got up from the couch. She noticed that her nose was still bleeding slightly. Her hand was blue and her face was seriously bruised. She opened her blouse and saw a bruise the shape of a large handprint across her breast. As she walked toward the bathroom she felt pain in her legs, in her breathing, and in her face and chest.

How can I go to work tomorrow? was her first thought. *I want to call Dad* was the second thing she thought. *No, he'd come and kill Greg. He really would. I'd better not tell him. Maybe I should just quit work and go back home.* Her thoughts continued to race. She got washed up and put on face makeup that Wendy had left and went downstairs to the car. She drove to the Ace Hardware about a mile away and bought a new lock and a dead bolt for the door.

"I don't understand, I just don't understand," she just kept saying as she installed the lock and drilled a hole for the dead bolt. With each turn of the screw her hand ached but soon it was done and the time was almost eleven p.m. She went to the phone and called Ms. LaSterna. Maria had given her her home number and they had become close friends. Not go-out-to-eat-pizza friends, but great friends at work.

Maria answered the phone in a sleepy voice. She wasn't a night person. She wasn't married and she lived by an exact schedule. Her bedtime was ten thirty. But she hadn't gotten to sleep and so she answered after only two rings.

"Hi, Maria, this is Goldie."

"Hi, Goldie, what's the matter?"

"I think I broke my hand. I wasn't looking and I fell down and think I broke my right hand."

"Have you seen a doctor?"

"No, but I think I'm gonna go to the hospital if it's alright with you."

"Absolutely, go see the doctor and take tomorrow off and call me and let me know how you are and what the diagnosis was. Are you really okay, Goldie, you don't sound very good?"

"I'm okay, I just fell down."

"That doesn't sound like you. You are usually so very coordinated. Are you sure that's all that happened?" Maria was astute and she knew Goldie well enough to question whether she really had fallen down or not.

"Yeah, that's all that happened," Goldie responded, feeling like a liar.

"Okay, take tomorrow off and go see the doctor. I think you should go tonight."

"Thanks, Maria, you're great!"

"Just get well, you've got to go to school Monday. They won't wait for you and I can't, so take tomorrow and if you need to take the rest of the week off, but please be in San Diego Monday. I'm counting on you."

"I'll call you tomorrow and tell you what the doctor says."

She hung up and looked at her right hand, which had now turned completely blue from the base of the fingers to the end of the palm.

"I guess I'd better go see a doctor right now," she said out loud.

She drove to the Hollywood Hospital. It was quarter after twelve by the time she got there. She went to the emergency entrance and filled out the forms. Maria had said the company had really good insurance, but Goldie had never used it before. She showed her insurance card and they escorted her into a little room where she sat on the Gurney and waited. The nurse came in first and looked at her. She looked at her hand and at her legs, which now had also turned blue from the fall and hitting the corner of the couch. She looked at her face and at her breast.

"Looks like someone beat the crap out of you," she said in a questioning voice.

"Oh no, I just fell down the stairs going up to my apartment," Goldie responded. She didn't sound very convincing. She wasn't a good liar, probably from lack of experience.

"Your admissions form says you're not married. The guy who did this to you should be put in jail. Don't protect him; he's a son of a bitch. Any man who would hit a girl is a coward."

"No, I just fell," Goldie insisted. She hadn't had to lie much at home and she just didn't have that convincing look that good liars acquire.

"The doctor will be in shortly. Do you need something for pain?"

By now Goldie was hurting. She was hurting all over, but especially in her right hand and in her chest. Although it would be hard to say where she hurt the most, even her legs and cheeks and back and arms hurt.

"Yes, if you could, I'd love something to take away this hurt," she answered, almost so quietly that she was scarcely audible. The doctor came in five minutes later. He looked busy even though there were only three other people in the emergency room that Goldie could see.

He examined her for almost ten minutes. He listened to her heart, her breathing, her back, her stomach, and asked her to move certain parts, including her hand. He sent her to x-ray with a note for the radiologist. The note said, "X-ray only the hand and shoulders. Do not photograph the lower body."

Goldie was still in a lot of pain and as the nurse hadn't given her anything to stop it yet. She was used to suffering in silence. Her mind went back to the farm where two years earlier she had gotten pinned against the inseminating stall by a bull. That really hurt. The bull had followed a cow that had dried up and was probably in heat. So when she shooed it into the stall, the bull took the opportunity to push her against the steel cage with its hip. It took three months to feel better but eventually the pain and bruising went away.

This hurt isn't as bad as that one, she thought.

She was wheeled back into the cubicle in the emergency room from the x-ray room and the doctor came in about five minutes later.

"It looks like two of your right metacarpals are fractured. It's a hairline break but I'm gonna put you in a cast, which you'll need to wear for a couple of weeks. You also have some serious subdural hematomas and it looks like your jaw was displaced. It's come back but you're going to have some pain in your mouth for a week or two. I see on your admittance papers that you're not married?"

"No, I'm single," she answered, wondering if she should tell the doctor about Greg.

"Well, you probably know that you're pregnant. But what you don't know is how serious this kind of injury can be in relation to your child. 'Falling down stairs' can cause you to abort the child in a minute."

"No, I don't want an abortion!" Goldie spontaneously answered in an almost argumentative voice.

The doctor could see she didn't understand his use of the term so he further explained.

"You can abort a child naturally. You can also cause the body to abort the fetus when you subject your body to physiological stress or injury. Carrying a baby is a very delicate process; you must protect yourself and your baby. I used the term abortion in that sense, not in the sense of forcibly taking the child from you."

Goldie understood immediately.

"Yeah, I've got to be more careful going up to my apartment."

"My examination reveals that you were hit several times. Probably by a man. You clearly didn't fall down the stairs. You want to tell me about it?"

Goldie started to cry. She knew he knew the truth but she didn't want to get Greg in trouble. She still loved him.

"He was just drinking and I told him about the baby. I should have waited. He's really a good man. He was just shocked. It was all my fault. I should have planned better. The telling could have waited. I should have known."

She started to cry again.

"Good men don't hit people they love. You are a very beautiful woman. No one should ever hit you. You are worth much, much more than that."

The doctor seemed to be so very kind and seemed to care more than just professionally about Goldie's health and feelings.

Goldie couldn't remember when she had been called a woman. It took her by surprise that a doctor would say it. This was a young doctor, probably in his mid to late twenties. She instinctively looked at his left hand, something that Wendy had taught her to do.

"Always look at the ring finger. If you see a ring or the impression of a ring, don't go out with the guy, it only spells trouble," Wendy would say.

But this guy had no ring and no signs of having a ring. His face showed no signs of being married and neither did his talk. He wasn't really flirting with Goldie. Just seemed to be commenting. There was probably nothing to it.

"I could get this guy off your back. I know how and I do carry some weight with the authorities here in Hollywood," he said, looking her in the eye with sincere concern.

"No thanks," Goldie said with just a hint of interest.

"You know the law requires me to report this. It's really out of my hands. How about having coffee with me tomorrow and talking a little more about it?" the doctor asked very politely and very sincerely.

"I'd love to have coffee with you, as long as we don't talk about me."

"Okay, I can do that. Can I pick you up, or do you just want to meet at a coffee shop?"

"The way I feel tonight, or this morning," she said, looking around for a wall clock, "is that it'd be okay with me if you picked me up. I don't know if I can drive."

"So why don't you stay here tonight and I'll release you in the morning when you wake up. That'll let you get some sleep and also help you feel safe and protected for tonight. I'm off tomorrow. How about three or four?"

"Four's great. And yes, I think I'll stay here until the morning. But I've got to get back to the apartment in the morning for a couple of hours," she said, not knowing exactly why she chose four over five or three.

"Like I said, the law requires me to report any symptoms of abuse, both physical and mental, that I might find. I've got to report this."

"Please don't. He's never hit me before. I know he'll never hit me again. Please give him a chance. Greg says that the police are really prejudiced and he'd never stand a chance in court. Please, doctor, don't report this."

"It's okay, Golden. I'll note it on my personal log and not report it. Are you sure that's what you want me to do?"

"Yes, although I'd rather you didn't even note it on your personal report."

"Let's say it's a little insurance. If it happens again, I'll have it noted and I promise you, I'll send the son of a bitch to jail," he answered with both an affirmative voice and a little anger.

That was all Goldie could get out of the doctor. He had to go and see other patients. She hoped it was enough. If Greg found out she had reported him, he'd never see her again. The PA came into the room and wrapped the hand first with cloth and then with plastered roll that he wet in a plastic pan that the nurse had brought in. He gave her some ointment for her legs and face and chest and told her to apply it three times a day. He recommended she stay home from work for a couple of days. He gave her a prescription for pain and also gave her a bottle of pain pills he had in the cabinet. As she was leaving, the doctor gave her his business card. On the back was his home phone number.

"If you need anything at all, at any time, please call me," he said, smiling. He touched her newly cast hand at the fingers that were lightly coated with plaster at the base.

"I've got your address on the admittance form. I'll see you tomorrow. Are you going to stay here tonight?"

"No, I've decided that I need to do some cleaning and take a bath," Goldie answered, still in a lot of pain. She took the pills at the water fountain and walked out to the VW.

The drive home was tiresome. She had taken two of the pills before leaving the hospital even though the PA had told her to wait until she got home. Her hand still hurt and so did her chest and legs. Her face had a slow ache in it and she was sleepy. When she first got to her door, she pulled out the old keys and couldn't get the lock open. She swore and then remembered she had changed the lock. She put in the right key and went into her house. It was more disheveled than she remembered. She locked both the door lock and the dead bolt and went to bed.

Morning came late. The alarm didn't ring because Golden had not turned it on. She awoke to the morning sun streaming into her window.

"It must be after nine," she said out loud. "The sun doesn't get over the mountain 'til then." She rolled over and sharp pain stabbed her in the chest.

"Ouch! Oh, yeah, I remember last night!" she grumbled as she sat up on her bed and looked at the clock radio. It was quarter after eleven. She called work and talked to Maria for almost ten minutes. She didn't ever reveal that she had been beaten up, but did say that her hand was broken, just a hairline fracture, but just the same broken. She'd be back to work Monday. She asked if that was okay and Maria said slowly, "Yes, of course. Please take care of yourself. But remember don't come here Monday, go to San Diego!"

She then talked a little with Golden about men and especially abusive men. Her voice conveyed that she either didn't believe that Golden had fallen or that she suspected that there was something more to the injury.

"Maybe I can come by after work and see how you're doing?" she asked.

"I'd love to see you!" Goldie responded without thinking. Then she remembered that the doctor was going to take her out for coffee.

"Oh, I just remembered that I have to go some place. I'm sorry!"

"Okay, just take care of yourself. Remember that all abusive men will apologize profusely after they have hurt you, but they'll do it again anyway."

Goldie didn't think that was true of Greg, but she had seen a different side of Greg so she really didn't know. She just really didn't know.

It was almost three by the time Golden had eaten, bathed, and cleaned up the apartment. She felt her stomach to see if the baby was okay, even though she was still so flat that there was very little evidence of pregnancy. She began to wonder what she would do. She had to tell her parents, and she knew that her dad would be very, very, very mad at her for sleeping with a man before marriage, let alone sleeping with an Afro-American. She wondered what the child would look like. She wondered what gender it would be. She wondered what she would name it. Finally she wondered if she should abort or not. After all, her parents would probably hate the child, and if Greg didn't come back she'd have to raise it alone. Was she up to it? Could she do it? In her mind was the question of what she would do with the rest of her life if she had a child to raise. Where would she go? She couldn't go back to Angora. Nobody in that town would understand. Except maybe Mom. Dad would take her back too. She didn't know if he would understand, but he would take her back. Well, that was one option. The other, of course, was abortion. That would simply make the problem go away. Perhaps that would be best. But there was a huge moral issue there. One she had talked about so blithely and knowingly in high school. She had made all the arguments in debate class both pro and con, but now, now she was the pregnant single girl she had talked about. It was so different. It was so real now and so just pretend then. There was a knock at the door.

Golden walked to the door and looked through the peephole. It was Greg. She wanted to answer. She wanted him to hold her in his strong arms and tell her he was sorry. But she didn't, she let him try his key, and she let him knock again and again. Finally he left a note and pushed it under the door and left. She waited for a few seconds and then went to the door and picked up the note.

"I know you're home. Your car is in its parking place. Will you please meet me tomorrow morning at ten to talk? I only want to talk. I promise I won't touch you. I just want to talk. We can meet at the coffee shop on the corner of Wilmington and Fifth...please."

Golden read the note over and over. What was he saying? Did he want to make up?

Could she do it? Could she ever trust him again? What explanation could he give for hitting her and breaking her hand and bruising her body? Maybe he just wanted to tell her that he wasn't gonna pay for the kid. Maybe he wanted to take her to an abortion clinic like he had said last night. She remembered Wendy who had said she knew some friends who do this all the time and would only charge a couple hundred bucks.

Maybe, just maybe I should consider... Just then there was another knock at the door. Golden hesitated to go look at the peephole again, fearing he would see her shadow or something, but she went anyway. Outside was the doctor. She opened the door and said, "Come in. I need to go freshen up. I'll be right back." She went into the bathroom and looked at her face. It was horrible.

"How could he have said I was a beautiful woman? I look like crap!"

She put on some base and even a little powder and lipstick and came out.

"Hi. I'm sorry I look so bad. You know bruises, they always get worse before they get better."

"I wasn't looking at your bruises. I see enough of them at the hospital. I was looking at you. You are a very beautiful woman. Come on, I think I'll take you out some place better than a coffee shop."

Goldie was a little frightened. This was a medical doctor. He was certainly educated and could go out with anybody he wanted. So why her? She shrugged and said, "Great, I'd really like to go somewhere else anyway."

The doctor drove a Honda Civic. It was pretty new and well appointed, but she had expected a Lexus or something like that.

"I hope you like my car. I just got it. I'm still on the last six months of my internship, so I don't make a lot of money."

"It's great. I mean it. It's really just great," Goldie answered, and for a second her mind flashed back to the '49 Cadillac and Jeff. He was so very good to her. *I'm so stupid*, she thought. *Jeff would have given me the world. He probably would have even moved to California for me. Oh well, what's done is done.* Her thoughts changed as they drove past some very old buildings that were weather worn from the eastward sea breeze.

They drove north on 101 until they were well out of town. The beach drive was wonderful. Goldie hadn't ever been this far north and she enjoyed the scenery and the jagged cliffs with the surf pounding against them in an incessant effort to change the landscape. Sorta like Greg trying to get back into her apartment, pounding at the door, but never really getting through it. Perhaps he didn't really want to. Or perhaps he only wanted to hit her again.

"I know of a great German restaurant up north about fifty miles. You up to going that far?"

"Yes, it sounds like fun. Thank you."

"I don't think I've ever met a woman as thoughtful as you. You don't need to thank me for inviting you to dinner. It's I who am thankful for the time you've given me. I know I said I wouldn't talk about your injury, but let me just say this. You are much too beautiful to be hit. You are much too great a person to have to tolerate that kind of treatment. Please consider that."

"I will, thank you."

"There you go again. You don't have to thank me. Okay, let's see, do you like German food?"

"I don't know. I don't remember ever eating it."

The rest of the evening was great. Eric never mentioned the cost of anything. He offered her anything she wanted and begged her to have dessert. He was so very kind to her and not once, no not once, did he cut her down, mention her injuries, or even allude to her being pregnant. The restaurant was in a castle-like structure up by the Seven Flags park. It was very exclusive, and like the Hyatt the waiters couldn't do enough for you. The food was really tasty and big enough portions that she felt like she was home. Goldie couldn't believe she ate everything on her plate. She was a little embarrassed when Eric smiled and said, "Well, we'll have to come back here. You need to try some of their other dishes too."

Goldie smiled and started to apologize for eating every crumb on her plate but Eric smiled and said he was glad he didn't waste any money.

"Besides," he said, "you need the nutrition to heal your bones."

She laughed; he laughed. He reached over and took her left hand and pressed it gently.

"I think I've enjoyed you and this night more than I have anything else for a very long time. You are so very sincere and so very fresh. It strikes me strange knowing your condition. How could you have stayed so very beautiful and innocent and still have gotten pregnant? Maybe that's exactly how, you were just too innocent."

He smiled again and looked deeply into her eyes.

"I don't think I'm innocent. But thank you for the compliment," Goldie answered, wondering what he saw in her eyes.

The ride home was also very nice. She put her head on his shoulder and fell asleep. In what seemed like only a minute or two he gently woke her.

"Golden, we're home."

She awoke not with a start, but opened her eyes and looked at the doctor and then remembered she had just gone on a date with him.

"You should call me Goldie. Golden is what my mom used when she was mad."

"I've got a couple of shifts to do tomorrow, but I'd like to see you again," Eric said.

Golden's eyes flickered, showing some hesitancy. But she thought, *Well, I'm not married and he seems to really like me.*

"Yes, I'd like that too," she said quietly.

The doctor walked her up to her apartment and kissed her goodnight. It was a good kiss. Clean, simple, but seemed to express a kind of warmth and caring that she had not experienced before. She liked it and smiled and looked him deeply into his eyes as she closed the door. *Maybe,* she thought, *maybe life is okay after all.* She almost started to sing when her mind went back to Greg. The whole thing seemed so confusing. He had loved her. She couldn't bring herself to believe that he was just wording his promises to love her and keep care of her for the rest of his life. No one could do that. No one could lie like that. He was so sincere. And when they made love, he always kissed her so passionately. He always swore that she was the only one he loved or had ever loved. No, no, no one could fake that. He did love her and she knew it. But could she live with him? And what about the baby? And what about his mood changes?

"I'm so tired," she said out loud to herself.

Her bed was still unmade. It was so very unlike her. She always made her bed before leaving the house. She fell backwards onto the bed and it reminded her of her pains in her chest, her face, her hands, and legs. They all stung as she hit the not-so-soft bed.

"Crap! I better take some more of those pain pills or I'll never get to sleep."

She got up and walked to the bathroom where she had put the bottle. She went into the kitchen where she had a little cooler for some bottled water. Greg had said not to drink the LA water. He said it was horrible. So did Wendy so Goldie didn't. She bought a bottle of water each week from the Culligen Man and then threw them in the cooler. She just had to use at least four bottles every two months. Goldie poured a big glass of water and sat at the kitchen table and drank it with the pills. She was tired. She still was wondering whether to call Mom and Dad or not and still wondering whether Greg would love her, let her keep the baby, marry her, ever see her again.... Her mind raced on and on for about fifteen minutes and then the pain pills hit her. She was sleepy and walked into the bedroom, and for the second time in her life fell onto the bed and went fast asleep without disrobing or even getting under the covers.

⇢•⇠

Thursday morning. Thursdays are always great. Even if you have to work, they seem like a vacation. Somehow they seem like you can choose what you're going to do. It was the next to last day of the workweek for most, but usually Goldie's day off. Goldie didn't set the alarm again this morning. She slept in. Not as late as yesterday, but still, it was after eight when she got up. She called work just as a matter of course. Maria wasn't there so she just said she'd be in Monday. She was feeling better. The pain in her right hand had subsided and the bruising in her face was turning yellow. *It'd be gone by Monday night*, she thought. Then she remembered that she was going to San Diego Monday and would probably have to leave really early in the morning or go Sunday night. The company wasn't going to pay for Sunday, but she figured she could stay with Wendy and drive down from San Clemente.

"I really need to clean up this apartment," she said out loud.

She had lifted up the couch, cleaned the kitchen, and vacuumed the living room, but not as well as she usually did. It all seemed so not real, so just imagined, not that the bruises weren't there to prove it, just that even they now seemed to be fading faster than their color. The only real evidence left would soon be the cast. She took off the sling and bent her elbow. It seemed to bend so slowly and even hurt a little, but after a couple of times she could move it freely without pain. She sat down on the couch and looked at the empty apartment. Too many things had happened so quickly. She realized she was not a child anymore. She realized she was an adult, a pregnant adult.

At ten Golden decided to call her mom but not tell her about the accident and definitely not tell her about the baby, but just to talk. She needed someone to talk with where she didn't have to build walls or pretend. There was no need to protect herself from Mom. She would love Golden no matter what. She was someone with whom she could just be herself and not have to protect any part of her. That was Mom. She could say anything to Mom and Mom would understand or at least she would love Golden without demeaning her and without saying she was wrong. Mom's love was unconditional.

The conversation with Mom went just as Golden had expected it to go. Mom was great. She was sweet and she loved and missed her daughter. They talked about work and about the weather and when Goldie might be coming home. Jeff was leaving town Monday and Mom thought it might be a good time for Goldie to come home, if she wanted to. Goldie of course said she wasn't coming now but told Mom about her promotion and about the school they were sending her to. Golden told her mother about a friend who had gotten pregnant outside of marriage and with a man of another race. She said the friend and her boyfriend had gotten into a fight and separated and asked Mom what she thought she should tell her friend to do. The phone went silent for several seconds. The time seemed like an eternity to Golden who wished she hadn't asked the question. Mom came back in a clear voice and said she didn't know. She was sorry the girl had gotten herself into such a mess but she really didn't know. Abortion was out of the question, but maybe she could have the baby and give it up for adoption. There are a lot of people who would love to have babies and couldn't.

The conversation continued without going back to Goldie's friend and without resolving the problem presented. Goldie sensed she had said too much but Mom hadn't reacted badly, so she probably didn't know. Dad was out feeding the cows or something. He almost never took a day off. Mom said they were going to take a week off next spring or maybe this fall and come and see Goldie, that is if she hadn't come home first. In which case they'd take her anywhere she wanted to go. The conversation ended and Goldie hung up. It was nice to talk with Mom and she did get some resolution to her problem. She knew now with certainty she wasn't going to have an abortion. She'd probably give the baby up, but she wasn't having some doctor or worse, someone else, tear it from her womb.

"This is crazy, I'm getting like Wendy trying to second-guess Mom and leaving clues. I've got to tell her. I can't have a baby without telling Mom and Dad."

It was twenty after two when she finally finished cleaning the apartment and doing her laundry. She sat down on the freshly vacuumed couch. She looked at the clock hanging on the kitchen wall.

"Yes, I think I'll go. He deserves a chance to tell me why. He deserves the chance to apologize. I'll probably not take him back, but I need to give him the chance to see what he feels and why he attacked me."

She got up and went to the bathroom and brushed her hair. She didn't put on any makeup and she didn't even change her pants she was cleaning in. She drove to the coffee shop and walked in. It was five after three when she got there and she didn't see Greg.

He probably left when I wasn't here at exactly three, she thought. *Oh well, I guess it's for the better.* As she turned to leave, in walked Greg. He was dressed exceptionally nicely and had gotten a haircut. He looked straight into her eyes and his eyes scanned her with some surprise.

"Sorry I'm late. The barbershop guy took longer than I thought he would."

Goldie thought she'd play this one out for her benefit.

"Well, you always said that a person who's late is late because they don't think the meeting is as important as whatever else they are doing."

"Nothing is more important to me than this time with you. Please forgive my lateness. Let's get a seat."

They waited without speaking to each other for the waitress who sat them against the wall by the window. Goldie felt comfortable there. People walking by could see and she could walk out without Greg getting physical.

"What's wrong with your arm?" he asked timidly.

"It's my hand. You broke the bones in my hand."

"I am so sorry, I had no idea. Sometimes I don't know how strong I am. Please believe me, I honestly didn't deliberately attempt to break anything or hurt you in any way."

"How can you say that? You pushed me and slapped me and was gonna slug me. You certainly did attempt to hurt me."

"I know it's no excuse, but I was drunk. If you can forgive me, I promise I'll never do anything to you again. I'll never get drunk again and I'll take better care of you than I ever have. I love you, Goldie, I love you, and I have never been so miserable in my entire life than I have been in the last two days."

Goldie was impressed. Greg was pleading and his eyes had filled with tears. He looked directly into her eyes again and she into his. His gaze seemed to penetrate her soul and she thought he really meant what he was saying.

"Greg, as you know, I'm pregnant and I won't have an abortion. It hurt me when you asked if it was your child. You know the truth, Greg, so why would you ask that if not to hurt me? So, like I said, I'm not having an abortion. I love you and want your child with or without you."

"It's okay, honey. I want the child too. I'm so very sorry I hurt you. I love you and want to live with you for the rest of my life. Let's get married. I bought a ring and I think it'll be great to have a baby in the house. We'd have to rent a little apartment somewhere or stay in yours for the first six or seven months. We only need one bedroom for now. Then when the baby comes we can get another apartment with two bedrooms. I love you and didn't plan on proposing in this way but now that we're here and I've blurted it out, please, please consider marrying me."

All the ugly words he had said in the apartment came back to her. How could he be so black and white? One minute nice, the next mean. One minute in love with her and the next angry and accusatory. But now he was proposing, just as she had wanted. She was a little scared. In her heart she wasn't sure if she really wanted to get married. It seemed so very permanent. Would Greg be a good father? She really didn't know. He was gone so much and he was, in truth, not very dependable. Still he made good money, and usually gave her whatever she needed. Dad was gone all the time too. But at least he was always reachable; Greg wasn't.

Goldie was formulating carefully her answer when Greg slipped out of the bench-seat and knelt down beside her. He reached into his pocket and pulled out a box, a little purple felt-covered box. He opened it and in it was the biggest ring she had ever seen. More than twice the size of the ring Jeffery had given her. It must have been three or four carets. It was huge and gorgeous.

Goldie couldn't help herself. She reached over and took the ring and put it on her hand. It fit perfectly. She held it up to the light from the window and to her surprise, everybody in the restaurant began to clap.

"Yes, honey, yes, I'll marry you!" she almost shouted. Everyone clapped and cheered.

"When can we do it? And how do you want to do it and where do you want to do it and…" Goldie was interrupted with Greg's hand held up to the square meaning stop, he wanted to say something.

"I'd just like to be married by a JP. We can do it tomorrow, or Saturday. I'll take you on a great honeymoon."

"I really wanted to invite my parents. I know you don't know them but they have been and are so very important to me. They can't make it until next spring. On the other hand, I'd really like to be married for several months before the baby comes. I'll call them tonight. So on second thought, yes, yes, I'd love to marry you tomorrow!"

"Okay. Great! I'm sorry about suggesting you abort the baby. I'd love to have it and I'm excited about your pregnancy. You know we can make love up to the date of your delivery," he added with a look that shouted, "I need some sex today."

"I know, sweetheart. Would you like to come over to my place for a while?"

"I wish I could. I really really do. But I've got to meet with a client and I've got to get some money for our honeymoon."

"I love you, Greg. I'm sorry about the way I treated you too. It was mostly my fault, I just didn't know how to tell you about the baby." Goldie honestly in her heart thought she was mostly to blame for the fight.

"No, honey, I just wasn't thinking right. It was probably the beer. You know how I get."

Greg left and promised he'd be home by 9 p.m. and Goldie went back to her apartment. There were three messages on the phone. One was from Maria. She said she was worried about Goldie and asked if she was okay. She said to call her.

Golden called and promised to be in San Diego on Monday, which was only four days away. She said she was feeling much better and had some great news to tell her. Goldie wasn't sure she should tell Maria she was pregnant, but she would tell her she was getting married. So she told her about the proposal and that they were getting married tomorrow. She timidly re-asked if it was okay to take Saturday and Sunday off. It was a courtesy; she knew that she was scheduled to have them off anyway.

"Of course, I already told you to. But remember, Monday morning at 9 a.m. you have to be at the training center in San Diego."

"Oh yeah," Goldie said, remembering she had to go to San Diego instead of showing up at work. "I promise to be there. Thanks for everything, Maria, I don't know what I'd do without you."

"You'll find out if you're not at the training center Monday morning." She laughed a little laugh, not a giggle, but a chuckle.

"Hello, Mom?"

"Hi, darling, how are ya feeling?" Mom asked. It was kinda funny that she'd ask how Goldie was feeling. It implied she might know or suspect she was pregnant.

"Okay, Mom. Actually, I'm doing great. Remember me telling you about Greg?"

"Sure I do, sweetheart, I remember everything you say to me."

"Well, Mom, he has asked me to marry him and I accepted. I know it seems a little sudden but we've been dating for quite a while, and I love him."

There was silence on the other end of the line for a long time. Then Mom spoke. Her voice wasn't the same as normal.

"We, um, where are you going to get married? And when?" Mom asked in a shaky voice.

"I knew you and Dad couldn't make it right now, but we've decided to get married by a justice of the peace tomorrow. And when you come up, we can have a bigger wedding if you'd like. I know this isn't how you wanted it, Mom, but I love him and I have to go for two weeks to a training center in San Diego, and I want to do it before I go."

Goldie's voice wasn't convincing. It seemed hesitant to Marge. There was something Golden wasn't saying. Something important. Marge remembered the story about Goldie's friend; she knew it was really her daughter. She knew in her heart that her daughter was probably pregnant and was probably marrying someone that Jay may not approve of.

"We'd like to meet our new son-in-law. Couldn't you wait a couple of weeks for Dad to get someone to watch the cows an' do the milking?"

"I love you, Mom. No, I'm not going to wait. I've got to be in San Diego Monday so there's no point in coming for at least three or four weeks. I know you'll love Greg. I hope Daddy loves him too."

"If you love him, honey, we'll love him. We'll send you a wedding present and…"

"I'm sorry to interrupt, Mom, but I have to go. I only called to tell you I love you and miss you. Please come this summer, I know you'll be glad you did."

"Bye, honey," Marge said with a cry in her voice.

"Bye, Mama. Tell Dad I love him."

⁂

Marge listened to the dial tone for four or five seconds before hanging up.

I guess children grow up and do what they want. She didn't seem convincing to me. But she was determined. Maybe there's something wrong with Greg, maybe he's missing a leg, or is older, or something.

Marge went on talking to herself for another twenty or thirty minutes. She knew the real answer, she knew he was probably black or Asian or something. She fixed dinner and waited for Jason.

Jason came in at 7:10 that night. He hadn't cleaned up the holding pen for several days and it was almost knee high in cow pies. He used the little front-end loader to scoop up the droppings and stack them in a corner behind the hay barn for fall and spring spreading. The spreader was an old wagon with a spinning wheel at the back, driven by a gear on the back wheel. The wagon was at one time pulled by a couple of work horses but since has been modified to be attached to the end loader, which he uses for almost everything on the farm.

"Sorry I'm late, honey. I had to clean up the holding pen. I wish Goldie would come back. You know, one never knows how much help he gets until it's gone."

"Speaking of Goldie, she called today."

"Damn, I always miss her calls. She knows when I'm in the house, why doesn't she wait until I'm home?"

"She's getting married."

"When?"

"Tomorrow. She says she can't wait and doesn't want a big wedding. I'm worried about her, Jay. This isn't what we had planned. This isn't what I wanted. I'm really worried."

"I can put you on a plane. You'd get there tomorrow. You know I can't go, but I can send you," Jay said.

"Let me call her friend Wendy, wasn't that her name, Wendy?"

"The lion girl? Yeah, I'm pretty sure it was Wendy. Do you have her number?"

"Yes, I got it from Goldie when she lived there. I'll call tomorrow morning."

"Kids grow up, they do what they want to. I love you, Marge, but she is grown up and making her own choices. All we can do is be here for her, love her, and occasionally send her some money or whatever she needs for help."

Jason was that way; he accepted most things and tried to make the best of what he was given.

"What's for dinner? I'm starving," he said.

Jason was the kind of man who said what he felt and let it go. Sometimes it seemed a little uncaring to Marge, but when push came to shove, Jason had always been there for her and Goldie.

"Polish sausage and sauerkraut. I cooked up some corn too and baked you a potato. Hope you like it, it's a little different."

"You're great, Marge. Thanks."

Jason had always been complimentary to Marge. He loved her and told her often.

The rest of the evening they talked about Golden. About what might have happened to her to make her marry without the church or without any fanfare or ceremony. Jason suggested that she might be pregnant, but Marge said no. She said there was no way that Goldie would go to bed with someone outside the bonds of marriage. In her heart Marge wasn't really sure, but felt she needed to assure Jason. At least for now. Jason reminded her that they had slept together before they were married. But Marge dismissed it and went on sewing her quilt. The quilt had a frame that Marge put right in the middle of the living room and on the occasion that Jason wanted to watch the news or a TV show, it mildly annoyed him. He never said anything, though; he just kept moving the place where he sat when Marge moved around the frame, it was understood. Their marriage had specific roles and each role had been defined, not verbally, but through behavior and the culture each brought to the marriage, each person showing what was important to them and the level of their defense for that activity. So over the years the terms and bounds of each person's role had been ingrained into the hearts and minds of the others in the family. It wasn't a bad system. Everyone knew what was expected of him or her and also knew where he or she could expand, play, and grow. But now, Goldie had violated her terms of the roll. She had left prematurely and now was getting married. It wasn't like marrying Jeff. That was going to be an event. It was going to set her for life. No, she was marrying tomorrow with a justice of the peace and neither Jason nor Marge had any idea of who their son-in-law was going to be.

 The morning came. Jason was out milking. It was too early to call because California was three hours earlier, so Marge fussed, paced, and fixed Jason some breakfast. Jason came in and ate most of his breakfast. He had three cups of coffee, which was unheard of for him. About half way through his second cup, Marge saw he was going to drink more and perked up another couple of cups. Even Marge who never drank coffee drank a couple of cups. Jason didn't say much. But Marge knew he was worried because he fidgeted and kept talking about when Goldie was a little girl in school. At last he went out to inseminate some cows that needed to be freshened. The process would take him three or four hours but he said he'd be back at noon or so. Marge paced again and tried to call Wendy. She found her number in her address book where she put not just numbers but names and dates and people to see and things to do. It was sort of a day-timer without all the pre-made compartments. She had written in the back a calendar, using a quarter of a page for each day and she noted important dates there.

It was three in the afternoon when she finally got through to Wendy.

"Hi, who's this?" Wendy asked, answering the phone in a sleepy voice.

"May I speak with Wendy?" Marge said. She knew it was Wendy; she was the only one who ever answered the phone there.

"You got her," Wendy said.

"Wendy, this is Goldie's mother, Marge. Goldie called me and said she and Greg were getting married. Today! I'm not sure if there's a problem or what, but I'm really scared and nervous. I think that it may be a mistake. Her father and I wanted to give her a beautiful church wedding, and all that seems to be down the drain now. Do you know anything about it?"

"She's gonna marry him? Wow. I didn't teach her anything. I personally don't like him. He seems sleazy to me and I'm not sure he's everything he says he is. He does dress well and seems to have a lot of money. But usually those kind of guys are easy to get because they don't want to commit and neither do I, so that makes us both happy. Wow, Goldie, damn her, she's a great girl. I just don't think she's been in the big city long enough. She's still a little stupid."

"What else can you tell me about Greg? Is he good to her, does he love her? Jay and I are worried that there is something wrong with him. Goldie was hesitant to tell us about him."

"Well, like I said, he makes good money. But he is black. I mean he is of Afro-American descent."

"Oh, she didn't tell me that. Maybe that's what is so secretive. Does she really love him?"

"Yeah, she does, but I'm not sure that's enough. I know he hit her last week. And I know that she left him for a while, but I didn't know they made up and were gonna get married. Ya know, even in this day and age interracial marriages are hard. I hope she's got lots of guts, 'cause that's what it's gonna take. It's not that I haven't dated lots of people of almost every race, it's just I'd never marry a black man. When you marry, you get the whole family, friends, old girlfriends, etc., plus you get their culture and religion, you know. It's just really hard to make it when you start out with so many things against you. But Goldie is sure a determined girl. If anyone can make it, she can."

Before Wendy could go on, the phone went dead. Marge had hung up. She hadn't even said thank you or anything, just hung up. Wendy absolutely understood.

XI

THE WEDDING

It was Friday morning.

"Wake up, honey, it's after seven." Golden's voice had an air of excitement.

"Yeah, okay, I'm awake. What the hell's wrong with you? Why you waking me up at seven in the morning?"

"You're such a kidder! We're getting married today. It's the best day in the rest of our lives! C'mon, let's go get some breakfast. I'm treating."

"Well, now that you put it that way, I'd love some breakfast. We can take my car."

"'Course we'll take your car. We're not getting married in mine. How'd you do for getting money for our honeymoon? You got home so late last night, I didn't want to bother you. Did you get the dinner I left you on the table?"

"Yeah, but the meat was cold and I didn't finish it."

"Honey, I left you a note to put it in the microwave. Don't you ever read my notes? It's okay. I love you. I got today, Saturday, and Sunday off."

"Great, so do I. Except for a little calling I have to do, but I can do that from anywhere. What'd ya say we go up 101 to Frisco?"

"That'd be wonderful. I would love to see the coast and maybe we can go see the Redwoods and drive through that tree I read about."

"Okay, let's go get some breakfast. And then down to the city. Did you get the license yesterday like I ask you?"

"Of course. I wouldn't forget that!"

They went to breakfast at the Pancake House and Greg had three helpings of pancakes and eggs with sausage on the side. Sometimes he would eat like a horse and other times he wouldn't eat hardly anything. Goldie figured he hadn't eaten last night and was making up for it.

The marriage ceremony was short and by ten they were married. They went home to pack a few things and then they were off. Goldie wasn't like most women. She didn't pack the house to go on a three-day trip. No, she just took a small suitcase full of clothes and some makeup. Mostly makeup that Wendy had given her. Goldie had turned off her cell phone because she didn't want to talk with her mom right at that moment. She needed to feel free and needed to believe that she was independent. The feeling had grown in her since she learned of her pregnancy. Somehow it was her admittance to the adult world. She understood why Wendy had never grown up. It was because Wendy never did anything for someone else. She was singular minded, she wanted to enjoy life, and didn't want to reciprocate, although she had given to Golden her house, her food, sometimes even her car and her money. And she did give the men in her life what they wanted.

Maybe I'm wrong, Goldie thought. *Maybe each of us gives in the way we can to perpetuate our claim to life and to pursue happiness. Maybe her answers were wrong for me but right for her.* Goldie felt at last alive and at last an adult.

Greg was great to her. On the way up the highway, they stopped at a little restaurant, which served seafood. It was about half way up the coastline at almost three in the afternoon when they finally stopped and Goldie needed it. She was tired of sitting in the car. The coast was beautiful. It was so gorgeous that Goldie could hardly take her eyes off the ocean and the great waves that washed against the rocks like a relentless bull on a cow. Goldie loved the view. She loved California, and she loved Greg. He did have some quirks, but who didn't?

"Have some lobster or whatever you want," Greg said.

"Not yet, we've gotta have it tonight. We've gotta do our honeymoon right. You just don't get it. A honeymoon has to be orchestrated in an exact manner. This is the only honeymoon I will ever have and I want it to go perfect. I know that's asking a lot of you, sweetheart, but please just for me, just this once, let me be a little spoiled."

"You can be as spoiled as you want. I've got a little money and I'm gonna treat you like a queen."

She ordered the halibut and he got a hamburger. Goldie thought it strange that they would come to a seafood restaurant and get a hamburger, but it was okay. "If that's what he wants, that's what he gets."

They drove up the coast another hundred miles until they came to the cutoff that went over the hill to Salinas. As they passed through Whisky Town National Park, Goldie was awestruck at the beauty of the lake and the huge arch bridge that crossed over it. It was spectacular!

"I've never seen such wondrous beauty in my life!" she said. "Minnesota is beautiful in a million ways, but I don't think it has anything like this."

Greg smiled, turned to her, and said, "We'll stay in the Holiday Inn in Salinas tonight and tomorrow we'll go see the Shasta Mountain. It's just north on I-5 and if you go to the top of it, you can find the passage to the center of the earth. There are little people there who will help you if you know how to find them. Some say they are little because they live underground and need to be little to fit in the small holes and passageways. After that it's only a couple of hours to the Redwood forest. I think you'll love it there too."

Greg was being really good. He knew almost everything about the country and smiled and put his hand on her lap. She was glad she had decided to marry him.

As they came to the top of the hill just after the bridge, the right rear tire blew. It made a loud popping sound and in an instant started flapping against the tire well. There was a very small, narrow shoulder. Not wide enough to pull off onto. So Greg made a u-turn and drove back across the bridge to the park ranger station.

"I haven't changed my clothes from the wedding and this a thousand-dollar suit. Can you change the tire, sweetheart?" Greg asked in a pleading yet commanding voice.

"You should have seen the tractor tires I've changed on the farm. Of course I can change the tire," she answered in an extra perky voice.

Golden got out and opened the trunk. She found the spare and it was flat too. Undaunted, she walked into the park service office and spoke with the clerk behind the desk.

"Do you guys have an air pump here on property so I can pump up this tire?"

"How do you know it's not got a hole in it?" asked the uniformed male behind the desk.

"'Cause I looked at it and squeezed it and didn't get any air out of it. It probably has a slow leak, but it'll get us down to Salinas."

"Just a minute, I'll have to ask our supervisor."

The green uniformed, flat-faced male who was not only slightly overweight, but appeared to be as interested in Goldie's tire problem as a dead horse, slowly walked down the hall to an office near the end on the left and stepped inside. He was gone only for three or four minutes when out of the office came a middle-aged woman. She was dressed in a white blouse with black shoulder bands that had a gold bar on each. Her skirt was a red and light yellow flower print, which did not appear to be part of the uniform.

"I'm sorry, but we have specific instructions not to allow the public to use our equipment. There's an insurance issue in addition to our concern that if the tire explodes and damages you, we'd probably be liable. You may use our phone to call a taxi from Salinas if you'd like."

"No thank you. What is your name?" Goldie asked, looking at the nameplate over her right breast.

"Marty," she answered with a smile. The smile seemed to indicate that she might be willing to compromise. Goldie didn't hesitate.

"Maybe I could walk around the building where you keep your trucks parked and look at your equipment."

"I don't think there's a rule against the public looking at the kind of equipment we have here. I'd need to accompany you to make sure you don't steal one of our trucks," Marty said, smiling.

As they walked around the building Goldie looked into Marty's eyes. They were beautiful. They showed compassion and some hurt or disappointment that Goldie didn't understand. Goldie had learned to read people by looking at their eyes. As silly as it may seem, she had learned it by looking at animals' eyes. Horses were the easiest to read, but cows can also be read rather easily too. Dogs, of course, tell all with their eyes, but cats are a little more self-protective. Marty was easy to read. She had decided to live life as it came and to simplify complex situations. Goldie noticed she didn't wear a wedding ring and wondered how a woman so beautiful could go unmarried. Perhaps she choose to.

"I need to go look at our scraper, so I'll just leave you here by the air pump. I'll be back in a minute to show you around."

Goldie quickly ran around the corner and grabbed the tire, which was leaning against the Camaro's trunk, returned and filled the tire with air. It didn't have a noticeable leak so she was sure she'd make it to Redding. She waited for Marty. Marty seemed to have an internal power, perhaps a love of others or at least of life that Goldie hadn't seen in anyone else except perhaps her mother. Marty returned, smiling.

"I hope the tour was what you expected."

"Thank you so much. You are a gracious and giving woman. I'm on my honeymoon. We're headed to the Redwood forest, but we thought we'd stay the night in Salinas."

"Is that your husband with you?" Marty said rhetorically.

"Yes, he'd normally fixed the tire, but he has on his new suit."

"Perhaps he should have taken it off. We have a nice restroom and I'm sure he brought other things to wear. You need to establish the terms and conditions of your marriage early. All men want to know is how much they can get away with. If you establish that early, they know and most conform to your conditions. They need what you've got more than you need what they've got."

The conversation seemed out of character for a woman with so kind a face. Perhaps a man or two had deceived her. Perhaps she just instinctively knew men. In any case the words rang true to Goldie and she thanked Marty again and gave her a hug.

"Here's my card. I've written my home number on the back. If you end up needing anything call me. I sincerely wish you luck in your new marriage. Remember, you set the terms of the marriage."

"Thanks," was all that Goldie said. She rolled the tire slowly, thinking that maybe Marty had lost faith in the worth of human souls, particularly men.

"Where the hell have you been?" shouted Greg. "We've been here for twenty minutes!"

"Oh, hi, honey, the tire was flat and I had to talk the supervisor into letting me fill it up with air at their private pump."

"Okay, let's get the stupid tire on and get going. I want to get to Salinas in time to have dinner."

Goldie jacked up the car with one of those screw jacks. She hated them, they were slow and only went up about half as far as she liked. But the lug bolts came off easily and the tire went on with ease. It was changed in less than ten minutes. Goldie was dusting herself off and washing her hands in the restroom when Marty came in.

"Thanks again, Marty. I sure appreciate your kindness."

"You're very welcome. You take care, girl. I see in your eyes some trouble, some danger. Please, please take care of yourself."

"I'm okay, what you see probably is that I'm pregnant."

"Yes, I did see that. Good luck with your children."

There is more to her than meets the eye, Goldie thought as she approached the car. *Much more.*

They arrived at the Holiday Inn before seven, changed clothes and went to dinner. Greg kept looking at his watch and eating hurriedly.

"Thanks for a great honeymoon. I'm really having fun and I'm so in love with you," Goldie said, after devouring a steak bigger than she had ever had, even on the farm.

"How come you keep looking at your watch?"

"Oh, I've got a friend here in town that I need to go see. I sold him a car about a year ago and promised I'd look him up if I ever came to town."

"That's great. Can I go with you?"

"No, but I'll only be gone an hour. Why don't you stay and go swimming and watch a little TV. I'll be back before you know it."

"Oh, honey, please let me go. I don't want to stay alone on the first night of our honeymoon. I'll be good and only stand in the background and…"

"No!" Greg half shouted. "It's just business and you know what I told you about my business. I don't want you involved."

"Okay, honey. I think I'll go swimming." She sighed.

At that Greg got up and left. He casually tossed the plastic room key onto the table and kissed Golden on the cheek. She wondered why the cheek. Not the lips.

How funny, she thought.

A few seconds after he left, Goldie realized he hadn't paid for the meal. When the waiter came to the table she asked if she could charge the meal to the room and he said he'd check. He returned and said yes, that the room had been rented and a large cash deposit had been left. Goldie thought it funny that Greg wouldn't leave a credit card. It would have been so much simpler. *Oh well*, she thought, *that's Greg*. She went up to her room and changed. She found her swimming suit and as she put it on she looked in the mirror. She was showing a little already. *How strange*, she thought, *I must be making a really big baby. Well, that figures, Greg is a really big man.* She was a little sorry she was showing because she wanted to be thin and beautiful for Greg on their honeymoon and because she didn't want to explain to the girls at work yet that she was pregnant. As she turned sideways, looking in the mirror she decided she wasn't showing after all; it was just her imagination.

The pool was nice. It had a Jacuzzi that was hot. Golden loved hot Jacuzzis. She thought if the temperature was more than a hundred and five they were perfect. She swam in the pool and sat in the Jacuzzi for more than an hour. Finally she grabbed her towel and went up to her room. She had just turned on the TV when there was a knock at the door. She looked through the peephole, and to her surprise, it was the woman from the Parks Department. Goldie opened the door and said, "Hi, what are you doing here?"

"I'm sorry to bother you, it's just that besides being an officer for the Parks Department, I sometimes have a gift. I'm also a masseuse. Would you like a rub down?"

"Oh, I've never had one, and I'm sure my husband is going to be coming back in just a few moments."

"If he comes I'll give him one too. It's free. Come on, you'll love it."

"Okay, what do you want me to do?"

"Nothing, I've brought my own table and everything." At that Marty reached down and brought out a folded table with a nice leather top and strong steel legs that snapped down.

"Just lie here and let me go to work."

"But why are you doing this? I don't even know you," Goldie said.

"Today up at the office you said it was your wedding day. I thought it might be a good wedding present for you."

Marty went to work. She used a lotion, which was smooth and soft. To Goldie it felt great. As she rubbed her legs she asked if Goldie wanted her to rub harder or softer. Goldie replied she wanted to be rubbed hard, very hard. Marty was surprised at the musculature on Goldie. She was still strong and well built. Goldie said it was a carryover from her days on the farm in Minnesota.

"You know I have another special gift," Marty hesitantly confessed. "I'm a psychic."

"Really? Does that mean you read cards and palms and tell the future?" Goldie asked with a tinge of sarcasm in her voice.

"Well, sometimes. But sometimes I just get this feeling. I was cooking dinner tonight when I got a bad, really bad, feeling about you. Not that you're bad, no, but I'm afraid of this marriage. I know you just got married, and from rubbing you down and from your eyes, I'm sure you're pregnant, but I think you need to carefully rethink your commitment to this man. He gives off bad energy. He gives me the feeling that he is hiding something and that he is very untruthful."

"Well, I don't know about your feelings. You didn't really meet him and so I'm not so sure you could really tell me much about him. I love him and I know he's basically good. Sometimes he does things a little different than I would, but my mom said that there are no perfect men, not even my father. We as women just need to help them where we can and accept them where we cannot change them. Thanks for the massage, and for the advice. Thank you for taking your time to come and for your kindness. I don't think I want to finish this massage. Don't get me wrong, you're great and I feel a kindredness toward you that I haven't felt in a long time, but Greg is coming home and I want to be ready for him."

At that she got off the table and walked into the bathroom. Marty slowly folded up her table and leaned it against the bathroom wall. As Goldie came out she gave her a hug and looked into her eyes for what seemed an eternity.

"Please take care of yourself and your children." She turned and grabbed her table and left.

What a strange lady. She was nice, even kind, but strange, Goldie thought as she closed the door. She went to her suitcase and found a negligee. It was purple and made of fine-spun nylon, translucent, and on her it was beautiful.

Three hours passed and Goldie finally fell asleep on the bed watching *The Tonight Show*. It was almost a quarter after two when Greg finally came back to the room. As he entered he saw Goldie lying on the bed in the negligee.

I gotta admit, she is beautiful, Greg thought.

"I wonder what our kid will look like?"

He climbed into bed with her as quietly as he could, but Goldie awoke.

"Oh, what time is it, honey?" she asked. "I'm sorry I fell asleep. How did your night go?"

She asked so very sweetly and with so much love in her heart that Greg was touched. He was touched by her innocence and by her sincerity.

"It went okay," he said with a slightly slurred voice.

"Do you want to make love?" she asked.

"No, I'm tired," Greg answered. The answer disturbed Goldie. He had never said no to lovemaking before. But he probably was very tired. Goldie could smell alcohol on his breath.

❖

Goldie woke at six thirty. About an hour later than she usually got up for work. Greg was still asleep so she nudged him. He said he needed to sleep for a little longer and that he didn't want breakfast so he'd meet her down in the restaurant in an hour or so. Goldie went down the elevator to the restaurant. She ordered a big breakfast. She was hungrier than she had been in a long time. She again ate more than she ate when she was working on the farm.

Must be the baby, she thought. *I'd better not get fat. I know Greg hates fat women.*

In spite of the self-warning, she ate a three-egg omelet, toast, and two glasses of orange juice. She even had two cups of coffee. After breakfast she wandered to the front desk where they were giving away free coffee and donuts. As she was talking with the front desk manager, Greg came into the lobby.

"Hi, honey, you're up. They are giving away free coffee and donuts, or we can go get you some breakfast."

"I'll just have some coffee," he answered. Greg guzzled four cups and then turned and walked back up to the room. Goldie followed and they packed their clothes into the suitcases without saying much to each other.

They finally got out by ten that morning, which was great. It was Goldie's honeymoon. She didn't have to hurry or go to work or clean up the holding pen. She only had to enjoy herself. It didn't matter really that her husband hadn't come home until two last night. He loved her and she loved him. He was going to support her for the rest of her life and she was going to have his baby.

They drove up to Shasta, the little town just below the mountain. Greg and Goldie walked into a tavern at the end of Main Street and talked with some of the locals. The barkeeper knew of the little people and told them where to go on the mountain to find them.

"Sometimes you'll find them, and sometimes you can't. It just depends on if they want to see the big people or not. They call us the Top-Landers. You have to be careful, do not insult one of them or they'll take you down below and kill you. You'll never be heard from again."

Goldie smiled and Greg laughed. They drove up the mountain until the road ended in a circular culvert. You could see the snow from there and the backside of the glacier. Greg and Goldie walked down the path for better than a mile. It was beautiful and Goldie was touched by the majesty and beauty of the mountain. She was happy in her heart. Now she was married and her man was taking care of her. Her heart was filled with love and gratitude.

"Oh, darling, this is wonderful, it's so beautiful! Thank you, thank you so much for your love and goodness to me. I love you."

She took his arm and turned him toward her and hugged and kissed him. He smiled and held her tightly for a few seconds.

"It's okay, I love you too."

They came to a waterfall, a small one but beautiful. It flowed out of the little gorge on the side of the mountain above them about twenty feet. The stream fell a good three hundred feet. It was not a gusher but when the water hit the bottom a mist arose, which captured the sunlight and made a clear, beautiful rainbow. They walked to the pool at the bottom of the falls and Goldie drank from it. She smiled, said it was bitter cold, then cupped her hands, filling them with the water and took it to Greg but Greg refused to drink.

"There's probably animal shit in it. Besides, you should be protecting our baby."

"Don't be silly, after a fall like that nothing could survive," Goldie answered laughing.

They turned and returned to the car. Goldie was cold and Greg held her for a few more seconds. He opened the door and let her into the car.

"Incidentally I bought a tire last night," he said in a false gruff voice.

"Great! When I saw the flat one I knew it was a goner," Goldie replied, trying to perpetuate the ruse.

They came down the mountain and ate at the tavern. The keep asked if they had gotten a chance to see the little people, to which Goldie laughed and said, "Yes, and they were very nice."

"Well, ya gotta be careful, if you offend them you're as good as dead," the keep replied, probably forgetting he had said the same thing before they went up on the mountain. He said it keeping a very serious and straight face. Greg shook his head and drank a beer.

The trip up to the Redwood forest was great. They arrived in McKinleyville really late. It was almost nine p.m. McKinleyville is small town off of Highway 102 and just before you go into the forest. They rented a little bed and breakfast at a place called The Red Wood. It was great. The room had a big king-sized bed and a canopy covering it. There was a beautiful mirror framed in carved wood with an eagle carved in the two upper corners. Along the sides were various animals carved in the richly varnished red wood. Greg didn't go anywhere that night and they made love. It was great. Goldie had never felt so good. She was finally where she wanted to be. Life was great.

So was breakfast. They ate in the kitchen downstairs. It was early and Greg had gotten up almost without any begging. The food was cooked before their eyes on a regular stove and coffee was made to their order. Greg wanted really, really strong coffee. He said it was right if it melted the spoon you stirred it with. Goldie only wanted light coffee, so two pots were made. The woman doing the cooking owned the home and was cheerful and very pleasant. She told stories of the redwoods and told them the age of many of the trees. She said that some of the trees were there when Jesus Christ walked the earth. They were probably the oldest living things on earth. She expressed some fears about people cutting them. The forest service did allow some of the trees to be cut. You needed a special permit, which took forever to get, but the forest service felt the forest needed to be culled, to be trimmed so as to allow the old trees to keep growing and not let the younger trees take over by choking them out. It was what they called "controlled growth." The woman said she believed that nature would naturally select the trees and that the bigger trees were stronger and better rooted so they didn't need the help of the forest service. They left the bed and breakfast place with a packaged lunch made by Linda, the owner. She said she didn't usually do that but because it was their honeymoon and she really liked Goldie, she didn't mind. She made them a beautiful lunch including fried chicken potato salad and a couple of pickles with a bottle of lemonade. Goldie hugged her and thanked her and said good-bye in an almost cry.

They drove through the park. It was wonderful. Water falls, giant trees, trails, and Greg. They stopped at a little picnic area and had the sandwiches and a couple of sodas. It was late in the afternoon and Greg suggested they drive east for an hour or two, have dinner, and turn back toward home.

"Everyone has been so great. Oh, sweetheart, I'm so happy. Thanks for this time together with you. You know we've never spent more than a few hours together without interruption before. So this trip has been great!"

"Well, we're about out of money. I thought maybe we'd go down to Highway 20 on Redwood Highway and then turn on 20 east to Lake Port. Maybe stay the night and get up and leave by four or five in the morning."

"Sounds great. What time do you have to be back?"

"I've got some appointments late Sunday night. I figure if I drive straight through we can easily make it in a day."

"That's perfect. I've got to go to San Diego Monday and stay for two weeks. I know you don't want me to go, honey, but we really need me working right now and I really need to go to keep this job."

"It's alright, I'll get my things moved into your apartment while you're gone."

Goldie had hoped to move into his apartment, but she thought it was okay; after all, there was no need to keep and pay for two apartments. Hers was little but big enough for both of them at least until the baby was born. Besides, hers was less expensive.

The rest of the trip was great. Goldie saw some wonderful sights, some very beautiful country, and some great costal regions. They stopped in Williams and ate and then got back onto I-5 and headed south to LA. She slept most of the way home and when they got back it was Sunday night about ten. Greg changed clothes and said he wasn't sure when he'd be back. Goldie kissed him and he left. She wondered why he had appointments on Sunday and why so very late. She set the alarm and sat on the couch. The last three days had been everything she had hoped for. Well, almost everything. In any case, she was happy and she fell asleep. She fell asleep on the couch and was awoken by the slamming of the front door.

"How was your night?" Goldie sleepily asked. "Can I fix you something to eat?"

"I don't want any damn dinner, and next time have the balls to stay awake long enough to feed your husband dinner when he gets home."

Oh no, Goldie thought, *he's in one of those moods. Work must have gone wrong for him tonight. I'll try to comfort him.*

"Can I get you something to drink?"

Greg got up close to Goldie. His eyes were a little wet and dilated and he staggered just slightly. He put his arm out to the wall to support himself as he spoke to Golden. She thought he might be drunk but she could not smell alcohol on his breath. Perhaps just tired. Her dad sometimes needed to lean on the wall to support himself after a long day's work.

"Yeah, we got any beer?"

"I think so, honey, I bought you that Heineken German beer last week and put it in the fridge."

She opened a can and poured it into a glass and served it to Greg, who had collapsed onto the couch.

"I don't want one of these goddamn glasses. I just want the beer in the bottle the way it comes from the store!" he shouted, throwing the glass onto the floor.

"Sorry, honey." Goldie went back to the fridge and got another beer. She opened it and gave it to Greg. Greg guzzled it down and lay on the couch and fell asleep.

Five in the morning the alarm rang. Goldie got up, quickly showered, and grabbed the suitcase she had packed last night while waiting for Greg. Greg was still asleep on the couch. She kissed him on the cheek and he rolled over and groaned. She left and hurried down to her car. The drive to San Diego was lonely and a little troublesome. Still, she knew Greg when she agreed to marry him and he was the father of the child she carried. He'd be okay. She thought she'd remind him of his promise not to get drunk anymore after she came home.

The time in San Diego was great. Monday morning started with a class on installation and repair. It took all morning and each morning for the next five days. The company provided lunch, which was usually hamburgers and fries and a drink. Monday afternoon she began the management classes. The first was introduction to the management philosophy of GTE. That class was going to last all week and next week they would get into the specific skills and methods of managing people. Goldie had never managed anyone except a helper or two who came and did some milking or some stacking of the hay. She was excited; at nineteen she was going to manage women and men much older than herself. She was a little scared and a little worried too.

Evening came and she went to the hotel the company had picked out for her. It wasn't the Hilton, but it was nice. It was a small hotel about three blocks away from the training center and a mile or so from the beach. Goldie sat on her bed and read over the day's lessons. She was a careful note taker and a meticulous student. It only took her an hour to cover everything that was said in a whole day of lessons. It was actually easier than high school.

How funny, she thought. *Grown-up schools are easier than high school.*

I always wondered if I could make it in business schools, but this is a breeze.

She watched TV for only a half an hour and got disgusted at the stupidity of the programs. She decided to go to the movies. Goldie had tried to call Greg, but he didn't answer his phone. That seemed strange to her because he had a device on the phone that told him who was calling. Maybe he set it down or was in a meeting. He did attend a lot of meetings. It was part of his management duties.

As she was leaving to go downtown to see a movie, she saw a familiar face coming down the hallway toward her.

"Hi, Goldie, I was in the neighborhood and thought I'd stop by."

"Doctor, what in the heck are you doing here and how did you find me?"

"It's Eric, and well, I had to lie. I told them you desperately needed some medicine you hadn't gotten when you were at the hospital. So they told me where they had booked your stay."

Goldie laughed. "You're a sneaky son of a gun. It's nice to see you."

"Well, it's nice to see you too. Would you like to go get something to eat?"

"I was just on my way out. I was going to a movie and to get a hot dog or something."

"Good, I'll take you to get something better than a hot dog."

Goldie was glad to go. She didn't worry about the doctor being aggressive with her and she really liked him. She had almost forgotten she was now married, but once they entered the restaurant, which was a quiet Asian restaurant with lights down low and music playing in the background, she remembered.

Goldie became reserved and quiet. She suddenly felt guilty going out with a man while her husband was in LA working and trusting her. But Eric was so very kind and so pleasant to be with.

The evening went wonderfully. Eric once again attended to her every need and want. He asked how she was doing in school and how she was feeling with her baby. He made an appointment with her to give her a sonogram and talked with her about some of the problems of women having their first baby. He also warned her about drinking alcohol during pregnancy and told her neither to start smoking nor to be around those who do.

The night passed so quickly. Eric was sincerely interested in her. Almost everything he said was about her and everything he did was to attend to her needs and wants. It was so very wonderful that she had flashes of thoughts wishing she were not pregnant and not married. She decided not to tell him she had gotten married. She thought he might know anyway.

Eric suspected in his heart. He had tried to contact her during the past three days and was unsuccessful. He figured she was either out with her attacker or had gone back home to Minnesota.

The night ended with a word from Eric.

"Goldie, I did some research into your boyfriend. He's a dangerous man. You know he's been in jail. More than once. I couldn't find any evidence he worked for Mercedes and I couldn't find his address. Goldie, please re-consider. I don't think he's a good bet for a partner for life."

His words penetrated her heart like never before. Maybe he was right. Maybe there was something wrong with Greg. In lots of ways he didn't compare with Eric. But Greg was the father of her child and she remembered well the teaching of her father: "You make your bed, you have to sleep in it!" Well, Goldie certainly had made her bed and Greg was sleeping in it. He was good to her in so many ways. She had re-fallen in love with him on their honeymoon.

She got to the motel and said goodnight. Eric had been so very nice. As she walked into the room she thought about what Eric had said about her husband. She thought out loud, "No, no, Eric was just saying those things because he really likes me. Maybe he is just being protective like doctors sometimes do. Maybe his research is flawed. Greg is a good man. Maybe he's saying it because he knows Greg is black and he is jealous. It doesn't matter. I have married him and I will be a good wife. I will keep his house and raise our children and love him no matter what!"

She moved her papers from the bed, sat on the end, and disrobed and fell asleep.

<hr />

The rest of the week went well. Eric said he had rotation for the rest of the week and couldn't come back and see her. She never did tell him she was married. But he knew, he knew. On the weekend she went back up to LA, when she entered her apartment, she was surprised to see all of Greg's stuff lying on the living room floor. He hadn't put anything away. So Goldie carefully put each item away. There were a couple of large suitcases, which were locked, and Goldie thought they probably had personal stuff in them. She put them in the closet in the bedroom. They were heavy. As she put things away she marveled that she was in fact married. It seemed strange to her to be married, to have come to this point in her life. She realized she was no longer a child. No longer in high school, no longer able to go where she wanted and do what she wanted. She owed an allegiance to her husband and would consult him before she went anywhere.

It was after ten when Greg finally showed. He came in and stumbled against the coffee table. He turned on the light and started to say, "What the he…"

"Hi, honey, I got home at six thirty. They let us out of class at three today. So I came home. How was work?"

"Where the hell is all my stuff?"

"I put it all away."

"What about the two suitcases with the lock on 'em?" he asked in a rather demanding voice.

"Honey, I put them in the closet in the bedroom."

"You didn't open them, did you?"

"Of course not, they had a lock on them and I figured that they were personal stuff."

"Good, keep out of my personal belongings. Some things are for me only. Remember that when we're living together. I need some space and I need some things kept personal."

It sounded so cold to Goldie. "We're living together." Not now that we're married or when we share life, or in our home. It was okay, though. Goldie had some things she didn't especially want Greg to thumb through. Her diary, and pictures of her mom and dad, or even pictures of her farm or the horse she loved.

"Ya wanna go out?" Goldie asked.

"Yeah, seeing as how you didn't cook me any dinner."

"Great! Today was payday and I have a few bucks."

They went out to pizza. Goldie was famished and she ate five pieces. Greg, of course, commented on each piece as she downed it. She didn't care; she was hungrier than she had been in a year. When they finished she sighed. "Wow, I sure was hungry. The lunches at the training center are also really good and I seem to be eating more than I have for quite a while. Probably what happens when you get pregnant. But don't worry, I'll keep my weight down."

"You better. It's important to me to have a wife that looks like you look now, not like you're gonna look in a couple of months."

Goldie didn't quite understand the statement. Did he mean he wouldn't take her out after she was showing? No matter. She smiled and drank the rest of her root beer.

The rest of the night went well. They went home and talked for another hour. Greg didn't even turn on the TV, they just visited. Greg was jealous and suspicious of almost everything Golden did, but he repeated that he loved her twice. That in itself was a minor miracle; he almost never said he loved her. She knew it, but it was almost never said.

Saturday morning came and Goldie awoke at six. She got up and went into the kitchen and cooked some breakfast for Greg and herself. Greg got up and shaved and put on some clean work clothes. He came into the kitchen in a tie and shined shoes. He looked great. He smelled great too. Goldie asked what kind of aftershave lotion he was wearing, but he shrugged it off.

They ate breakfast and Greg announced he needed to go to work today. He left her a list of things he needed to have in their house and said he'd be bringing over some more of his stuff that afternoon. The list included a subscription to the newspaper, cablevision, and another telephone for his personal use. He insisted that he wanted his food cooked in iron cookware. Goldie agreed, her mom had always said aluminum caused Alzheimer's or at least brain damage.

Goldie hadn't bought much in kitchen wear so she went out shopping when Greg left and bought a hundred and fifty dollars worth of dishes and pots and pans. She got a special on knives, forks and spoons, which she thought were beautiful.

This is so great. I'm setting up my own home. I never thought I'd be doing this. I never thought I'd be having a baby. Wow, so much has happened in such a little time. I wish Mom were here to share this with me. She'd be so excited and so proud of me. I really miss her. I hope they can come next spring when the baby's born....

Her thoughts were interrupted by the clerk asking if that would be all. She carried everything out to her car and put it into the trunk. It was noon when she finally finished shopping so she decided to go get some lunch.

"I feel rich today, and good. I guess I'll take this stuff home and go out and have a Ruben. No, I think I'll have a Ruben first and then take the stuff home."

With that she got into her car and drove down Fifth to a sandwich shop that she had passed going to work and always wanted to stop at but never had. As she walked in she could smell the lunches cooking and it reminded her of home. Mom always cooked lunch when she was home. They were always great; even when they were only mac and cheese, they were always great. Mom prepared them and presented them as though she was a cook at a great resort.

I sure miss her, she thought and sat down at a table next to the window.

As she looked out the window she saw Greg's car. It was stuck in traffic so she got up and ran out to invite him in to have lunch with her. The light changed just as she got to the street and Greg, who was busy talking with a client, a grubby-looking black man with a beard and braided hair, a dirty shirt and cheep sunglasses, didn't see her as he sped away.

It's just as well, she thought, *I didn't want to have lunch with one of Greg's clients anyway. I'll tell him I saw him when he gets home tonight.*

The Ruben was great. Golden always had extra sauerkraut on it and this time she had some extra sauce. When she first bit into it, the sauce was so good that she called the waiter over and said she'd like more sauce put on the sandwich.

The rest of the day was spent putting away the things she had bought and cleaning up the apartment. It was small but she knew they could live in it until the baby was born. *I really need to get a doctor for my baby. I probably need vitamins and I should talk with him or her about losing weight. I don't want it to be Eric. He has been so very kind, and he seems to care so much, but I just don't want to be told that I shouldn't have married Greg. Besides, he's wrong about Greg. I don't think he has ever broken the law in his life. He usually doesn't even speed and although he talks badly about law enforcement people, I think sometimes he's probably right; they are prejudiced and probably have harassed him in the past. So he's got a right to be self-protective and a little paranoid.*

At four Goldie called Wendy and told her she was home from San Diego for today and tomorrow. She asked what she was doing and Wendy said she had talked with Goldie's mom and she should call her. Wendy seemed cold and a little withdrawn. Goldie knew she had done wrong. She still hadn't called Mom. She said her goodbyes and hung up the phone. Golden stood by the phone and debated for twenty minutes whether or not to call Mom. Finally she picked up the phone and dialed.

"Hi, Mom, how you doing?"

"Honey, we've been worried sick about you, how are you?" Mom usually asked how you were when she wanted to know everything that had happened. It reminded Golden of her date with Jeff when Mom asked how she was when she got home rather late.

"Well, Mom, I got married and I love Greg. I know you wanted a big wedding but Greg and I just couldn't afford it and I knew you and Dad couldn't leave this time of year, so we went to a justice of the peace and got married."

"Are you pregnant?" Mom asked. She had a sense about her that was almost psychic. She really already knew but she asked to give Goldie a chance to tell her.

"Yes, Mom, I am. I love you and I know you're a little disappointed that I got pregnant before I got married, but I love Greg and he'll make a great dad. He's hardworking, Mom, and I think Dad'll like him if he gives him a chance."

"Sweetheart, I love you. Please tell me what's wrong with Greg. I know it must be something because of the way you married him and because you never came and presented him to Jay and I. Tell me, I really need to know."

Of course she had already spoken with Wendy and knew that Greg was Afro-American, but she wanted both to confirm it with her daughter and to see if there was anything else she might not have told her.

"There's nothing at all wrong with him, Mom. It's just that I don't know if Dad will accept him; he's an Afro-American. But he's kind and good and the father of my baby. Please love us and accept us, Mom, please. I really need your approval and love to get through this pregnancy and to make sure Dad understands and loves him too."

"I know you love your dad, he really loves you and misses you, but he has lived a sheltered life and doesn't understand interracial marriages. He has criticized them to me in the past, so now I must tell him his daughter has done the very thing he is critical of? Okay, honey, I'll talk with your father. How are you doing physically with the baby? You got cramps, are you throwing up in the morning? How you feeling?"

"Yeah, I've got morning sickness, but I'm doing okay. I'm eating like a horse and am starting to show even though I'm only three months along. I get tired really easily too. And my appetite is so strange. Also when..."

She went on for another hour telling her mother everything. She told her how she met Greg and how very kind he was to her. She told her about their dates and their honeymoon. She told her about everything she could remember since she had come to California. It was almost six o'clock when she hung up.

That would make it eight or nine there, she thought. *Dad's probably coming into the house right now.*

Mom had given her some good advice, and Golden in her usual well-organized style wrote down all the suggestions Mom made and put them in the notebook she had bought for the school in San Diego.

Greg came home late again. It was almost ten o'clock when he finally arrived. Goldie had prepared him a lasagna dinner and had put it on "warm" in the oven. She had covered it with aluminum foil to keep it moist and had put the salad in the refrigerator. She had made some drink out of papaya juice and Kool-Aid that she thought Greg might like. She had made some peach cobbler, which was his favorite for dessert. He came in and kissed her and said he had eaten out and wasn't hungry. She offered the peach pie as a consolation and he accepted.

Goldie was disappointed that her first homemade meal of their marriage in their together apartment wasn't eaten. She had made the lasagna from scratch and was proud of it. She had used three cheeses to make it and filled the layers with cottage cheese like her mom had taught her. Greg's breath smelled not like alcohol, although there was some smell of alcohol there, but it smelled sorta sweet. Probably he had stopped and gotten some breath mints or something. Greg went into bed and straightaway fell asleep.

I wonder if he still likes to make love with me? Goldie thought. *'Course he does, he's just tired, he works so hard.* Goldie walked into the bathroom and picked up Greg's pants. She dutifully took everything out of the pockets and hung them up. His wallet was bulging with money so Goldie counted it. There was eight thousand dollars in twenties and fifties and hundreds.

We need to get a bank account, she thought as she put it back. Wrapped half way around one of the rubber band-bound money packets was a slip of paper with a note written on it. The paper was one of those roll-your-own cigarette wrappers. The ones with the guy with a beard on the cover. While cleaning his pocket she also found the original package. "How funny?" she said out loud, "Why would Greg roll his own cigarettes. He doesn't smoke that much anyway. Maybe with the cost of cigarettes these days, he's probably saving money. She read the note; it said, "P.u. at 9, take rod."

Maybe one of his clients broke the piston rod on his car, she thought as she put everything in his pockets on the nightstand by his side of the bed. It was after twelve when she finally got to bed.

Like clockwork Goldie awoke at five thirty. She got up and put on some coffee and started some toast. At six she ate the toast and drank a couple of cups of coffee. It was Sunday and for the first time in a long time Goldie felt like going to church. She had the baby in her womb and she felt closer to God than she had felt in a long time.

"I don't care which church I go to. Maybe Greg has a place he'd like to go," she said out loud. She went into the bathroom and as quietly as possible showered and put on makeup, and for the first time since she had left Wendy's place she put on fingernail polish. She quietly scrounged through her closet and found some clean fake patent leather shoes and a dress that she had always loved. The dress had always been a little large but it fit perfectly now. Not that she was showing yet, but her waist had grown. Her breasts too had grown and she imagined she could feel them stretching. The dress was a little snug on the top too, but Goldie liked it. She thought Greg would like the "busty" look and she smiled as she reflected on the night she got pregnant.

It was almost nine o'clock when Greg finally awoke. He staggered into the kitchen as usual. Goldie was ready for him this time. When he had first stirred she put in some toast and warmed up the frying pan for eggs or whatever else he may want.

"Good morning, sweetheart," Goldie said, turning from the stove in a sorta whirl to show off her dress.

"Where the hell is my coffee?" Greg answered, without even looking in her direction.

"Here you go, honey," she answered, undaunted. "It's fixed just the way you like it."

"Really?" Greg asked with an honest surprise in his voice. "Thanks."

"What would you like for breakfast?"

"Gimme a couple of eggs and some toast," he answered, finally looking up at her and gulping down the last swig of his hot coffee.

"I don't know how you can drink that coffee so hot. Doesn't it burn your tongue?" Goldie asked, trying her hardest to be noticed.

"What the hell's the story? How come you're all dressed up?"

"Do you think I look pretty? I thought maybe we'd go to church today."

"No, we're not going to your damn church. It's full of prejudiced whities. And I don't think I could even go to my old church. My ol' lady used to take me every week and I hated it."

"By your ol' lady do you mean your mom, or is there someone you haven't told me about?"

"Yeah, I meant my mom. I'm still not going to your church."

"So let's go to yours. Maybe your mom will still be there and I'd love to meet her. I'd love to go to your church with you."

"You really are politically ignorant. Don't you know they'd hate you for coming into one of our churches? I'd be like you had the right or you were one of us or something."

"I think I do have the right. And besides, it's God were trying to worship, not people's opinions. I am carrying your child. What else can I do to earn the right to go and thank the Lord for such a great blessing?"

"For Christ's sake, woman, okay, we'll go, but just for a hour."

Greg thought it might be a good time to show her off anyway. He didn't have much belief in God, but he did occasionally go to church to meet with friends and see his mother.

Greg put on his suit; he looked so good in it. Goldie thought she'd like to hold him and snuggle to him when he looked so handsome. He didn't shave but when Goldie mentioned it to him he said he was giving his face a rest. His hair was getting long again, but it still looked good from the last cut. He put it into a ponytail that morning and it looked good. They took the Mercedes.

Church was located southwest of LA. It didn't take long to get there. The roads weren't as crowded as they usually were on weekdays. It was a four-square church, which Goldie had never before been to. As they walked in, she found the chapel plain but beautiful. Everyone seemed to know Greg, and as they walked in and up the aisle they all stared at Goldie. She didn't feel uncomfortable, though. She met the reverend outside and now as he was going up to the pulpit he stopped and smiled at her.

"Welcome to God's house," he said.

"Hi, Father, thank you."

"They don't call me father, here," he said. "I'm a reverend, most people just call me 'brother.' But we're glad to have you. Please have a seat."

"I know some of your members are staring at me, but I'm grateful for your welcome. My husband and I are trying to get more God into our lives. We're going to have a baby."

At that the pastor stepped back and looked sternly at Greg. He didn't say anything more except "I've got to go do some preparations."

Greg's hand tightened on Goldie's arm and he squeezed so tight she thought it might break. He turned her to his face and said, "You don't tell anyone about your pregnancy, that's personal between us! Got it?" He shook her slightly but really strongly as he emphasized his point.

Goldie was surprised at Greg's reaction. She had assumed he'd be proud of having a child and would want to show her off. She thought maybe that's why he agreed to go to church that morning.

Church was great. They sang and the minister gave a great sermon. The church members raised their arms in praise to the Lord and some hugged the person next to them. Goldie thought it was great. She had never been to a church where the members were so actively involved in the sermon. One guy got up and played a guitar and an older woman sang a solo. She quite liked it, and even though her arm ached from Greg's squeezing it, she too raised her arms and sang with the rest of the congregation.

As they left the minister shook her hand again and said he was glad she had come to God's house. He asked if he could have a word with Greg and they stepped off to the side for a few seconds. Several other people came and shook hands with Goldie, and some smiled and said congratulations when she told them she and Greg were married. One older woman looked at her very carefully and asked if she was pregnant. Goldie didn't want to lie, especially because she was so very happy to be carrying the child of her husband and because she was in the house of the Lord, so she whispered, "Yes," and smiled so hard it hurt her mouth. The woman smiled too. She took Golden's hand and said, "You are a courageous woman. I wish you well."

Greg returned a little discomforted but didn't say anything about what the minister had said. Goldie was going to ask, but then thought she'd rather not spoil a great morning.

"Wanna go to the beach?" she asked, hoping he'd say yes.

"No, I've got some business to do this morning."

"Oh, honey, don't go and do it. Stay with me, I can make it worth your while," she said with a hint of sex in her voice.

"Look, woman, I've got business to do and that's how I support you, so don't push me!" he snapped back.

Actually, Goldie thought, *he hasn't given much to support us up to now. 'Course, I've been in San Diego for the last week and will be there next week, so maybe after I get home he'll get some groceries and pay the rent for next month. He did pay some of it this month and he's only just moved in so I guess I shouldn't be too critical.*

As they drove home Greg was mostly silent, but Goldie chattered on about the meeting and how much she liked singing and swinging her arms and praising the Lord. She said she hadn't done that before and she thought it was a great way to thank God for the baby and for her great husband. Greg just grunted. He finally proffered, "We won't be going back there for a while."

"Oh, honey, why not? I really loved it and some of the people were really nice to me. One woman came and asked if I was pregnant, and others shook my hand and some hugged me. Can't we go next week? I know you'd like it if you went."

Greg turned to Goldie who looked into his eyes in such a pleading way that all he could say was, "Yeah, maybe I'll have time to go next week."

At home Greg didn't bother to take off his suit. He went to the closet and picked up the two big bags Goldie had put there, kissed her good-bye and left.

I hate it when he does that, Goldie thought. *He never tells me when he's coming home or where he's going. As soon as I get back from training I'm getting him that cell phone he wanted from my office so I can call him. I don't know why I can't call him on his work phone, but that's okay. He's probably right, it's a tough world out there for his kind of man and that makes him very protective of his job.*

The hours passed and Goldie cleaned up the apartment spotless. She then walked down to Wiltshire Boulevard and window-shopped. She called her mom again later that night and watched some television. She couldn't stop eating but she was careful to only eat things like un-buttered popcorn and veggies with a little dip. Dad didn't talk to her. Mom said he was asleep, which was about right. It was three hours later there and she knew Dad went to bed at about eight or nine at the latest.

❖

"How's my girl?" Jay asked as Marge slipped into bed.

"She's okay, honey. She still has a little morning sick and misses us. Don't you think you could call and talk with her? She really needs you and loves you."

"Yeah, I miss her and love her too. It's just hard to think of her as pregnant and married. Especially to a black man! I can't imagine why she'd marry someone of a different race."

"Sweetheart, that doesn't matter now. She is married and she needs us."

"Okay, I'll call her tomorrow or Tuesday."

He rolled over and went to sleep. It was after ten.

❖

Greg got home at two thirty in the morning. Goldie kissed him and fell back asleep. Five a.m. came quickly and she arose, grabbed the suitcase and quietly left. She didn't put the coffee on because she figured he'd not wake up 'til nine or so but she left it all ready to be turned on.

School was even better this week. She studied every night. It was easy and she over-learned everything. A couple of the girls in the class came by her motel and asked if she wanted to go to a show on Tuesday, but she said no thanks, she really wanted to do well in the class. Maria was counting on her and she wasn't going to let her down. It wasn't every day that a young girl got the opportunity she was given and she knew it.

Tuesday and Wednesday went by and her dad hadn't called. Not that Goldie knew he had promised to call, it was just that she missed him and really wanted to hear his voice. He had always been a great friend to her and she had loved and admired him. He was everything she wanted to marry. He was stable and kind, and almost never got angry. Goldie knew why he wasn't calling. She knew that her mom had told him about her marriage and he was probably pretty upset. But she knew he loved her and so she figured that he'd call and support her in this very difficult decision. Maybe it was that she was pregnant. Although that shouldn't matter, once you married someone that's what happened.

The school week ended on Friday at ten a.m. They had a graduation ceremony and Goldie was the top of the class. She got an award from the teacher and an extra citation from the school. The manager there said she had a perfect score. No one had gotten a perfect score since they had started the school more than ten years before, so they gave her a free dinner for two and another twenty-five dollars. She was excited about it and couldn't wait to tell Maria. She was going to put the award certificate up on the wall by where she ran the switchboard. Other operators shared the space, but she figured it'd be okay. She was really proud of it. Besides she was going to be the assistant supervisor so she should get some privileges.

By the time the ceremony and everything was finished and she had had some lunch, it was two. She finally got out of town about three. Driving home, she thought about everything she had learned. She was surprised at how much they could cram into just two weeks of training. She thought about Dr. Eric. He was such a great man. He was willing to take her on even though she was pregnant and even though they knew very little of each other. What a strange thing. She wondered why, why would anyone want her? It wasn't that she didn't know that she was very attractive, she knew, but life was more than good looks; it was honest relationships. She wasn't sure she was able to develop an honest relationship with Greg like her father had done with her and with her mother.

Goldie wondered again why Eric would be willing to take someone else's baby in the package. It didn't matter. She had decided. In spite of Greg's sometimes selfish behavior and his volatile temper, she loved him. He was the father of her child and she was going to make it work. She knew she could change him. She knew inside he was a great man and with a little love and teaching she could change the bad parts and love the good. Traffic was heavy and going north on I-5 was hell. But she finally got home at six fifteen and walked into the apartment. It was a mess. Greg had of course been living there but he hadn't picked up a thing. He hadn't done a dish and he hadn't even made the bed. Goldie sighed and then started to clean up the house. First she put on some noodles for spaghetti and started to fry some hamburger. While it was cooking she picked up the living room and put all of Greg's clothes into a plastic bag to take downstairs to the laundry. She figured she'd wash tomorrow because she wasn't scheduled to work until Monday.

She was just mixing the hamburger and tomato sauce when Greg came home. He didn't want any dinner so Goldie covered it with plastic wrap and put it into the fridge.

XII
The Doctor's Appointment

Goldie had a great Monday morning. She told everyone about the training and about her time in San Diego. She was excited about how great the company was and her little part in it. She went down to the street corner and got a Starbucks coffee for everyone on shift, which cost her thirty dollars. Maria called her into her office and sat Goldie down.

"I heard from the school in San Diego. They said you were the top of the class."

"Well, I loved the class and I loved the material, and Mr. Wood was a great teacher."

"We're going to give you a raise and a promotion, Goldie. I know you've only been here a few months, but you show such promise that my boss, Mr. Howe, and I have decided that you would make a great addition to our management teem. We're putting you in charge of the midnight shift. You'll start at ten p.m. and finish at six thirty. There will be times when you won't get through by six thirty, but if you do your job well, I think most of the time you'll be through by then. You need to learn the four forms you have to do daily and the weekly report. In addition you'll need to keep track of the employees' hours and the number of complaints we get on any operators working. A big part of this job, Goldie, is leadership. That's one of the points of discussion I had with Mr. Howe. He wasn't sure that you could lead women older than yourself with confidence. I told him you could, so don't make a liar out of me."

"I promise I won't. I know I can lead our operators and even improve their time and lower the complaint level," Goldie responded with excitement. Maria continued to explain the duties and they conversed for another hour.

The rest of the day was spent in explaining to Goldie the specific forms used by her department and the time deadlines for those reports. It sounded like a pretty big job for Goldie; she wondered if she could do it. There was a projection form due monthly. There was an hourly report form; there was an economic projection form due weekly. In that one she had to project the amount of money her department was going to spend in the coming week. There were forms for customer complaints and forms for overtime. In all it wasn't four forms at all, it was more like twenty. Goldie wondered where Maria got the number four.

They gave Goldie a new nametag. It said "Ms. Coleman, Supervisor." Goldie was delighted to get it. It was a symbol of all her work and it made her feel great. It made her feel needed and important. She might have loved it even more than the raise. She was on her way up. Wow, what a great feeling!

The evening came. Goldie was late getting home and Greg was waiting.

"Where the hell have you been?" he asked in a demanding voice.

"Oh, honey, you'll never believe what happened to me today. They promoted me. I know I went to the school to get trained for a promotion, but I figured in a couple of months they might make me an assistant supervisor or something. But they made me the shift supervisor! Greg, I'm the full-fledged shift supervisor. Plus I got a dollar-an-hour raise and in three months after my probation as a supervisor, I'll go to salary. What'd ya think of that?"

"That's great, honey, but I've been sitting here for a hour, hungry as hell, and you are at work playing."

"Well, not exactly playing. I was getting promoted."

"What'd ya got for dinner?" was Greg's reply. He didn't even walk over and kiss her; he just sat down at the table. Goldie knew about hungry men; they needed to be fed first and then they would calm down and talk.

"Just a second and I'll get this dinner warmed up in the microwave. I made it especially for you.

Greg grunted and picked up the newspaper and started to read. In less than five minutes Goldie announced, "Spaghetti!" She said it triumphantly as she set a steaming plate in front of him. "Just a sec, hon, and I'll get you some milk or water if you want."

"I'll take a beer," he responded

"Sure, sweetheart, how was work today?" she asked as she sat down with her plate.

"It was horrible. I've got to get some material to a man and I've got to pay for it first and then collect. I hate that. That's not how to do business. He'd better have the bucks."

Goldie waited for him to ask her how her day was or if she graduated or if she was still employed or anything about her work so she could tell him about her awards and her great time in San Diego. He didn't.

"Well, guess what I got?" she asked, trying to stir some interest.

"I can't guess. What."

"I graduated from GTE's school of management and I&R, and I was the top of the class! What do you think of that?" she asked excitedly.

"That was great, honey," he responded, not going any further into the event. But Goldie wasn't finished, she wanted to tell him all about it. She wanted to show him her awards and tell him how great it would be at work. She wanted a little praise and attention for her accomplishments.

Goldie stood up and walked over to the end table and picked up her two awards. She held them up triumphantly and said, "Look, honey, I was the number one person in the class, I was top of the entire class, and Mr. Howe said no one had ever before completed the class with a perfect score. I'm famous!" She was so excited that it was contagious and Greg couldn't help but smile and praise her.

The rest of the evening went well. They talked about changing doctors for her baby. Goldie said it was because she had good insurance and why should she go to an emergency doctor when she could see an OB/GYN just as well. Greg agreed. He went into the bathroom and took a shower and then went to bed.

When Goldie got into the bedroom after doing the dishes he was fast asleep. She was disappointed. They hadn't made love or even visited for a week and she wanted to spend some time with him talking and loving. She got up, went back into the kitchen, and called Wendy. Wendy wasn't home so she read the only magazine she had in the house, a *Ladies Home Journal*. She had read it three times already but it was okay, she learned some new stuff. She read over her installation and repair class notes and thought at least she could become an installer if she failed at the operator business. *I'm gonna be okay*, she thought. *I guess I'll do all right in this world. I sure do miss Mom and Dad but I don't think I was ever meant to be a dairy farmer, or to marry Jeff or to stay in Angora.*

Tuesday was uneventful except that Greg had to work. He didn't go to work until after two but he was gone all night. Goldie thought it was a strange job. She supposed that he got paid extra for his long and unusual hours. Greg had explained that he was a problem solver and that in addition to his supervision of sales managers at various locations, he was also required to resolve customer complaints, which meant he usually had to meet with them after work or on weekends and at their homes, which, naturally, were scattered all across southern California. Finally on Thursday night Greg got home early enough to talk with his wife.

"Well, if you got promoted and a raise, let's go out to dinner. How about Rubens? I really like their prime rib."

"And I love their salads. How about you share some prime rib and I'll share some salad."

"Yeah, I'll give you a bite or two," Greg said, smiling.

At dinner, Goldie re-explained her promotion and talked about the forms she had to fill out and what Maria had said about her new duties. At length she finished and smiled. "So what do you think, honey?"

"You haven't said what shift or days you'll be working."

"Well, that's the part that may be a little disturbing. The only shift they'll give to new supervisors is the midnight shift. It's sorta an initiation thing, and also because they have a hard time keeping supervisors on that shift."

"So what time will you be home for me?"

"I don't have to leave for work until about nine p.m."

"All right, I usually eat before nine anyway. What about when you have the baby? Will they change your shift, or do you still have to work midnights?"

"I'll probably have to work this shift until another supervisor is promoted or leaves. I'm not sure how long that will be."

They talked until ten thirty. Greg had some business and took Goldie home and dropped her off. The rest of the week Golden trained and sat with Maria and learned about the company's policies and procedures. She sat with the girls and handled complaints and did international calls. All the girls liked her and it seemed no one was jealous or even unhappy that she was going to the midnight shift. She sat in with Maria while she counseled one of the girls who chewed gum and took pretty long coffee breaks.

The rest of the week passed so very rapidly. And then Monday night, her first shift as supervisor came.

It was great. Golden listened to the names of her girls and she listened to their complaints. It seemed so natural. She took the time to interview each of her seven girls. There were no males working nights, which seemed strange to her, but male operators were rare anyway. She set up her office and solved only four call problems. She did two international calls, which the girl at the board could not handle; other than that, the night went well. She stayed to talk with Maria who came in at eight forty-five. The conversation about work only lasted five minutes; after that it went to Goldie's personal life. Maria said she could see some sadness in Golden's face. She asked about it and Goldie explained that Greg was sometimes unkind, abusive, and selfish. She reaffirmed that she loved Greg and was determined to make the marriage work. Maria wasn't so sure. Maria said Goldie should consider leaving Greg.

"After all, he's not even contributing much to finances, let alone to you personally."

Sunday morning Golden awoke and after fixing breakfast showered and got into her Sunday best clothes. When she tried to wake Greg he just rolled over and said to leave him alone. So Goldie did. She went out to the car and decided to go to a church near her home. She didn't think it would be a good idea to go the Greg's church without him there. Golden drove for a few miles up Five and took off on a road near Ontario. When she had driven up a winding country road for a couple of miles she saw a Lutheran church, which was just getting started. The minister was standing out front greeting the regular members and visitors. She pulled in and parked in an empty space near the end of the row.

As she approached the front door the minister extended his hand and asked her name. She shook hands with him and said, "Oh, hi, I'm just passing by and thought I'd come in and hear your sermon. I feel like I need to be close to God right now. I'm so far away from my parents and my old home."

"Please do come in. We're glad you came," he responded in an almost canned voice. Even though Goldie knew he had probably said the exact same thing to a million churchgoers, his eyes were good. He looked at her intensely and deeply and when they shook hands she felt that he was a good man and a good minister. The sermon was on the Good Samaritan, about how we should care for others and not think of ourselves or our own personal comfort so much. It was good and Goldie decided to re-dedicate her life to teaching her child and helping her husband and not think so much about herself.

As she was leaving the minister again shook hands with her and invited her back. He was really sincere, but Goldie doubted whether Greg would like it there or not. She looked at the minister and asked, "I'm married to an Afro-American, do you think he'd be welcome here?" The minister was visibly surprised. He even stepped back half a step.

"Of course, we love all of God's children here," he answered. Goldie loved his sermon and believed the things he said, but she had not seen even one colored man in the congregation. She was beginning to look for those things. She was beginning to become more and more aware of the way people of different shape, background, or color were treated. She had even noticed that some people treated her differently when she was with Greg. For example, when she last went shopping, a grocery store clerk had made a remark about salt and pepper. Goldie didn't understand it until she got home and asked Greg, who laughed and said it was a racial comment.

Golden drove home. She got there at two and Greg was still asleep. The coffee was burnt because it had sat all day with the heater on and had evaporated down to almost half of what she had left. She dumped it out and remade a pot. Greg liked fresh coffee and he usually bought some fresh ground vanilla or some other flavored kind. When Goldie shopped she would go to Safeway and grind up some of their beans and take them home and make a pot. She was becoming a big coffee drinker. She'd have two or three cups in the morning and two or three cups in the afternoon. She picked up Greg's clothes and hung up the suit. It had to be dry-cleaned but his shirt, shorts, socks, and handkerchief needed to be washed. She took the things out of his pockets and set them on the end table by the bed. There was an assortment of "strange" things, most of which she had no idea of what they were. His wallet was partially opened and she looked inside. There were a dozen hundred-dollar bills and in his pocket was a roll of twenties rolled up and held by a rubber band. It seemed curious to her to keep money like that, but she figured that it must be a lump sum kept separate for payment or something.

On Tuesday they finally decided to go see a doctor. Greg knew a doctor his mom had used who was an OB/GYN. Goldie looked and he was on the list from work that Maria had given her for doctors who accepted the insurance she had. The appointment was made for Thursday morning at 11:30. Goldie was looking forward to seeing a *real* doctor and not just an emergency doctor. She had tried putting Eric completely out of her mind.

Thursday morning came but Greg had to work. He said he'd meet her there if he could get away. So Goldie went alone. The doctor's office was in south LA, about eight or nine miles away from the Hollywood apartment. It was clean and well kept and the clientele were mostly younger women. She wasn't sure she would like the doctor and she was a little afraid. Up to now she had never been to see anyone specifically for her pregnancy and she wasn't sure what they did. After filling out a raft of forms and giving the receptionist her little red insurance card, she sat and read a magazine.

Almost three quarters of an hour past and finally a nurse peeked out of the closed, white-painted door. Sticking only her head out and craning around the corner, she said, "Ms. Coleman?"

Goldie got up and walked back into the room with the nurse. She measured her and took her weight. She then guided her into a little room with a white translucent paper covering the narrow table-couch. She took her blood pressure and temperature and said, "Sit down and the doctor will be with you in a moment."

Goldie started to doubt if she was going to like it here. Or if she was going to like this doctor. She hardly had time to think it through when the door opened and in stepped the doctor. He was an older man with gray hair, glasses, and a very kind smile.

"Hi, I'm Doctor Bates. How are you doing?"

"Hi, Doctor, I'm Goldie Coleman. I'm pretty sure I'm pregnant."

"Okay, let's first get a work-up on you and do some blood tests and get you going. How far along are you? Do you know?" he asked cheerfully.

"I'm pretty sure I'm close to three months along," Goldie answered with some hesitancy. Gates noted the change in her voice and looked her in the eye and asked, "Are you married?"

"Yes, but I wasn't when I got pregnant," Goldie answered, feeling like the doctor may have crossed over into some of her very personal space.

"Please don't feel embarrassed or uncomfortable. I want you to have a beautiful baby, and I don't judge anyone. I just needed to know. It makes a difference in what I may prescribe. Now let's see, I have another client named Coleman, she's an older woman, an Afro-American. I don't suppose you're related."

"Probably," Goldie responded. "My husband said you treated his mother here."

"So you're married to Greg?" the doctor asked with some surprise.

"Yes!" Goldie exclaimed. "I'm pregnant with his baby."

"Great, if you'll just urinate in this little cup and take off your clothes. You can put on this robe and I'll be back in five minutes."

He handed her a paper cup, pointed to the adjacent bathroom, and folded a paper bag that opened into a sorta robe. It tied in the front or back, Goldie couldn't figure it out, but she dawned it and tied it tightly around her waist. She seemed so vulnerable with her clothes off, holding a cup of her urine and waiting for the doctor to return.

Maybe this was part of having a baby. Maybe one had to go through this to understand what was really happening to her body.

In any case ten or fifteen minutes passed and the door opened again. In walked the nurse and the doctor. The nurse was smiling this time and she seemed very nice and friendly. Still, Goldie wasn't sure she wanted to expose herself to the nurse. She figured that the doctor was enough, but did the nurse have to be there too? The doctor took the cup from Goldie who had been holding it like it was something of great value and handed it to the nurse. He then waited for her to return. While he was waiting he took some blood. Goldie didn't like needles and she hated being stuck in the arm. But the doctor was good and only made one poke. Usually, like the last time, they made a million sticks before they found the vein. He drew three little tubes of blood out. It seemed a lot of blood for a simple pregnancy test and Goldie spoke out. "You gonna dry me up?"

Gates laughed. "No, you've got plenty more in your system. I just need to run several tests and I need enough to do each test separately."

The nurse returned and labeled the tubes of blood and then stood by while the doctor examined Golden. He looked at her breasts and her lower parts and made the usual grunts and nods. He then said he'd like to look at her with a sonogram. Goldie wasn't sure what a sonogram was, but he was the doctor and she figured it couldn't be any more embarrassing than what she had already been through.

The doctor sent the nurse out to get the instrument. She returned with a tray that had a TV on top and a bunch of instruments under it. The doctor untied her tight waist knot and put jelly all over her stomach and abdomen. He then put a cold, flat, round instrument on her abdomen and began moving it around. The television screen showed gray and black and white silhouettes, which seemed to move as the doctor moved the disk. Inside the shadows you could see what seemed to be the shape of a baby. The doctor took almost ten minutes and re-looked several times. He even had Golden roll sideways, to which the nurse whispered something into the doctor's ear and he said, "Yeah, it looks like it," ignoring curious Golden. The doctor put on the stethoscope and listened to her tummy for another three or four minutes.

Goldie started to ask what was happening, but the doctor shushed her. When he finished he had her sit up and the nurse brought the back of the table upright so Goldie could lean on it.

"Well, Mrs. Coleman, I have some news for you," the doctor said. He didn't smile and Goldie got afraid for an instant.

"What? I'm okay, aren't I? The baby's okay, isn't it?"

"Oh, you're okay. But the baby isn't a baby, it's twins." The doctor smiled ear to ear. "Congratulations, you are going to be the mommy of two babies, and I think they're boys. It might be a little early to tell, and the images are a little cloudy, but I think I saw a penis."

"Twins? I've got twins?"

"Yes, and you're about as far along as you said. So we're going to start you on some vitamins and we're going to monitor you very carefully. When you leave, please make an appointment for next week. After that, I'd like to see you every two weeks for the next four months and for the last two months we'll be seeing you every week.

Goldie left the doctor's office mostly happy. She wasn't sure if having twins was going to be more painful than just one, but she thought it probably would. She went to over to work and finished setting up her new office. She had been working for a week before they got all the old supervisor's stuff out and got her a new desk. Maria had given her the little room next to the break room and a computer, which the other supervisor didn't know how to use very well, but she did. It was wired with a connection so she could listen to any of the operators while they were helping customers.

She stayed for a couple of hours overtime to see how the afternoon shift girl ran her department and made notes of all of her advice, which was volumes. Maria had given her lots of advice but it was in the form of council. It was sort of wise sayings and advice on how to treat the operators when they got in disputes or came to work mad or were just having a bad hair day. Maria was really a good employee and fast becoming a good friend. Goldie told her about her pregnancy and that she had twins. Maria smiled and told her not to mention it to any other supervisors. The company might not like having to give her maternity time so soon after spending money to train her as a supervisor.

When she got home it was after six. Greg hadn't gotten home yet, which made Goldie glad. She called Wendy and told her everything. All Wendy could say was, "Wow."

They promised to meet next Saturday and go slumming, but Goldie wasn't really sure she would show. After she hung up she fixed some dinner for Greg. She wasn't really hungry and she was trying to decide whether to call her mom and tell her not only that she was pregnant but also that she had twins. She decided to call her Saturday morning, because then she'd have enough time and energy to tell her everything. Goldie loved her mom. Marge had been both a great mother and a good friend.

Greg called at eleven thirty and said he wasn't going be coming home tonight. He said he had to go back up to Redding and finish a deal he had going there and would be home Friday late. Goldie wanted to tell him in person and Greg didn't even ask how it went at the doctor's, so she let it go. She fell asleep on the couch watching *The Tonight Show* and woke up with a pain in her back. It was almost two a.m. and she staggered into the bedroom. It was her day off. She was sort of mad at Greg. She had good news for him and he didn't even ask how the appointment went. She figured he had gotten busy and forgot. But he shouldn't be forgetting. This was important. Damn him. Why did he have to be that way? Oh well, Goldie figured she'd make it up tomorrow when he got home. She'd make love to him and tell him about the twins.

Goldie went in to work to finish her training. Maria was great and took her through the forms she had to fill out again. This time Goldie understood all of them and was very competent about doing the samples that Maria had put on her desk. She shared her office with the afternoon shift girl, but she had two of her own filing cabinets and her own passwords on the computer. She was feeling important and still a little scared.

Greg got home at about twenty after nine that night and he was a little "squirrelly." That's what Golden called him when his eyes wouldn't focus clearly and he staggered slightly and even his speech was a little slurred. She couldn't smell alcohol on his breath but she knew he must have been drinking. Usually he'd go to sleep and sleep until two or three the next day. Goldie dutifully fixed dinner for him and hoped he wouldn't ask about the doctor. She didn't want to tell him when he was like that. She wanted it to be a moment to remember.

"Ya got anything for me to eat?" he asked in a mildly demanding voice.

"I sure do, sweetheart, I fixed one of your favorites, lasagna, and it's hot and ready." Goldie was trying to be as kind and sweet as possible. She really hated it when he was this way, but she thought she understood. His work was really stressful and he sometimes needed to let off steam.

"What'd ya got to drink?"

"I made some of your vanilla coffee," she answered, hoping to get as much of it down his throat as possible.

Greg didn't answer but sat at the table and looked demandingly at Golden. She served him and he ate voraciously. When he was almost done with the dinner he looked up and asked, "Well, how was the doctor's visit? What happened? Do I have to buy any prescriptions or are you gonna have a normal baby?"

"Well, honey, I think you're gonna be surprised. I'm healthy. I do have to take some vitamins and watch what I eat. I also can't have anything alcoholic to drink for the rest of the pregnancy but other than that I'm in great shape." Greg grunted approval. There was a pause and Goldie smiled.

"Now for the really good news. We're having twins!" She said it with as much excitement she could muster, hoping it might waylay any negative reaction from Greg. He was so unpredictable, but Goldie was feeling so glad that she was having twins. It had taken most of the day for her to ingest the fact that in her body were two little lives. But now that she had, it seemed such a great thing. She was going to be the mother of two little boys. *Wow, what a blessing.*

"What'd you say? We're having twins? My God, how am I supposed to feed and clothe twins? Twins? I'm going to bed."

With that he rose and walked into the bedroom and without taking off his clothes he fell onto the bed and went fast asleep. He was sprawled across the bed and it was difficult for Goldie to get in. She had cleaned up the kitchen and started the dishwasher. Generally she didn't run the dishwasher during the night because Greg complained that the noise kept him awake, but she knew nothing would wake him up now. She thought that he took the news well. After all, having twins is a pretty big shock. Men seem to not have the same thinking pattern as women; they seem not to care about the important things like having babies. Like having twins. Goldie thought it strange. She knew that there was much about her husband she didn't understand.

As she lay on the outside corner of the bed, not able to get comfortable and afraid to move Greg's huge leg, she decided to find out more about him. *Tomorrow,* she thought, *I'll do some checking, just some private checking. I really need to know more about this man I am married to. I'll also call Mom tomorrow.*

She drifted off to sleep and awoke with a pain in her neck and lower back. She got up and didn't make coffee for Greg. She knew he'd probably sleep until three p.m. and she'd be back from work by then. It was Friday and she looked forward to Monday when she would have to be to work at ten p.m.

THE EYE OF THE BEHOLDER

❧•❧

Work went well. Maria had a ton of things to do so she didn't pay much attention to Goldie. Goldie arranged her office and went through the paperwork one more time to make sure she knew everything. She took a long coffee break and talked with the girls in the office. Most were excited about her new job as a supervisor. Some were jealous, but even they liked her and respected what she was doing. She told everyone that she was pregnant and they all congratulated her. They decided to throw a shower for her at the office even though she would not be working with them anymore. One of the girls said the night people didn't know her and probably wouldn't throw her a party and every pregnant girl needs a shower, so they would do it. They planned the party around the breaks of the girls. A third would take a break and then the other third would come in and take a break and then the last third would come in and take a break. By then it was almost time for the first girls to take another break. Goldie learned a lot about the girls in those break sessions. She thought it might be a good way to learn about her girls; just stay in the break room for the first few days. Well, maybe not stay in the room but at least be there at one of the break times for each group. Golden was learning leadership qualities. She was also growing up very, very fast.

The end of the day came and Maria came and asked Golden to stay a few minutes. Golden went into Maria's office and sat on the chair in front of her desk. Maria came in and sat on the corner of the desk rather than in her chair across from Goldie.

"You are learning about people," Maria said without any opening conversation.

"Yes, and I think I'll be a good supervisor. At least a better one than I would have been yesterday."

"We have become friends in the time you've worked here, Goldie.

I hope that friendship continues. I want your paperwork turned in on time and I want it to be accurate. I want you to come in and report to me every Tuesday morning. You can stay over and I'll try to get here by 8:15 or so."

"Okay," Goldie answered with a hint of question in her voice.

"Let's get together once or twice a month on your day off too. Is that okay with you?"

"Oh, I'd love to. You have been such a good friend and a great supervisor. I want to thank you for this chance. I want to thank you for your friendship."

"Well, let's keep working together and we can do some good here in our corner of this company. I noticed the girls are having a shower for you. I understand how important that is; just remember what I said about telling everybody about your pregnancy. It could lead to some problems."

Maria stood up and Goldie stood up and Maria gave her a hug.

"I think you're a very brave girl," Maria said without explanation.

When Goldie left work, it was after three. She drove by the house to see if Greg was still there and to her surprise he was gone. She didn't fix dinner. She had gotten her check and so she decided to take Greg out for dinner. She drove over to the church that she and Greg had gone to. She wanted to talk to someone who knew Greg before she married him. Someone who knew about him and his mother and his lifestyle. Maybe someone who could help her fill in the blanks.

The minister recognized her immediately.

"Welcome, I thought you'd never come back," he said with a quiet sense of honesty.

"I like you," Goldie responded. "I like you because you are an honest man. My father is an honest man like you. He doesn't go to church as much as he should, but he is very honest and simple. Simple by choice, not by intelligence."

"What can I do for you?" the minister answered without any circumspection.

"You could tell me about my husband. I am pregnant with twins and now I want to know more about their father."

"I think that's wonderful! When are you due?"

"I'm about four months along. So what can you tell me? Did he go to church here as a child? What's his mother like? Does he have any brothers or sisters? Do you know where he works? I can't seem to find his place of employment. I know he works because he is always going out and doing business and he brings a lot of cash home, but I have called and not been able to find him at any of the Mercedes Benz companies here in the valley."

"That's a lot of questions to answer. Please come into my office and let's talk for a while."

They walked down the aisle to the front of the church and around the pulpit. Behind the pulpit was a set of offices and a back door. The second door on the right was the office of the priest. It was decorated plainly but did have an overstuffed chair and a beautiful oak wood desk. The priest walked around the desk and sat in the chair. He sat carefully. He did not plop down, nor did he tilt it back and look condescendingly at Golden. He sat quietly and leaned forward on the chair with his arms bent and resting on his elbows. His hands were folded together with the fingers intertwining.

"None of us go through life without a strong will to survive. Those who don't have it die early. Life is too complex and too difficult to package into some brief philosophical statement. Your husband has had some difficulties. To answer one of your questions, yes, he did come here as a child. I haven't seen him for several years, but his mother still comes once or twice a month."

"Why doesn't he introduce her to me?"

"Mothers are sometimes judgmental. Sometimes they don't hesitate to say what they feel. I think he may be afraid to present you to his mother. You are of a different race, which in some parts of their culture is considered a violation. Sometimes Greg may have been or done some things that he doesn't want you to know about. That may also be a factor. With your pregnancy, especially with twins, I think his mother would be delighted. I'll speak with her. I know she will want to meet and visit with you.

"I don't think Greg works for Mercedes Benz. I think you should sit down with him and talk directly with him. I know he could get a good job and with the advent of children I think he should. Men need to take responsibility for themselves. Not just because society asks us to work, but because we are responsible for not only ourselves but for the children we bring into this world. We must stand up and shoulder that responsibility. So please, sit down with Greg and talk straight to him. Tell him you carry his children, his seed. I think, or at least hope, he will understand and give you truthful answers."

"I'm not sure I understand. If Greg is not working for the car company, where's he getting all his money?"

"You'll have to talk with him about that," the priest answered, looking away for just an instant. "I will go see his mother and talk with her. She will probably call you. Can you give me your number?"

"Of course." Goldie gave the minister her number and the times when it would be best to call her.

Goldie drove home wondering. She turned over and over what the priest had said to her in her mind. *He's right! I'll take him out to a good meal and talk with him.* She planned the entire evening as she drove home.

When she got home Greg still wasn't there. She sat down, tired from the day's work, and brewed herself a cup of coffee. Greg came home at about nine thirty and looked exhausted. He came in and sat in the recliner and tilted it back.

"Damn, I have had a rough day. What's for dinner?"

"I thought we'd go out. I got paid today and I'm excited about starting my new job Monday, so I thought we'd go out for dinner."

"Great! Let's go to Red Lobster. Let me make a couple of calls and we'll get going."

"Sounds good, honey. I'll straighten up my hair and put on another dress."

In twenty minutes they were both ready and left. They drove to the Red Lobster east of Hollywood toward Pasadena. Greg liked it; they had eaten there once before.

Greg ordered scallops. He loved scallops. They were great in the white cream sauce that the restaurant made. He had a couple of red wines and a great salad. Goldie waited until he was through with the salad and was comfortably eating his scallops.

"Honey, do you remember last night? I told you that I am pregnant with twins?"

Greg stopped eating and stared into her eyes. He looked for what seemed to be the longest time. Then he shuddered, "You told me that?"

"Yes. You were a little tired and went to bed, but I did tell you."

"Twins? Do you know if they are boys or girls?"

"The doctor said he thought they were boys."

"You could still have an abortion. I don't know if I want to raise twin boys. I don't know if I even like kids. Will it stop you from working?"

"No, honey, I'll keep working. As for an abortion, you know how I feel about that. Can I ask you a question?"

"Yeah, go ahead," he answered, taking another bite and not looking up.

"Where do you work? I'm not trying to be nosey but we're married and I'm carrying your twins and I know you don't work for Mercedes Benz. So where do you work? How come you have so much money sometimes and other times you need five from me just to get some coffee. Do you have a bank account that I don't know about? Where do you go at night if you're not working for the car company? How…"

Greg interrupted. "Look, I paid the rent this month and I bought groceries. What the hell else do you need to know?"

"I need to know what my husband does. I'm part of you. We are a team and we are having a couple of other people come to us from Heaven. I need to know."

"Okay, bitch, you wanna know. Great. I'll tell you what I do. I'm a drug dealer. Not just your average street dealer, no. I'm one of the main guys. I distribute and move my product to the second-level people. I also sell to street dealers. I am increasing the size of my area. The guy I met in Redding needed some oil. He was having a hard time getting what he needed because of a bust, so I moved in and set him up. It's a little way to drive, but it's good money. So there you have it, I'm a drug dealer."

"How can you do that? You know, everyone knows, what drugs do to people. It destroys life and ruins our kids. How can you do it?"

Goldie was truly surprised. She was in fact shocked. She couldn't believe what she was hearing.

"I do it because first it pays very well, secondly because the whities of this world have oppressed me and I can't get a good job, so I do what I can to make a living. And also because I get whatever I want in drugs for free. And while we're talking, I'd like to add that you can't testify against me because we're married. Also remember this, bitch, if you ever so much as mention to anyone, I mean anyone, that I deal, I'll kill you and the kids in you!"

Goldie sat silent. She was in shock. She shook her head slowly. She began to cry, not audibly, but tears rolled down her cheeks and she began to tremble. She bit her lower lip so hard that it began to bleed. Greg, seeing her reaction, reached over and took her arm. She tried to pull away but he griped it hard and pulled her to himself.

"Look, I still love you, you are my wife and you have my babies in your body. I don't want you to leave and I don't want you mad at me. I've got a big score coming in two weeks and we can take a few days and go on a trip. I'll stay out of trouble and I'll cut down on my meth."

Golden knew what meth was, but she didn't realize he was using it. Apparently that was why he would sleep all day after he had been going all day and all night.

"You can't go home," he said. "Nobody in Minnesota would accept you with two black babies and no dad. Besides, I won't let you go home. If you try to leave me I will hunt you down and kill you and your parents."

"You say you love me in one breath and in the next you say you're gonna kill me. What kind of love is that? I don't think you love me at all and I don't know if I still love you! But you're right, I've no place to go, even Wendy wouldn't take me pregnant, it would ruin her lifestyle. So here I am, stuck," she said, trembling. Silent tears ran down her cheeks. She didn't shout, she just softly said it.

"Look, we can make it. You work and earn pretty good money. I bring in a lot of money too. I'll buy you a house and get you some nice clothes. We'll be okay."

"I don't want any of your druggie friends coming around my house. I don't want to see them. I'll have to think about us, but for now I don't want you touching me!"

Golden knew she had some new control over her husband. She was scared about his threats, but she knew that he would be scared too. If she told on him he'd go to prison, so she knew she had some power. Now she was going to use it.

XIII

Birth

Months passed. Goldie called her mom almost weekly. She worked at the phone company and improved the stats so well that she got a Christmas bonus. Greg kept his word and they went on a very nice trip. He spent lavishly on her; in fact, Golden hadn't realized how much money Greg had. They went down the peninsula of Baja, California, and stopped in several fishing villages. They took a ferry across the Gulf of California to Masatlan and stayed in a very nice motel there. Golden was showing and so she bought a single piece bathing suit, which she put on when they went swimming. They swam in the ocean and in the beautiful pools the resort had. They ate great food. Finally Golden let Greg make love to her. She was internally unhappy with his drug dealing, but he had been so nice and had not mentioned since the date at Red Lobster anything about his business.

He brought more money home and made sure she took her vitamins. All in all he was a good husband. He still stayed out some nights, but Goldie was working anyway and so it was actually better. Sometimes he'd come home and sleep beside her all day. Sometimes he'd sleep for two days straight. But usually when she came home, she'd make him some breakfast and a cup of mud and he'd leave. He bought a new car. Goldie didn't like it; it was a Cadillac Le Mans, a sporty convertible that Golden thought would be good for picking up girls, and she resented a little that her husband was out on the streets with a new convertible while she was at work. But in general the marriage was going well. They argued almost every day about some point or other, but Greg did try to treat her better now that she was pregnant.

※

Golden had started going to church almost every Sunday for the past four months. Greg accompanied her only twice, but she had decided to go with or without her husband. Her schedule changed and sometimes she had to work Sundays, but she'd go after work if there was a meeting scheduled after noon. She didn't go to the place on the southwest side of LA; she went to a Lutheran church near her home and work. It was a mostly white congregation but the minister was open about her marriage and treated her well. There were also several Afro-Americans in the crowd too. Goldie had picked them out the first day and went to talk with them. They were pleasant and a couple of them had children. The two younger men knew her husband and she wondered how.

※

Golden was now very pregnant and her due date was coming up fast. She couldn't sit well and she couldn't stay standing for more than an hour or so. At the last visit to the doctor, he said it could be any time. He was right. Golden was on the job and solving an overseas calling problem when her water broke. She called the hospital and told them she was coming in. One of the girls at work insisted that she drive Goldie to the hospital because she thought Golden couldn't make it alone. The North Hollywood hospital was only fifteen minutes away and with late night traffic it was no problem getting there. Golden had started labor the minute her water broke and by the time they got to the hospital, the pains were coming fast and hard. Goldie called Greg on the cell phone she had given him and told him she was having the baby. He said he'd be there as soon as he could.

Labor was only three and a half hours, which surprised Golden because she had read that first births take longer and especially with twins. Both babies were delivered and both looked good. They were boys. Goldie had called her mom too. It was almost three when her water broke, which would be six in Minnesota, so she knew Mom would be up cooking breakfast. They had talked yesterday morning for a couple of minutes. Mom comforted her and reminded her to pray and thank the Lord for the babies.

She fell asleep after the birth and was awakened by Greg who showed at about 8:30 a.m.

"I saw the kids," he said when she had barely opened her eyes. "They look good. Have you seen them?"

"Of course, honey, I was there when they were born. They brought them in about an hour ago and I nursed them. Wow, that's gonna be a handful."

"They don' t look like me," Greg said.

"Honey, all kids are born puffy and wrinkly. Give them a couple of days and I think you'll see that they have your eyes and nose."

"You gonna continue nursing them?" he asked with an implication that he didn't approve.

"Yes. Momma nursed me and in school I learned that babies get a lot of good immunities from my milk. Besides, it's a way to show that I love them."

THE EYE OF THE BEHOLDER

"Are you sure they're mine? They are white and have blond hair."

The question upset Goldie. She had been faithful. In her heart she still didn't trust Greg, but she hadn't any evidence that he cheated on her. Still there were sometimes several days that would pass where they didn't make love. Not like when she first married him. He wanted to make love every day, sometimes twice or three times a day.

"I have never made love with another man. Ever in my life. You know that."

Greg did know it but it surprised him that the babies were white with light hair. Both had blue eyes. They were identical twins, not paternal, and they were really beautiful.

Even Greg had to admit they were the best looking babies in the nursery.

Greg left. Goldie stayed in the hospital for only two days. The doctor would have released her a day earlier but one of the twins was a little jaundiced and he wanted to make sure it cleared.

Golden was resourceful. She got permission to go downstairs to the nursery and nurse the babies four times each night. She had to hire a baby tender because the company nursery was only open during the day, but she talked with Maria and Donald, the vice president of that office, and they gave her permission to have the babies on property at night during her shift. They mostly slept during her shift, but three or even four times a shift she'd have to go down and nurse them. She took her mobile phone that the company rigged to connect to any outside callers the girls referred to her. Golden began to love her children. She began to understand some of what her mother was trying to teach her. She began to understand some of the struggles her mother had faced. She began to mature again.

When she first changed the babies' diapers, she was disgusted and sickened by the smell, sight, and mess. But that changed. She loved the babies and they needed her. Greg was very little help with the children. He had become more of a boarder than a husband. Occasionally he would be kind and take Goldie out for dinner, but generally he would leave if she had been too busy with the babies to make him the exact kind of dinner he wanted. He stayed out more lately and came home only to sleep. They didn't talk about his business; Goldie would keep the strange things she found in his pockets in the cabinet by the bed. Occasionally she would take three or four hundred dollars from his wallet when he came home with a load of cash and leave him a note that rent or the phone or the water or something was due. He would always question her about it the next day or when he was up when she got home.

The twins grew. They stayed blond haired and blue eyed. Greg played with the children very little, and Goldie didn't care. She called her mother and told her about the children and both Grandma and Grandpa sent gifts. They finally came out to California for a visit when the children were just turning two. Greg had gone up to Redding, on purpose, to avoid meeting them. It really hurt Golden's feelings. Greg was Greg. Golden had begged him to quit dealing. She pointed out that they could make enough money to get by with her job and if he would just get a real job. He could do anything he wanted, she didn't care, but in spite of it all, she still loved him and worried that he would get caught by the police or, worse, be shot by another dealer.

Mom begged her to come "home." She said that GTE also had offices in Minnesota and that she could get a job there too. Dad was his loving, soft-spoken, unassuming self. He loved the twins and nicknamed them Jay and Jayjay. They could only stay a couple of days and when they left they left Golden with a little money, which they instructed her to use only on the grandkids and herself. Mom regretted not having met Greg, but Dad said he knew the guy was up to no good, else why wouldn't he meet his in-laws? He also invited Golden to come home. She said she would consider it.

It wasn't that Goldie didn't want to go home. She was falling out of love with Greg a little more each day. There were times when he was so good, and there were times when he was not so good. He wasn't home nearly as much as he had been before the kids were born, and if Goldie didn't steal the money from his wallet, he would never offer to pay anything. They had moved to another apartment when the kids turned two. One bedroom was just too little. Goldie had gotten two more raises since the birth of the children and had put in for a day shift. Maria had been promoted to general manager over the entire external communications department. Goldie continued to have the best stats in the department and her girls loved her.

One Tuesday morning when Goldie was reporting to Maria, Maria told her of an ad Kimberly Clark diapers had put in the paper for kids to model their wears. Maria thought Goldie's kids were really beautiful and she had always said they should be in the movies, so she told Goldie about the ad. Goldie thought it was a good idea and when she got home she told Greg about it. Greg was still up and changing his clothes. He agreed. "Yeah, let's take 'em down and see if they can do anything besides eat."

The babies did really well. Jackson was the best behaved, and he preformed so well that the director said he was a natural. Jason fussed a little but was better because he laughed in front of the camera and the director was overjoyed at that.

The studio said they'd call Goldie if they decided to use the kids. Goldie was really happy. On the way home she couldn't stop talking about how great the babies were.

"I'm sure they'll use our kids!" she said to Greg, who drove without saying anything.

"If they do, don't use our last name. I don't want a million fans coming around our house."

"Oh, honey, fans don't come to babies' houses, that's just for the bigger people. People who vicariously satisfy their own need to be famous or to have sex appeal or to have money or to sing etc., etc., but no one ever comes to ooh and ahh over babies."

A week passed and the call came. The Kimberly Company offered them a thousand dollars a shoot. Goldie was to bring the babies with a change of clothes, diapers, and food. They said a shoot might take five or six hours. The number of times they'd shoot the babies would depend on how the first commercial did.

The commercials did great. After the first television program came on with babies, they got five more calls from other advertisers. Greg said he'd negotiate the price of the shoots, but it turned out that the companies would only pay up to two thousand dollars for each shoot. They had a set price and it wasn't negotiable. This wasn't stardom; it was commercialism at its best. They said kids were a dime a dozen and they could get other children easily. They said that the only value of the twins was that they were first twins and second that they were very good on stage. Also it saved them from running an ad and interviewing and screening a million other kids. Goldie was excited and had called her mom and dad. She told them when to watch the kids on TV. Mom was delighted but felt it might be commercializing the kids too much. She said don't take too many contracts; the kids need time with their mother and not as much time out on stage.

For the next year and a half the kids did commercials once or twice a week. Other companies such as clothes for kids and toys for kids and baby food and high chairs and safety seats and even floor wax were calling and using the kids in their commercials. The twins had a great appeal. First they were identical and so they were interchangeable, and second, seeing them together was enjoyable for the viewer. Moms quickly attached themselves to the twins, and in the supermarket Goldie would often have some mother recognize the twins and come over and talk. Most women were great, but there were some who were either jealous or vicariously living out a dream through Goldie and her twins. All in all it was usually fun and sometimes tiresome.

The fact that Goldie worked nights was a blessing. Even though she had put in for days, nights allowed her to take the kids to shoots and gave her time to get them ready and now they had developed a routine. Even Greg worked much of his day around Goldie's schedule. Goldie didn't get much sleep, especially on the days she had to get the kids ready for filming and take them and bring them back.

Greg was zero help. He grumbled a lot when Goldie didn't get home in time to fix his dinner. That is when he was there. Many a night she would fix a good dinner and he wouldn't make it. Their relationship deteriorated even more. Greg stayed in it because Goldie was making as much as he and she stayed in it because deep in her heart she felt it was better for the kids to have a father, any father, than none at all. Besides, she couldn't go back now. Her job was good to her and she felt needed there. The kids were great and she loved them. She had stashed about ten thousand dollars from the kids' filming by telling the contractor that she wanted 20% of their money put into an account for the kids. Goldie was smart; she had gotten an agent early on and he did all the contracts. All she had to do was show up with clean and cute babies. The set people re-dressed the kids and fed them and even had a teacher on set for when they were waiting for lights or set men or any other of a million things that always made a shoot two or three hours longer than the contractor had said.

A family magazine came and asked to shoot the kids just before going on set. They offered to pay six hundred and fifty dollars so Goldie said yes. She took the money and stashed it. The problem is that there are counters and noncounters in this world. Greg was a counter, Goldie was not. Goldie thought that money should be used as needed and taken care of, but not hoarded and especially not counted as the worth of the person who owned it. She was like her father; money was necessary to get things done, it was a means to an end. Not Greg; he thought it was the end. It was hard to keep a savings; Greg would withdraw large amounts and promise to replace it. Occasionally he did but within a month he'd withdraw it out again. Goldie knew she couldn't take more out of the kids' money or he'd figure it out. He had to look at every check and then criticize the agent for not getting a better contract. He threatened to call the agent several times, especially when he was drunk or high, but Goldie always gave him the office number and, of course, at ten at night, no one was there.

For the most part Greg had stopped being affectionate. He still demanded making love every time he came home, but even in lovemaking he had stopped saying the things that made Goldie fall in love with him in the first place. Still Golden hung on. She frequently begged him to stop with the drug dealing. She said they made enough money he didn't need to do that anymore. He could get a decent job and she would help and they'd make it just fine. But Greg always argued that without his money they'd never make it. LA was a tough place to live and it was expensive.

There were the early mornings when Goldie came home to find Greg up and waiting for her. It was always the same; he needed money. Golden had told him she needed to have her own checking account because she needed to keep track for taxes and for the kids. He granted her an account but insisted that his name be on the withdrawal form so he could get money "in case anything happened to her." She agreed but found that he frequently would withdraw money and forget to tell her.

Sometimes on weekends they would send the kids to the baby tender. Goldie didn't trust the baby tender. She thought she was a druggie and that Greg kept the money she gave him to pay her and instead gave her drugs. As the weekends passed, Goldie found herself drinking. She even took some ecstasy and some coke. She was scared of coke but ecstasy didn't seem to be addictive and so she found herself taking it occasionally. It was easy to get from Greg, and he delighted in her taking it. It seemed to smear her sainthood. She reasoned that because Greg seemed to love it so much, there must be something to it. She smoked a joint a couple of times with him when she got off work. Just to relax. But she found she didn't think as well that night when she went back to work and she could see herself putting things off that she normally would do right away. It made her too casual, so she stopped.

Greg still hit her occasionally. Maria said to leave the bastard and put a restraining order on him. One morning, a Saturday, just after getting home from work, Goldie found Greg there in the kitchen sitting, smoking a joint. The kids were awake and crying in the bedroom.

"How long have the kids been crying?" she said.
"Who gives a shit. You feed 'em, they're your kids!"
"They're your kids too."
"I'm not so sure. They sure as a hell don't look like me."
"I don't know what you mean by that. If you're implying that I had sex with someone else, you couldn't be more wrong. I have never made love with any other man in my life. You know that, I have told you a hundred times."

One of the problems with druggies is that you have to repeat everything to them ten or twelve times. Then after a couple of days you have to start over and re-repeat again. Greg answered, "Yeah, well, they're not exactly black, are they?"

"No, they did not inherit your skin color, but they are definitely your kids."

Goldie sometimes thought they were hard to control and seemed spoiled. Still she loved them. In many ways Goldie still loved Greg too. She couldn't help herself; sometimes he was kind and good, usually when he was sober. When he was not on pot or meth he sometimes would show that he really cared for the children. Sometimes he actually treated Goldie with love and respect. He still promised to quit using and dealing when he wanted love or sex or food, but it never happened and Goldie soon realized that it never would happen. She was stuck with this man and there was nothing she could ever really do to change him. She had his children and she had a job. She really enjoyed her job. The people loved her and she was very good at solving problems. She had gotten raises and commendations for her good work. Her mom frequently coaxed her to come back to Minnesota but she couldn't go back to Angora, there was no way. She had come too far and become another person. The girl she left behind was gone. She wasn't even sure her mother really knew her now. She was stuck. Both by choice and circumstance. Even Greg had said she was stuck. He still threatened her with the death of her parents if she told on him or left him. Goldie never did tell her mother that Greg was into drugs. She knew what her dad would do. She wouldn't endanger him, not her dad, he was too important to her.

Once Jay offered to bring her home, pay for any college or university she wanted to go to, and take care of the kids while she got trained. He said she didn't have to clean the stalls and all she'd have to do was get on the airplane. Goldie didn't say much. She knew Greg would kill both her parents if she left him. She just quietly declined.

So Goldie was trapped, trapped by her own choices and her own foolishness. Trapped by her desire to discover and by her naivete. She was trapped by her children and by the love she had for a man who turned out to be untrue. One who had turned out to be all the things she had spoken against in high school and the kind of man, in her heart, she hated.

Life was beginning to be difficult for Goldie. She now had to struggle with the children, with her job, with her husband, and with all the social implications, which were constantly crashing down on her. She was beginning to understand the fact that her husband was a druggie. What that meant and what it meant for her. It was very inhibiting; she had to be careful about what she said and did. She had to be careful about her car and her house and even her garbage. Greg had taught her how to play the game and even though she was not a dealer, she had to play. She had to protect her husband. So she had to deal with people who would meet her husband every time they would go to dinner or to the show. They all would look at her suspiciously and Greg would sometimes send her away and sometimes have her watch for cops. She now knew how to spot a user in a second. They all had the look. Most of them were paranoid and the rest were washed out, either mentally or emotionally. All of them showed in the face fear or nervousness.

She was constantly on the lookout for the police. When she drove she always watched her mirrors and found herself downing the cops, even though she had never been mistreated by one of them and as a child she had been taught to respect and admire them. But now they were enemies. People to be feared. She did not want to get pulled over and she did not want to answer any questions from them. So she always drove the speed limit, stayed in the center lane, and signaled for every lane change and turn.

There were other things, other elements. Her husband didn't love her anymore but for some reason, probably the money, he hung on to her. She thought maybe he liked owning another human being. Perhaps he liked the power it gave him. His drug dealing went up a step. He was made a senior partner and manager in a cartel running LA. With the change he got less kind and less considerate. Perhaps the stress of the children combined with his work. But it translated into the same thing; he was unpredictable and dangerous. Goldie never, never asked about how his work was going. It was important to her not to know. She didn't want to know because if he should get caught she could honestly tell the police she knew nothing. He was gone a lot more now then he had been before. He would sometimes leave for two or three days and not call or even give her warning that he was leaving or when he'd be coming home.

Early in August of their fifth year of marriage he came home and told her he had lost the car permanently. It was a major turning point. He didn't say it but it was clear he was demoted. They took away his car and put him back on the street. Now he was borrowing money from her almost daily and his portion of the rent was seldom paid. Goldie was doing very well at work. She was in line to move up to days because one of the day shift managers had quit. Maria still really loved Goldie and they had now become more than just supervisors and employees; they had become real friends and went out to lunch frequently. Goldie also now frequently hired baby tenders to watch the children during the day. She didn't sleep much, maybe four or five hours per night. Greg was sleeping more now. He was taking more drugs and so, of course, Goldie slept less, took care of the kids, and did all the shopping and other household duties in addition to working a fifty-hour week. She was still working nights and got home about 8:00 a.m. Greg was seldom up and usually wasn't even there. He very seldom was awake or waiting for Goldie anymore. When he was there he'd demand breakfast, would gobble it up, and then just grunt. He seemed to be smoking more and more marijuana now besides the meth and other drugs he was taking. It was hard for Goldie to understand; it made both him and her unhappy. Why would someone persist in behavior that was self-defeating and destructive? Behavior that destroyed the most important things in the world, their wives and children? It didn't make sense to her.

He had begun to hit her again. She called the police a few times. They'd come, talk with him and her, and he'd promise never to do it again. He was never arrested because usually Goldie would deny anything had happened. She seldom had facial bruises so the cops couldn't see any damage. When they left Greg would apologize for hitting her but reinforce that if she ever told on him again he'd kill her. She believed him.

The children were really beautiful. They were so cute and so precious, they were learning to talk and walk and Goldie loved it. The people with the commercials loved it too; she had more offers than she could possibly take. The kids were making as much money in one shoot of three or four hours than she made in a week's worth of work at GTE. Some days if they got two shoots done in a day she'd get $3,000. Goldie was making less than fifteen hundred every two weeks so it was nice that the children brought in the extra money. They moved in to a nice three-bedroom beautiful apartment near downtown Hollywood. It was expensive but well appointed and close both to work and to the studio where they usually shot the kids' commercials.

There were many nights when Greg would come and talk with Goldie and they would share their time and even their love together. Greg didn't make love like he used to; still Goldie loved the time together and when Greg wasn't on drugs he was usually kind and considerate and even loving. He didn't ask to make love every time he was home anymore. Goldie thought he might be having an affair. She knew how very, very sexually active he had always been. Goldie would ask him about it but he seldom told her anything except how very much he would like their marriage to continue. And even to improve. Goldie wanted the marriage to improve too. But she doubted if would. It was just that she had been trained to be so against drugs. She had never liked them. Even in high school she was occasionally offered a joint but she always threatened to tell on the seller so they stopped offering. But now she was living with a man who sold them. He sold to all buyers, even children. He sold to people who would damage their income, sacrifice their families, violate all their personal integrity, and would do almost anything just to get a hold of more self-gratification.

They still went places, out to dinner, or to a mini golf course, or to a movie. Goldie sometimes would get four days off on a weekend and they'd go north or east for a couple of days. Greg always would leave the family at night to do some business. Goldie had acquired about three weeks' paid vacation so one evening late on Saturday night when she did not have to work she sat down with Greg and said, "Let's go on a vacation, sweetheart."

Even Greg thought it was a good idea to go on another honeymoon. Goldie said they could make life good again. She wanted to make her marriage work. She was getting desperate. Life was stagnant for her. Unless it changed, she knew the marriage would collapse.

"We could look for a real job for you. I know we could find one that you could do and it would make me and the kids so happy and proud of you."

Greg answered that he was getting back "up" in the company and soon he would be re-promoted. He did say that he'd consider the different job idea but that he needed a couple of weeks off.

They decided to go south, maybe down along old Highway 395 and then cross over to Highway 10 and go east, passing through Texas and on over to Florida. They'd have three weeks of paid vacation. Goldie really wanted to do some good with it. She wanted to repair her marriage and she also wanted to scoot up to Minnesota and see her mother and father. Goldie figured that her father needed to meet Greg and spend some time with him.

She called Mom and asked if she could come home for a few days. Goldie knew there was a rift in her relationship with her father but she loved him and she knew he loved her. She still knew better than to tell him what Greg did for a living. Goldie sensed that Jason knew something was wrong with Greg and his employment, so the negative feeling stood and there really was no cure for the difference. Still she was anxious to go back to the farm, to the home of her childhood, and see it again. See her mother again and hug her dad again. In spite of all the differences she knew they would love the children and would be really glad to see her.

Mom knew the truth, or at least sensed it. She would often tell

Goldie on the phone to leave Greg even if she didn't want to come home. She'd say she didn't understand Greg's nature. Goldie knew if she left him he'd kill her or worse the children. So, all things considered, her mom's arguments didn't matter. Goldie couldn't leave her job and she couldn't leave her husband. She had become a woman and she could not go home again.

They went down to El Paso and went across the border into Juarez and spent a little money. They bought a piñata for the twins and ate at a restaurant. Greg had some Tres X's beer. You usually can't get it in the states; they sell Dos X's but not Tres X's. So Greg enjoyed the lunch/dinner and they stayed the night at the old Coronado hotel in El Paso. They had made arrangements to meet the Kimberly Clark Company in Chicago to shoot the kids in a commercial for training pants. The children had to meet with producers first and then they would shoot the commercial. They had to remain in Chicago for three days but they got an extra three thousand dollars so Greg was pretty happy about it.

They were scheduled to go to St. Paul in Minnesota where they'd get the opportunity to shoot the children again. The producer so liked the children that he made arrangements for a second commercial. It was wonderful; every time they shot the children they got a check that allowed them to continue their vacation with more money. Greg went out in Chicago for the evening, leaving Goldie at the hotel alone. She got the hotel babysitter to come and watch the kids and she went down to the bar. She made it a point not to drink at all during the week, but on her days off, or when Greg would clearly choose drugs over her, she would go get a couple of drinks. She seldom got drunk, but she did drink until she felt a buzz or until she felt nothing. She wondered how long she could continue to sell the kids in commercials before they would not be useful to the baby companies. What would she do then?

Greg in most ways on this vacation was really good to Golden. The vacation was great for both him and Goldie and good for the twins too. It was even especially good for Greg who could buy all the drugs he wanted for himself. At least he wasn't selling. At last they arrived in Angora, Minnesota. It was beautiful there and Goldie sighed a deep heartfelt relief at finally being where she grew up. He house seemed like the same palace in the same field and the same barn, the same mommy and daddy. But they were older and wiser now. Goldie noticed things about her mother that she had never noticed as child. She noticed the stately dignity of her father who, even though he was nothing but a dairy farmer, had great wisdom and great understanding.

The first night they ate dinner quietly. Greg complimented Goldie's mother several times about the delicious meal. The next day they went to the woods where Goldie showed Greg where she swam in the ice cold water and where she played as a child. She took him to her high school and introduced him to her high school teacher. The teacher didn't react well, but was very polite and really sincerely loved the children.

Goldie told Greg all the things that made her who she was. She even told him the story about the lion and Wendy. Goldie was so very different than when she had left six years before and yet inside and in her mind she was still the same. She had matured, she realized and understood life in ways that her parents never had or in their present circumstances never could. Still, she was glad to be reunited with her parents. Even if it was for a short period of time, she was home and happy. Happy in a way that she had never been before. She understood now more than she ever had in her life. She re-fell in love with her parents. They were so good. Jay was even kind to Greg and not once made reference to his race or fatherhood.

It was their second night in Angora and had to be their last. They all gathered at the dinner table at about 7:30. It was after a day of traveling and seeing the town and surrounding area. Goldie even went horseback riding which Greg. He was a horrible rider and fell off twice. He couldn't get the horse to turn and couldn't get it to go forward even after kicking it and swearing at it. Goldie laughed and laughed. She thought Greg's adaptability in the country would have been better. It was good for her. She was on top here. All of her life with Greg had been in the city. He was in charge there. He knew the streets and the people there. He was good at city life but he did not know the country. It was different here. It was as though Goldie had come back to the kind of life she knew. She realized then and there that she would have to come home. LA wasn't really her home. This was. The thought took hold in her mind and in her subconscious. She began to plan a way to escape.

After dinner Greg went up and went to sleep. Goldie sat on the swing on the front porch. Mother came out and sat beside her.

"Goldie, you know we love you. We love the children; they've been such a joy to tend and to take care of. I know you were always true to Greg but I don't think he deserves you. He is not a good man. Jay says that he sees in him some very dark places and your father is afraid he might hurt you. Has he ever hit you?"

"No, Mama, he hasn't," Goldie said with hesitancy.

"We can't understand why they are blond haired and blue eyed. Even you aren't blond." Marge looked deep into Goldie's eyes.

"Oh, Mama, I don't know why it happened that way. Who cares, the children have been such a joy to me. They are my life. I've been little upset at having to put them in daycare and to have to show up to get them ready for a shoot after I've been working all night. But they bring in more than three thousand dollars a month. That's more than I make. I've gotten hundreds of offers for contracts from different companies. They even wanted the kids to act in a television series. But I just couldn't do it. It would mean I'd have to quit my job, and they really need me at work. I'm important there and I'm loved. The kids are so good at home and I love them so much. It would be really hard to come home now. And yet, I feel such a comfort here. And I know that I was not really meant for life in Los Angeles. I just don't know what to do. I really don't."

"Dad thinks that your husband uses drugs. He probably is spending your money to buy 'em."

Marge was speaking to Goldie assuming that she didn't know. She spoke to her like she was still in high school. Goldie understood. Mom hadn't been there, she didn't know.

"Mom, I know he sells and uses drugs. But I'm trying to get him to quit. I thought if I brought him out here he might see the other possibilities in this world and quit."

"Your father had better not find out about this. He would kill him, honey, you know he would. He'd take his gun and kill the man."

"I know, Momma, please don't tell him. I love Dad and all it would do is get him thrown in jail. It wouldn't change anything. I think when I go back to California, I'm going to file for divorce."

Marge wasn't as dumb as Goldie had thought. She answered, "He'll threaten you. He'll probably try to force you to stay. If you leave and divorce him then you can tell on him and he's probably really scared of that. So please leave him first and then get a restraining order on him and then file for divorce."

"Okay, Mom, I'll call you and tell you when it's started. I love you. I'm sorry that I…"

Mom interrupted, "You don't have to be sorry. You trusted, you loved, and you have the most beautiful children I have ever seen. I love you, Goldie."

Mom had always said she knew Goldie would find her own way. She was sad that her daughter had fallen in love with a "no account" drug dealer. It was a slap in the face to her. She thought of all the things she had taught he daughter. All the things she had learned in school. It was an assault on all that her father believed. Marge knew she couldn't tell Jay. And yet she had never in all their years of marriage kept anything from him. She had never deceived him and while they, like most of us, had had some quarrels, by and large they lived in trust and honesty. She knew Jay absolutely despised druggies and in particular those who sold them.

Their parting was sweet and Goldie longingly kissed her daddy. She kissed her mama and smiled. The smile was one of those "I trust you, please don't let me down" kind of smiles.

Marge pulled her close to her and looked deeply into her eyes. She whispered in her ear, "Sweetheart, you don't have to do this. You don't have to live like this. You can come home anytime you want. I'd love to help you with the kids. Just think about it." She then kissed her on the cheek as she walked to the car were Greg was waiting impatiently.

They said their goodbyes and Grandma kissed the children. Grandpa gave them some dulse de leche drops and took their 50th picture.

The drive home was long and tiring. They took Highway 80 mostly and stopped at a couple of places. On the way they stopped in Salt Lake City at the Stockton Tree Hotel. They got the kids to bed and made love. Greg was excited. In fact more excited than he had been in many months. Still his lovemaking was not the same as it had been. It was different for Goldie now too because she was beginning to know she would leave him. Even though she was afraid he might hunt her down and try to hurt her, she hoped that if she moved home, her dad would protect her. She did want to be through with him. She did want out of the marriage; it had gone full circle. He and she had been married six years; Goldie had improved and increased her earnings and her ability to earn. By herself she had become the shift manager and had gotten several awards and three raises. She had increased the percentage of her check that they put away for retirement. She had put double indemnity on her personal insurance and gave it specifically to the twins. She had also increased the amount of savings she put away. In all she was a very careful planner. And now she was ready to leave him.

She thought she might get a job with GTE in St. Paul. That wasn't too far from Mom and Dad. Maybe, just maybe, she'd meet a good man there. One who was willing to take the twins and love her.

Maybe that was hoping for too much. She thought she'd settle for just a little house and a job with GTE. She was pretty sure she could get that. Goldie knew that the money from the kids wouldn't last forever. Sooner or later they would outgrow their attractiveness and the companies would stop calling. So even though she had gotten bonuses and three raises, she still brought approximately the same amount home. Greg didn't know the difference. He had never worked a steady job in his life. She just told him that the phone company was cutting back and so nobody got raises this year. He never looked at her check because she had it direct deposited. When he needed money he'd look at the balance on the checkbook and take whatever he needed. Sometimes it would leave them short, but Goldie always had spare money from the kids' commercials and money she put into a separate account that Greg didn't know about. She kept the savings book in her desk at work. She knew she would have to provide for the family.

The children were fussy sometimes and Greg would yell at them. Goldie would have them stop at McDonald's and get the kid's meal. The kids loved it and they loved the toy that came with meal. The kids would get hamburger dressing and lettuce all over their car seats and all over the rest of the back of the car, but in general they were great and Goldie loved them.

※

It was late Saturday evening when they finally pulled into their apartment in Hollywood. Exhausted, Goldie tucked in the children and Greg went to the bedroom to lie down. He was not down for long when the telephone rang; not the regular house phone but his cell phone, the one that Goldie had bought and given to Greg to keep in touch with him. Later she learned that he used it to call the dealers under him. So Goldie had unknowingly provided him with free access to all of the dealers. In fact she could easily be charged with being an accessory to his drug activities. He said he had to go, she nodded, and he left. She bolted the door closed after he'd gone. He'd have to knock to get in because she also put the door chains on the door too. Greg had bought a blue Camaro. He was constantly fixing it. Goldie still had the little ol' VW.

She had asked Greg for a new car several times. Greg would say no, that the VW was good enough and he didn't want to spend more money on a new car when this one worked good enough. It was true; the VW had not ever broken down. It started every time and had been extremely reliable. She said she had wanted really badly to get a bigger car, mostly for the kids. She said that they could not sit comfortably in the back of the little Volkswagen. Greg sat in the front when he went with them to do a shoot or when his Camaro wasn't working. He said it wasn't that the car was that much too small or could not accommodate them, it was that it wasn't the kind of car she wanted as a manager for GTE. He was right, Goldie wanted something with a little more class. She was even sometimes embarrassed to take the children to the set because they came in an old Volkswagen. Every time she asked Greg he would say absolutely not, they were fine with what they had. Goldie worried about Greg's Camaro. It didn't work well. It would quit and break down frequently. But Greg loved it. He had built into it some compartments, which were impossible to be accessed without some special tools. So when it broke down he'd have to spend enormous amounts of time and money repairing it. That irritated Goldie because it was generally her money. There were times when Greg came home with a lot of money. One evening he came home with $30,000 cash. Goldie asked how much of it was theirs to spend and Greg said, "It's all mine."

Time drifted by. Goldie worked as a supervisor. In three weeks she got the shift change she had hoped for. It wasn't a promotion, but it was a significant increase in her status. She was a day supervisor. There were supervisors still on night shift and afternoon shift who had more time in than Goldie, but no one could deny Goldie's statistics. She had the lowest complaint record and the best worker attendance record. Only one of her girls had missed more than one day in six months. It was a reflection of her competence as a leader and her spirit as a friend. She had made friends with all her employees.

There is always one or two who deviate from the friendship type of management. Those who don't want to be friends with the boss. They need to complain and if they are friends with the object of their complaints, they become both hypocrites and, worse, not listened to. So they make it a point not to become friends with the boss. It feeds their "Oh, poor me!" complex.

Greg continued his selling. But there was something changed. He began to suspect that Goldie was planning on leaving him. Her behavior toward him had finally changed. She did not serve him like she used to. She did not stretch herself to make him coffee or dinner or even clean up the room. He was right; she had given up on the marriage and was looking for the opportunity to leave him. She had planned it out. She would leave him when he was away. She wanted to take her things. The things she had worked so hard for. She'd leave the TV and she'd leave the furniture but her jewelry, her clothes, her photos, and the kids with their clothes and things she had to take.

She made sure the car was registered only to her. She took Greg off the insurance policies including her personal policies at work. They wouldn't take him off the company life because they were still married and she had to get a power of attorney or other legal document disallowing him. She thought it too complex; besides, after she left him she'd close the accounts and collect whatever earnings had been made by the insurance. Also she had changed into her sole name the other account and the insurance on the kids plus the company retirement into which she had been putting double the amount as both insurance and a savings.

So Goldie waited to get all that arranged. She planned to leave him in nine months around December. It was May now so she had plenty of time to get the rest of the policies changed and to get the kids ready for the move. She had done it to her mom and dad and she loved them so she knew she could do it to Greg. She'd just leave. Goldie decided not to tell her parents that she was leaving until she was out the door. Her dad might try to come and get her or do something that might let Greg know. Jason was very protective and in that mode he could be dangerous.

Unbeknownst to Goldie, Greg also noticed the difference in treatment. He soon realized that Goldie was planning to leave him. On a late Thursday evening Greg had stopped off at the Cantina Bar. It was where he met his northwest side pushers. The usual scenario was to go to the bar and sit in the far corner table, order a couple of Dos X's and wait. The bartender would watch and see if anyone was watching or any new people were in the bar. After ten or fifteen minutes he'd call Iglesias and tell him that Greg was "in position." Iglesias would come. He lived around the corner and down Calle Blanca so it would only take him five minutes to get there. Iglesias would walk in, order a beer, and look for a place to sit. If Greg was in his usual seat, he'd walk over to him and ask him if he'd mind some company. If he used any other greeting Greg would know there was something wrong and would say "no," he'd rather drink alone.

This night all went as it usually did. Iglesias went to the bar and sat with Greg. Greg didn't give him a new supply. He took his money and then told him he'd deliver the stuff later tonight. He leaned over the table and said he needed to talk about another matter that was very important to him and ultimately to this end of the cartel.

"What'd ya got?" Iglesias asked.

"I married this blond bitch from Minnesota and she gave me a couple of kids. She's now thinking about leaving me. I wouldn't give a shit but she knows everything about my business and if she's not married to me, I know she'd rat."

"You only got one choice, man," Iglesias proffered.

"No, I got a couple or three. I can force her not to leave me by promising to kill her parents or the kids. Or I can let her go and take the kids. Or I can cap her. The last option has, obviously, some dangers. What'd think?"

"Like I said, I think there's only one option. Cap the bitch. You can always give the kids away. But she needs to disappear."

"Maybe I'm just paranoid. She probably won't rat. She'd probably go back to Minnesota and live with her parents."

"It's not her I'd be worried about. The cops will go to her. They will pressure her. You know the drill, they'll threaten her with charges of conspiracy, aiding and abetting, accessory to the crimes, etc. They'll promise to keep her out of prison if she rats. Believe me, amigo, she'll squeal like a pig. She's not gonna go to prison and leave her kids for a guy she doesn't love, for one she's planning on leaving anyway. I say off the bitch!"

"Okay, Ig. I'll think about it. I'll meet you back here in an hour. Thanks."

Greg got up and left. He didn't finish his beer. That had never happened before in ten years of dealing with Iglesias, never. An hour later Greg came in with a grocery bag. It was a double paper bag. He had gone to the store and bought a couple of items and asked for two of the big paper bags. Safeway offered either plastic or paper bags and they were glad to give him a much larger bag than the groceries needed. Greg would put the lettuce and bread and coffee on top of the drugs and carry it with one arm out of the car to the bar. Every week he'd change delivery methods and places, but they always first met at the bar. After checking the surroundings, Iglesias came and sat down by Greg. He said he'd bought some groceries for him. Greg took the bag without much conversation and left. Iglesias always wore peasant clothes. Farm worker type with a little mud on the pants and a torn dirty shirt. He was hard to mark as a pusher. He looked so very innocent and so sincere. Like an exploited farm worker who came to the US to feed his family. He wore a ring that helped with the image and he made sure someone very inexperienced cut his hair. It gave the appearance that he didn't have enough money to get a professional haircut so he had his wife cut it. He wore work boots with field mud on them. All in all Iglesias was a very hard dealer to spot. He drove an old Chevy and always obeyed the traffic laws.

Greg went back home. Goldie had fixed him dinner. She was consistent. She knew she had a duty and she had to fix dinner for the kids anyway so she usually fixed dinner for Greg. He seldom was there to eat it and often even if he was there he didn't eat. But tonight, now he had decided, he ate hardily. He complimented Goldie on her meal and said he didn't have to go out that evening. For an instant Goldie thought he might still love her. She thought she could be okay with him and maybe the marriage could be saved. It was only a passing thought. After a moment's thought, she re-resolved to leave him. That night he made love to her. It had been three weeks. But it was good. He was passionate and considerate of her feelings and needs. Goldie loved it when Greg treated her kindly and loved her. He even helped with the dishes and held Jackson while she changed Jason.

Goldie woke up in the morning happy and once again was reconsidering her decision to leave Greg. If he could be the way he was last night every night, she knew they could make it. She got dressed and dressed the kids. As she was leaving to take the kids to the daycare center, Greg called after her. She had gotten up early and fixed him his coffee just the way he liked it, so she was surprised when he called her. She walked into the bedroom where Greg was sitting on the corner of the bed with a cup of coffee in his hand.

"Yes, honey, what can I do for you?" she asked with honest sincerity.

"The VW has a couple of things I need to fix on it. I figured you could take the Camaro today and I'd work on the Bug."

Goldie had been asking him to fix the door latch. Sometimes when she drove it would come open when she went around a right corner. She had been asking him to fix the gas pedal too. It would sometimes stick and at a stop sign or corner and the engine would race. So she was pleasantly surprised when he offered to fix them. *Wow,* she thought, *I need to give him love more often.* She smiled and said, "Thanks, honey, I'd really appreciate that." He tossed her the keys to the Camaro and she bundled up the children and left.

Greg took the car to make a couple of deliveries. He stored most of his drugs in a storage shed, which was rented by a third party, who got a fourth party to actually do the renting. Greg always drove around the storage area twice before entering. If anyone was there loading or unloading he'd wait until they had left. The shed was in El Cajon down a dead-end road. It was built in a field that used to be a tomato farm. The farm went broke and the owner built the shed. There was almost no place someone could lay in on the shed and watch it without being seen. Greg knew the spots where one would have to hide to watch the shed and he always checked them before going to the shed. He never told his up line where he kept the stash and he never told his dealers. He never cooked in the shed either. And he made sure the front of the shed was filled with furniture.

This day he went to the shed, put together two packs for dealers, and put them in the VW. His Camaro had a secret compartment he had built to stash the drugs, which he usually used. Today he was extra careful and hurried to make the deliveries. In the back of the shed was a small steel safe. It had all his coke and a bunch of money in it. The meth was stored in the dresser, the third drawer down, and the pot he put in the bottom drawer of a white kitchen stove. Other pills and some horse were stored in plastic baggies and put behind a large picture with a removable back. To any agent worth his pay, their location would have been obvious. It was the only picture with the plastic clips holding the back of the painting on. You just swiveled them around and pulled the cardboard off the back. The picture frame was one of those deep gold lace, carved frames. This one was about two inches thick, which made for plenty of room behind the painting to stash baggies up to an inch thick. You could get fifteen or twenty bags into the frame with ease.

After the delivery, Greg went back to the shed. He was now stashing money in the safe. He'd stopped giving Goldie money, but he still paid for the rent and his car and insurance. She was responsible for all the food and clothes and utilities and her own car and insurance. She was also responsible for all the extras such as eating out, paying the daycare center, all the apartment furnishings, dishes, etc. And, of course, gasoline. Gasoline was expensive, so were clothes for the kids. They were still in diapers. Goldie was trying to get them trained, but to date she hadn't succeeded. Sometimes they were good and sometimes they were just babies. She had to buy the laundry detergent and pay for the washing and drying. All in all, Goldie was responsible for the entire house. Greg even had her pay some of the rent when he didn't have enough to make it.

Greg picked up from the shed a knife, sharpening stone, and some money. He then went to the wrecking yard just outside of El Cajon going toward El Centro. He wandered around the junkyard for almost an hour, looking at all the VWs on the lot. He found two that were the same year as Goldie's and carefully removed the hose for the gas, the wiring for the ignition and battery charger system, an entire break line, and the rubber connector on the steering column. He also picked up a new right front passenger seat. He paid for them and loaded it all into the VW and drove home. When he got home he parked the car in the back where he usually fixed the Camaro and very carefully replaced the front seat. Greg left the bolts loose so the seat would come out if the car got into a collision.

He then measured the gas line and the electrical line that came from the generator to the battery. He put all the things for the VW in his toolbox, put the box in the shed, and took the brake line into the house together with the sharpening stone.

In his room he set the brake line on his bed. He had crawled under the VW and found a place where the break line was attached to the underside of the car. He measured it both from the connection to the master cylinder and to the tire in front and marked exactly where the line would rub against the body frame if it came loose from its attachment to the wall of the car. He had to make sure that when he reattached this break line that he didn't leave any wrench marks on the attachment nuts and that he could put it exactly where the old one had been. Of course without the holding clamp.

He worked on the brake line for almost three hours. It was almost worn through, not quite, but almost. He then went out to the VW and crawled under it and also rubbed the stone against the wall of the car where it would rub naturally if it had come loose. He then removed the holding screw and clamp for the line at that point and loosened the screws that held the clamps in front and behind that place. He then returned to the apartment and got the entire brake line, took it downstairs, and installed it. He figured he'd install it now and it would in a few days break. He'd check it every day so he'd know exactly when it was about to give out.

The next thing was the gas line. The gas tank was in the front of the car and the engine was in the back. The gas line was metal up to where it connected to the filter just before going into the carburetor. The electrical wire that came from the distributor to the coil could be moved to cross the gas line. Greg thought that if he could shorten the wire and make it rub against the rubber gas line connection, it would wear through the line. If the rubbing stripped off the insulation of the wire, the electricity would ground when it hit the gasoline and the grounding spark would cause a fire. Probably not an explosion, but a fire that would spread rapidly through the car, melting the hose, which would cause more gasoline to pour from the tank and then cause the entire car to burn up. With luck this reaction would occur so rapidly that Goldie couldn't escape and be burned to death. It would also destroy any evidence of tampering with the breaks or the gas line.

One more piece of damage Greg planned to do. He'd wait until the break line began to leak and then replace the rubber connector on the steering wheel shaft. The steel shaft comes down the column from the steering wheel to the gearbox that connects it to the tires. Right at the point of connection there is a rubber disk that connects the steering shaft with the shaft coming out of the gearbox. If that breaks then there is no connection and thus no steering. But it couldn't happen too soon. First the new parts had to get some wear. They had to look like they were part of the car and that they had been there all along. This would take a week or two. So about a week before the brakes began to leak, Greg would replace the gas line and the connection disks and send her out. When the steering disk broke, Goldie would of course immediately push hard on the break, and with a little luck the action would lunge the break line and the steering column forward and finish splitting all three lines and the car would crash and burn. Greg put all his hopes in the plan. It wasn't foolproof, but Greg figured it was impossible to trace back to him.

Goldie continued to work. Now that she was on days, she worked directly under Maria. Of course she had always worked under Maria, but now she could go into her office and talk out a problem or discuss an employee. It was better because she now had time to get all that done on the job and didn't have to stay over on her own time.

One of the problems was that it was more difficult to take the children to their taping sessions. The commercial people had a specific schedule that could not be violated. They wanted the kids at the studio at a specific time and if they weren't there, they'd cancel the contract. Goldie was late only once. The director came to her and said, "There are no second chances in this business. We're paying for the set, the actors, the camera men, and a host of other costs, the least of which is your kids. Either have them here on time or we'll get someone who will."

With that he walked away. Goldie got the hint and was never late to another session. Maria was pretty good about letting her go early on the days when the kids were being shot. It was only a couple of times a month. Occasionally more, but in general every two weeks or so. Sometimes a month would go by and they'd not get a contract. They had an agent and he was pretty good about booking them for shoots. The types of commercials in which they could be shot were changing. They were no good for diapers now, but they still were good for baby food and for children's clothes and training pants.

It was the first week in June and Greg had been dumped again. He was passed over for the regional distributor because he used too much and he was way too familiar with his buyers. He not only knew them but also would smoke and shoot with them.

On Friday, Goldie came home at three forty-five in the afternoon. She had left the twins with Greg because he said he had nothing to do that day so she asked if he would watch them. It not only would save money from the daycare, but Goldie thought maybe Greg would enjoy being with his children. When she got home, he was sitting on the front porch of the apartment. It was an upstairs apartment, three bedrooms and two baths. Goldie liked to have her own bathroom, and Greg agreed, she could change the kids there and he didn't have to bother with the mess of their clothes and occasional potty accident.

The apartment had both an elevator and a staircase, which went upstairs. It was in a Spanish circular pattern with a lawn and swings downstairs in the middle of the apartment so the kids could play and not be able to go out into the street. Each apartment had a little veranda coming out of their front door onto which most of the tenants put a barbeque, little table, plants, or kids' toys. Around the veranda went the walkway, which connected the apartments upstairs to each other. So one could walk around the entire second floor on the walkway by going up any of the five stairways. It was an expensive apartment complex and had only two- and three-bedroom apartments. In addition to the playground for the children, it had a swimming pool with a kid's pool and a Jacuzzi.

Outside the ring of apartments on the backside was the parking lot. It had covered stalls and a large cement parking space for guests. You could get to the parking lot from your apartment by taking the elevator; the doors opened both front and back or you could also take the back stairs down to the parking lot. The management of the apartments had put a little gate on the back stairs ramp to keep the children from going out to the parking lot or worse to the road. The gate was about five feet high and keyed commonly to all the apartment keys. Parents could open it but the kids could not.

Each apartment had two car stalls, one of the features that convinced Golden to rent there. Greg parked his Camaro in the stall next to Goldie except when it was broken and he'd take it out to the guest parking lot, which was way too big to ever be filled up with guests, and work on it. The management would let tenets change a tire or even do brakes or change an air filter there but they didn't want an engine rebuild taking place on their property. Greg pushed the limits. He had the head off the Camaro twice and grease all over the ground. The management asked him to clean it up and to not do that kind of engine work on the apartment property again. He, of course, didn't comply.

So this day when Goldie got home, she found Greg, half asleep, smoking a joint on the veranda and one of the twins asleep in the high chair with a mess of food in front of him and all over the floor beneath him. She couldn't find the other twin. She first looked in the bedroom and then downstairs in the playground. She panicked. She woke Greg up, yelling at him, "Where is Jackson?"

Greg opened his eyes and rolled them upward and to the right. He sighed and said, "What the hell's your problem? I put him in the Bug because he wouldn't shut up."

Goldie ran down the hall and down the stairs. She didn't wait for the elevator; she ran down the back stairs and out to the visitor parking lot. The VW was there, up on jacks with all the windows closed. The outside temperature was eighty-three degrees but when she opened the car that had been sitting in the sun all afternoon, it was at least a hundred. Jackson had passed out and was lying on the front seat. He was not sweating; he was dry and hot. She picked him up and he started to cry. It wasn't a regular baby cry. He didn't scream, he only cried a soft, raspy cry. Goldie took him upstairs and pulled Jason from the high chair. Jason was covered with food from head to foot and his face was smeared with peanut butter.

Goldie said as she grabbed Jason, "I'm taking Jackson to the hospital. I think he's got heat stroke." She turned and left. Greg grumbled something about her being a bitch and if she'd take care of her children this wouldn't happen. At the hospital she encountered Eric. She hadn't seen Eric for almost three years. He had gone to Chicago for two years but had come back. He'd tried to do family practice but found it didn't do for him what emergency practice did. Somehow he loved the thrill of life and death medicine. So he had gotten back to the Hollywood Central Hospital just three weeks before. He looked at Jackson and shook his head.

"This child has heat stroke. It's *very* serious. How did this happen?" He spoke to her like any other patient.

Perhaps he doesn't remember me or recognize me, Goldie thought. *It's all for the better.*

"I'm going to have to keep him hear for tonight. I'll start him on saline right now and we'll put him a cool, air-conditioned room." The doctor didn't ask permission, he just made the statement and expected it to happen.

Goldie was scared; the doctor had said it was very serious and she knew if he said it, considering the kinds of patients he sees, he meant it.

Eric looked over at Jason. "You should clean the baby after he's eaten. Otherwise the rotting food gets bacteria, which is easily transferred to the child. Most children will re-eat food left on their face and clothes."

Goldie was a little hurt by the doctor's statement.

"I'm a good mother, Doctor. I had to leave the children with their father today while I went to work. He fell asleep because he works nights and accidentally left Jackson in the car."

"I'm going to report it to the child protective services. They'll be contacting you."

"Eric, don't you remember me?" Goldie asked, hoping to mitigate what seemed like a harsh decision. Eric stopped and looked into Goldie's eyes. He looked for a few seconds and his expression changed. It softened. He smiled.

"Yes, Goldie, I remember you. How have you been?"

"Okay. I work a lot, but I've been promoted to manager of days. It's a good job."

"When we make a decision, sometimes it's irreversible. At least its effects are irreversible. Your children are your most important responsibility. You need to think about that. The baby will be okay. Come in in the morning and get him. About ten would be okay."

Eric smiled and shook his head side to side.

"I hope you found what you wanted."

He turned and walked over to the desk and told the PA to admit the baby and get him in a cool room. He instructed the PA to monitor the child and to take some blood samples. Without talking again to Golden, he turned and left the emergency room.

Goldie came home without the baby. Greg asked where she had been. She reminded him that he had left the baby in the car and she had to take him to the hospital. She told him she left the baby at the hospital for the night. Greg got mad. "Couldn't you just bring him home? We can give him water as easily as the stupid hospital."

"It's more complex than that. The doctor said he had heat stroke and needed to be observed for a while. He took some blood to make sure his electrolyte count was okay too."

Greg's eyes narrowed. "They took blood from him? You stupid bitch, don't ever let them take blood. Ever!"

"From you I can understand, but from our child, I would think it's a good idea. They can find what's wrong and fix it."

Greg was squirming. He stood up and said he had to go take care of some business. Golden softened, as she usually did.

"Wouldn't you like for me to fix you some dinner? I can make you anything you'd like."

"No, I'll be back later."

He stood, and without going into the apartment, turned and walked down to the elevator.

Goldie sighed. All she really wanted was for him to change a little. Inside she hoped he'd love her and the kids and want to be a father. He was good in some ways. She just needed to change his regard for some things. If she could change him, he'd be a great husband and father.

No, she thought, *that's why I'm leaving him. He won't change. He had a million chances but he just won't do it.*

Goldie thought about how long it had been since he had made love to her, not just sex, but made real love. *Some of this is my fault,* she thought. *If I really tried to love him, to give him the benefit of the doubt, he'd probably respond in the positive.*

Goldie had these battles with herself frequently. She just really didn't want to give him up. Maybe it was that she didn't want to fail in the thing most important to her, her family. She also didn't really want to leave work. She was loved there. The day girls were really glad to have her. The company also had treated her excellently. There were the usual power games, but Goldie hadn't played any of them. She had accepted whatever instructions she was told to do and did them. She had a way of softening harsh instructions for her workers.

She'd get them into the coffee room on their breaks and explain the reason for the change and what the girls would have to start doing. It always turned out really good. So while other shifts were complaining about the new changes, Goldie's shift was happy and content. The management noticed that and rewarded her accordingly.

The battle went on inside her head. Should she just accept Greg and stay at work, or should she carry out her plan and leave? In the end she always went back to leaving him. She now figured she'd leave in December.

She returned to the hospital at 6:30 a.m. Jackson woke and fell back asleep. He was doing much better. Goldie called Maria and said she wasn't coming in. Saturday was usually Goldie's day off anyway, but Maria had scheduled a managers meeting, which she said would last a couple of hours. Maria said the meeting was very important and said Goldie really needed to be there. Goldie said she'd come if she could bring her baby. It was agreed and Goldie showed at 10:30 a.m. for the meeting with Jackson.

For the next three weeks Greg kept the VW home with him. He said it needed a bunch more maintenance, like the oil changed and the valves adjusted. The valves on the older VWs need to be adjusted every ten to fifteen thousand miles. They are solid lifters and the tappets get out of adjustment. Greg explained all this to Goldie and she took the Camaro to work. It was well painted and looked better than her VW so all the employees commented on it. Goldie explained that it was her husband's car and she was only borrowing it for a few days until he got hers fixed.

XIV

An Accident

It was Friday evening, July ninth. Goldie left work early to get the children to a shoot. She had to come home and dress the kids and get them ready to take to the makeup people at the set. She loved the children more than she ever thought she could. They were her life. And she knew that they had to be taken away from Greg. The tests from the hospital had come back with traces of phenobarbital in the baby's system. The CPS came and retested both the children. They came out clean so they dropped the case. The investigator said sometimes they get false readings on kids because they take cough syrup or something else that triggers the blue indicator for certain types of drugs in the system. Goldie knew the truth and told Greg if he ever gave the kids drugs again she'd kill him. He laughed. He said they kept crying and so he gave them just a little to "calm 'em down."

Her days off were changed to Sunday and Monday. They got changed every couple of months. Each supervisor had to take a turn working Saturday and Sunday or Sunday and Monday or Friday and

Saturday. This week she was off Sunday and Monday. She had another shoot scheduled for Sunday and was glad she was off. She spent Sunday morning getting the children ready for the shoot. It was for Gerber baby food. The Gerber people were always enjoyable and pleasant. Goldie went out to lunch after the shooting and left Maria with children. Goldie and Maria had become pals and Maria loved to tend the kids. She said anytime Goldie wanted to give them away, she could give them to her. They chatted for a few minutes and Golden left.

※

About four thirty Goldie came back and picked up the kids from Maria. She was driving the Camaro because Greg was still fixing the VW. Jackson had a slight cough and Jason seemed to be developing flu symptoms. Goldie said she would come back if Greg wasn't home by seven. Greg showed up about 8:30 and Goldie hadn't left yet so she stayed. Greg sat in the living room watching television, drinking beer, and smoking a joint with his legs up on the beautiful rosewood table that Mary had found at an antique store and had bought for Goldie. Goldie did the dishes and came in and sat by Greg. She put her arm around him and she looked into his face. It was full of concern and worry. He showed fear and a distance to Goldie she hadn't seen before. She tried to comfort him but he ignored her. At about midnight Goldie said she was really tired and was going to bed. Greg grunted, "Okay, go." She went into the bedroom and got into her night clothing, climbed into bed and fell asleep.

It was about 3:00 a.m. when she was stirred by Greg. "Get up, it's time to go get me a beer," he said.

Goldie groaned, "It's three in the morning, can't you do without another beer?"

"Look, bitch, all I ever get from you anymore is a few lousy bucks.

You don't make love with me anymore, you don't talk to me anymore. I seldom even see the damn kids."

"That's because the television baby tends 'em. Half the time, you're off in la la land when I need you to help with the children. If you'd take the time to play with them, you'd love them," Goldie answered. She now rebutted Greg's accusations frequently. She loved the kids and wasn't going to take a lot of crap from him.

"I need a beer and I'm too drunk to drive. Take the Volkswagen and go."

Goldie awoke. She still had on her pants under her bathrobe. It was a sort of signal that she wasn't going to have sex. She seldom wore pants but she felt good in them and put them on after work to get things done around the house. She grabbed the VW keys and went downstairs. As she was leaving she asked, "Why can't I take the Camaro, it's a better car. Besides, I need my gas to get to work and take the kids to their filming."

"Because the damn thing's broken! Take the VW!" he answered in his intimidating voice.

Golden knew better than to fight or argue with him when he was drunk and especially when he was trying to intimidate her. She wondered how it had got broken when she was driving it this afternoon and it was working perfectly. But she knew that whenever she rebelled, he reacted physically against her. She knew better than to respond. She walked down the stairs and out of the apartment. She was mad but remembered how important the children were to her. She wasn't going to leave until she got the transfer back to Minnesota. She hadn't officially put in for it but she had talked with Maria about it, so she watched the board for openings in the Minnesota office and when she saw one she was going to put in for it.

Greg would never follow her there. He was so deeply involved in his drug deals that he could never leave the LA area. Maybe that was the answer. It was better than filing for divorce here in LA and suffering whatever consequences might befall her. She didn't love him anymore, but she did fear him. He seemed to like the kids. Not because they were such beautiful children or even because they showed love to their daddy, but because they brought him money. For all his drug dealings, he really didn't contribute much to the house. Since his demotion, he mostly just drank and complained.

Goldie walked to the parking lot and started the VW. The gas gauge was only about a quarter full but that was plenty to get to the 7-Eleven, which was up I-5 about fifteen miles, but she'd rather go there than search around town for an open place and then hope they had either Heineken or Bud.

She started the car and put it in gear. When she let out the clutch, the slight jerk forward pulled on the gas line and it split open very slightly at the place where it had been cracked and worked by Greg. The brake line also had finally split and was dripping break fluid, not a lot, but a good pump on the break and it too would split open.

The car had been good to Goldie. She always used it to go to work and to take the children to the studio for filming. The Volkswagen had been well used. It had worn the tires, which now needed replacing, and the interior had been worn by the kids and by time. The dash light was out so it was hard for Goldie to see the instruments after dark. That was one reason she didn't like to drive at night. It was really not a great night car. They had taken it when they went home to Minnesota because Greg said it would save on gas. It ran well and did great on gasoline. But its time was almost done and Goldie was making enough money now that she didn't have to worry about buying a new car. She even had managed to create a third separate savings account in the bank that Greg didn't know about. It was mostly for the children, but she thought she'd take some money out of it to buy a car when she got back to Minnesota. She also had figured the kids could help pay for at least part of their college. So she put a third or more of their earnings into an account. She hadn't told Greg about it because she knew he would insist she withdraw it whenever he needed money.

Goldie thought she would take Interstate 5 north. The roads wouldn't be crowded at this time of night and she could get off on the Rowena exit and pull right into the 7-Eleven. She'd get some beer and get some gas.

She pulled out onto Melrose and then turned right on to 101. She went down old 101 to 110 and turned east on it until she came to 5. She swung onto the interstate and headed northbound. It was mostly uphill but the VW was a good climber and she got up to 65 pretty fast. She had only driven for two or three miles when she smelled smoke. She looked into the mirror and saw smoke coming out of the engine.

"Damn," she said, "I wonder what the heck is wrong." She relooked at the gas gauge and the other instruments. She looked again at the gauges as she passed under a freeway streetlight. The temperature gauge was climbing. Goldie signaled and pulled from the left lane to the center lane and then started to the right lane. She pushed on the brake pedal. At first it started to slow down but then the pedal faded and went clear to the floor. There was no brake at all. It was early in the morning. She figured she could cross to the right shoulder. Traffic was light but there was a curve in the road ahead and she had no brake.

At the point of the curve was a bridge. She grabbed the emergency hand brake and pulled it up hard. At first the back tires squealed and then the car started to spin. At that very moment, an old blue Chrysler came around the corner and clipped Goldie's skidding car on the left rear end. The VW spun with the hit and Goldie was thrown from her car as the door swung open and the seat came off its mount. The car continued skidding across the freeway and collided with the wall just behind the shoulder. By then it had become engulfed in flames. Goldie rolled like a rag doll for thirty feet or so and then stopped lifeless on the pavement.

The alien driver of the Chrysler was drinking and speeding. He pulled over to the shoulder and got out of his car. The VW was now completely consumed in flames. He could see Goldie lying in the second lane. At first he thought she was dead, but as he started to go out to her, she stirred, partially sat up, and looked at the Latino. Her head was bleeding and it looked like her arm was broken or out of joint. He looked back at her. He saw desperation and fear but more than that he saw a subtle realization that she knew she was going to die. At that instant they both knew, somehow they knew.

Golden looked out from her bleeding face with defiance. She had both moral courage and a powerful will. Out of nowhere a Kenworth rounded the curve. His lights found Goldie lying in his lane. He slammed on his brakes. He sharply turned the truck with its 52-foot trailer to the left. The trailer was loaded with kids' playground equipment. It was heavy and as the truck turned, the trailer broke loose and skidded sideways still traveling north. It began to tilt and then broke loose and rolled over, falling onto Golden and crushing her in an instant. The Kenworth tractor flipped over when the trailer broke loose from the plate holding it. The huge tractor rolled twice, then came to a stop a few feet from an overpass, which dropped down about thirty feet to the lower road. The driver was stunned, bruised, his shirt torn and the radio, which flailed around during the roll, had cut his chest. Bleeding but not badly injured, he sat, seat belted, in the overturned truck for a few seconds and then realized that the trailer had most likely hit the girl in the road.

The Mexican was terrified. In Mexico you'd be in jail just for being there, let alone actually hitting the girl. He looked at the scene and could see the driver of the truck trying to get out; he hesitated for a couple of seconds and then ran to his car and drove off, leaving the driver of the truck, Goldie, and the VW that was now so completely burned that the flames were starting to die. He reasoned to himself that he didn't know any first aid anyway and when the PD came they would surely blame him; after all, he was illegal. So he ran. The radio on the truck still worked. The truck driver radioed the police. They were there with an ambulance in less than ten minutes. A homeowner who saw the fire from her window had already called the fire department.

The paramedics could see Goldie's body under the truck. They got the tow truck to use its cable and pull the trailer off her. They didn't even try to revive her. She was dead and her body was so badly crushed that they just covered her. Her head was bloody and her chest completely smashed. The body had been half way pushed out by the rolling trailer so her head was clear of the trailer but the lower half was still lying under the end of it. Swing sets and steel pipes used for making jungle gyms were scattered along the freeway. The CHP closed all the lanes and diverted traffic off the freeway at the exit. Southbound traffic was also diverted to the right lane. The paramedics sent the body to the hospital in Hollywood, were Eric was acting as the emergency physician. He pronounced her dead. When Eric saw her he began to cry. He still, for some reason unknown even to himself, loved her. He shook his head as he covered the body. The coroner showed up a half an hour later and said he'd leave the body at the hospital until it got identified.

She was such a beautiful girl. I wonder why she had to die this way. Eric felt it strange that she would be out at this time of night. He didn't have the report of the accident, just the information from the paramedics that brought her in.

The fire department quickly put out the last vestiges of the fire on the VW. It was mostly destroyed. The seats and the engine compartment were completely blackened. The gas tank had melted. Gas tanks that are almost empty burn much better than full ones. There's more oxygen and that enables the gas to burn or explode. The PD ordered the car be towed to impound and held for further investigation. It was loaded onto a tow trailer and taken away.

The police came to the hospital and took a report from the truck driver. The paramedics took him because of his bleeding head and some suspicion of internal damage. Eric checked him out, gave him a couple of stitches over the left eye, bandaged the skin abrasions and lacerations on his chest, and gave him some pain pills and a shot for infection and typhoid. The driver filled out some more forms. He had said that when he came around the corner he had seen another car there. A Chrysler, he thought, and a Mexican man standing next to it, looking out into the road at the woman.

The truth is that most people can't tell a Mexican national from a Guatemalan, but they classify all the Mexican and South American people as Mexicans. It's a little offensive to the Mexican people, but they usually don't say much.

The accident investigator took careful notes. They tested the truck driver for alcohol and took some blood for drugs.

The police officer on the scene had noticed the left front door of the VW was open, the seat in the road. He had also noted the damage to the left rear. It was evident that another car had been involved in this accident. A hit and run. The police put out a bulletin based on the description of the truck driver for the Mexican and his Chrysler.

Greg had been called and he showed up at the hospital at about 7:00 a.m.

"Where the hell have you been? I called you three hours ago."

Eric was mad. He was mad at Greg and he was mad that a beautiful, great woman had died. She had needlessly died.

"I had to get a baby tender and get the kids to her. Who are you?" Greg gruffly replied.

"I'm the emergency room physician. Ms. Coleman was brought in to me at about 4:30 and I called you at five a.m. Please follow me to the morgue. You need to identify the body."

They walked down the hallway and downstairs where the hospital had a temporary morgue.

Greg looked at the body. She was recognizable, and he didn't even flinch. He looked at her and said, "Yeah, that's Golden."

Her hair was pushed back and scraped off on one side. Her face was partially crushed and ground down by the sliding trailer. In her eyes, which were still open, you could see her defiance, her strength even in death. She was self-willed and strong. Greg looked at her for a couple of minutes. He didn't cry or even react, just looked. He still had alcohol or something in his system and he swayed a little. His voice and sentence construction also showed it. He turned away and then turned back, re-looked at the body, and confirmed that it was his wife. He asked for her purse. The police said they had taken everything out of the VW and that it was in their custody for now. They said they had to take her and have an autopsy done to make sure the accident was the actual cause of her death, to which Greg readily agreed. He said he wanted to make arrangements for the funeral. The officer in charge said it would only take three days and then he'd release the body and she could be buried by Thursday or Friday.

And so was the death of Golden. Dreams shortened, and life and love forgotten. Eric did a little research on the net and found her parents. He called at about 8:30 California time, which was eleven thirty Minnesota time. Eric told Marge her daughter had died. When Eric told her, she dropped the phone and fell to the floor. It was a few seconds before she picked it back up. At first she demanded to know who was making this very stupid and wicked joke up. But after Eric re-identified himself and explained what had happened, she knew it was true. The truth was that Marge really knew early that morning anyway. When Jason had got up to do the cows, she told him that she had had a very bad dream. She dreamed that she saw her daughter at a wedding. It wasn't with Greg; it was with an angel or Jesus Christ or some other heavenly being. The dream seriously disturbed her and she had planned to call Goldie today and tell her about it. She said thank you to Eric out of habit. There was nothing to thank him for except for telling her. She hadn't gotten a call from the PD, and so she was glad that this doctor was kind enough to call her. Usually doctors are reluctant to call across the country and tell parents about the death of their children. Most of them let the police or someone else make that kind of call. Not Eric, he felt personally involved and felt that in some ways he knew Goldie's parents. He preferred telling them in preference to having the cold call from the PD sergeant to whom most of the officers left that duty.

Jason came in after spreading some dung on the hay fields. It was about noon.

"Hi, honey, got any lunch for me?"

Marge hadn't made it and she hadn't gone out to tell Jason of the death of her daughter. She had just sat in the kitchen chair, with the phone still off the hook, and wept. When Jason came in and saw her, he walked over and put his arm around her shoulder. He hung up the phone and kissed her tenderly on the cheek. He instinctively knew. Marge would only cry like that with the death of her mother or her daughter. So he knew.

"What has happened to Golden?" he asked.

"She is dead, Jay, she is dead."

"How can that be? Are you sure your caller isn't mistaken or she hasn't been misidentified? How can that be?" He repeated, "How can that be?"

They discussed what Eric had told her and then they called the LAPD. They called the hospital, but Eric had gone home. They spoke with the secretary who said she was not allowed to give out that information over the phone. Marge got upset and shouted into the phone, "I live in Minnesota, my daughter has just died, and you can't tell me anything about it. You're the stupidest girl I have ever known," at which she hung up the phone.

When they called the PD, they told them they would call back, which they did after five minutes. They were checking the number and making sure it was the residence of the parents of the deceased. For the first time in thirty years Jason didn't milk the cows that night. He had called over to tell Jeff's parents. They sent over Simon, Jeff's younger brother, and he did the milking.

"I think I'm going to close the farm and retire," Jason said after sitting for more than two hours on the couch and not speaking.

"Yeah, maybe we can travel," Marge answered, not really wanting to travel or really even answer her husband.

"We're going to have to go get the body. I'd like to bury her here."

"Okay, I'll try to get somebody to milk the cows while we're gone," Marge answered, not really knowing what she had said or why.

XV

Postmortem

After Greg had made some arrangements for the children, he called the telephone company and told them of Goldie's death. He drove over to the company offices that afternoon and showed Maria a copy of the police report. Maria wept bitterly and openly. She shook her head and looked with the hateful eyes at Greg.

"What was she doing driving at 3:00 in the morning?" Maria asked.

Greg answered by saying how she sometimes couldn't sleep. That she had worked nights for a long time and couldn't get it out of her system so she went for drive.

"I have to do some paperwork," Maria said. "Goldie had a seventy-five-thousand-dollar life insurance policy and she had some savings here in the company bank. She also has some insurance for the children. Please call me by Friday or next Monday and I'll have a check for you and a some release papers. You'll need to bring me a copy of the death certificate and a statement by the police that the death was ruled an accident."

Greg was surprised at the amount of insurance she had. He knew she had some insurance and she also had some vacation pay coming. She also had her last paycheck coming but he didn't know about the insurance on the kids and he didn't know about the savings. Greg was very, very happy to learn that it would be more than a hundred thousand dollars when the double indemnity paid. He thought about the children and their insurance.

"How much insurance is on the kids?" he asked flatly.

"It's about 50 thousand dollars each. That's with double indemnity. If they die by accident," Maria said. She could barely talk with him. She knew what he was and she hated him. But she was trained to be efficient and to solve problems. The insurance was there for the kids, and she was going to dispatch it as soon as possible

"I knew I had some bucks coming but I never realized it would be more than a hundred and fifty thousand dollars," Greg declared with some glee.

Maria walked away. She stopped and turned and said, "You can pick up your blood money Monday."

Greg left. He was completely unaffected by her comment.

❧•❦

Greg made the initial funeral arrangements. The autopsy showed that she had been crushed and killed by the truck. The police found the abandoned Chrysler near the border and assumed that the Mexican had returned to Mexico. The car insurance company settled and paid 50,000 dollars for the death. Greg took the check and went home to the children who were crying and fussing. The baby tender was really mad at them and complained vehemently. She said she did not want to continue tending his kids. Especially now that Goldie had died. The truth was that she tended only because she wanted her drugs. She definitely did not want to be the children's new mother.

She had tried to feed them some cereal but they wouldn't eat. Both the kids had a cold and their noses were running.

Greg was frustrated with the children and had no idea how to take care of them or what to do with them or how to feed them They cried and fussed all the time and Greg had never changed a diaper in five years. He didn't like the smell and he didn't really even like the kids. They, of course, had messed in their pants and he did not want to touch them. Goldie had the kids potty trained but the baby tender didn't ask them and they needed reminders to go to the bathroom. Ms. Gillian had not changed them and she had not put them in clean clothes or even cleaned up the breakfast mess. She left without much conversation with Greg.

So Greg was left alone with the kids. Usually he'd just wait for Goldie to get home and she'd change them, but now he was stuck. He called around and found a baby tender who said she could watch the children that evening and she would watch the children when he went to the funeral. But that she would not and could not be a permanent baby tender. She was a college student and couldn't spare the time. She was a member of Greg's mother's church and he got her name from Mom. Greg told his mother about the death of Goldie. Mrs. Coleman spoke harshly to Greg.

"She was the best thing you ever came up with. You should have taken better care of her. She gave you children and devotion and even love. Sometimes, Gregory, you're really stupid."

She hung up the phone and Greg loaded the kids into the Camaro and took them over to the baby tender's.

The funeral went well. Greg still had not called Goldie's parents so he had no idea that they knew of the death of their daughter. Greg didn't really care. He was rid of an extremely dangerous liability. And to his delight he was rich. With the car insurance and the company double indemnity and her savings, Greg had acquired more than two hundred thousand dollars. He had never in his life had that kind of money. It was his to dispose of at his will. He took the babies back to Ms. Gillian who agreed to tend them for the next four days. He left them in her apartment. He also agreed to pay her both in money and with some drugs.

The police did call on Greg after three days. The investigator said he was just clearing up the case and asked him if he had called his wife's parents. Greg said no, that he had been too upset and grieved and had forgotten to make the call. The sergeant shook his head in disgust. "You're a peace of shit," he said and walked away, shaking his head. He had pulled Greg's record and knew a little about him.

"What a lucky stiff. Gets a blond with a good job and she dies and leaves him insurance and kids," the detective said. He wasn't able to develop any evidence that would indicate that Greg was in any way responsible for the death of Goldie. So they closed the case. Of course, Goldie's parents missed the funeral. When they got there Sunday afternoon, they were glad that they hadn't gone to the funeral. Mostly Greg and his associates attended it. Jason called and asked Greg if they could please take the body back to Minnesota. To which Greg answered, "Sure, it's no damn good to me."

Greg was rude and unkind to Goldie's parents. He allowed them to take the children to the hotel for a couple of days while he returned to the telephone company and collected the insurance. Marge and Jason fell in love with the kids in an instant. They were both beautiful and intelligent. They had grown a lot since their visit.

While they were with the kids at the motel, Greg's mother called and asked if she could come and see Marge and Jason and the kids. She seemed sincere and surprised Jason by showing concern for the children and despair about the death of Goldie. He asked Greg's mother about the children. She had come to the hotel to visit and see the kids. Only once did she defend Greg.

Goldie's mother had begged Greg to let her take the two children back to Minnesota. She said he could come and see them any time he wanted to. She said she'd even put them on an airplane and he could have them for a couple of weeks in the summers. But Greg answered, "No, they're my kids and I love them."

Greg was really not a part of his own family in the sense that he ever played with the children or even helped Goldie take them to filming sessions, but they were his children and he had a claim on them. He said he was moving as soon as he could find another apartment. His plan was to move back to the Watts area. There he would be king. With two hundred thousand dollars, he'd have anything he wanted. He would raise his children there, using his mother and his ex-wife as baby tenders. He also planned to keep Alicia Gillian. She was good for any last-minute tending and he knew she'd do anything he wanted. She was poor and loved coke.

Goldie had obviously not left a will. She had no idea she was going to die. She had designated payment of some of her insurance to a college fund for the kids. But it was to be administered by her husband. She believed she would live to be old enough to see the children grow and go to college or marry.

Jason and Marge loaded the coffin on to an airplane and flew back to Minnesota. They didn't talk much on the way. Marge wept off and on all the way home. When they got back to Angora they had a brief graveside funeral. Jason had a paid for a plot next to this father and he had called ahead and told them they were bringing the body home. The hole was dug and the funeral was short. Jeff and his family came. Jeff cried openly and shook all over.

"I just don't understand it. I loved her. I would have given her California if she wanted, I would have given her anything."

The funeral ended and Marge and Jason, Marge's mother and friends went home. It was a hard time for Marge and it was an even harder time for Jason. He had loved his daughter so much. He had forgotten how much he loved her. He was unhappy with her choice of mates and he just didn't know how to convince her to come home. But now she was dead.

"How could this have happened? How could this possibly have happened? What did I do wrong to have my daughter leave me and go to California? What did I do wrong that made her leave? That made her go to California and make love with a nigger?"

Jason hated Greg. He hated him not because he thought he had deliberately murdered Goldie, but because he knew that Greg had treated his daughter so poorly and that his daughter deserved so much more. Goldie was a wonderful, sweet, caring, and intelligent soul and a great mother. It was then and there he decided to see if he could sue and get the children away from Greg.

Jason picked up the phone. He turned to Marge.

"I'm calling an attorney, Marge."

He called an attorney in St. Paul. The attorney said he had no standing in California. He'd be glad to help Jason, but the attorney told him he'd need to call a California attorney. Someone who knew the laws there and could represent Jason and Marge well. The attorney knew the name of one who was reported to be an extremely good legal eagle. The St. Paul attorney said, "His name is Brian Goodfell. He specializes in cases of a complex nature, those that might need some careful legal maneuvering. The problem with California is that the law is pretty specific about leaving kids with their biological originators. He's pretty expensive but they say you get what you pay for, so I think it's probably worth it. Of course it's up to you."

"I don't care. I just don't care what it costs. I've got to get my grandkids out of that man's hands," Jason replied.

The attorney gave Jason the California attorney's telephone number. Jason carefully noted it down and thanked him for all the legal help he'd always done for them on the farm. Jason hung up.

"Okay, Marge, we've got the number of a California attorney. Do you want to pursue this? I'm sure it's gonna cost us a buck."

"What else can we do? Let the children grow up with that monster? No, I don't care what it costs, I want to raise our grandchildren."

He dialed the California number. It was an attorney whose office was in San Clemente, strangely enough in the same town where Goldie had originally gone. Bryan was a good attorney. He listened carefully to the case. After Jason had finished telling Brian much more than he needed to determine the likelihood of winning, Brian said, "I think I can help you. We need to meet and explore the different kinds of approaches. Can you come out here?"

"I run a dairy farm and it's really hard to get away. I'll need a couple of weeks to make arrangements."

"We can't afford to wait that long. The longer the children are with Mr. Coleman, the less the chance that the court will uproot them. I can fly out to St. Paul in the morning. Can you meet me there?"

"We haven't discussed your fee," Jason tendered with hesitancy.

"I'll pay for my own flight there. We'll discuss what needs to be done and when we have decided in which direction we're going to take this case, then I can give you a fair figure for my fees."

Jason and Marge were waiting at the Minneapolis/St. Paul International Airport. The flight got in at 10:30 a.m. Rather than go back to Angora, they went to a restaurant. Jason said it was a two-hour drive back home and then to come back would be a waste of Mr. Goodfell's time. So they went out to a Wendy's hamburger place.

Brian carefully listened to everything both Jason and Marge said. They rehearsed the entire history of Goldie and then waited for Brian to respond. Brian looked at both of them for a few seconds and sighed.

"We can re-petition Greg for the children. The problem is that we haven't anything he wants. If he hadn't gotten the money, I'm sure he'd give them up for a buck. But that's not possible now. I am dubious that we can appeal to his sympathies. We can demand a custody hearing in which we can show that Greg and the children are not only incompatible but that it is in the children's best interest to have them be raised by you. In order to do that, we're going to need to investigate Mr. Coleman's background in order to show that his lifestyle is not healthy nor contributory to the children. Further we will need to show that your lifestyle will be significantly better for the children than his."

"How much will this cost us?" Jason unabashedly asked.

"My fees will need to include the fees of a private investigator who will do the background on Greg and some legal research for our side of the case. The best PI I know costs about 300 dollars per day plus expenses. I'm not sure how long it will take him to do the background. But the problem is time critical. We will need to file for a hearing and get our case before the judge as quickly as possible. My fees, including legal research, approximate court time and an approximation of the PI fees, together with filing fees, will be in the neighborhood of twenty thousand dollars plus. That's a low estimate. It may be as much as forty thousand dollars. There are several factors that influence that. So I am left to say if you don't have at least thirty thousand, you should not pursue this case. Also you should know that our chances of success are only about fifty-fifty."

Jason looked at Marge, whose eyes were wide open and her mouth had dropped.

"That's a lot of money, Marge. I don't think we have that much, even in our savings."

Marge shuffled in her chair.

"What's the cost of human lives? How much is too much to save the lives of our grandchildren? I know we own the farm free and clear, can't we get a loan on it?"

Jason answered instantly. "Yes, honey, we can. If you want to do it, I can do it."

"You'll have to come to California and be there for approximately two weeks," Brian interrupted.

"It's your choice, Marge," Jason said, turning to his wife and taking her hand.

"I choose to help," Marge said in a final and firm voice.

"Okay," Brian said. "I'll need ten thousand up front to get the papers filed, the PI hired, and to get some legal research done."

Jason reached into his coat pocket and pulled out a wrinkled checkbook. It looked as though it had not been used for months. In fact it had not. Jason seldom wrote checks and was very cautious about using the checkbook. He wrote a check for ten thousand dollars and said he'd take Brian to the bank here in St. Paul to cash it. Brian agreed.

After they had cashed the check and made arrangements with the airlines for a ticket for Marge and Jason, Brian went back to the motel he was staying in. It was an upper-class motel but not an extravagant one. Brian would not stay in a cheap motel, but he did try to use good judgment in spending the clients' money. He would meet with the Bradleys at his office in two days. It was short notice and Jason was hard pressed to find someone to run the farm. There was a farm labor hall in Minneapolis that Jason had called before. He called and asked if anyone there could run a dairy farm. The man said he had a guy that had worked dairy farms in the Angora area. Jason said send him up. He didn't even ask the name or age of the applicant. There was only one, so Jason took him.

⇒•⇐

Jackson arrived at the farm that evening at almost ten p.m. Jason recognized him and welcomed him in.

"Jackson, how have you been? I haven't seen you in twenty years!"

"Well, I'm okay. I quit working five years ago, but my boy in California got into some trouble and needs quite a bit of money, so I came back to see if I could go to work and send him some."

"I don't know if you knew that Marge and I married. We had a little girl...." He paused and gulped. "She was killed in LA a couple of weeks ago. We've got to go there and see if we can get her twins away from the father."

"I met Goldie on the bus. She was a very sweet girl. She loves you very much," Jackson answered.

"She spoke a little of you," Marge said. "I think she named one of the twins after you."

"Probably not," Jackson answered. "But we did talk for three and a half days. She wanted to see what the rest of the world was like. I guess she won't have that chance now."

Jason changed the subject. "We've got to fly out tomorrow afternoon. Get up with me in the morning and I'll go over our procedures. Please clean the tits off good. I don't want any cases of mastitis when I get back. You can stay here in the house, in my mom's old room. She died six months ago. Goldie couldn't even get back for her funeral." He shook his head and held back a tear. Jackson was not so noble. He had tears running down his cheeks.

"I'm so very sorry she is gone. You must know that she was very, very concerned with you and loved you very much."

⁂

Jason and Marge left on the plane the next day at four in the afternoon. American Air landed in LA at 5:20 LA time. Marge commented that it had seemed more like three hours than one. Jason laughed for the first time since the death of his daughter. They caught a cab to the Holiday Inn in East LA. When they got to the inn, Jason called Brian's office. Brian was still in. He was doing some research on custody laws and he had assigned his paralegal to do research on definitions for terms such as "unfit," etc.

"Hello, Mr. Goodfell?"

"Yes, how are you, Jason? How was your flight?"

"It was okay. I forgot how I hate to fly, but the plane was big and the ride was comfortable."

"Okay, listen, we've got to act fast on this. The first thing I'm going to do is tomorrow I'll file for a hearing. In order to get a hearing I've got to have bases. I found that here in California grandparents have standing for custody of children when the parents are shown to be incompetent or incapable. I've called Mr. Robert Bosley, the PI I told you about. He'll be here in the morning. Can you be at my office at ten in the morning?"

"Sure. I can rent a car here at the hotel so we'll see you in the morning." Jason hung up; he turned to his wife. "Well, here we go, honey. I hope we're up to it."

The rest of the evening was spent in the hotel room watching TV and going out to eat. They ate at the hotel restaurant. Jason didn't really want to see the city.

Ten a.m. came early. Brian briefed the Bradleys for almost an hour before Robert showed. The secretary sent him right in.

"I thought you said eleven," Robert said as he sat down on the end chair.

"I did," Brian noted. "I thought I'd brief Mr. and Mrs. Bradley first and invite you in to tell them what you do and get an estimate of what it will cost them."

"Well, okay…I'm Robert Bosley. I'm a private investigator and my fee is pretty standard. I charge four hundred dollars a day plus all expenses. That includes all my meals, my stay at a local motel, and my gas. I charge forty cents per mile. That covers things like tires and oil and other incidentals. If I need another agent to assist with the investigation, I charge a flat one hundred and fifty dollars a day for him with no expenses. I first need to hear what needs to be done in your case before I can give you an estimate on what this investigation will cost."

Jason looked Robert in the eye. "I don't want to give my money away to you or anybody. How do I know you'll do what you say before I pay you?"

"Some of it you won't. If I interview ten people, some at bars and some at their homes, I'll keep a log. Of that you'll have a record. But if I go to Ontario to get a lead, I'll charge you the time and the mileage and you'll just have to trust me. The bottom line is that not all investigations turn out to be what the client wants. You have to pay me anyway. All I do is gather the facts and report them to you. I never bend them and I never mis-report. So if you have any doubts, please, please, don't hire me."

Jason turned to Marge who was also looking Robert in the eye. "I think this guy is okay," Jason said.

"So do I," Marge confirmed.

Brian interrupted, "Okay, if we're settled on using Robert, let's get down to explaining to him what we need."

Marge and Jason agreed and they simultaneously started to tell Robert the history of their daughter. Brian let them talk for about ten minutes until they got to the part where she died and then Brian interrupted again. "I or they will brief you more on Golden when you need information. For now here's what we need." He explained about the background on Greg and the need to show he was an unfit father. He explained they thought he might be selling drugs and about his lies on being employed by the Mercedes Benz Company.

Robert left Brain's office after being given only a few workable details. He was used to getting scant information from clients. Most attorneys don't know what was really needed to do a good investigation. Some attorneys know the law really well and know what they need in court but have no idea on what is needed to get the kind of information needed to win the case.

Robert started at the hospital where Golden was taken after the accident. It was important to know whether the report said she died at the scene or at the hospital. He walked in and asked the receptionist if he could talk to the doctor who saw Golden Fern Coleman. She said it was the emergency physician and he was just getting off duty. She said he worked until ten a.m. and his shift had ended an hour ago but he had to finish cleaning up an emergency patient and setting a cast.

Robert walked back into the emergency room and asked for Dr. Eric. As Eric came out of the double doors from the emergency holding area, he looked right into Robert's eyes. His face was tired, even though he was very young for a doctor; he carried a tired face.

"What can I do for you?" he asked suspiciously.

"My name is Robert Bosley. I'm a private investigator looking into the death of Mrs. Golden Coleman. What can you tell me about her death?"

"About Goldie, I could tell you a lot. I loved her. But more importantly, a strange thing happened last night. Her twin boys came in. They had overdosed on Robitussin with codeine. I looked at the bottle; it was more than ten years old. Apparently the kids were given at least four or five tablespoons of it to stop their coughing. The babysitter administered the dosage. The youngest baby, Jason, just died an hour ago. I'm waiting for the coroner and the PD."

"One of the twins just died?" Robert asked, not believing the doctor was talking about the same person. What about the other child?"

"Jackson is comatose, but it looks like he's gonna be okay."

Eric had both a very tied and disgusted look. He continued. "Yeah, first the mother, and then in a week or so, the baby."

"And the baby died of a cough syrup overdose?" Robert asked, still not believing what he was hearing.

"They both came in with respiratory distress. Codeine causes depression of the neurological signals to the muscles. Jason was breathing shallow and had a rapid pulse. So did his brother but not as severe as Jason. We started work on them immediately, but it was too late for the little one. The paramedics said they talked to the babysitter that showed them the bottle of cough syrup. The paramedics said that the baby tender said Greg had left her the bottle and instructed her to give each of the kids four or five tablespoons. He reportedly said that ought to keep 'em quiet." Eric reached into his white blood-stained scrubs and pulled an almost empty bottle.

"The paramedics gave it to me to make sure that what was in the bottle was in fact Robitussin. I looked at it and sent a tablespoon to the lab. Sure enough it's cough syrup with codeine. Some of the syrup has evaporated over the years so it's even more concentrated that it was originally. The syrup, incidentally, is for adults. The prescribed dose for adults is one or two teaspoons every four hours."

Eric shook his head in disgust. Robert took the bottle. He looked at it and thought; *Well, it's not much good as evidence now. No latents, and no chain of custody. It's gonna be hard to prove that this was the same bottle containing the syrup that caused the overdose.* He was going to keep it but could see the doctor was guarding it like some sorta proof of criminal behavior. Robert knew that the babysitter would blame the father and the father would, of course, blame the sitter. The bottle looked old and the label was smudged. It looked as though it was not prescribed to Greg. That may also be a problem. His thoughts were interrupted by a voice coming from the entrance doors.

"Doctor Eric?" a man said, walking up the hall. He was a cop. You can spot them a mile away. It's the nature of their attitude. Not just the blue sports coat, or the pleat in the shirt, or even their authoritative walk; it's a combination, and once you get an eye, you can spot 99% of them even though they are trying to work undercover or undetected. Most narco guys know that. Of course there are some who fool you, but they become like the people they are trying to catch. It's a catch 22, you have to become like a druggie to fool them and when you do, it becomes hard to remember whose side you are working for.

So up walked the cop. He introduced himself as Lieutenant Woods. He was with LAPD and carried that air that made him establish that he was in charge from the first encounter. The doctor, who should have been in charge, yielded to his overbearingness and answered his questions as best as he could. Robert stayed to listen but was soon asked to leave by the lieutenant. He wasn't a great cop. He didn't even ask who Robert was or whether he was there about the death of Jason. How funny, you'd think a good cop would want to know all the elements in a case. Robert walked down the hospital hall to the set of pay phones hanging on the wall like little children waiting to be noticed. He picked up the first one and called Brian.

It took a minute to get through to his secretary but after telling her the message was very urgent, twice, she interrupted Brian's consultation with another client and put him on.

"Brian, this is Robert. You're not gonna believe this. The younger baby, Jason, died last night. He was given four or five tablespoons of Robitussin with codeine and had respiratory and heart failure. He actually died at about seven this morning. The PD is talking to the doctor and I'm sure they'll go to the baby tender who gave the kids the medicine. She is claiming that the father told her to give the kids the cough syrup and that she was only doing what she was told. I'm on my way over to see her. The PD came and I got her address from the lieutenant by looking over his shoulder at the report. He was looking through his papers for her name and on the top of the report sheet was her address."

"My God, Jason died last night? Are you sure it was our Jason?"

"Yeah, I'm sure. The doctor also said he loved Golden. I think the kids look a little like him, at least from the picture I got from Marge, so I'm gonna look into that too."

Brian cleared his throat. "I'll call Jason and Marge. I don't know what they'll say. Don't do much more until I see if they are still wanting to take care of the remaining kid. I also will need to see what they want to do about the funeral."

He hung up without saying good-bye. Robert walked slowly out of the hospital. At the admissions office he was able to talk the clerk out of the doctor's address and phone number. He figured the doctor would not be getting home for several hours, so he'd wait 'til tomorrow to call him.

The baby tender was about 33 years old. She looked fifty. She was clearly a user. Probably getting her stuff from Greg. She invited Robert in cautiously. Robert told her he was not a cop and that his job was to help clear her of any wrongdoing. She said that the police had said she might be charged with manslaughter or worse. She was scared. Robert asked her if she thought Greg would admit telling her to give the kids four or five tablespoons of a drug. She said she had called him after the cops left and he was on his way over. Robert thought it might be better if Greg didn't see him at this point in the investigation, so he talked with Alicia for another five minutes and left. He asked if he could return and visit with her. She agreed.

As he left Robert spoke Spanish and complimented her, which made her comfortable and more willing to talk with him. He implied that he could be of some advantage to her in the event she was charged and said that he'd testify for her at the initial indictment hearing. That's assuming that the grand jury would issue an indictment for her in the first place. Robert wasn't sure; he'd seen them ignore this kind of stupidity and he'd seen them charge the activator with murder two. So you just didn't know. But he did know that the PD would give it to the DA, and if he figured he could get an easy conviction, he'd go for it. Over the years Robert had learned that cases had little to do with protecting society and a lot to do with making the prosecutor look good. If the case were a "walk in the park," the prosecutor would take it and use it as evidence of his or her skills as an attorney. The person being charged seldom had much to do with the process except that the cleaner they were, the less likely it would be a park walk and so the more likely that the prosecution would decline to prosecute. They'd always say something like, "There is not enough evidence to conclude that the act was deliberate. But we reserve the right to re-open the case should we get more or different information."

It was all bull. Just words protecting each party's position. Making sure they came out looking good. And having little to do with the perpetrator or even the crime.

As Robert left the apartment complex he saw the blue Camaro pull into the apartment driveway. He thought it strange for the father to go to the babysitter before he went to the hospital where one of his sons had just died and the other was still comatose.

Robert had also left a bug in her apartment. Nothing as complex as the CIA uses. Just a bug that you can listen to on your car's FM radio. It's good for about a thousand feet, although Robert had picked 'em up from as far away as two blocks. You tune your radio to a dead spot on the FM dial and the transmitter broadcasts to that. Once you got a voice, you'd put a tape by the radio to record the conversation. That way the listener doesn't have to remember and can re-examine what was said in light of other evidence as it gets collected.

Robert put a little sticky cloth tab on the back of the transmitter so he could stick it where it would pick up conversation and not be seen. This one he put under the coffee table in the living room. Robert felt gum under there and knew she didn't clean it often or ever.

After writing down the plate number of the Camaro, Robert drove down around the corner. He waited until he saw Greg get out of the Camaro and walk up the stairs. Then he pulled into the space just below the apartment. He had been careful not to let Greg or Alicia see the rental car he was driving. Initially, Robert had parked around the corner and walked up the back stairs. The conversation was very, very interesting. They had already begun to speak before Robert could get his radio tuned to the bug.

"Why the hell did you tell them you gave the kids the medicine?" Greg shouted.

"The paramedics asked if they had taken anything. I said sure and showed them the bottle. They took the bottle and put it into their bag. They looked at the kids who by then had stopped talking to me and stopped playing and stopped doing anything. They just fell on the floor and were asleep, but when I tried to wake them, they wouldn't budge and they were not breathing right. I didn't know what else to do but call the paramedics. I sure didn't want them to die."

"Well, I'm denying that I told you to give the little shits that much cough syrup. I'm gonna claim I didn't know you were giving them anything at all."

Robert heard something banging down.

"Where the hell does that leave me? You can't hang me out to dry for this one! All I did is what you told me to. I didn't know it would kill 'em. You said it would just make 'em go to sleep."

"Look, you stupid bitch, you want anymore ice, you'd better take the fall for this one. If they ask, I'll tell them that I didn't know it would hurt 'em either. The kids were insured, it's a lot of money. A lot more than they make prancing around in a stupid diaper. I'm collecting for the stupid bitch tomorrow. I'll have enough money to retire. You play your part and you'll never need anything again. I worked the whole thing out. It worked, it all worked so damn well."

"What'd mean it worked?" she asked. "This wasn't on purpose, was it?"

"You really are a moron. She was going to leave me. I needed the bucks and I had to have the security that she couldn't rat on me. The bitch was gonna leave me. Here's your stuff." There was a pause. "Just tell the cops you didn't know there were any drugs in the medicine and they were really coughing badly. You can't be held responsible if you didn't know it would hurt them. I've gotta go, I'm meeting a user at the high school. She pays for her fun with my fun."

He got up and left. Robert laid low in the rental as Greg pulled away. He followed him back to Greg and Goldie's apartment. While he was in the apartment, Robert heated a screwdriver, a Phillips, with a cigarette lighter and pushed the hot tip into his left taillight lens. He'd need to follow him at night and one way not to lose a car you're following is to make a little hole in the plastic taillight; that way you can see the white pin hole from a long way away and don't need to follow so closely. Also if you loose them, they are easier to reacquire.

It was five in the afternoon. Greg had stopped by the hospital and ID'd the baby. He was questioned by the PD and asked to come in for some more questioning. Robert figured Greg would go to the high school pretty soon. Robert labeled the tape while waiting and an hour passed. Another hour passed and another. He must have fallen asleep. His story to Alicia about a high school girl may have been bull.

Robert had hoped it wasn't because if he could get some pictures of him dealing, that would be powerful evidence that he was an unfit parent. Also he almost admitted killing his wife. At least he intended her death. Robert decided that tomorrow he'd go to the junkyard and look at the VW.

※

It was ten after nine at night when Greg finally left the apartment. He must have taken a long nap. He drove south toward the Watts area. Robert got a little nervous following a man into Watts after dark. Mostly because a rental car is easily spotted there. Greg stopped at a 76 service station, gassed up, and talked with the teller for about five minutes and slipped him a little white envelope. Robert got a picture of the exchange and the money given.

Greg then took I-5 south and drove all the way down past San Diego. He could follow from a good distance because the white light from the screwdriver hole on the left taillight showed up like a beacon. Greg went on down to Chula Vista. There's a train station right next to the Mexican border and he stopped there and waited. It was almost two fifteen a.m. when someone showed. A Mexican national. He was carrying a briefcase in one hand and in the other a small box. One just large enough to hold in his hand. His fingers wrapped half way around the box. It looked to be cardboard, white and brown in color, with some red writing on it. The man walked halfway across the street towards the train station, stopped and looked both ways, not looking for traffic, but probably for cops. His eyes focused on Robert's car. Robert slunk down in the seat and hoped that the darkness would not silhouette him. Usually you can't see a person sitting in a car in the dark if his head doesn't form a silhouette against the back window. He looked for a few seconds and then walked over to Greg who was sitting on the concrete bench under a plastic booth that was probably built to protect the train passengers from rain.

When they met, they both almost simultaneously looked around to see if there was anyone else in the area. Robert had his cameras out. He had both an infrared camera and a standard camera loaded with 400 ASA film. The briefcase was exchanged as was expected, and then the small package was given to Greg. He hurriedly put it into his overcoat pocket. It bulged out and was easily visible through the coat.

After putting the box into his coat pocket, both men looked around again. Robert wondered what could be in the box. What was so valuable? Greg pulled out a very thick manila envelope, which the seller immediately opened, Not taking out the money, but carefully counting it while Greg stood watch. The transaction done, they both scurried off like gutter rats.

Greg drove back to LA. On the way he stopped at three places. Each time the same behavior pattern. Caution, then walking with the buyer to an isolated location, looking around, then the exchange. Greg would always open the briefcase in the car and take out only whatever amount he was selling to that particular buyer. He'd leave the briefcase in the car. After delivering he'd always very carefully count the money. Greg was even more careful about the money than the man in the Chula Vista train station. Then they departed.

Each time Greg labeled the envelope with the money and put it in a small compartment in his car door. At the third stop Robert got a glimpse of where Greg was putting the money. He would open the door and twist the speaker for the radio, which was located at the lower front part of the door. The twisting looked like a combination, twice forward, and once back. The speaker came out and a small compartment appeared into which Greg put the money. He appeared to be very good at drug dealing. He was succinct and careful. He did not engage in lengthy conversations with the clients and always counted his money before closing the deal. With some he counted before giving the drugs to the customer and with others after. It must have been a matter of trust or experience.

The day dawn was breaking and even though Greg had slept half the day before away, he went home. Robert figured he'd have a few tokes and go to sleep for at least part of the day. Robert followed him home and after watching the apartment for fifteen or twenty minutes, Robert drove back to town. There was a little restaurant just down the street from the city offices so he went there and had a little breakfast and a couple cups of coffee. The offices were supposed to open at nine so at five till, he headed over to find out where the VW had been towed. The clerk gladly gave him the information when he told him that he was part owner of the vehicle and wanted to see if any of it could be salvaged.

At the junkyard the VW had been put in a reserved corner. The yardman said that the PD might still have some looking to do because the lady driving it had died. But when Robert explained he was representing the insurance company and showed his PI ID, the guy let Robert look at the car. Robert crawled under it and looked at the brake lines. One was broken, just 19 inches after the line came off the master cylinder, right where it was attached to the wall of the car. It was hard to tell whether it had worn a hole in it by rubbing against the frame or if it had been tampered with. Robert got out his magnifying glass and looked closer. He could see pliers marks about four inches from the brake and some evidence that the line had been very slightly twisted. The wear pattern did not match the wear pattern on the wall of the car. Robert knew the break in the line could not have been due to natural wear. He took a couple of pictures of the line.

Then he looked at the gas line. A small electrical lead had been put across the gas line and at the point where a urethane hose extended the copper line as it went into the carburetor. The connection was old and cracked and mostly melted, but when Robert bent the line, he could see fresh black rubber down deep in the slit where the melted copper wire laid. That kind of new rubber cannot come from wear. Robert took another couple of pictures. He was a very careful examiner. He next looked at steering mechanism. The steering column appeared to also have been tampered with. The rubber pad between the steel column and the connecting gearbox at the end of the steering column had clearly been torn. It didn't appear to just be worn. Once again, by using the magnifying glass, Robert could see pliers' marks on the rubber. He took some more photos. It appeared to him that the car was deliberately damaged in several ways to insure an accident.

It is very difficult to prove that the intent was to take a life, and just as difficult to show that Greg or anyone specific did the damage to the vehicle. It is almost impossible to show a link between the death of the vehicle operator and any damage that may have been done to the vehicle prior to the wreck. It is less difficult to show who did the damage or changes to the vehicle, but in court a good defender can create doubt. Most defense attorneys will argue that in the first place you have to show that their client did the damage, in the second that the damage was intentionally done to injure the specific person in question, and finally that the end result was foreseeable and the intention of the accused. So in general all this was just supportive evidence, none of which is absolutely probative in and of itself. Just the same, Robert took photos of the entire car. He took photos of what was inside the car, inside the glove box, and of the tires, the windshield, and of course the doors. He wanted to remove the back seat and see if there was anything there but the yardman came back while he was inside the car and told him he could not do that because the police hadn't cleared it yet.

Robert thanked him and gave him a twenty. He knew it was a minor violation to let him look at the car when it was impounded and saved for evidence. The guy thanked him and apologized again for not allowing him to look behind the back seat.

Robert called Brian. Brian said that the grandparents were coming in to his office at five p.m. and could he meet them there. Robert said, "Of course." And the conversation ended. Robert hadn't had any sleep for the past twenty-four hours, but he couldn't sleep now. He still had to follow Greg and see if there was any truth to the high school girl story.

He drove back to the apartment on the chance that Greg was still there and to his astonishment and fortune he was. Robert could see him in the kitchen drinking some coffee and pacing back and forth in front of the window. At twelve thirty Greg left. This time he drove over to the high school in Northwest Hollywood. He walked over to the fence and leaned against a tree just outside the fence. He stood there for about four or five minutes. It was lunchtime. The school had two lunches because of the number of students; the first started at twelve and the second at twelve forty-five. A very thin young girl, probably 15 or 16, walked over to the fence and spoke with Greg. Robert snapped a photo. Greg nodded at the girl and walked over to his car, got in, and sat.

Within five minutes the girl came out of the school walked across the street and got into the front seat. Robert took a couple more photos. He put on his telephoto lens and zoomed in on the two in the car. It looked like the girl said, "Okay, let's go." Upon which Greg started the car and drove off. Robert followed. They went west and then north on 101 to the beach. The same beach where Greg and Golden had made love that fateful night six years ago. They parked the car at the road's end and walked down to the beach. Robert couldn't follow them down the path to the beach without being seen and there was no other access. He drove to the next beach road. It was less a mile north. Robert pulled in and parked. He got his camera and took the telephoto lens.

He walked down the beach toward the place where Greg had taken the high school girl. There was a rock formation that jutted out into the sea and which blocked anyone from walking down the beach to the place where Greg was. Robert, holding his camera up in the air, walked into the water. He didn't know if it was going to be too deep for him to walk, but it was the only chance he had. The water immediately went up to his chest. The surf was pushing him and pulling him and he almost fell three times. In spite of the surf, Robert was able to walk to the point of the rocks and climb up onto them. He climbed up and over the rocks and looked down on the isolated beach. He wasn't surprised to see Greg undressing the teen. He took a dozen photos. They went back into the little cove and made love. Robert got some good photos.

They started to get dressed and Robert hurriedly climbed down the rocks, walked into the ocean, and around the rock and up to his car. He hurriedly drove back toward the parking spot of Greg's car. Greg and the young girl were walking toward the car. Robert pulled over about 250 yards from where Greg had parked. It was a good place. Other cars had pulled over to go to the beach so he blended in and wasn't noticeable. Robert put back on his telephoto lens and waited. They got in the Camaro and Greg reached down somewhere under his dashboard and pulled out a small white envelope. It had a lump of something in it, which Robert figured was meth. The girl smiled and they drove back to the high school. Robert got on his cell phone and called the Hollywood PD. "I'd like to anonymously report a girl at the high school on Beaver Street has just bought some drugs from a guy named Greg, driving a blue Camaro, with a special plate number, 'the guy.' They are south bound on I-5 at mile marker 15."

"Thank you, please hold, and I'll transfer you to our narcotics division," was all the secretary or dispatcher said. Robert rapidly hung up. At this point in time he did not want to be identified with an investigation on Greg. The moment he got on the phone with narcotics they would make him identify himself or trace the call and ID his phone.

Greg dropped the girl off at the school and smiled. It was two thirty so there wasn't much school left. She smiled too and they parted ways. Robert took some more photos even though they would probably be worthless in court. They didn't show her using the crystal, nor did they show anything but maybe statutory rape. In California some judges would throw the book at you and others would dismiss it with evidence that the girl consented. The pictures of her and Greg were pretty clear, but even that wasn't proof that he gave her drugs in exchange for sex. You'd have to prove that the material in the envelope was in fact an illegal drug. Pretty hard without getting it, which would be pretty hard without a warrant.

PI's do have some advantage over the police in those areas they don't have to read anyone their rights and they can search without a warrant. Of course they're liable if the search doesn't prove fruitful but sometimes it works out good. Robert watched the school until 3:15 when the girl came out and got into a car with an apparent boyfriend. She took out the little white envelope and put a little of it into a homemade pipe. She lit it up and took a drag and gave a drag to her boyfriend. They went home to her house and Robert noted the address and took a couple of pictures of the stuff they were smoking. It would be hard to use as evidence. The defense would ask if Robert ever lost sight of the girl and then point out that she could be smoking anything in the world and that she could have gotten it from anyone because she had had contact with hundreds of other students during the time she was in school. So legally connecting what she was smoking with Greg was a problem and secondly proving that it was a narcotic would be very difficult.

It was quarter after four so Robert left the house and drove to Brian's office. He arrived at five ten and walked in. The secretary had gone home and the grandparents were there sitting at the attorney's desk. The woman was weeping. Robert knocked and Brian signaled for him to come in.

"What ya got?" Brian asked.

"I can show the car was deliberately damaged. I can show the husband Greg dealing drugs to a minor and buying and selling. I can show Greg probably with neglect towards the kids. I also got the doctor to tell me that the babies were given an overdose of Robitussin with codeine, according to the babysitter about four or five tablespoons. The Robitussin was about ten years old. I haven't gotten to the prescription to see to whom it was issued, but the baby tender gave the kids the drug. She, of course, claims that he told her to do it and she didn't know there was codeine in it. He, of course, will say he never told her to give the kids any of it. The funeral is scheduled for tomorrow afternoon. I think I should be there to see who comes and see if I can get any more info on Greg's friends and family. Sometimes that gives us leads. There is a lot of work to do to bring this thing together. I don't know if I can do it as fast as you need it done. When is the first hearing and when do you need my case?"

Brian said the case would be heard in one week. Monday at ten a.m.

"I can get you some help if you could use it. Also we need to know what the entire case is gonna cost," Brian said, and both Jason and Marge turned and looked at Robert.

"I won't charge you any more than I'm already charging. I'll personally pay the help. But I do need a pretty competent person; this isn't your average domestic case. In total it's going to take me at least ten days, which includes court time and write-up time. That total is four thousand dollars plus expenses of motel, gas, food, write-up expenses and mileage. I calculate that my total cost will be approximately eight thousand dollars. It might be less but that's the approximate bottom line."

Brian turned to Jason and Marge.

"It's up to you. I think we can get Jackson from this guy. But it costs a lot of money and it's going to take some time. I don't know if you have either."

Jason cleared his throat. Not just the incidental hack, no, he cleared long and deep. Then he turned to Marge and smiled.

"I think we should let it go, honey. I know you really want the baby. I know you really miss our daughter, but I think it's too risky."

"So we let a child go to hell, just because it's risky to try to save him. And I know our money is low, but we can get a loan on the cows, on our equipment. We can even get a loan on our house. Please don't leave little Jackson to this animal."

Jason turned back to Robert. "So you think your total costs will be eight thousand or less?"

Robert hated to give exact figures because there were always contingencies, but he leaned forward in the chair and said, "I'll charge you no more than eight thousand dollars regardless of how much time or investment I have to do on my part."

"So we're talking about seventy or eighty thousand dollars to get a child to live with us? Right?" Jason said, looking right into Marge's eyes.

"It's not just a child. It's Jackson. It's our child's child. Why do we go to church if in the end we want our things more than we want to give, to love, to care for our grandchild?"

Jason turned to Brian.

"What are our chances? Give me the bottom line!"

"It's hard to say. I'd give us at least a 75% chance of winning. What do you think?" he asked, turning to Robert.

"I think we can show this guy an unfit parent. I also suggest that we test the baby and see if he really is the father. The kid's white, blond hair, blue eyes, what are the chances of Greg being the biological father?"

"Golden would have told me if she had had an affair with anybody else," Marge said in a slightly defiant voice.

"I've done a little background on Wendy, and anyone who lives with and goes out with that girl probably won't stay a virgin long," Robert answered pointedly.

Brian listened intently and then agreed with Robert.

"We'll need to time it just right. I think it will be easy to get a court order, but if we do it too soon he may rabbit with the kid, and if we do it too late it will appear as a desperate attempt to the judge."

"We're gonna have a tough time getting blood from Greg. He's a user and doesn't want any legal proof of his habit," Robert proffered.

"I can make up a non-disclosure waiver for the blood analysis promising they won't look at anything but the comparison of gene type to the child."

"Any chance we can not get that waiver delivered on time so the blood people accidentally discover the level of drugs in his system?" Robert asked, smiling.

"Maybe," Brian answered. Turning to Marge and Jason he said, "Well, it's really up to you. I'm sorry these cases cost so much. There is a mountain of paperwork and investigation and preparation and interviews and depositions to be done. If you'd like to check with another attorney or anything like that please feel free to do so."

"No, we're going to do it," Jason said with some defeat in his voice.

"Okay, Robert, your help is a man called Carl Olden, he's good and he is sincerely interested in saving the child. I'll call you tonight and tell you where to meet him tomorrow."

"Okay, I'll need him to help me with the funeral so see if we can meet early."

❖

It was after ten when Brian called. Robert had gone down to the restaurant to eat. After eating he went down to the hot Jacuzzi to soak. He was just walking back into his room when the phone rang. Brian gave him Carl's phone number and address.

Robert called with some reluctance. He usually worked alone, but he really needed the help this time. There was too much to do and too little time for him to do it all alone. Carl was not only very pleasant, he seemed to be competent. As they talked Robert learned that Carl had served as a Navy SEAL. Robert was impressed. He also learned that Carl had done some investigation on his own and so he did have some experience. Carl expressed a willingness to do whatever was assigned him. An unusual quality for someone who had the authority and status of a Navy SEAL. They made plans to meet for breakfast early.

Five a.m. came early. The alarm on the end table started playing classical music. Robert loved the masters, especially Tchaikovsky. Robert rolled over in the bed and thought, *Maybe I can sleep for another fifteen and still make the six appointment*. He reached over, turned off the alarm, and rolled back over and closed his eyes.

"No, I gotta get up, shower, shave and get going," he said out loud.

He rolled over and almost fell off the bed.

"What I need is a good cup of coffee."

After his shower and dawning of clothing he walked to the restaurant downstairs. Carl was already there.

"Hi, I'm Robert Bosley. You been waiting long?"

"No, I just got here five minutes ago."

"Okay, let's have some breakfast and discuss what needs to be done today and decide who will do what."

They both ate a good breakfast and decided to go to Jason's funeral together. They also decided to each take a different part of Greg's background and go get some data. Robert told Carl about his exchanging drugs for sex with the teeny bopper and that he had gotten some pictures. Carl was impressed.

"The defense will probably make a motion to suppress, so we'll probably need to introduce it first as a witness statement from me. He'll then make the motion but that way the judge gets to hear it even though it might be suppressed. He'll still have it in his mind."

"Can he get away with suppressing important information like that? I thought the court wanted to hear all the truth in a case?" Carl naively asked.

"No, courts seldom want to hear all the truth. Courts are mostly word games. The one who can manipulate, express, and circumvent the most wins," Robert said sarcastically.

"So what are we doing?" Carl asked.

"Just giving Brian enough tools to make the best word scenario he can. If he has all the facts, he can manipulate them to make a good argument and case for his clients. It's simple: convince the judge, win the case."

They left in separate cars. Carl had brought a good camera with a telephoto lens. Robert was impressed. He assigned Carl to photograph all the people at the funeral and who spoke with whom. Carl didn't understand why that would be important, but Robert said it might. He also asked Carl to take photos of the cars, and who was driving them. Finally he asked him to take pictures of the emotions expressed by the guests as best he could.

When they got to the funeral, Carl pretended to be a reporter and went up to the entrance. The entire attending population was Afro-American and he stood out like a sore thumb. They denied him entrance. He stepped away from the entrance and looked into the bushes where Robert was hiding. Robert just shook his head. Luckily no one saw him looking and so no one discovered Robert. Carl busily took all the photos he was assigned to and even talked with some of the ladies and others attending the funeral. There was about a half hour given for viewing before the funeral started.

At five minutes to nine, Marge showed up. She was wearing a blue dress with a black patch on her right shoulder. She was the only one not dressed almost completely in black. She was white so at first she was denied entrance, but the doorman asked Greg, who nodded, and they let her in.

During the services, Carl talked with some of the drivers of the vehicles, mostly hired limo drivers, and with others. There was one woman who identified herself as Martha Coleman. Carl asked if she was related to Greg and she answered with a sarcastic grin.

"Yeah, I'm his wife."

Carl had brought a small microcassette, but he hadn't turned it on.

"Oh, when were you married?" he asked as nonchalantly as he could muster.

"We've been married for almost eight years. We haven't been living together for the past five or so, but we've been married."

"So you never got a divorce?"

"No, But it's okay. He had that white bitch, the kids probably aren't his anyway. I figure now he has some money, he'll come back to Mama."

She turned and walked away.

"How come you are not in the funeral house with the rest of the people?" Carl said to her back.

She turned and laughed. "I wasn't invited, an' the guy at the door wouldn't let me in. That's okay too, I'm gonna get the prize anyway."

She turned and walked to her car, a little Ford Taurus parked across the street in front of someone's driveway, got in, and drove off.

Robert had been busy writing down all the plate numbers and watching an older lady who was invited to go in but refused. He suspected she was probably Greg's mother. Why she didn't go in wasn't clear. Maybe she didn't like funerals, or maybe she didn't approve of the children or the marriage or maybe she was unhappy with Greg.

Robert motioned to Carl to talk with her but she had walked into the lobby of the chapel and sat down outside the assembly hall.

The funeral was short. In less than an hour, the doors opened. A couple of women came out and you could see they had been crying. Most came out without any signs of emotion. Greg came out, emotionless. He looked around, probably for the woman who had claimed to be his wife. He shook hands with several of the older people and walked over to the woman who Robert suspected to be his mother. He spoke to her with his head turned to her ear. She shook her head in the negative and turned and walked away. She spoke with a couple of the others who had attended the funeral. She talked intimately with an older gentleman. She hugged a couple of other women and walked slowly to the limousine where her son waited. The baby's body was in the back. She scooted in and kissed her son on the cheek, but still didn't say anything more to him.

Carl followed the procession to the airport where Greg and Marge had agreed to take the baby and bury it next to his mother in Minnesota. There was a short ceremony at the airport. Greg's mom took some more pictures. Carl followed and also took pictures, mostly of the faces of the people. When the film was developed, they were great. Carl really did have the knack and intuitively knew whom to take a picture of and when.

Robert waited at the funeral home until everyone had left. He walked up to the man closing the door and asked if he could talk with the director. The usher led him into the office off the lobby and knocked on the door. A man in his late fifties appeared at the door and asked if he could be of any assistance. Robert started off by saying he hadn't lost anyone but wondered if he could talk a little about the funeral that had just finished. The director said of course and asked what Robert's interest was. Robert lied and said he was the agent for the insurance. The director said he didn't personally know Greg and was contracted by Greg's mother. He said he hadn't spoken with Greg even though he had tried to talk with him in order to make the eulogy more personal and effective. Greg was never home.

Robert got a photo of the guest list in the lobby while he sent the director to see if he could check if the grandparents had contributed to the costs of the funeral. He also took a couple of photos of the director and assistants whose pictures were hanging on the wall above the desk. The casket selected was the least expensive one the parlor offered. Brian had already made a petition to take the body and bury it next to the baby's mother in Minnesota. Marge's friend was waiting there and would bury the baby. When they returned they would have a graveside service.

Robert left and went back to the address of the girl who had given sex to Greg in exchange for some drugs. He had swung by the library last night and cross-referenced the address. Ms. Reynolds owned it. Robert didn't know if she was the one living there or if she only rented the place. Generally the Polk index will tell you if the place is rented or lived in by the owner. It said it was not rented. Robert really wanted to talk with the high school girl. He hoped the mother wasn't home. As he pulled up the cul-de-sac, he saw the same old Ford that her boyfriend drove her home with the last time. It pulled up to the curb, they kissed and argued a little, and she got out of the car, turned and gave him the finger and walked up the steps to her front door. He squealed off. Robert got out of the car and walked up the walkway. He knocked.

She opened the door saying she had said "no" and was startled to see the face of someone else.

"Hi, I thought you were someone else. Whaddya want?"

"My name is Robert, I'm a private investigator and I'd like to talk with you for a couple of minutes."

"I don't know. You guys are spooky. Don't ya have to show me some badge or something?"

"Sure," Robert said, opening his folding wallet where his PI ID with his picture and name and number were splattered across the little plastic enclosed card. She took it from him. That always made him nervous. Usually he'd never let someone take it. It had been his experience that sometimes they wouldn't give it back.

"Whaddya wanta talk about?" she asked in valley girl slang, giving him back his ID without really even reading it.

Robert sat down on one of the three chairs sitting on the front porch and she followed suit.

"What's your name?" Robert asked.

"My real name is Linda, but everyone calls me Crystal," she said.

"I want to make you a deal. I have some photos of you and Mr. Coleman. They are very incriminating. Not only for statutory rape, but for drug dealing and use. I'm willing to give you the photos and the negatives, if you call and tell both the cops and a judge, which I'll name, that Greg traded sex with you for drugs. You can do it anonymously, but you have to do it and I have to see the report come out of the police department. You'll have to tell them your age and where you go to school, but before you do that, get a commitment from them that they will not try to identify you. Make him look like a predator. Make him look like the son of a bitch he is. Finally, don't tell him we've had this conversation, or I'll have your ass in jail in five minutes."

"Let me see the photos," she asked timidly

Robert took out eighteen of the more than thirty and showed her making payment for the drugs, the sex, the smoking with her boyfriend. The pictures had a time and date stamped on them.

Robert hoped she didn't know the law too well. Actually the pictures didn't prove anything except she had sex with an adult. The little white crystal ball could have been salt. She looked at the pictures for almost ten minutes. Her mouth dropped open.

"So you'll give me the pictures and the negatives? And you won't tell anybody, not the cops, not my mom, not Greg, nobody. Right?"

"I give you my word."

She looked into his eyes for a couple of seconds. Then she leaned down to tie her shoe. She had no bra on and her breasts hung exposed. Robert looked away. When she came up she said, "Ya know, no one's home right now. Wouldn't ya like to come in and have some coffee?"

She wasn't unattractive. She was young and well built. Her face was pretty and she seemed to know what she was doing.

"Thank you," Robert responded. "Life's too short for me to go there." He stood up and said, "Remember, tell no one that we had this conversation, and make those two calls. I'll contact you the day after tomorrow. Give me your phone number and I'll call. Or if you prefer, I'll come by."

"No, no, don't come by here again. Call me before 7:30 p.m. That's when my mom gets home from work. How will I get the pictures and negs? From you?"

"I'll keep my word, the minute I know you made the two calls, I'll put them in your mailbox before you come home from school, but after your mom leaves."

"How can I trust you?" she asked, getting a little braver.

"Because I'm honest and because you don't have much of a choice. I could go to the police right now. But so far I haven't."

"How come? What's in it for you?"

Robert didn't answer. He would have liked to tell her about the death of Greg's wife and child, but over the years he had discovered that too much information is a dangerous thing for a teeny bopper druggie to have.

Robert walked down the stairs and looked back to make sure she had gone into the house. He didn't want her to see his car or get the plate number. He wanted to make sure she had as little information about him as he could give her. He wasn't sure if she even really caught his name, she never called him by it. He was pretty sure she didn't read the ID he had handed her.

❖

It was after six. Robert wondered if Carl was able to trace that marriage thing or not. He got on his cell and called Carl. Carl answered in a tired voice.

"Hi. How'd it go with you?" Carl said when answering the phone.

He must have one of those caller ID phones, Robert thought.

"It went pretty good. I talked to his sex partner, the high school girl who he was supplying drugs to. She's gonna call the PD and the judge. I've gotta get the name of the judge from Brian and call her back and give it to her. She's gonna call both of them tomorrow, I hope. Were you able to get any more information at the cemetery? Also were you able to run that girl's story about being married to Greg?"

"Yes, I got a lot of info for you. Let's get together in the morning. I've gotta do some personal business tonight, but let's meet for breakfast."

"Okay, same place. Let's meet at eight."

With that Robert hung up and pulled into a Sizzler to have a steak.

⋗•⋖

The rest of the evening Robert spent reviewing all the events, cross-referencing the names on the funeral parlor sign-in book, and trying to build a character picture of Greg. He spent almost three hours compiling the data he had gotten so far, particularly on Greg and his activities. First there was the VW; clearly the break line had been somehow filed until it was cracked. Robert still wasn't sure how it was filed, clearly not by a file or saw because it resembled wear except for the wear patterns didn't match the wear patterns on the body and there were places that, when examined with a magnifying glass, it was clear that the wear was new. The same with the gas line. Even though it was mostly melted, and the wire cutting across it appeared to have worn a groove into the line that eventually caused it to leak. Had Greg insisted she take the VW when he sent her out on the night of her death? There was probably no way to tell. But it seemed reasonable, especially if his intent was to kill her or at least do her great bodily harm. The child was still a puzzle. Why would he want to kill the boys? Robert made a note in his palm to check with the telephone company and find out how much insurance was carried on both Golden and on her children. He finished compiling all the documents and all the information he had by three in the morning and went to bed.

The alarm rang at seven. Four hours' sleep was not enough. But he got up and took a quick shower and gathered his notes. It was quarter to eight when he walked into the restaurant. Carl wasn't there yet, so he ordered a pot of coffee. Robert took out his notes and his conclusions from last night and planned the day. First he would go to the telephone company. He would send Carl to the city and then to the county to see if he could find a marriage record on Greg prior to his marriage to Golden. If he couldn't find a record, he would send him to the mother's house. She shouldn't be hard to find. Her name was on the funeral list on the top of the page. A space reserved for the next of kin. Her last name was not Coleman, but she may have remarried.

After the telephone company visit, he would go to the PD and see if they got the report on the rape (statutory) by Greg. Robert was pretty sure he could get the info from the PD, but not so sure the judge's secretary or clerk would give it up. The last place he planned to visit on that day was back to the doctor's place. He suspected the doctor had a personal relationship with Golden and he wanted to see just how far it had gone. Maybe the doctor was the father of the children. That might explain Greg's desire to kill him. He also had to go see Brian tomorrow and report what he had done to that point and what else needed to be done. Brian would give him the schedule for the hearing and he'd know how much more time he had to finish the investigation. He also had to meet with the grandparents, probably in their hotel room, and tell them what he had discovered and what else he thought he could do. Probably get some more money; he was running low. The motel, car, and food were costing him more than he had anticipated. Also he had given $350 to Carl for gas and food and he had shot more than six rolls of film and used five microtapes so he'd need more tape and film.

Carl was five minutes late. He apologized. It was okay. Robert could see he was good. He must have been a good SEAL; he knew what to look for and what to write down. He even took some good photos. He had a one of those new electronic cameras; they were great. He loaded it up on his laptop and showed Robert all the people at the funeral. He showed him who was talking with whom and got a good photo of the woman who claimed to be married to Greg. She had bragged about her name, so Carl figured that she would be listed as Mrs. Coleman. He said he'd check and see if he could get some more info from her. Robert told Carl the name of the mother and said she probably lived in the greater LA area. She dressed well so probably not Watts, but he wasn't sure. Carl said he could find her.

"You need anything else from her except the marriage angle?" he asked.

"Yes, see if you can get any info on the marriage date and place and check to see if there is any divorce record. You'll probably have to start at the county records and go from there. They were probably married here in LA, so with any luck it should be pretty easy. We also need any info on previous criminal behavior. When you find the mother, see if she thinks the kids are his and see if she liked Golden or not. In general get all the information you can from her. I'd pre-make up my questions so she doesn't divert you. Then even if she wanders, you can get back to the right questions. I have found if you don't, you get off talking with the person you are questioning and before you know it, you've missed the chance to glean good information."

Breakfast went well. Carl was a careful eater. He ate pancakes made with wheat and buttermilk and drank bottled water. He didn't have any coffee either. Robert told him he'd call him and tell him when they needed to meet with Brian and also they needed to meet with the grandparents. If Carl was busy, perhaps he'd meet with the grandma and grandpa alone. But for sure he needed Carl at the meeting with Brian. Robert also said he needed all the information, facts, and conclusions by Carl written up and printed on paper with the name type and case number at the top of the page. Carl again thanked Robert for letting him work with him and reviewed what he was going to do that day. Robert paid for breakfast and gave Carl another fifty for gas, food, and other needs.

At the police department, the clerk said he didn't know anything about a call from anybody claiming statutory rape, especially in exchange for drugs. Cops are almost impossible to bribe, but if you "good ol' boy" them, you usually can get the information you need, providing it's not really important to an investigation or clearly restricted by the captain or somebody with authority. Robert told the clerk how he used to clerk when he was a cop.

"They made me do it once every three months for a week. Too cheap to hire a full-time desk sergeant."

"Yeah, I know, you'd think the great city of LA could get some permanent desk guy; instead they use anyone who might have been injured. Too cheap to pay workman's comp so they put you on what they call limited duty. What a bunch of crap!"

It wasn't long before the sergeant was looking in the incoming log for a report. He found it. Robert thanked him and offered to get him a *real* cup of coffee. The sergeant said if he found one on his desk, he'd drink it. Robert went outside to a coffee shop nearby and got a big cup of some Hawaiian Kona brew, took it up, and without saying anything, left it on the front desk. The sergeant smiled.

⇒•⇐

It was almost noon by the time Robert left the police station. He drove back to the Hollywood hospital. He asked for Dr. Eric. He told the nurse he just needed a couple of minutes to talk with him a little more about the Coleman death. Dr. Erickson came out of the emergency room; his whites had a bloodstain on the right lower half, but the rest of him was clean.

"Hi, Doc. I don't know if you remember me, my name is Robert Bosley, I'm a PI investigating the death of Mrs. Golden Coleman."

"Yes, I remember you. How is your case going?" he asked.

Robert felt a trust in Eric he hadn't felt for many years. The guy seemed sensitive and full of integrity. Almost never had Robert revealed details of an investigation to one of the people in the investigation, but he blurted out, "The case is going well. We found out that Greg was still married to another woman."

The doctor looked blankly at Robert. He even stepped back a step and then sighed. Not a sigh of relief but a deep hurt and anger sigh.

"What more from me would you like to know?" he asked.

"Are you the father of the children?" Robert asked.

"No, I knew Goldie well. I took her out a couple of times and treated her when her husband or boyfriend beat her almost to death."

"Did you report the assault to the police?"

"Yes. But she kept saying she fell down and the investigating officer, a uniform, said he wasn't gonna press charges just on my say-so. Particularly because no other charges had ever been brought against Greg."

"You said you took her out?"

"Yes, I really liked her from the first time I met her. She had a kind of innocence that I loved. She also was really bright and full of life. When I examined her she was pregnant. I told her she had a positive reading on the blood test and even she was surprised. Later I drove down to San Diego and took her to dinner."

"So you definitely didn't get her pregnant?" Robert asked, looking Eric right in the eye.

"No, not that I wouldn't have, but she was already pregnant when I first saw her. When we went out we didn't make love. Just talked."

"You mean you take out a very beautiful woman, one who you say is innocent and vulnerable, and you don't even try to make it with her?"

"No. I was an intern when we first met and I was working 80 hours a week. Not only was I tired, but also I am an honest man. She didn't want it. So we talked."

"About what?"

"Her boyfriend, who I think was by the second time we went out then her husband. She didn't say, but I kinda put two and two together and figured it out."

"What'd you say about her husband?"

"That he was a rat. He had a criminal record and had spent a couple of times in jail. Also he had been arrested seven times where the charges were dropped because they didn't have enough proof to get a conviction and the DA wouldn't take the case."

"You don't have that written down anywhere, do you?"

"Of course. I got it from the county court records. I'm not much of a PI, but I figured I'd check the county."

The doctor walked with Robert to his locker in the back of the emergency room and took out a thin stack of papers.

"It's all here."

"You know the kids are white as snow, don't you?"

"Yeah, I know. I treated them, remember? Maybe I was wrong about her being so innocent. You think I oughta take a blood test?"

"Not if there's no possibility of you being the father to the kids."

"You think Greg had something to do with her death?" Robert asked.

"Probably not directly, but yes, I think he did."

"Thanks, Doc. May I call you if I come up with any other questions?"

"Absolutely. Here's my card. Let me put my home number on the back."

Robert left the hospital with a sick feeling in his stomach. The doctor obviously knew even more than he was saying. Probably afraid of being accused of stalking or homewrecking or something. Still, it would be easy enough to check the dates of when they went out and compare to the term of her pregnancy. He was also willing to have the blood test done on himself. Those things go to his innocence, at least as far as being the father of the twins goes. He obviously was trying to steal her away from Greg. Probably would have been much better for her if he had succeeded.

Two thirty. Robert had a change of plans.

"I think I'll go down to San Clemente and visit with Wendy. She must know if Golden was sexually active," he said out loud as he got into his car. He reached into his sports coat pocket and turned off the recorder, took out the tape, and wrote down the date and time of the conversation.

"What a strange case," he said as he started the car and drove over to I-5 and south. Traffic wasn't bad yet. It was still early enough before the five o'clock rush that the southbound traffic hadn't started. On the way down Robert called Brian and asked when and where he wanted to hook up. Brain said that Jason and Marge were in the Ramada just south of Pasadena and were hoping to see him tonight at about eight. Robert committed to it and asked if Brian could call Carl. Brian said he didn't have time and Carl didn't need to be at the meeting anyway. Normally Robert would have conceded the point, but he felt that with the information that Carl had gotten, it would be nice to report it to the grandparents.

"Is it okay if I call him and invite him? He's got some really good stuff."

"Why don't you meet with me at four and we can all go over the details of the investigation to this point?" Brian asked.

"Can we make it five? I'm en route to San Clemente to see Wendy."

"Yeah, be at my office at five."

Robert called Carl and he agreed to meet at Brian's office at five p.m. Robert figured that he and Carl could report and then go together to see the Bradleys.

Wendy was home. She said she had a date that she expected at four thirty so he only had forty-five minutes or so. Robert came straight to the point. "Was Golden sexually active while she live here with you?"

"Hell no. I tried to get her to put out a little. After all, those guys spend a lot of money and they expect something in return. But she wasn't putting out. She loved going on the dates. We went out three or four times a week, but to the best of my knowledge, she never put out until she did it with Greg."

Wendy was smart and in the know. Robert sensed that she was also a very unequivocal truth teller, at least to him. He was sure she lied to the boys, but in this case Wendy obviously loved Goldie and wasn't concealing anything.

"What do you think of Greg?"

"I think he's a son of a bitch. I encouraged Goldie to date anyone who would treat her with courtesy and had enough to spend a little money on her, but Greg was always funny about money. He carried a lot, but he seldom put out. He just got you where he wanted you and then pretended to either not have it or that he'd get it tomorrow. He did sometimes pay Goldie back, and sometimes he treated her great, but other times he was selfish, mean and if you ask me, really stupid."

"Can you tell me how and where they first met?"

Wendy told Robert the story of the spilt drink and of the first time Goldie went out with Greg. She told him about their first sexual encounter and how Goldie had called her and told her all about it. She told him about her home in Minnesota and about Goldie saving her life in the forest.

The doorbell rang. Wendy abruptly stopped and said, "This is my date, gotta go."

She got up and Robert followed her to the door. As they got to the door he asked her one last question: "Do you think he killed her?"

"I really don't know. I do know he was and is a drug dealer. I got that from several friends, some of whom buy from him, but I don't know. If you're thinking she had an affair and he offed her because of the white kids, I'd have to say no. She'd a told me if she had sex with anyone else. The doctor came to see her in San Diego. I was hoping she'd make it with him, but she said no. I honestly don't think she has ever had sex with any other person than that bastard."

She opened the door and Robert excused himself and left. It was four ten and he hurriedly drove north. Traffic wasn't bad northbound. Most of the cars were leaving LA and so it wasn't too bad going north. At the I-5 and 805 exchanges he was stalled for about fifteen minutes, but he got past that and got to Brian's office at five ten. He'd called Carl when he got into the car at Wendy's and Carl said he'd be at Brian's by five.

Robert unloaded the disk from the recorder and put the time and date on it. He had a little plastic holder where he put each tape. So far this case had only used six tapes, which was less than Robert thought he'd have used by now. He walked up the stairs and into Brian's office. Carl was there. He had been reporting to Brian all that he had discovered, all the information he had developed. Robert came in on the last of it but asked him to repeat it because he needed to correlate it with what he had done. Carl proudly said, "I've got him by the balls. He was married to ol' Martha eight years ago, and they never got a divorce!"

"Are you sure? They might have gone to Tijuana and got a quickie?" Robert probed.

"No, I checked Tijuana and the other border towns in Mexico. I also checked the other counties here in California. You have to live in Las Vegas for six months to get a divorce there, so to the best of my knowledge, they're still married. The son of a bitch is a bigamist!" Carl said with a smile. Both Robert and Carl looked simultaneously at Brian. He wasn't as impressed as even Robert thought he should be.

"That's good info. You got anything else?"

"It's more than good," Carl said. "It's great. Can't we now have the marriage annulled and give the kids to the grandparents?"

"It's not that easy here in California. We've got to show that the biological originator, i.e. Greg, knew he was still married to Martha and that he's not a fit parent." Brian was obviously pleased with the report but not as excited as both Robert and Carl.

Carl proceeded to tell Brian about the people he had spoken with in the apartment where they were presently living and the one where they had first lived. Neighbors said that Greg would leave the kids alone outside of the apartment while he did business inside. He also left them sometimes for hours while he slept. Carl had reports from three people who were willing to testify that he was drunk most of the time and the rest of the time he was abusive with the kids.

Brian made fastidious notes and said he needed Carl's report written up and on his office desk in the morning. He turned to Robert and said, "What have you got, Robert?"

Robert made his report and said he still needed to talk with the mother, and to go see the dealer in San Diego. He thought he could put some pressure on him to roll. He showed the photos of the car, the gas and brake lines, he showed the photos of the trade of drugs for sex. He played back the conversation with the girl, with Wendy, with the doctor, and with the PD.

"I think we should test the little boy. I'm not sure he's really the son of Greg. He's white as snow and Greg is black as night."

Brian interrupted. "Let's talk about that in a minute. I think you both have done an excellent job. I'll meet you at the hotel tonight at eight. Why don't you go get something to eat? Let me lead the conversation with Jason and Marge. I'll be specific about what information I want you to give them. Okay?"

"You bet," Robert said.

Carl sat thinking about it. As they left he asked Robert why he couldn't just tell the clients all he had discovered. Robert laughed quietly.

"Because some of it is unprovable and clients tend to blurt out anything they know that they think will damage the opposition. Also if you don't tell them all you have, but tell them you have quite a bit more not quite ready for them, they will be more willing to pay. It's a matter of working the facts."

Carl wasn't satisfied with the answer, but he settled for it. They went to Subway and had a sandwich. Eight o'clock came and everyone got to the motel on time except Brian. He was about five minutes late. His lateness made it uncomfortable for Robert and Carl. They sat and talked about the weather here in California as compared to the weather in Minnesota. The grandparents were also nervous and Jay paced back and forth while they talked. Brian got there and apologized for his tardiness. He led the conversation and told them in essence what the investigators had discovered about Greg. Brian then went, without letting the grandparents ask questions, to what his legal plan was. It was to show that Greg would be not only unable to raise Jackson, but that he was an unfit parent. Brian would show this with my photos of him and the teenage girl and with his criminal record, and with evidenced that he dealt drugs. The conversation lasted almost an hour.

Robert spoke for a couple of minutes. He suggested that Brian might introduce the racial difference. That little Jackson would have a difficult time adjusting to living in the Watts area because he was Anglo and that might create a social stigma that would be very difficult to overcome. Robert finally suggested that Brian get a court order to test Greg and Jackson to see if he really was Greg's child. Marge was offended, but Jason thought it to be a good idea. Brian said it could backfire. "If the tests show that Greg is in fact the father of the child, it will give him an advantage."

"What kind of an advantage? The man is a drug dealer, immoral, and a killer of children?"

Jason's voice level was up and his face had reddened.

Brian answered, "Sometimes what we know and what we can prove and finally what is admitted into court are entirely different things. I know it is frustrating, Jason, but the only way we can win this case is with evidence, not anger."

Brian paused and then turned to Marge, who was sitting on the bed.

"Okay, so do you want to test him or not?" Brian asked.

"Yes. If he's not the dad, then we've got a great shot of taking home our only grandchild," Marge perked up.

"Okay, Robert, can you get Greg served?" Brian asked.

"I don't want him to see me yet. I'll have Carl serve him. How soon can you get the court order?"

"I'll try to get it first thing in the morning. Come to my office by eleven and I'll have it for you. Where is the baby now?"

Robert looked at Carl.

"I think he has been put in CPS for the time being. Do you know Carl?"

Carl looked up from some of the papers he was reading. His answer seemed a little slow. Robert figured he was a still in a little shock that the marriage information wasn't the clincher.

"Yes, yes, the baby is still with Child Protective Services."

"Okay," Brian answered. "Robert, you go get the blood from the kid there and, Carl, you serve and get blood from Greg. Let's get this done tomorrow. We've got four days to court, folks, so let's get going."

Robert then reported on what was left to investigate and how much time it would take.

"I still need to talk with the dealer in Chula Vista. I think I can get him to roll on Greg. If he does, Greg will be spending some time in jail, and you'll get the kid. Also we need to get some records of his criminal history and do a broader search of any arrest record he may have. We also need to get written testimony or a deposition from neighbors about how he treated the children. Only Brian can do that, so it's his call. Also, we need to see what the DA's going to do with the baby tender. There are a couple more loose ends we need to tie up, but I figure four more days and we should be done."

Turning to Brian, Robert asked when the hearing date was set for. Brian said he had tried to push it up even more because Jason and Marge needed to get back home, they had the farm to run and they were running out of money.

"It's still this coming Tuesday at ten a.m.," he said. "So you've got your four days."

"It's gonna take a day to coordinate all the data and write it up. When do you need to discover?" Robert asked.

"Tomorrow morning, but we can introduce some documents in court. I'll just tell the judge and Greg's attorney that we just got certain documents and they need to be introduced. He'll probably object but I'm sure the judge will allow it a couple of times before he looks at us with a jaundiced eye. The defense can look at them in court. He won't be happy with that, but I think we can get away with it."

Robert left the hotel a little nervous. Carl also was a little disappointed.

"How come we didn't tell them the marriage was bogus?" he asked, implying they should have told the grandparents everything they had. .

"That's Brian's call. There might be some legal maneuvering he's got in mind. I don't know. I've learned to trust Brian. It's one thing you learn as a private investigator. You do your job and the attorney does his. You can't be all things to all people. I really make an effort to just do the best I can and let the system work. Sometimes it does and sometimes it doesn't. This case looks great. I promise you we'll show that he was married to a second party in court."

The answer was a little unsettling to Carl, but he accepted it and asked if they were going to meet tomorrow. Robert said he was gonna go check some of the other counties and maybe drive up to Sacramento to see if he could pull any records on Greg at the state level. He paused and then said, "On second thought, I think I'll go on down to Chula Vista and see if I can find the dealer. I've got a pretty good picture of him, so I'll go ask around. Maybe I can meet with him and see if he wants to deal. Let's meet tomorrow morning and I'll give you a couple more things to do, if you can, and I'll go south."

"I have some business at eight, so it'll need to be before or later at eleven or so."

"Great, I think I'm gonna sleep in. I'll see you at eleven. Let's meet at that pizza place off Wiltshire, you know the one where the Jacksons sometimes eat."

Carl thanked Robert again for letting him come along and help. Robert shook his head and smiled.

"You've been great. I couldn't have done half of it without you, thank you."

No alarm, just Robert lazily opening his eyes. He had been up for the last two days, so when he looked at the alarm clock on the stand by the bed he wasn't surprised to see the time. It was ten to ten. He rolled over and sat up on the edge of the bed. He sat for only a couple of minutes and then stood and sort of staggered toward the bathroom. The shower was slow and relaxing. The warm water felt good. It seemed to relieve him of the tensions of the case and help him focus on the things he needed to do today. Carl was on time.

"Okay, Carl, why don't you go talk with the mother. I've been meaning to do it, but just haven't had the time. Time is now not on our side, so go take her to lunch or something and get as much information as you can out of her. We need to know a little about his history, see if she'll tell you about any criminal activity he has been involved in and ask about his marriage to the other girl. Get as much info on that respect as you can. See if the old wife is pulling a money game. Also see if Greg knew he was still married to her. Talk as much as you can about his drug dealing. See if Mom knew about it and if she did see if she could tell you any more about it. After you're done with that go see the neighbors in both apartments again and get either written statements or appointments for a deposition. Take your recorder and tell them you are taping them. And finally go see Maria, you know, Goldie's supervisor at the telephone company. Can you get all that done today?"

"Yes, I'll be 'til midnight, but I'll do it."

"Great! You've got my cell, and I've got yours. Call me if you need anything or if you get something really hot. I'm heading down to Chula Vista. I don't know when I'll be back, but I'll call you and set up a time to meet."

Robert ordered a couple slices of pizza and a salad and gobbled it down with a soda. He got up and left a ten to pay his part of the bill. Carl stayed and had some spaghetti.

The trip to Chula Vista was tiring. Traffic was horrible. Robert reaffirmed to himself that he would never live in LA. Traffic was just too much. It was after three when he finally got to Chula Vista. He started with a couple of Mexican bars. He showed the picture and pretended he was a buyer. Before going into the bar, he took off his suit coat and put on a checkered lumberjack wool shirt. It was hot, but he rolled up the sleeves and said he was from Oregon. After a couple of drinks he found an obvious user who told him that "Ortega" came in about six or seven times a week. That he lived down in Mexico, in Tijuana, and it was easier to see him down there "'cause it's across the border."

Robert got some general directions from people in a couple of bars that Jamie Ortega frequented. He spoke Spanish fluently and so it made it easier to talk to some of the Latinos. He decided to go on down to Tijuana and see if he could find Ortega. It was about six p.m. when he walked across the border. Nobody inspects you coming in if you're walking. You just have to look like a local, or a rich tourist. Robert resembled a tourist, although probably not rich. He was carrying his boot pistol, which was no problem. Nobody ever searched you unless you were going into the interior. He carried it just in case. Over the years Robert had only used it a couple of times, but there were times when it had saved his life. It was a .40 semi-auto Glock with eleven rounds, including one in the pipe. Robert had bought it in Phoenix from a newspaper add. It wasn't registered. It had cost him right next to six hundred bucks, but it was worth it. Glocks are light and very accurate and extremely durable. The .40 caliber had a very good one-shot kill rate, probably the best in handguns. Robert had loaded it with a 180-grain hollow point and a hot load of powder.

Robert checked around and found the bar that Ortega usually

frequented. He went there and drank a bunch of sodas with a cherry on top and a thin straw. The drink looked like a rum and coke so he blended in.

It was almost nine thirty when he saw Ortega come into the bar. Robert knew him immediately. Not just by the pictures but also by the way he walked and carried himself. He remembered the guy from the Chula Vista encounter. Ortega walked over to the bar and without saying a word was served some tequila.

After a couple of drinks Robert approached him. He spotted Robert right off. Most druggies are paranoid. So when Robert approached him he watched him carefully. Ortega knew immediately Robert wasn't a user. But he didn't look like a cop so he figured he must be a PI.

"Your on the wrong side of the border to do anything stupid," Ortega proffered.

"I'm not here to do anything stupid. I've got a proposition for you. It'll make you some money and keep you out of jail and able to continue to do business on the other side."

"What do you got? I'm really doubtful I'm going to jail. I'll give you five minutes." He looked at his watch. Robert pulled out the photos and then said he had confiscated the stuff from Greg and it came back positive. He said there was no problem in chain of custody and with his witness and the photos he had Ortega by the short hairs.

They talked at the bar for almost an hour. Finally Ortega said, "Look, let's go over to my place. I'll give you the information you want on Greg and you can do what you want to with it. But I get the pictures and the negs too. Otherwise you can go screw yourself."

Robert followed him over to an upstairs apartment on the west side. It was an old building, and the apartment was ragged and unkempt. They walked up the stairs, Robert behind Ortega. Robert thought the set up seemed too easy, but Ortega didn't have a lot to lose, and there is no honor among thieves, so maybe he would give up Greg. Ortega had said he had some receipts and a couple of other really incriminating evidence against Greg that he would give up in exchange for Robert not ratting on him.

They walked into the living room. It had an old couch with material worn down and torn on the corners and on the armrests. The cushions were matted down in the middle and darkened from either hair oil or something else worse. The windows were covered over with black garbage bags that were taped to the sill. A pile of dishes was in the sink that was visible from the front door as was the stove and tiny refrigerator. The opening to the kitchen went half way across the room. The rest was a wall that also was one side of the hallway to the bedroom. There was only one row of open shelves on the kitchen wall where there were a couple of cups and plates. The rest were sitting in the sink together with a million flies and some rotting food. On a plate in the middle of a little table that sat half in the kitchen area and half into the living room there was an old piece of meat that Robert could smell even from the door. The table had a plastic tablecloth, which was red and black checkered and worn through so you could see the threads under the missing plastic in spots where elbows had set.

Ortega walked over to a small dresser against the wall opposite the kitchen and pulled open the top drawer. He shuffled through the drawer for a few seconds and then turned slowly around to Robert and raised a .357 Smith, cocked the hammer, and smiled. Robert's eye immediately went to the trigger finger. It was moving. He dove to the floor behind the couch as the first shot rang out. He rolled over back into the area just shot as another exploded in his ears. He reached into his right boot and pulled out the Glock. A third shot penetrated the couch and into the floor an inch from his face. He jumped up and fired. Ortega was expecting him on the other end of the couch because he had already fired at the end where Robert was. Robert fired only one shot but it punched into the chest of Ortega. He looked surprised. His arms went limp to his side and he looked again down at his chest. Blood was saturating his shirt and dripping down onto his belt, partially clotting there and then falling to the floor. Slowly he shook his head in the negative. His knees began to buckle and he swayed from side to side for a second. He made a slight cough and blood came out of the left corner of his mouth. He tried to raise his arm, to return fire, but somehow didn't have the strength. He realized he was dead, and that any effort to raise his pistol would only get him shot again. His eyebrows wrinkled and he looked at Robert again in wonder. His eyes dilated and his mouth opened and he fell. He fell straight forward, his head hitting the corner of the coffee table in front of the couch. It didn't matter, he was dead. Robert walked around the couch and kicked the pistol out of his hand, reached down and felt the carotid artery. He was dead.

In Mexico, nobody kills another, even in self-defense, and stays out of jail. Robert disarmed himself, wiped off the Glock, the clip, and the holster and threw it and the holster down on the floor. He wiped Ortega's neck and everywhere he had touched. It was a shame to give up such a good weapon. He then realized they might get some DNA off the holster because it had been strapped to his leg. He picked it up and planned to dump it into a garbage bin on the way out. The garbage collector would find it, but he could sell it. Because of its value he knew the garbage man would never give it to the local police. The reason he left a good and expensive Glock was that if he was checked going across the border, they'd hold him. That was one thing he didn't want. With a little luck, he'd have time to get out of Mexico before the body was discovered, providing the neighbors hadn't called the PD and they were on the way.

He opened the door with his handkerchief and turned the lock so it would lock when he closed it. He then quietly walked down the stairs and across the street. He walked another block, put the holster into the top of a garbage can, and hailed a taxi who took him to the border. At the American entry there was a pretty long line of people. He couldn't understand why there were so many people at that time of night, but he stood in line hoping that the TJ police wouldn't find the body, at least not for the next half hour or so. Finally he got to the booth.

"Of what country are you a citizen?" the INS officer asked.

"US," Robert responded.

"Please step over to the secondary inspection," the officer said.

Crap! Robert thought. *If I'm here when they discover the body, they'll close the border down and I'll be in deep shit.*

"Hi," Robert said to the secondary officer. "I didn't buy anything, just went over to get a taco. I love the street tacos."

"I hate 'em," the officer responded. "You never know what's in 'em and how long they have been on the stand with a million flies crawling all over them." The inspector looked at Robert for a second and then smiled. "Okay, you're okay, you can go."

What a relief, he didn't even search me, Robert thought as he walked away. As soon as he had cleared the metal gate, he walked hurriedly toward his car, which was parked in the park parking lot behind a chain link fence. The gate was still open. As he was getting into his car he saw the red lights come on and the Mexican police closing the border. There were a couple of Federales talking with the supervisor at the POE gate. Federales are the top cops in Mexico. They can shoot you without asking any questions and seldom even get written up for it. They have absolute power and if you're arrested by one of them, you'd better have a lot of money, or know the President of Mexico, because if not, you're going to jail and it's going to be a long time before you get out.

Robert drove off thanking his stars he had gotten out in time.

That was a dead end, in more ways than one. Maybe Robert could use the incident to intimidate Greg. *No*, he thought, *I'd better not. This whole affair stops here and now with me. I can never tell. It's not that the killing wasn't righteous; it's just that in Mexico there are few righteous judges. The US is frequently willing to extradite citizens back to Mexico for major capitol crimes. So the death of Ortega will have to go down as untold, unknown, and never spoken of.*

It was after midnight. Robert dialed up Carl in hopes of catching him still awake. He answered and asked Robert how his trip went. Robert answered saying he couldn't find the guy and dropped it at that. They made arrangements to meet in the morning at 7:00 a.m. and Robert sighed. He knew time was now getting very, very short. Carl had had some success and was anxious to report. There was a little pancake house on old 101 that Robert liked and they planned to meet there.

He got to the motel and flopped into his bed. He was so very tired, and yet the events of the day and especially of the evening scrambled across his mind.

I should have known when the guy asked me back to his apartment, he thought. *I should have spotted the trap. I should have danced with the girl in the light blue dress. The dip was good at the party....* His mind began to wander and he was soon fast asleep.

The morning came early. Robert got up at six and showered, shaved, and dressed. Traffic wasn't too bad and he made it over to the pancake house by ten after. Carl was there and enjoying a stack of waffles covered with strawberry topping and whipped cream. Robert sat down and ordered a cup of coffee. Carl gobbled his waffles and smiled.

"Whaddya got?" Robert asked.

"I spoke with the mother again yesterday. She gave the name of a friend of Greg's, one who she said would be very interesting. I went to his house and he was indeed very angry at Greg. Greg had reneged on a drug deal and had cheated him out of some money. His story is like this...Carl told of how this guy, named Adelbert, had been conned into robbing a 7-Eleven with Greg. Greg put a ski mask on and Adelbert waited in the car and drove. Greg went in with a gun and held up the store. As he was leaving he shot a hole in the ceiling and tipped over a couple of display racks. Adelbert drove away thinking they'd got a lot of money. Greg said he only got three hundred and fifty dollars. He gave Adelbert a hundred and said because he did all the work he'd keep the rest. He promised to make it up to him by bringing him some smack for cost for the next month or two. It never happened. Greg charged him the same and said if he said anything he'd kill him.

"The cops found Adelbert and questioned him, but he kept silent. Even though they offered him immunity for the name of the guy he was with and promised him prison if he didn't cop. He remained silent and the cops didn't have enough evidence to prosecute. It turned out that the clerk had written down the license plate number but had gotten one of the digits wrong. The public defender said if they took it to court, he'd eat the kid alive, so the DA declined to prosecute.

"The guy told Carl he'd testify but he wanted immunity from prosecution and 500 dollars. In exchange he'd give up the pistol used in the robbery. He'd taken it and stashed it under the seat when Greg came out and never gave it back."

This was really good info. In California any robbery with a weapon gets you mandatory prison time. With any luck, they could pin this on Greg and he'd be in prison and the grandparents could walk with the child. Robert told Carl to go to the PD and search the records and find the date and place of the robbery and see if they coincided with the story Adelbert was telling, then to go to the robbery division and see if they wanted info on the case. Make a complete report and call Robert when he was done. After that he was to serve Greg the blood papers and if necessary take him down to be tested. He was to take a Hollywood PD officer with him if he thought Greg would be any trouble.

Robert went to the telephone company and talked with Maria. Maria was extremely stressed. She had given Greg the second of three checks before she knew that Jason was dead. The first check was from the company insurance. It totaled one hundred fifty-three thousand dollars. The second was her savings, vacation pay, and the last week of pay. It totaled eight thousand three hundred and thirty-eight dollars and twenty-three cents. Greg informed her of the death of Jason after getting the checks and demanded she pay him Jason's death insurance too. She said she needed a death certificate and a letter of clearance from the police department before she could give him that money. He got mad and said he'd be back on the morrow.

Robert interviewed Maria for almost an hour and a half. She told him she knew that Greg was a dealer and that she had told Goldie. She said Goldie was planning on leaving him and had put in for a transfer to Minnesota. It hadn't come through yet. She told Robert about Goldie using the kids in commercials and that she thought Goldie had stashed a large portion of that money in some bank account for the kids. She gave Robert the name of Goldie's agent and some other details.

Robert left and thanked Maria for all the information. He told her that Brian would probably need her in court, and that the preliminary court date was Tuesday. He said he could get a subpoena but didn't really want to take the time. Maria said if he'd have the attorney call the office, she'd get permission to be off without them having to get a subpoena. Robert left. He got to his car and called Carl on the cell phone. Carl answered after six rings.

"Did you get that robbery checked?"

"Yes, Albert's story checks out. Right down to the place, the date, and the shot in the ceiling."

"Alright, I'll go see the DA and see if I can get him to present the case to the grand jury. With luck we'll have Greg in jail before the hearing Tuesday."

"That's in two days," Carl reminded him.

"Crap, today is Sunday? What the hell are we going to do? We still have four or five days' work."

Robert had been so busy he had forgotten the day.

"Brian said finish up today and cut it off."

"Well, I can take the rest of today and tomorrow morning to finish. He's got to do the prelim stuff so maybe I can take most of tomorrow."

"I don't think so," Carl retorted. "Brian said he needed us in court at the onset."

"Okay, you go, and tell him I got delayed for a couple of hours. I'll go see the DA first thing in the morning and by the afternoon, I'll go get the blood test results. Tonight I'll go talk to the priest at the church. You go back to Brian's and get a subpoena for the mom and Greg's wife and deliver it. The mom'll be at the hearing anyway, but I want her and the wife subpoenaed as hostile witnesses. In the morning I'll also go back to the hood and see the barkeep. I think I can get him to talk to the cops about Greg's meetings there. After you serve Mom, go serve the doctor. I'll go see the CPS and see if they have anything. Tomorrow night I want you to meet me at the motel. I'll get an office for us at the motel and we'll write the whole thing up."

The rest of the day didn't go went well for Robert. He decided to talk with the DA at his home instead of going to his office Monday morning. The prosecutor was a little mad that Robert had found his home. After the conversation about a violation of his personal privacy, he said he didn't think he had enough to open a case and file for prosecution on Greg. The DA said that the only witness was an ex-con and that his credibility was really poor. The kid who was clerking at the time clearly stated that the assailant had a ski mask on and he couldn't pick him out from a lineup. Robert said he had the gun and if they had a bullet they could match the barreling. The DA said they never found the bullet, and the gun was coming from an ex-con.

The DA finally said that the case was also so old that he wasn't sure he'd get away with re-opening it, especially if he had to give immunity to Adelbert. Robert left the DA's home really unhappy. He had gone there with high hopes. He figured it would be a good case and an easy one to make. The DA could add it to his credits and in all probability Greg would cop a plea once presented with the testimony of Adelbert. Robert had recorded the conversation with the DA and thought he might use it in court or at least play it back for Brian and the grandparents. It was all for naught. The DA didn't think it was a good case and said with a smile that he wasn't going for it.

Robert went over to the minister's place. They talked for almost an hour. The minister admitted that he knew that Greg was a dealer, but he wasn't willing to testify. He said that in his congregation there were several people who depended on his silence and he wasn't going to take the little faith they had away from them. The minister also admitted knowing that Greg was married but said that he didn't know whether he had gotten a divorce. In general, he was of no help. He did say that he was fond of Goldie and thought her to be a really good mother and wife. He said he didn't believe that Greg killed her or the child.

The bar was on the way back, sort of, and Robert was a little reluctant to stop. But he was really needing at least one witness who was willing to testify that they knew Greg was a dealer. His name was Sam, really Samuel, but everyone called him Sam. He was friendly and informative. He said he didn't use and didn't want people selling at his bar. He said he was willing to testify that Greg came in and met the same three or four people at least three times a week, but that he couldn't say that they were buying drugs. He never saw any drugs. He also said that the DEA had come in and asked him when and where they met and he told them, but anytime there was a strange car parked in the neighborhood or anyone strange in the bar the deal was off and both people would walk. So DEA never got anything. Robert asked him to come to court on Wednesday morning. He said he would.

When he left the bar it was seven thirty, way too late to go see CPS. He'd have to do it in the morning. Robert got back to the hotel and went to the front desk.

"I'm gonna need a room with a computer and printer and scanner for most of tomorrow evening," he said to the front desk manager.

"Shall I add the charges to your room or is this a separate charge?" the manager asked.

"Add it to my room. How much do you charge?" Robert asked as a second thought.

"Our guest computer rooms are seventy-five dollars per night, or if you are going to use the room for less than three hours, it's twenty-five dollars per hour."

Robert took the room and asked to have two tables put into the room and four chairs. He went up to his room and took another shower, laid down on his bed and fell asleep. He spread all the info he had across his bed and was about to organize it when there was a knock at his door.

That's gotta be Carl, he thought and walked to open the door.

"May I help you?" Robert asked, surprised that it wasn't Carl. A young blond valley-type girl stood at the door. She was dressed in a pale blue-checkered blouse and a light green skirt. It was short like the ones they used to wear in the sixties. She was beautiful and as Robert searched her eyes for a hint of drug usage or for a meaning for her being there, he could see neither. She was carrying a rather large black purse, which was trimmed with brown leather and some gold metal clips. The purse looked like it could easily conceal a weapon.

"I hope so. Are you Mr. Bosley?"

"Yes."

"May I come in?"

Robert knew that it was dangerous to invite a woman into his room. There was the chance of her screaming rape, which would disrupt the hearing. There was also the chance of her being armed and he having to struggle with her to prevent being shot, or worse yet, turning his back on her and getting killed. There were also a thousand other possibilities so Robert hesitated.

"Perhaps it would be better if we went downstairs and conducted your business in the lobby."

"No, what I have to tell you is important. If you don't want to hear it, okay, but I think you will."

"Come in," Robert responded, still with some hesitancy.

She walked into the room and Robert, against his better judgment, walked in front of her and took all of the papers off the desk, which sat at the end of the room next to the glass sliding door and collected the papers spread across the bed. The glass door opened onto a patio. The patio was barely large enough to put a little round table and chair on it, but it made the room look larger and more luxurious. Robert opened the curtains. Not that it did any good. They were on the third floor, but it was making a statement to the girl. He slid the table a little toward the middle of the room and motioned the woman to sit down. She sat and crossed her legs, which made the skirt slide up even further. Robert looked for a second.

This one's a beauty, he thought as he sat down.

"What can you tell me?" he asked, cutting out all the introduction bullshit and getting to the chase.

"I want to hire you," she said. She reached into her purse and pulled out a hundred-dollar bill. She pushed it across the table. It didn't slide; the table was leather trimmed on the outside with what appeared to white ash wood and brass buttons holding the stuffed leather trim. The middle was high-gloss varnished oak. Robert had spilled some coffee on the table the day before and it had dried there, leaving the table sticky in the middle. There stopped the hundred-dollar bill. She looked Robert in the eyes for the first time. He examined her eyes. Now he could see some fear and some hate.

"I'm involved in a case right now. Even if I weren't, my fees are generally four hundred dollars a day plus expenses."

Robert's fees sometimes varied depending on the case and even sometimes on the client.

"My name is Jennifer, I am the mother of Linda. You probably know her as Crystal. I know she has been buying drugs from this drug dealer. I think his name is Greg. I want to put a stop to it. I hate the son of a bitch and I know you do too. All I want from you is where I can find him. He doesn't go to the apartment in Hollywood much and I haven't time to sit there and wait. So I'm paying you a hundred dollars to tell me where I can find the bastard."

Robert was surprised. She didn't look old enough to have a

sixteen-year-old daughter. She looked like in her middle twenties but clearly that couldn't be.

"How old are you?" Robert asked

"I'm thirty-two," she answered with some pride.

"If I give you an address where Greg is staying, what are you going to do?"

"Now that you're in my employment, you can't tell on me, can you?"

"Not usually," Robert answered, hoping it would get her to tell him what he wanted to know.

"Okay, I'm going to kill the asshole. He got my daughter on drugs and now she steals money from me. She goes out with the shit of her school and I know she's had sex with 'em. I don't mind if my daughter grows up, but I didn't want her sleeping with everybody on campus, especially for money."

Robert sensed she didn't know about Crystal's affair with Greg.

"What good will it do your daughter if her mother is in prison for murder?" Robert asked.

"They won't catch me. I know exactly how to do it and I won't get caught. He's a dealer. If I kill him making a deal, the cops will think the sale went bad and a buyer shot him. The buyer will run, fearing the cops will suspect him or fearing the shot was meant for him. No problem."

"Not a bad plan," Robert said. "But it won't make your daughter better. She'll just buy from somebody else."

"No she won't! I'm putting her into a rehab place tomorrow."

"How did you find me?" Robert asked, knowing the only way was through Crystal.

"Linda and I talked last night. She told me everything. She was afraid of going to jail. You got her scared."

Robert was surprised. First she would have to have noticed his name, then how in the heck did she know where he was staying?

Probably called my office and said she had a meeting with me and forgot where I was staying. I'll have to talk to Angie about giving out that kind of information, Robert thought. Then he asked, "Did she tell you that she gave sex to Greg in exchange for drugs?"

"That's a lie. I know she'd never do that. She's basically a good girl."

Robert pulled out some of the pictures from the manila envelope lying on the bed. His plan was to make the mother mad enough to testify against Greg at the hearing. Jennifer looked at the pictures in amazement. Her hands holding the pictures slowly fell to her lap. She wasn't the confident sexy girl that had come to Robert's door. Now she was broken.

"I had no idea. How could she have sex with that bastard? He's older than I am and he's black!"

"The want of drugs does strange things to people," Robert answered, now wondering if he had gone too far.

"Tell me where he lives. I'll pay you another hundred," she said.

"If I did, I'd become an accomplice. Now that you've told me your intentions, I can't tell you his address." Robert really wanted to tell her. It would solve all his problems. Greg dead and the world would be a better place. But that just wasn't going to happen.

"Take your two hundred back. I can't help you. But maybe you can help me. Will you be willing to come to court and testify that Greg sold your daughter drugs?"

"Yes, I sure am."

"We need to meet in Mr. Goodfell's office at seven in the morning. Here's one of his cards with the address on it. Please call if you can't or won't make it. I'm sure we can beat this guy in court. With your testimony and other evidence I think we can also get the cops to charge him with statutory rape against your daughter. We'll send him up the river for eight or ten years."

"I'll be there," Jennifer answered. She got up and walked to the door. Robert politely opened the door. As Jennifer was leaving, Carl was coming down the hallway. He turned and acted like he was opening another room door. Robert spoke up.

"Carl, this is Jennifer. She's the mother of Crystal, the high school girl in our investigation."

"Oh, I wasn't sure if you wanted me here at this time," Carl answered a little shyly.

"I only wish," Robert answered.

He turned to Jennifer who had extended her hand for Carl. Carl shook hands with her and she politely excused herself. As she walked down the hallway Carl shook his head and said, "I'd a given you another hour."

"Any other time I'd a taken it. I've got a room for the report. Did you bring everything you've collected?"

"Yeah."

"Okay, leave me with what you've got and I'll get started collating it for tomorrow night."

※

In the morning Robert spent more than three hours at the CPS. They would not tell him anything and in the end asked him to leave. He went to the lab and got the blood tests and also had to wait there for two hours. In all the day was almost a loss. Robert went back to the motel and opened up the computer room and called Carl. He had two computers put into the room. When Carl got there at about 5 p.m., Robert had already set up all the paperwork by date and incident. He asked Carl to write up everything he had done. First on an outline page showing the hours, and secondly classifying all his investigations in order of what he felt was the most useful to Brian first. He was to write up a narrative and make footnotes for explanations when necessary. Carl stacked a bunch of papers on the table near the computer Robert would be working. Robert looked down at the pile and said, "We're probably going to need some coffee."

Carl got up and went to the restaurant to see if he could get a pot and some sugar and cream.

Robert took all of the recordings out of his briefcase and laid them out in a chronological row. He reached over and took the envelope on the top of the pile. It was the blood report. He had completely forgotten about it.

"How the hell could I have forgotten about this? It can make our case." He sighed and opened the envelope.

"Crap. The bastard was the father," he said out loud just as Carl was reentering the room.

"What do you got?" Carl asked.

"The probability that Greg is the father of the twins is 98%. I just opened the blood test. So I guess we can wash that one. Go figure, he's black as coal and his kids are white as snow white. I sure was wrong about that one. Looks like ol' Goldie really was true to him. The plus is that he shows positive for meth, cannabis, coke, and a slew of other things like angel dust. Brian said he didn't think we could get that into testimony because Greg had not consented to anything but the DNA. We still got a ton of proof showing him to be a dealer and a thief and married to someone else the whole time he lived with her."

"I don't see how the case can go any way but ours," Carl answered.

"You never know about courts. Nothing in our world is so arbitrary. I have seen judges rule and justify the stupidest interpretations of law. And juries, I can't even talk about juries. One time when I was a border patrol agent, the jury went out on a smuggling case. They had fifteen witnesses who said they were going to pay the driver to take them to LA. The jury came back with a 'not guilty.' So I asked the foreman what had led him to that conclusion. He answered, 'You can't trust those Mexicans, most of them will lie to get out of having to go back to Mexico.'"

"I couldn't believe it. The guy had it all wrong. The jury had it all wrong. So as for me, I never count on anything until I have it in my hand."

Carl and Robert worked until four thirty in the morning. Carl complained for the last two hours.

"I never knew that PI work was like this. Writing this whole thing up has been harder than the investigation."

Robert laughed. "All the work we do is of naught if the attorney can't present it in court. This part is probably one of the most important parts of the work. Besides, where else can you stay up all night and review what you have done and write it up?"

"I don't know, nor do I care," Carl answered with some irritation.

As they were parting, Carl promised to be in Brian's office at seven in the morning. Robert was going to be there too. The court time was ten so Robert would give the report and answer any questions Brian might have and leave. He still had to go see the DA about whether they were going to go on the babysitter. As Carl got up to leave, Robert invited him to come up to his room and get some sleep. There were two beds there and he was welcome. Carl thought it over and said, "Yes, after all it would take me thirty-five minutes or more to get home and then I'd only get an hour or so sleep before having to drive down to San Clemente to Brian's office."

They got to Brian's office at seven ten. Brian scowled at Robert, but then smiled.

"The Bradleys still aren't here. Brief me with what you've got."

Carl went first and then Robert. The Bradleys came in at 7:30 and Brian signaled them to sit down. They listened intently to Robert explain, in order, what he had developed.

Jason got real excited when Robert showed photos and played tapes of Greg dealing drugs. Marge got excited when he showed the photos of Greg cheating on Goldie. The air of excitement in the room was high and Robert finished his report with stats that showed that Goldie was probably murdered by Greg. Robert said he was going to the DA with that and to see if he was going to go on the baby tender, Alicia. He said he'd show the possibility of murder and show the DA the evidence he had for drug use, including the photos of Wendy.

Robert said he was pretty sure the DA would go on something even though he had declined on the robbery. With all the new evidence he'd probably indict Greg, and that would make it great for this hearing because the judge would summarily give Jackson to Jason and Marge.

Robert left and drove straight to the DA's office. He had made an appointment two days before so the DA was expecting him. The assistant DA came and invited Robert into his office. They talked for twenty minutes. Robert showed him all the photos and all the evidence. He also told him he had tapes of all the conversations. All the assistant would say was that he would look into it. He asked for the photos and Robert gave them to him. He had printed duplicates so he was okay with handing over all the evidence he had gathered. He did not give the DA's office the tapes but promised if they needed them he'd copy them and send the DA the originals.

Robert left the DA's office a little disappointed. He didn't know whether they were going to go for an indictment or not. The assistant did say that he would check with his boss and see if they would convene a grand jury to hear the case. Or maybe add it to cases being presented to the grand jury next week.

Robert got to court at 11:15. Brian had already made the pleas and the judge had asked the defense if he was prepared. The defense was a good attorney. Greg had the money and he had hired the best: Mr. Lloyd Hansen. The guy specialized in family law and had twenty years' experience. Brian was a little nervous. Hansen had a reputation of being ruthless and he was very qualified in family law.

XVI

The Hearing

After the introductory statements were made by both the plaintiff and the defense, the judge made a statement: "Gentlemen, I have read your briefs. The principal purpose of this hearing is to determine if the remaining child, Jackson, is best served by staying with his father or by being placed with his grandparents. Plaintiff, you may call your first witness."

Brian stood up. "We call Martha Coleman."

Brian had served almost all the witnesses with subpoenas. Martha stood up, approached the bench, and was sworn in. Brian began.

"Please tell the court your name."

"I am Martha Coleman."

"What relationship do you have with Mr. Coleman, the father of the child in question?"

"I am his wife. We were married in Las Vegas in June of 1976."

"Do you have any proof of that marriage?"

"Yes. Right here." Martha held up a marriage license and certificate. Brian took it and introduced it into evidence.

"Were you ever divorced from Mr. Coleman?"

"No. We separated for a few years, but we were always married."

"How often do you see your husband Greg?"

"In the last couple of years at least once a week. He comes over and complains about the 'white bitch' and I take care of him."

"What do you mean, 'you take care of him'?" Brian asked.

"I feed him real food and we make love. He usually spends the night."

"Did your husband know you were still married?"

The defense attorney stood up. "Objection, he's asking both for an inappropriate conclusion from the witness and for knowledge not necessarily held by the witness."

"Sustained," the judge answered. "You can't ask this witness what only the defendant would know."

Brian withdrew the question and then said he had no further questions.

Hansen stood. He walked slowly toward the witness and asked, "Did Greg ever ask you for a divorce?"

"Yes."

"Didn't he in fact give you the papers to file and even the money to file for a divorce clear back in September of 1982?"

"Yes, but…"

"Just answer the question," Hansen snapped.

"So for all you know, Greg thought you had filed the papers and you were divorced."

"No, he knew. I told him lots of times I never filed those stupid papers."

"Do you remember the dates or times when you allegedly told Greg you were still married?"

"Not the exact dates but…"

Hansen interrupted again. "If he had asked you to file divorce papers and had given you the money to do so, isn't it natural for him to expect that you completed the task? You do complete assignments, generally, don't you?"

"Yes, but..."

Hansen interrupted again. "Thank you. No further questions."

Brian stood. "Your honor, we would like to make a motion for a summary judgment granting of the petition based on the established fact that the marriage was invalid and an act of bigamy. We therefore make the claim that the defendant has no standing and that the child should be awarded to the plaintiff."

The judge didn't flinch. He looked at Brian and said, "Judgment denied. Even if the defense knew he was married to another, he still has claim to any child of his creation, especially when there is no living mother. You may call your next witness."

"We call Mrs. Eva Coleman."

Greg's mother came to the stand and was sworn in. She stated her name and address and her interest in the case. Brian only needed one thing from her. Did Greg ever tell her that he knew he was still married to Martha? She said he had. The cross examination was designed to impeach her and Hansen did a good job. He questioned Eva and showed she was mad at him for the death of Golden and especially the death of the little child, Jason. Brian got up and tried to get the mother to say that she knew that her son was a drug dealer, but Hansen objected and the objection was sustained.

"We call Robert Bosley to the stand."

Robert walked to the stand and was sworn in. After establishing his role in the case, Brian began by trying to establish the character of Greg.

"Mr. Bosley, did you do a background check on Greg Coleman?"

"Yes I did."

"What does Mr. Coleman do for a living?"

"He's a drug dealer."

Hansen stood up and requested to approach the bench. The judge signaled both attorneys to come forward.

"This line of questioning is purely demeaning to my client and is without foundation. Furthermore my client is not on trial here. This is a custody hearing only. I move to exclude any information that goes to any alleged criminal conduct on the part of my client."

Brian looked incredulously at Mr. Hansen.

"Your honor, this hearing is to determine the fitness of Mr. Coleman to raise the child. Surely his method of support and his personal character needs to be examined."

The judge considered the arguments for a few seconds.

"Mr. Goodfell, this hearing is not specifically about the character of Mr. Coleman. It is only a hearing to determine where the child would best be served. The nature of this hearing is only for the determination of two factors, namely first to decide if Mr. Coleman has a legal claim on the child and secondly to determine if that claim, if valid, can be overridden by the claim of the grandparents of the child, that is, is there a pressing reason to take the child from its father and award custody to the grandparents. Information about the character of Mr. Coleman is only admissible in so far as it can be shown to demonstrate Mr. Coleman is incapable of providing, loving, and teaching his child the things necessary to becoming an adult capable of contributing to our society."

"We believe that what Mr. Coleman does to earn money goes directly to his ability to teach the child correct social skills and to teach him to become integrated into our society."

Brian had raised his voice. This motion to suppress was extremely critical to his case. It could not carry without weakening his arguments substantially.

The judge said, "I will consider your arguments. For now, I will allow only testimony that goes to Mr. Coleman's ability to raise and teach the child."

With that the judge signaled both attorneys to return to their tables. He seemed cold and apparently refused to consider cultural and other issues that most assuredly would affect the child.

"Mr. Bosley," Brian continued, "what evidence do you have that Mr. Coleman is a drug dealer?"

"I observed him selling. I also observed him trading drugs for sex with a 16- or 17-year-old high school girl."

"Objection, admission of evidence not established. Also, we object to introduction of opinion of the witness and finally we object to the painting of Mr. Coleman as a villain without any probative evidence."

"Sustained."

"I'd like to introduce photographs taken by Mr. Bosley."

"May we approach the bench?" Hansen asked.

The judge nodded. At the bench the judge asked to see the photographs. Brian gave him the 18 best photos showing the defendant and the girl both having sex and Greg giving her a package.

"These photos can't tell us the age of the girl nor can they tell us what was in the package given to her. You have put the cart before the horse, Mr. Goodfell. Objection is sustained."

Brian walked back to his table. He read through some papers and again approached Robert.

"Mr. Bosley, did you have occasion to talk with the girl in the photos?"

"Objection, the girl in the photos can't possibly be qualified to determine Mr. Coleman's ability to raise his child."

"Sustained."

Brian was losing this very important part of the case.

"May I introduce the photos into evidence, your honor?"

"Unless you can show that these photos go to Mr. Coleman's ability to raise the child, I will not allow them introduced."

"They clearly go to his ability to raise a child. What kind of a father has sex with a child and gives her drugs in exchange? Certainly the court will consider that behavior as detrimental to the raising of a child." Brian was a little frustrated. It seemed clear that this evidence was an indication of Greg's ability to properly raise the remaining child.

"Objection sustained. You have not shown any connection to Mr. Coleman's sexual behavior and his ability to raise his son. I will disallow the introduction of these photos into evidence.

"I will, however, allow the plaintiff to introduce evidence that goes to proving that because of Mr. Coleman's occupation, whatever it may be, he is unable to properly care for his son."

Brian walked back to this table. He read a couple of notes he had and approached Robert.

"Mr. Bosley, in your experience, does the behavior of Mr. Coleman fit the pattern of a drug dealer?"

"Absolutely. I followed him both to Mexico and around south LA and photographed him making drug deals."

"Objection, no evidence has been produced that he was making drug deals. For all the witness knows he could have been selling jewelry or tickets to horse races."

"Sustained."

"Did you talk with anyone else about the character of Mr. Coleman?"

"Yes, I spoke with Mrs. Eva Coleman, his mother, Ms. Martha Coleman, his legal wife, with his minister, and with the doctor who attended his wife, Golden, both at the time of her death and other times. I also talked with the neighbors of Greg and Golden and with friends of both Golden and Greg. Finally I spoke with the baby tender for the children and with a guy named Adelbert."

Greg squirmed for a second and then whispered into Mr. Hansen's ear. Hansen nodded.

"Which neighbors did you speak with?" Brian continued.

"I spoke with the people living on both sides of the Coleman apartment and with two people living in the back of the apartment."

"What information did you gain from them?"

"All of the neighbors said that Greg seldom took care of the children. That he left them in the car he was repairing, did not feed nor change them, and drank and slept most of the day away."

"To your knowledge was any of this behavior reported to the authorities?"

"Yes, CPS has two reports filed by the neighbors on two separate occasions."

"We'd like to introduce into evidence the report files taken by the CPS." Brian walked to his desk and took two folders to the bench. The judge looked at them and gave them back, upon which Brian took them to Hansen who looked at them for an extra long time and then said, "We have no objection."

"Your witness," Brian said. He had calculated that the defense might bring up issues that he wanted to explore but which would be objected to if he introduced them, so he gave up questioning Robert to set that stage.

"My we approach the bench?" Hansen asked. The judge nodded. "I'd like to make a motion for recess to allow me to prepare motions to suppress. Much of what the plaintiff is attempting to introduce is vague or missing from his case brief, which as you know is a violation of court rules. The pre-court disclosure document did not tell me anything of this course of examination."

"Do you have any objection, counselor?" the judge asked, really as a courtesy more than an actual inquiry.

"No," Brian said.

He and Hansen stepped back to their tables and the judge said the court would recess until ten a.m. Tuesday morning. He added that he didn't want this hearing to turn into a two-week affair.

"Your honor, we would like to reserve the option to recall this witness." Brian wanted to use Robert again after he had established that Greg's principal motivation was the collection of the insurance money. He would then recall Robert and show that Greg was using the money to purchase drugs and sell them.

"So ordered," the judge dryly said.

Brian met with Jason and Marge and Robert and Carl right there in the courtroom.

"What Hansen is going to do now is make a motion to suppress any statements about Greg's sale or use of drugs. He'll also make a motion to suppress any unsubstantiated statements or evidence about other criminal behavior. If the motion carries, it will stop us from presenting our theory about the death of Goldie. It is, obviously, extremely important that we introduce that information."

Brian looked at his notes and said he'd like to meet with the DA for a few minutes and see if he could get them to go on what he had on Greg. He then made arrangements for everybody to meet in his office later that day and he left.

As he was leaving Jason grabbed Robert by the arm and asked him to come to dinner with Marge and he. He also invited Carl.

⁂

That afternoon they met in Brian's office and discussed the case. Brian informed them that the DA didn't think they had enough to take Greg to trial and he wasn't going to present it to the grand jury without more proof. Jason was unhappy. But Brian assured him that we were doing well in court and that he was sure that the judge would award them custody of Jackson.

Dinner was good. They went to the Holiday Inn restaurant. At dinner Jason pointedly asked Robert if he thought they would win the case. Robert thought for a few seconds and answered, "Yes, in fact, I'm sure we will win. Even if the defense gets all our criminal evidence suppressed, the judge will see it. He knows that Greg is a dealer and he's not gonna let that son of a bitch have the child."

Carl also assured him that even though the defense had won a few motions, they so far have been able to introduce evidence that clearly indicts Greg. Marge cried and complained about the judicial system.

"Why can't you just tell your side of the story? Why can't the judge just listen without all these motions? If he did he'd surely realize that

Jackson would be better off in Minnesota than in the Watts area. All he has to do is look at Jackson; the kid is white."

They parted company with both Robert and Carl assuring the Bradleys that Brian was a good attorney and that they would prevail in this court hearing.

⇾•⇽

Ten a.m. came and they were all back in court. Brian had called the CPS and subpoenaed little Jackson. He had also called around to some of the judges he knew and asked how to present before Judge Rochelle. Most of them said he was a "by the book" judge. Brian figured that was both good and bad. But now that he knew, he'd change his tactics a little.

"I would like to call Maria LaSterna to the stand."

"Objection, your honor, the plaintiff once again is introducing superfluous information to the court. We stipulate that the defendant got insurance money from the telephone company. Of course he did, he needed to raise the children and the money was lawfully his."

Brian shook his head. "While we can clearly argue that the money was in fact not lawfully his, he wasn't legally married to the insured, we concede that that is not the purpose of this hearing. We do submit that the witness has a bearing on what the mother of the children told her about her husband. We invoke the dying statement clause to allow for this hearsay."

"Objection overruled. Confine your questions to character of the father as it relates to his ability to raise the child."

Maria was sworn in. She sat in the witness chair nervously.

"Miss LaSterna, in what way are you acquainted with Golden Coleman?"

Maria moved the microphone around two or three times before she spoke.

"I was her friend at work and her supervisor. We also spent lots of time visiting each other after work."

"Did Golden ever talk to you about her relationship with her husband?"

"Yes."

"How did she say her marriage was going?"

"We had gone to lunch together a week before her death. She said that she knew her husband was dealing drugs and..."

"Objection."

"Overruled."

"Go on, Maria, what did she say about her relationship with her husband, not making reference to his drug dealing?"

The judge looked at Brian.

"This is not a jury trial. I'm not impressed," he said dryly.

"She said that he had beaten her and that he had said he hated the children. She said that he questioned whether they were even his and said she was lucky they made money in the commercials; otherwise, he would dump both her and the kids."

"What did you say when she told you those things?"

"I told her to leave the bastard. I told her..."

"If you continue to use unacceptable language in the court I will find you in contempt," the judge said, only because the defense was about to object.

"I told her I had heard from lots of other people that he was a rat. That he only stayed with her because she brought in a regular paycheck."

"Did Golden talk with you about the defendant's regard for the children?"

"Objection, that's stretching the hearsay rule too far."

"Overruled, I will allow the question."

"Yes, Goldie came to me on many occasions to tell me that Greg was not taking care of the children. In one case she said she came home at four a.m. and found one of the twins asleep in the Camaro parked outside. He hadn't been fed nor had his diaper been changed."

"Was that the only such incident she had spoken of?"

"No more than a dozen times she reported similar incidences."

"Was Golden insured at your company?"

"Yes, she had our regular seventy-five-thousand-dollar insurance with a double indemnity clause."

"Did your company pay that money to Mr. Coleman?"

"Not only that money, but the children were also insured. I believe that he collected forty thousand dollars for Jason's death."

"When Mr. Coleman came to collect the insurance, did he speak with you?"

"Yes, he read the insurance papers and said, 'It's about time the bitch paid off.'"

"So in total Mr. Coleman collected approximately a hundred and ninety thousand dollars from the insurance companies. Was there anything else you'd like to tell the court about Mr. Coleman's behavior at the time of your encounter with him?"

"Yes, we also paid him a death benefit from the company funds of twenty-five thousand dollars. He demanded all of it be paid on the day he came in even though I recommended he keep some of it in our trust fund for the children when they got to college."

"Children?"

"Yes, he came to the office twice. The first time was the day after the death of Golden. Jackson hadn't died at that time. I told him we needed to get the paperwork together and he'd have to come back for his wife's insurance. He made a fuss, he said we owed it to him and we'd better have it within the week. So I hustled and got it for him. By the time he returned to collect, the baby had also died. We checked with the DA's office to see if they had any intentions of filing charges against him for the death of Jason, but they unequivocally said no. They said the death appeared accidental and that Mr. Coleman was not a suspect in the cause of it."

Interestingly enough, the defense kept quiet during most of Maria's testimony. Brian thanked her for testimony and gave her to the defense.

"Miss Maria LaSterna, how many girls do you have working for you at the phone company?"

"Thirty-four, counting all shifts."

"Have any of them ever come to you and told you their husbands were not up to snuff?"

"Of course."

"In fact, have any of them who are married come to you and *not* told you their husbands were failing as fathers?"

Maria hesitated, thought and then quietly said, "No."

"No further questions."

Maria walked down off the stand and stared or rather glared at Greg. Hansen turned and asked to approach the bench. The judge nodded and he and Brian walked up to the bench.

"I submitted three motions to suppress, your honor, have you read the motions?"

"Yes, I have. I am upholding all of the motions. This is not a criminal trial and as such I don't want evidence presented here in my court that will be used in any criminal trial. Nor do I want evidence presented in this hearing to be used in a grand jury indictment. Have you received copies of the motions, Mr. Goodfell?"

"Yes, your honor, they were in my box this morning."

"Have you looked over the things listed in the motion?"

"No, I haven't had the time to carefully study them."

"I will remind the plaintiff that this is only a custody hearing. This hearing will end tomorrow at or before eleven a.m. I will now recess this court until one p.m."

The judge hammered down the gavel and both attorneys walked back to their respective tables. The judge got up and walked out.

Robert, the Bradleys, and Carl gathered around Brian.

"The motions carried. Anything that pertains to potential criminal indictment of Greg is excluded. Further all witnesses except those whose testimony goes to his ability to raise and teach Jackson are excluded."

"How can he do that?" Marge asked, almost crying.

"Because this is a custody hearing, not a criminal trial. But don't worry, the judge knows our arguments and they will be considered. Also the fact that we have shown that the child is probably illegal and that Greg is never home will significantly influence the judge."

Brian said he was going to stay and study the motions to suppress and that the rest of them could go to lunch. After lunch Brian called Carl, who testified about his investigation. Most of his testimony was objected to and the objections sustained. He did manage to get in a reference to the robbery at the 7-Eleven, but at the bench Brian was counseled not to violate the restraining order again or he'd be fined for contempt of court. He next called Greg's mother back. This time in her testimony she stated that in her opinion she didn't feel that her son was capable of raising a son with his work schedule. She also said he was inattentive and didn't have the ability to properly train a child. She wasn't crossed. Brian again tried to ask her if she knew what her son did for a living but an objection was made and sustained.

Brian called Jackson but the judge would not allow the five-year-old to testify. Brian called Wendy, who testified that she knew that Greg was "no good." She told how Greg and Golden met and about the abuse. Hansen only asked her three questions: Did she approve of the marriage? Her answer was, of course, "No." Had she ever seen Greg hit Golden or anyone else, and did she think an Afro-American had a right to raise a white child? The last question made Wendy mad.

"What do you think? You take a little white child and put him in a neighborhood with nothing but black children? What's going to happen? I'll tell you, he'll be destroyed!"

Brian didn't re-direct. He didn't re-call Robert. Robert was upset about that. He had a lot of other information to give out. Brian concluded and rested.

Hansen had listed Greg as a witness but decided not to put him on the stand. He presented to the judge papers, which he had gotten from the lab that tested Greg. Greg had told him and he did exactly what Brian feared. He used the test to prove that Greg was the biological originator of the children. He pointed out that the reason the plaintiff had failed to mention that they had required the test was that it conclusively showed that Greg was, in fact, the father of the twins. Rochelle looked at the documents and asked if Brian wanted to look. Brian answered that he had a copy. The judge admitted them into evidence.

The judge recessed court until the morning. He said he'd only allow short summations on the morrow. He further said that he'd have a decision tomorrow afternoon at about three.

<hr />

In the morning Brian was ready. He had spent most of the night preparing his closing arguments.

"We have shown the character of Mr. Coleman to be questionable at best. We have raised issues about his attentiveness to his children with statements made both by Mr. Coleman's neighbors and by the CPS records. We have shown that Mr. Coleman was a bigamist and that he probably knew full well he was. We have shown that Mr. Coleman is immoral and have presented photos of him having a sexual relationship with a female whose age is clearly not half of his. We have witness from the defendant's mother that he is not a good father and that he should not be allowed to keep the child. We have clearly demonstrated that Mr. Coleman was at the least negligent in the care of the children, which resulted in the death of the younger twin, Jason. And while we understand that the nature of this hearing is not criminal nor can it admit criminal evidence, we ask the court to consider the large volume of evidence presented that shows that the death of Golden may not have been entirely an accident. The testimony given about the money clearly goes to Mr. Coleman's motivation.

"Finally, your honor, we point out that the remaining child, Jackson, has been born with his mother's skin color. And while we are not trying to say that one race is better or more adapt at raising children, we are saying that raising a white-skinned child in the Watts neighborhood will result in significant damage to that child. We are not sure if the marriage of Mr. Coleman will remain in tact after this hearing, but we do know that Martha Coleman is not related to the child and cannot possibly have the love and care that the parents of Golden would have. Nor by any stretch of the imagination is the setting here equal to the kind of peace and love that would be provided in Minnesota. We are very willing to share custody. If Mr. Coleman would like to take Jackson for summers or holidays, we are more than glad to accommodate him in any needs he has to love and be with Jackson, but we have clearly shown that he doesn't have the time nor the inclination to attend to the child.

"We pray the court will realize that the grandparents are the best place for the child to be raised. They have both the time and the interest and the years of experience to give Jackson a perfect childhood. Please, therefore, place the child in the custody of Marge and Jason Bradley."

Brian walked to his desk and sat down. Marge was crying and Jason was stern.

Brian looked at them and smiled. He was sure they had prevailed.

The defense stood up. Hansen began his closing remarks.

Robert started as Hansen concluded after almost twenty minutes of oratory. He prayed the court would find for the father. He turned and abruptly sat down.

The judge ordered all parties to reconvene at three p.m.

Three came. The judge unceremoniously walked to his bench. He sat and the entire courtroom sat down without being told to by the bailiff. He shuffled the three or four folders on his desk, opening the first and making a note on the paper pad next to the gavel and then turning the pages and making another note. Closing the file, he went to the next. It seemed like twenty minutes passed in silence, and then he spoke.

"I have considered the arguments of the petition carefully. In California law, section 218, paragraph 24, we are clearly told that barring evidence that the 'biological parent' will inflict physical or extreme mental harm on the child, the child should remain with its parent as opposed to the grandparents or other petitioners. The evidence presented did not convince me that the father would inflict either physical or mental damage to the child in question. I therefore rule that the child will remain with its father. I grant reasonable visitation rights for the grandparents, which can be made with the father."

He hammered down the gavel.

Epilogue

Brian saw Jason and Marge off on the plane. They didn't finish paying their bill. Robert didn't collect any more either. Carl was seriously stunned by the decision. Brian was very surprised. Robert was very disappointed. Brian mentioned that the judge had made a whole bunch of errors and that they could easily appeal his decision. Jason just shook his head.

"We're out of money," was all he'd say. He didn't even ask about visitation. They got on a late plane that night and were gone.

Robert went home, having not made much money by the time he paid Carl and the motel bill and the car rental and all the other expenses. He found another Glock at a swap meet out in El Cajon. It was not as smooth as the one he had thrown away, but he knew a guy who would hone it down for him.

⇒•⇐

Almost ten months after the decision Robert was sitting home reading. He had done a couple of cases since, but somehow he didn't feel as confident. He didn't feel as sure about the judicial system. He had decided to take a job with a resort as the director of security. He was going to give up the PI business. As he sat there in his living room reading the magazine published by the FBI on crime stats, the phone rang.

"Hello?"

"I'm not going to tell you who this is. I am going to tell you to get back to California and make another petition for the little boy. The father is dead. He was killed in a drug deal and his wife doesn't want or deserve to raise the child. Incidentally Linda went to a rehab for teenagers and came out okay. I did what I said I'd do." She hung up.

Robert knew who it was. He couldn't help but smile. Ol' Greg had been killed and little Jackson was probably going to go to Minnesota. Robert slowly placed the phone back in its cradle. He didn't call Brian, he didn't call Jason, he didn't do anything. He just sat there and smiled.

Greg's mother called Jason and Marge and told them to come and get the child. Not to use the courts, not to do anything but come and get Jackson. She said she'd have some money for them too. Not much of the children's savings and college funds were left, but she did have some.